When Deception Meets Desire

"Why have you come, Virginia?" he asked.

"I want to know what love is like between a man and a woman."

When he didn't speak, she said. "He took my virtue, Macrath, not my heart. Never my heart."

He pulled her close slowly, so slowly she might have turned her head or escaped from him easily. She didn't, only tilted back her head, praying for a kiss.

Softly, he placed his lips on hers.

The kiss deepened, becoming something she'd never felt, as if their combined need created a maelstrom between them. She was left gasping for breath, but when he would've pulled away, she gripped his shirt with both hands and pulled him back to her.

"Teach me," she whispered.

KAREN RANNEY

The Devil of Clan Sinclair

AVON

An Imprint of HarperCollinsPublishers

AVON BOOKS
An Imprint of HarperCollins*Publishers*
10 East 53rd Street
New York, New York 10022-5299

First Avon Books mass market printing: August 2013

Avon Trademark Reg. U.S. Pat. Off. and in Other Countries, Marca Registrada, Hecho en U.S.A.
HarperCollins® is a registered trademark of HarperCollins Publishers.

Printed in the U.S.A.

10 9 8 7 6 5 4 3 2 1

Prologue

London
September, 1868

Please let him be there. If he hadn't come to the Duke of Bledsoe's ball, she didn't think she could bear it.

He must have been invited. She'd done enough hinting to the duke's daughter that she'd be very, very pleased if Macrath Sinclair was invited, along with his sister Ceana.

She'd waited so long already, a whole day, since seeing him. She'd told herself that all she had to do was be patient a few more hours. That refrain had sung through her mind all during the time her maid had dressed her hair, when the gown needed a few last minute stitches to keep one of the silly bows in place, and when her gloves were handed to her. Only one more hour, she'd thought as she was inspected by her father and Mrs. Haverstock, turning in a slow circle so her appearance could be judged.

To her surprise, neither her English chaperone nor her father had said a word. Nor had her father frowned, his usual expression in her presence. He only nodded, a sign to precede him into the carriage, Mrs. Haverstock following.

The carriage wheels had been too slow. Her heartbeat

had been too fast. Hours, decades, eons later they were finally at the Duke of Bledsoe's home, only for it to take forever before the carriage got to the head of the line and they could leave the vehicle. Because of the crush of people, there was another interminable wait to climb the steep stone steps, and yet another to enter the ballroom.

Would he like her hair? Her maid had done it in an intricate style tonight. What about her new scent from Paris? She'd thought about him the moment she uncapped the flacon, wondering if he would think the rose scent too strong. Would he think her high color attractive? She couldn't help herself; the thought of seeing him after an absence of twenty-four endless hours reddened her cheeks.

Dear God, please let him be here. Please. She'd promise a dozen things, only let him be here.

She heard Mrs. Haverstock behind her, greeting friends. Moving away, she scanned the crowd for a sight of him.

Thank you, God. There he was. There, just beyond the pillar in the ballroom. Standing there, looking out at the crowd as the music surged around him.

She made herself wait, watching him. He was so handsome in his elegant black evening dress. He stood on the edge of the ballroom, a man with the studied gaze of a person twice his age. His stature was of someone who knew himself well, who'd gone through his own personal battles and won his wars.

Several women stopped, their looks intent. Suddenly, she felt a fierce possessiveness, and wanted to clamp her hands over their eyes to stop their acquisitive looks.

He was hers.

He turned in her direction, his eyes lighting on her. There it was, the smile she'd been anticipating. Slowly at first, dawning with merely a quirk at the corners of his lips, growing as she walked toward him.

She wanted to race to him, throw herself into his arms, press her hands against his chest and feel the solidness of him. Otherwise, she might believe she'd dreamed him, conjured him up from a lonely girl's prayer and a wishful woman's yearning.

He was as perfect as any daydream could create him, but he was no illusion. He was Macrath and she was enthralled.

"Are you well?" she asked on reaching him. A full day, nearly twenty-four hours, had passed since she'd seen him last, and anything might have happened in the interim.

The smile she'd watched from across the room was now directed solely at her. How wonderful, that an expression could have such warmth, like the sun spearing directly into her.

"I am well, Virginia," he said. His voice, warm and low, held a roughness that chafed her senses. "And you?"

She was just now starting to heal. The last day without seeing him had been unbearable. She was shriveling up inside for lack of one of his warm smiles. Without seeing his beautiful blue eyes and hearing his Scottish accent, she was not quite herself.

How did she tell him something like that? It seemed like he knew, because his smile faded and he reached out one hand to hold hers.

She could hear people around them, but it was like a bubble surrounded Macrath and her. No one was important. Nothing else had weight.

"You're beautiful," he said.

She smiled, pleased he thought so. Few people did. She was too retiring to be noticed most of the time.

When she just shook her head, he said, "You're the most beautiful woman in London."

"You're beautiful as well," she said. She didn't mean

handsome, either. He was a gift from God, a creation of masculine beauty.

Even his laugh was glorious.

"Will you dance with me?" he asked, still holding her hand.

He seemed as loath to relinquish it as she was to step back. Prudence dictated that she do so, at least until Macrath spoke to her father, but prudence could go to blazes for all she cared now.

She was gloriously, madly, spectacularly in love with Macrath Sinclair and she didn't care who knew.

"I'd rather go into the garden," she said, daring to tell him the truth. She wanted another kiss from him, another stolen embrace.

"It looks to rain," he said.

"Do you care?"

"Not one whit."

"I don't either. Besides, it's forever raining in London."

"You'll find that Scotland is the same in some months."

"I won't care," she said. "It will be my home."

"Soon," he said, the look in his eyes growing more intense.

Perhaps she should thank Providence that the weather was souring. Otherwise, she might make a fool of herself in the garden, demanding kiss after kiss.

"Virginia," a voice called, breaking the spell.

She blinked and turned her head to see her father standing not far away.

Her stomach dropped, and she looked up at Macrath with apology in her eyes.

"I'm sorry," she said, "but Father's calling me."

"I understand. Shall I accompany you?"

"It's best you don't," she said. "I've no doubt done something wrong."

"When I meet with him tomorrow, I'll tell him the press of business demands a speedy marriage. We'll be in Scotland before you know it."

She would be with him wherever that was: in a corner of the garden, in a vestibule in the ballroom, in a hallway, a servant's stair. The location didn't matter, as long as she was with Macrath.

She squeezed his hand, then turned and reluctantly walked away, glancing back with a smile. Her father led her to an anteroom and closed the door.

"I'll not have you making a fool of yourself over that Scot," he said.

She held herself stiffly, as she did whenever he issued a dictate. The slightest indication that she disagreed with him would only make the punishment worse.

Now, she concentrated on the floor between them, hoping that he wouldn't see her inability to look him in the face as disrespect.

"I'm sorry, Father," she said.

Docility was better than rebellion. Easier, too, because she'd once tried to debate a point with him and had been severely punished for doing so. Her governess had taken great delight in using a birch rod. The lesson being that few things were worth physical pain.

Macrath was, and she wondered if her father knew it.

"People will look at me and wonder at the lack of control I have over a female in my own household."

She'd heard a variation of that comment all her life. Ever since coming to England, however, it had grown more difficult to listen to him, and maintain some appearance of humility while doing so.

"I'm in love with Macrath, Father," she said, the first time she'd ever admitted such a thing to him. She glanced up at him to find his eyes had narrowed. "You've agreed that Macrath could call on you tomorrow," she hastened to say.

After that, her future would be assured. She would be Macrath Sinclair's wife.

"I've already picked out your husband and it's not that Scot."

Her hands were still clasped in front of her. She bowed her head again, her gaze on the crimson patterned carpet. She'd think of anything but her father's words. Her mind, unaccustomed to joy, had forced her imagination to produce something more familiar, her father's derision.

"You're going to be a countess, daughter. How do you feel about that?"

She was going to be sick.

Slowly, she lifted her eyes, unsurprised to find him smiling.

"But you agreed to meet with him," she said.

"It's done, Virginia. We've just now finalized the arrangements. You're to be married within the month to the Earl of Barrett."

Turning, he extended his hand and a woman stepped out of the shadows. "Your future mother-in-law, Virginia. The Countess of Barrett."

She gave the woman barely a glance, intent on her father. She said the one word she never said, one tiny word she'd learned had no power in the past. Perhaps it would work now.

"Please."

The world halted, stilled, hung on a breath of air.

"There's no fussing about it; the deal has been struck."

"But you agreed to meet with Macrath."

He scowled at her. "I won't tolerate your rebellion, Virginia." Turning to the woman, he said, "I'll have her chaperone take my daughter home, your ladyship. Perhaps a few weeks of contemplating her future will make her grateful for it."

The woman merely nodded.

"There won't be any entertainments until after your wedding," her father said.

Did it matter?

She'd be confined to her room, but she didn't care. She'd sit and stare out at the world, her body in one place, her soul and heart in another.

Virginia only shook her head, unable to speak, flooded by a sense of despair so deep she was certain she was bleeding inside.

Chapter 1

London, England
July, 1869

The ferns near the window wiggled their fronds as if they wanted to escape the room.

Virginia Anderson Traylor, Countess of Barrett, wiggled on the chair and wanted to do the same.

She sat in the corner of the parlor, swathed in black. Her hands were folded on her lap, her knees pressed together, her head at the perfect angle.

How many times had she thought about this scene? In the last year, at least a dozen or more, but in her imagination she'd always been surrounded by weeping women rather than sitting a solitary vigil.

She stood, unable to remain still any longer. She'd been a good and proper widow for nine hours now. For the last four, she'd watched over her husband's coffin alone.

Her thoughts, however, had not been on her husband.

A dog howled, no doubt the same dog that howled for three nights straight. Ellice, her sister-in-law, thought he'd announced Poor Lawrence's death.

The parlor where she sat stretched the length of the town

house. Two fireplaces warmed it in winter, but now it was pleasantly temperate. The room had been refurbished with the infusion of money she'd brought to the marriage. The wallpaper was a deep crimson, topped by an ivory frieze of leaves and ferns. Four overstuffed chairs, upholstered in a similar crimson pattern as the wallpaper, squatted next to a tufted settee. A half-dozen marble-topped tables, each adorned with a tapestry runner, filled the rest of the available space, their sharp corners patiently waiting to snare a passing skirt.

No doubt Enid meant for the room to be the perfect showplace in the Earl of Barrett's home. What her mother-in-law had accomplished, however, was a parlor reeking with excess. Even the potpourri was overpowering, smelling so strongly of cloves that her nose itched and her eyes watered.

The coffin was crafted of polished mahogany, wider at the shoulders and narrow at the feet, with three brass handles on each side. A round brass plaque over where Poor Lawrence's heart would be was engraved OUR BELOVED.

Not *her* beloved, and he hadn't shown much love toward his family. The hyperbole, however, was expected of them. So, too, all the mourning rituals that would be carried out in the next year.

Perhaps Lawrence had arranged for his own coffin and the plaque was a last thumb in the eye to his wife, mother, and sisters.

For her sitting, she'd insisted the top of the coffin be lowered. The other members of the family would probably want to view Poor Lawrence once more.

"A bad heart," Enid had called it. A bad disposition as well, although perhaps she shouldn't fault him for being angry at the circumstances he'd been dealt. A semi-invalid since birth, he'd been limited in what he could do, to the point of being imprisoned in this house.

Poor Lawrence was what she called him in her thoughts. To his face, she'd been a proper wife. "Dearest husband," she'd said on those occasions when he allowed her to visit him.

"Dearest husband, how are you feeling?"

"Dearest husband, you're looking better."

"Dearest husband, is there anything I can bring you?"

He never answered, only slitting his eyes at her like she was an insect he'd discovered in his food.

Lawrence was, whether it was right to say such a thing about the deceased, a thoroughly unlikable person. Yet John Donne, the poet, stated that every man's death was a loss to be experienced by all mankind.

With age, Lawrence might have changed. He might have become a better person. He might have even been generous and caring.

How foolish it was to ascribe virtues to the dead they never owned in life. Lawrence wasn't a hero and he wasn't kind. Look at how he'd thrust them all into poverty.

She could easily understand his antipathy toward her. After all, didn't she feel the same for him? Why, though, would he treat his sisters and mother with contempt? Why punish them when it was obvious they hadn't done anything but treat him with kindness and care?

Every day, Eudora and Ellice called on their brother. Even if Lawrence wouldn't see them, they still returned, time after time. Eudora selected books she thought he'd like to read from their library. Ellice relayed stories to him of their days and the world outside the house.

Enid was as fond as any mother could be, worrying about Lawrence's health, querying his attendant about his cough, his color, his weakness. Despite his wishes, she insisted the doctor make regular visits, and listened when his examination was done.

What had Lawrence done to repay them? Guaranteed they would forever be dependent on others.

He could, just as easily, have given some of her father's money to his mother—or to her—to ensure their future was secure. Or he could have spent it on personal property not subject to his will.

But he hadn't done anything kind or caring.

At least, now, she would never again have to pretend to be a loving wife. These sleepless hours were little enough sacrifice for such blessed freedom.

Custom dictated the curtains be drawn, but she'd opened them at midnight, unable to bear the closed-in feeling of the room. The mirror was swathed in crepe. Candles sat burning on the mantel beside a clock stopped at the time of Poor Lawrence's death.

The room celebrated death, but she'd never been afraid of death. She was not overly fond of the dark, heights, or the ocean, however, and she detested spiders.

"The world is not going to swallow you whole, Virginia," her father had said more than once. "There's no reason to be a timid little mouse."

She circled the bier, her fingers trailing over the polished top of the coffin, closer to Poor Lawrence in death than she'd ever been in life except one time, the night their marriage had been consummated, six months after their wedding. On that occasion, he'd kissed her, so passionately it jolted her. The coupling, however, had been a painful experience, one she'd not wished to repeat. To her relief, he felt the same and they never touched again.

Enid, Dowager Countess of Barrett, pulled open the sliding doors of the parlor, then closed them just as quickly.

Her mother-in-law was stocky and short, her shoulders as wide as her hips. When Enid headed toward her, it was like facing a solid wall of determination. Enid's brown eyes could be as warm as chocolate sauce. Now they were as cold as frozen earth.

"Have you decided?"

Even though it was just before dawn, her mother-in-law was dressed in a black silk dress with jet buttons. Her hair was pulled back from her round face and contained in a black net snood. Although she wore a full hoop, she expertly navigated the room filled with furniture, moving to occupy a chair close to the bier.

"What you propose is so . . ." The words trailed away.

"Practical? Logical?" Enid asked.

Virginia walked to the window, trying to find some way to respond.

"Do not think Jeremy will support us, my dear. He will banish us from this house with a quickness that will surprise you. What he doesn't do, his harridan of a wife will. They'll care nothing for what happens to us."

"Would you?" she asked, glancing over her shoulder at her mother-in-law. "If the situation were reversed, would you care for Jeremy and his wife?"

"And their brood of children?" Enid sighed deeply. "I don't know. They're badly behaved children."

Virginia bit back a smile. Yes, they were, and she dreaded any occasion when she had to encounter Jeremy's seven children.

If Lawrence had left behind one child, they wouldn't be having this conversation.

Her mother-in-law was a planner, witness her brilliance in arranging a marriage between Lawrence, an invalid, and an American heiress. One thing Enid hadn't been able to do, however, was inspire Lawrence to bed his wife on more than one occasion.

She rarely called Enid "Mother," falling back on a habit of not addressing her at all unless it was in the company of others. Her own mother had died at her birth, a fact she'd been reminded of endlessly as a child. Not by her father, who seemed surprised when she was trotted out for his inspection at Christmas and during his one summer visit. A succession of nurses and governesses, all hired to tend her and keep her out of her father's way, ensured she knew her entrance into the world had been accompanied by the greatest tragedy.

She couldn't even imagine her mother's disembodied voice on this occasion. Would she have sided toward logic and survival? Or would her mother have been horrified at Enid's suggestion?

"Something must be done," Enid said. "You know as well as I."

The title was going to pass to Lawrence's cousin, Jeremy. He was a perfectly agreeable sort of person, pleasant to Virginia when they met. She didn't see anything wrong with him assuming the title. The problem was, everything Lawrence had purchased since receiving the bulk of her estate: the numerous houses, parcels of land, dozens of horses, farm equipment, and furnishings. Lawrence had ensured they would also go to his cousin by willing them to the "male heir of his body." Without an heir, the property traveled back up the family tree to Jeremy.

Without any cash or assets they could sell, they'd be penniless.

All she had was her quarterly allowance, and it wouldn't buy more than a few bottles of perfume. She had her mother's jewels, but they were more sentimental than valuable since her mother evidently had not been ostentatious in her dress. One good ruby brooch and a carnelian ring could be sold. How much would those bring her? Not enough to care for all the people who needed to be supported.

They were in dire straits, indeed.

Unless she produced an heir to the estate.

What Enid was proposing was shocking. Somehow, she needed to get with child and quickly enough that he would be viewed as Lawrence's heir.

"It's a solution to our dilemma," Enid said. "Have you given any thought to it?"

She nodded. She'd thought about nothing but their situation in the last four hours. God help her, but here in this room with her husband's body in a casket, she'd thought about nothing but him.

Macrath.

Chapter 2

London
A year earlier

When they'd arrived in London, Virginia had no idea she'd be heartily tired of the city within the month.

Tonight's ball was the third in two weeks, and the tenth engagement. Through it all, she saw the same people in different attire. The muscles of her face ached from smiling. Her feet hurt from walking on hardwood floors in her thin kid slippers.

She wanted to put her feet up, first, and second, she couldn't wait to read the broadsides her American maid had smuggled to her. Her father had come to her room, interrupting them, so she'd folded them quickly and stuffed them into her reticule, and all night she'd been dying to see what the talk of London was now.

She slipped away, retreating to their host's library. Settling into the corner of the settee and tucking her feet beneath her, she retrieved the broadside and smoothed it with her fingers.

On Monday an inquest was held at the National School, before Mr. Worley, coroner, to inquire into

the cause of the death of Thomas Newbury, a boy
who was found dead with his throat cut in a pea-
field, near Haversham.

> *A sad, a cruel dreadful deed,*
> *To you I will unfold, The murder of a little boy,*
> *As base as e'er was told;*
> *Murdered by a cruel man,*
> *At Haversham we hear,*
> *Near the town of Newport Pagnell,*
> *In the county of Buckinghamshire.*

"There's a better light over here," a masculine voice said.

Startled, she dropped the paper, then bent to pick it up, pressing it against her chest.

"I do apologize," she said. "I thought the room was empty."

She glanced toward the two massive leather chairs arranged in front of the fireplace. The speaker wasn't visible.

"As you can see, it's not," he said.

"I'm sorry. I didn't mean to interrupt your . . ." Her words trailed off.

"Reverie? Contemplation? Solitude?"

"Yes, all that," she said. "Your musing. Your considerations. Perhaps even your meditations."

He peered around the side of the chair, his smile surprising her. Or was it his intent blue eyes she saw first?

Her father always said she looked half finished. God had certainly taken the hue from her pale blue eyes and given it to this man. His eyes were such a startling blue she noted them from across the room.

The color reminded her of midnight over the Hudson, when the sky seemed like a curtain behind which a celestial lantern hid, revealing the night to be not black at all, but a deep and rich blue.

"My escape, most like," he said. "Are you doing the same?"

"I'm afraid I'm doing worse than that," she said.

An eyebrow lifted. "Are you absconding with something belonging to our hostess?"

"Of course not."

She debated whether to confess. To her father, a broadside was coarse and common. No one in proper company ever confessed to reading them. Nor was she to associate with people who did so.

"I was reading a broadside," she said. "About a horrible murder."

"Were you?" He didn't frown in dismay at her. Nor did he suddenly seem coolly aloof. He merely relaxed there, a handsome stranger who had evinced more curiosity about her than anyone had since arriving in England.

She stood, walked to the two chairs, and without invitation sat in the one beside him. What a handsome man he was. His mouth and eyes seemed paired in humor. His face was lean, the planes of it sharpened rather than shaped. Nothing about him was soft or genial, but she wanted to smile at him as she stared.

While she couldn't tell since he was seated, he seemed to be tall. His shoulders were broad enough, taking up the width of the chair. His legs were stretched out in front of him, crossed at the ankles. If there had been a roaring fire in the fireplace, she could understand why he'd escaped the entertainment. Since the evening was a temperate one, he must have retreated here for privacy.

She wanted to apologize for intruding. Instead, she handed him the broadside.

"It's about a murder of a young boy."

"Are you given to studying murder?"

She sighed. "I'm not very brave," she confessed. "I don't

think I could bear an actual murder. But I do like reading about things that would terrify me otherwise. Besides, I'm very interested in what's going on around me. How can anyone not want to know what's happening in the world?"

"I thank providence for people like you."

"Do you?" she asked, surprised. "Why?"

"I own a company in Scotland that prints broadsides."

She sat back, clasping her hands together on her lap. "Are you jesting? Or making fun of me? I realize a great many people don't think highly of broadsides, but why would you say such a thing?"

He handed back the paper, smiling at her. "I wouldn't think of making fun of you," he said. "What man in his right mind would ridicule a beautiful woman?"

Now she truly knew he was jesting. No one ever called her beautiful. Smart, perhaps, when she was dressed in the fashions her father had ordered. Perhaps even handsome when her hair was done correctly and she stood straight and tall, as her governess always instructed. But she'd never been called beautiful. Not even once, by the kindest person.

Her cheeks warmed and she was instantly filled with two conflicting wishes. She wanted to flee as quickly as she could. Yet she wanted to stay and talk with him at the same time.

"It's called the Sinclair Printing Company," he said. "We operate in Edinburgh. Have you ever been there?"

"This visit to England is my first outside New York," she said. "I'm from America."

"I discerned that," he said with a smile. "From your accent. It sounds almost English, but it's not."

"You are not the first person to say that," she said, looking down at her reticule. "My nurse was English and maybe I speak the way I do because of her. But everyone else has an accent, too. Such as yours. I could tell you were from Scotland."

He leaned his head back against the chair, his hands resting on the arms, the pose of a man at ease.

She didn't feel the least relaxed.

For the first time since she'd come to England, she was speaking with a truly handsome man. Even better, he was talking to her, and they were conversing about something more important than the weather.

"Do you print newspapers as well?"

"We do. Well, I don't. I don't run the company anymore. I'm involved in something else."

His name was Macrath Sinclair and he was in London, he told her, to escort his sister.

For the next hour they talked of politics and broadsides, books and plays. Each thought London overwhelming at times, with traffic an endless obstacle. Each thought Londoners unbearably arrogant, topped only by the French, who were arrogant and smelled bad. Neither had an affinity for English food, or the melodramas of the day, preferring to read instead. His humor was dry yet he was polite enough to laugh at her few jests. They talked of everything, some subjects not considered proper in mixed company. She was, however, as she'd told him, fascinated with history and, too, intrigued by English politics.

"I'm an American," she said, "and supposed to mind my manners. I'm not to be too inquisitive."

"Have you always minded your manners?"

She smiled. "I have, yes."

"That's right. You're not very brave. Are you really so cowardly?"

She sighed again." I hate heights," she said, "and spiders."

He merely smiled at her, so charmingly that she found herself breathless.

With great regret, she left him finally, glancing back as she made her farewells, thinking that the miserable voyage to England had been worth it if only for this night.

Chapter 3

London
July, 1869

The eastern sky was growing pink. A day would pass, then another, and finally Poor Lawrence would be laid to rest.

"Can you think of some other answer?" Enid asked.

Virginia turned to face her mother-in-law.

"The law does not see women as people, Virginia, but only as a man's limb. His leg, his foot, or whichever appendage you want."

For a moment, a ghost of a smile appeared on Enid's lips, then vanished.

"Your entire inheritance is gone, Virginia. Everything your father left you."

"Did Lawrence do it on purpose?" she asked. "Did he want us desperate?"

Enid tapped her fingers against her lips as if holding back improvident words. Finally, she sighed deeply. "I don't know. I don't know. I would hope he hadn't."

They regarded each other somberly.

"Search your memory, Virginia. Is there no friend of

Lawrence's? Or a person who might have come calling on my girls?"

Macrath. In this room, he seemed even more substantial than Lawrence in his casket.

Had Lawrence any friends? She'd never seen any visitors to the house. The closest to a friend was his attendant, but Paul was paid to be devoted.

As far as her sisters-in-law, Ellice was only sixteen and Eudora didn't seem interested in attracting a suitor.

"You do agree, don't you, Virginia?" her mother-in-law asked now.

"I'm not sure I can do such a thing," she said.

But, oh, to see him again. To smile at him once more.

"May I speak frankly, my dear?"

When had she not?

"Sexual congress needn't last long," Enid said.

Poor Lawrence hadn't been interested in sexual congress. Or perhaps he simply resented being a pawn in his mother's schemes. She had evidently been included in that resentment. Poor Lawrence had retreated to his suite of rooms early on in their marriage, rarely emerging.

"Seduction isn't all that difficult, Virginia. All you need do is suggest your willingness and the male will do the rest."

She had the most absurd wish to giggle. Her mother-in-law was giving her lessons on debauchery.

"However, you need to copulate regularly. You're young and healthy. Nothing should prevent your getting with child."

She felt like a chicken, scolded because it hadn't recently laid an egg.

"Is there no one to whom you could appeal?" Enid asked. "No one at all? Wasn't there someone before you married Lawrence?"

Macrath. Dear God, was she a terrible person for having kept him in her heart all this time?

She turned and faced the window again. Streaks of yellowish light bathed the street in front of the town house, stretching to illuminate the park in the middle of the square. She wanted to throw open the sash and breathe in the cool dawn air. She wanted to be gone from this place, from Poor Lawrence.

"Yes," she said, speaking to the window. "I know of someone."

Macrath.

Was he married? Nearly a year had passed since she'd seen him, and yet she could conjure him up so well he could be standing there, his dark blue eyes intently fixed on her.

What would have happened if her father had allowed her to marry Macrath Sinclair? Would her life be filled with joy, or the insane excitement she always felt when he was near?

Her heart stuttered around Macrath. Her palms became moist. Her emotions were too close to the surface, almost as if she were preparing to shout in joy or weep in despair.

A magnificent man, Macrath Sinclair, one who'd commanded her thoughts even during her marriage.

She'd almost been brave once, because of Macrath.

"He lives in Scotland," she said, feeling her heartbeat escalate as she spoke.

"All the better, then," Enid said. "Far enough away no hint of scandal will touch you."

"No hint of scandal?" she asked, turning. "What kind of a widow would travel in such conditions?"

"One who does so in secrecy," Enid said. "In the dead of night, if need be."

"Could we not appeal to Jeremy's generosity?" she asked.

The Dowager Countess of Barrett sighed audibly. "I have already done so. He is sensitive to our plight, he says, but will not attempt to break the entail. Don't expect any help from that quarter."

Now was the time for her to protest, to say Enid's suggestion was foolish. Try as she might, she couldn't see a brighter future for them, not with Poor Lawrence spending her fortune in such a profligate way.

"Do you have the courage, Virginia?"

No, she didn't. But what other option was there in the face of such unfair laws? A woman had no rights to anything, least of all her own money.

The door suddenly opened and her two sisters-in-law entered. Virginia was engulfed in a flurry of weeping, black silk and arms enfolding her in a comforting embrace.

"Dearest Virginia," Eudora said. "How are you faring?"

Enid's oldest daughter was tall, gliding when she walked. Her demeanor and poise was of a woman twice her age. Every once in a while, however, Eudora smiled, and the expression hinted at a younger and more carefree girl, one capable of mischief.

She wore her hair parted in the middle and swept into rosettes on either side of her head. A matronly style but one suiting her, as did the black she now wore. Even dressed in mourning, one noticed her dark eyes and long lashes, a creamy complexion, and full pink lips.

"Is she Mediterranean?" someone had once asked about Eudora, and the question had reminded Virginia of lithographs she'd seen of Roman women, even to the prominent nose and regal looking brow.

If Eudora had any flaws at all, it was that she loved to shop. A few times each week Virginia accompanied her, walking through the Pantheon, the Burlington Arcade, Davie's warehouse on St. Martin's Lane, or the Soho Bazaar.

They invariably returned empty-handed from each one of their outings, simply because Lawrence refused to give them any pocket money and Virginia's quarterly allowance wasn't that large.

"Oh, sister, was it awful?" Ellice asked.

Ellice was the opposite of her taller older sister. She fidgeted. She squirmed. She could not sit still for more than a few minutes at a time. Her brown eyes were always sparkling with curiosity. "Why do you suppose" was the phrase starting most of her conversations. Her brown hair was always coming loose, and she was forever being lectured by her mother on comportment, manners, what to say and when. Unfortunately, she had, on more than one occasion, offended people by speaking what was on her mind.

If Eudora was Enid's joy, Ellice was her trial.

Virginia had never considered they might be the saving grace of her marriage. Eudora and Ellice had become her sisters in truth.

"I'm fine," she said, answering both of them.

Stepping back, she met Enid's gaze. The three of them and all the servants in the house were dependent on her decision. She honestly didn't know what would happen to them once Jeremy ascended to the title.

"I'll consider it," she said to Enid.

"Consider it quickly, Virginia."

With a few parting words, she left the three of them to sit with Lawrence's coffin. Eudora wept with quiet dignity. Ellice was noisier and more effusive. Enid, like her, was concerned more with survival than grief at the moment.

Slowly, she closed the sliding doors behind her.

"I would be happy to assist you in any way, Countess."

Startled, she turned to find Paul Henderson standing there, watching her.

Paul was an extraordinarily handsome man. With his dark brown eyes and thick brown hair, he garnered a woman's attention. His features were perfect as well, even if his mouth might be considered a bit too large. Of average height, he was more muscular than most men of her acquaintance.

He would need to be, having been Lawrence's attendant. Paul had bathed him, cared for him, acted as valet and secretary. In the latter role, he'd summoned the solicitor whenever Lawrence wanted to spend more money. Paul had gone to Enid and told her what Lawrence was doing. Because of his warning, they had some inkling of their dismal future. Otherwise, they wouldn't have known until after Lawrence's death.

Paul had been in Lawrence's employ for five years and was considered almost a member of the family. Or as much as the Earl of Barrett would consider anyone beneath him to be part of his inner circle. Poor Lawrence was, regrettably, a snob, which was probably why he'd looked down his patrician nose at her. Her only pedigree had been a fortune, and she didn't even have that now.

Paul's eyes sparkled at her, and held what she perceived as a glint of humor, hardly proper for this moment. She moved aside so he could enter the parlor. Instead, he stood there studying her.

He made her uncomfortable and always had, as if he saw through the pretense of her marriage. But, then, he would know better than most, wouldn't he, caring for Lawrence as he had?

He knew how many times she'd visited her husband, how many occasions Lawrence agreed to see her, and how long each of those visits lasted.

Did Lawrence complain about her after she left? She wouldn't have been surprised. Paul was a confidant, and since she'd never seen anyone visit Lawrence, probably his only friend.

She took a step back.

Something about Paul bothered her. She didn't like the look in his eyes when he studied her, or the small smile playing around his mouth.

With Lawrence dead, was there any reason he should still be employed? All their expenses must be examined closely from this moment forward.

"I would do anything to assist you. Anything at all," he said. His smile vanished, but he didn't look away. "Please consider my offer."

Dear God, how much had he heard? She wouldn't put it past Paul to listen at doors. Yet how could she blame him for doing so, since it was how he'd gathered the information about what Lawrence had done?

She'd kept her concerns to herself. If she'd confessed to Enid that Paul made her uncomfortable, her mother-in-law would have simply looked at her with her nostrils flaring and a pinched mouth—an expression stating, without words, that she was being American and foolish.

"Thank you," she said, moving away from Paul.

He followed her, coming entirely too close. She stepped back but he only smiled, tracking her until her back hit the wall.

Leaning close, he spoke softly. "Are you afraid of me, Virginia?"

"Of course not," she said, pushing her fear down. She wouldn't let him see how panicked she was.

But when he reached out and trailed a finger down her cheek, she shivered. His eyes narrowed but he didn't move away.

"I wouldn't hurt you, Virginia. You'd enjoy it."

Grabbing a tendril of her hair, he wound it around his finger, pulling her closer.

She froze, keeping as still as she could even when he breathed against her temple. Closing her eyes, she prayed he'd move away.

Instead, he pressed a kiss to her cheek.

"I would promise you would feel nothing but pleasure in my arms, Virginia. You might come to yearn for it."

She slid to the left, ducking below his arm, scurrying down the hall. Turning, she looked back to find him studying her intently, almost like she was a mouse in truth and he a hungry cat.

In that instant, she made up her mind to travel to Scotland. Macrath would be at the end of the journey, and she'd somehow find the courage to seduce him.

Chapter 4

Four days later Virginia settled into the coach trying to prepare mentally for her journey. Dawn crept on the horizon, bathing the rooftops pink. A faint honeysuckle-tinged breeze cooled her cheeks. Birds nesting in the nearby trees called out a morning song, bidding her be about her task.

Lawrence's funeral had been the day before, and Enid lost no time making arrangements. They were to travel only by carriage. Even the stops at the inns were to be done surreptitiously. Her maid, Hannah, and the coachman would arrange for rooms, and she would use the back entrances. No one was to know the newly widowed Countess of Barrett was on her way to Scotland.

Her father had insisted she be given a diverse education. Therefore, she was prepared, if she must, to be a governess. Perhaps a man of wealth would want a slightly used countess to instruct his daughters. She could easily see an American hiring her, bragging about her title, "She's an American, you know. Became a countess. My gals deserve the best."

Getting a position wouldn't help the rest of them, however. Someone might employ Eudora, but where would Ellice go? What would happen to their mother? She could not, however much she tried, imagine Enid trimming hats.

How would they earn their living?

They had no time left, not enough for Eudora to finally be serious about finding a husband. Ellice was too young, and she doubted Enid had given any thought to remarriage.

She, herself, would not countenance marrying again. Her union to Lawrence had been distasteful enough. The only saving grace was he seemed to dislike her presence as much as she'd grown to dislike his. But what if she married a man who insisted on bedding her every night? That would be a worse situation.

Enid reached into the carriage, pressing a cup of warm chocolate into her hands.

"A fortifying beverage," her mother-in-law said.

She finished the chocolate and returned the cup. Sitting back against the cushions, she adjusted the leather gloves over her hands. She didn't see the back of the town house, Hannah arranging the baskets of food in the storage area below the carriage seat, or Hosking, the coachman, standing by the open door.

Ceana Sinclair told her in the beginning that Macrath was a brilliant inventor.

"He makes ice, Virginia," she had said. "Just imagine, his machine can generate ice for you any time of year."

He made ice, of all things, and in that small way Macrath Sinclair was playing God. Yet, in this journey she was about to make to Scotland, so was she.

London
A year earlier

"Why are you looking so distressed?"

Virginia turned at his voice. Her mood abruptly became better as she smiled at Macrath.

"I'm to be personable this evening," she said, tugging on her gloves.

A bad habit of hers, according to Mrs. Haverstock. A lady never draws the eye to aspects of her appearance. *Tranquility is as vital to a lady as beauty,* the woman often said. *An aura of peace is a quality you must cultivate.*

"I've never known you to be anything but personable," Macrath said, moving to stand beside her. They looked out over the dancers from their place on the terrace.

She sighed. "That's because you're too much like me. We'd much rather talk about scientific experiments than people or politics."

"But your dancing partners don't?"

She glanced over at him.

Tonight he was dressed in formal black, his gold and black vest a brilliant example of embroidery. His black hair was brushed back, the perfect frame for his unforgettable face.

When she looked at Macrath, she remembered those museum visits with Mrs. Haverstock, and all the statues unearthed from various places and brought to England. A Greek god, a Roman citizen, men with faces that lived on through millennia because of the placement of strong bones and features. Macrath's face was similar, but brought to life because of his intense blue eyes and a mouth that fascinated her. She liked to watch as he talked, the way he formed the letters. How he smiled when she didn't expect it.

"I've noticed how popular you've been tonight."

"It's father's money," she said. "It makes people very polite."

"On the contrary, I think it's you."

She glanced back at the dancers, feeling a surge of warmth at his words. Macrath could change her mood from dreary to delighted just with a smile. Conversely, when he wasn't at an event, it seemed to drag, each hour tied to a tortoise.

"I have heard excessively about horse racing tonight. Or gossip. People are very interested in other people."

"Politics is about people," he said, "and you're interested in politics."

She considered the matter, then nodded. "You're right. I have no place being judgmental, do I?"

"As long as we're listing your faults, I suspect you aren't to be on the terrace, either."

She smiled. "Yet you're standing right beside me."

"Perhaps I've been sent to teach you how to be more personable," he said.

"I'm not to be seen with you as much," she said. "People will get the impression that you've singled me out, which would be off-putting to other potential suitors."

"I hear Mrs. Haverstock in there somewhere."

She nodded. "Mrs. Haverstock possesses many opinions about a great many things."

"Mostly foolish ones, I think. The woman's daft if she thinks you're not personable. You're more intelligent than any woman here, and more beautiful." He glanced at her. "What would you rather be, intelligent or beautiful?"

She thought about the question for a moment. "I should say intelligent, shouldn't I? Intelligence would last you your whole life, while beauty fades. But what woman doesn't want to be considered beautiful?"

"You needn't worry. You have both."

She turned to him, placing one of her gloved hands on his arm. "The opinion of a friend," she said.

"Not just a friend," he said. "She's right in one regard. I have singled you out."

She dropped her hand, even though she liked touching him. Eyes were everywhere, and someone was sure to tell either her chaperone or her father that she'd been standing too close, and was too intent in conversation with Macrath Sinclair.

"Have you?"

"Not just a friend," he said again. Turning, he drew her back into the ballroom.

As they started to dance, she looked up into his eyes. If she were a more courageous woman, she'd tell him the truth.

She'd singled him out, too.

London
July, 1869

One of Paul Henderson's first memories was of his father telling him he needed to learn his place in life. Even as a child, he ascribed to a higher role, a better spot in the hierarchy that was English society.

As the son of a chimney sweep, he'd started working with his father at the age of five, sent up into narrow, airless chimneys with a brush and a rag with orders to do good or he'd have his ears boxed.

On Sundays the old man gustily sang in church, striking him on the shoulder if he didn't participate as well. He'd grown to loathe "All Things Bright and Beautiful," his father's favorite:

> *The rich man in his castle,*
> *The poor man at his gate,*
> *God made them, high and lowly,*
> *And order'd their estate.*

Upward migration rarely happened in the United Kingdom. From the time he was twelve, escaping the life of a flue faker by running away, he'd been determined to be more than what God had made him. He wanted to go to America, one of the few places where a man was allowed to climb the rungs on a societal ladder.

Until then he'd become a stable boy, working harder than the others, watching and learning from the men who rented the carriages. At seventeen he'd applied as a footman at one of the great houses, again learning from those who weren't aware they were being studied. He spoke with precision, always watching that hints of his childhood accent never appeared.

For ten years he kept his own counsel, woke an hour earlier than the rest of the staff, and learned to read thanks to a maid who'd been willing to teach him as a labor of love. He never stole, always performed each duty flawlessly, and on those odd occasions when he failed in some measure, promptly acknowledged his error.

By the time he was thirty, he'd saved some money for the trip to America. After hearing of a position open to care for an invalid earl, he'd once again applied, this time with glowing letters of recommendation, and a confidence about his appearance gained through years of sidelong looks and coy female smiles.

He hadn't planned to fall in love with the Countess of Barrett. He hadn't wanted to feel an odd possessiveness about her. Why he did was understandable, given the circumstances in this strange household.

She didn't feel the same for him. Like most servants, he was invisible. He went out of his way, however, to ensure she was aware of him. He conversed with her. He brought her tea. He complimented her.

Four days ago he'd offered to take her to his bed and get her with child.

She'd rebuffed him. She didn't realize he was the best solution to the dilemma the Earl of Barrett had created.

If it hadn't been for him, they'd never have known until too late.

They owed him something for his loyalty.

Lawrence had thought it a wicked jest to give him money. He'd taken it, and tucked it away in his savings even as he hated the man. Lawrence hadn't been generous; he'd given away the money solely to wound his wife.

The woman who was, even now, entering a carriage with her maid, intent on Scotland.

What was in Scotland that she couldn't find here? No one could love her as much as he did. No one could comfort her like he could. Not one person could protect her as well as he did.

He forced a smile to his face as she turned to stare right through him. She glanced away, not seeing the love he freely offered.

From this moment on he would have to change things. He wasn't going to be invisible to her anymore. No, he was going to ensure she knew exactly how he felt.

Chapter 5

Drumvagen, Scotland
July, 1869

Virginia had expected Drumvagen to crouch on top of a mountain like a brooding medieval monster of black stone.

Instead, Macrath's home was so unexpected she could only stare.

Built of gray brick the color of London soot, the house was massive and square, with four tall towers on each corner topped with a cupola bearing a different animal-shaped wind vane.

Twin sweeping staircases extended like two embracing arms in front. She'd never seen its like, even in America.

What was she doing here?

The wind ruffled the strange growth on either side of the road. Stocky purple flowers swayed amid fields of yellow blossoms. The mountains in the distance hinted at wildness, that Scotland was not sunk into history like England.

She pressed her fist against her chin, bit her lips and studied the approach. She had asked Hosking to halt the carriage on the side of the road, needing the time to compose herself. Hannah sat silent beside her. A good English maid, her mother-in-law had said when she'd announced the girl's employment last year. Someone who would know English society.

Hannah and she were nearly the same height and size. The girl's hair was brown, her eyes hazel, green flecked with amber. When she chose to smile, she was attractive, but was the perfect lady's maid, rarely showing any emotion.

As to society, Hannah hadn't been tested in the last year. The only society Virginia had seen was when she'd accompanied Eudora shopping or to an occasional dinner party or a ball. As a married woman, she was considered enough of a chaperone, and was forced to sit with the older widows and matrons.

Several American women had married into English society. When she greeted each of them, it was with the hope they could compare experiences, possibly find some common ground. But each woman she met appeared to be radiantly happy. But then, none of them had been married to Lawrence.

What would her countrywomen think about her mission? That it was the height of idiocy and immorality, no doubt. The same sentiment she would garner from her sisters-in-law if they knew. What story had Enid given them to explain her absence? Conversely, they might view her presence here as an act of courage. Each of them considered her brave for coming to England to arrange a marriage.

She hadn't been brave at all. She'd simply been her father's daughter, and her father, once he was set on a certain course, could not be dissuaded.

No, she wasn't at all courageous, especially at this moment, staring at the house perched so close to an angry sea. She didn't like the ocean, and seeing it now brought back memories of the voyage to England.

Her father had laughed at her fears.

"How do you propose we get to England, Virginia, if it isn't aboard ship?"

She hadn't answered him, as was the case with most of his questions. She only smiled and retreated to her stateroom when he allowed her to do so.

Now was not the time to be as cowardly as she had been then. So many people depended on her. Her mother-in-law, her sisters-in-law, and the staff, who would no doubt be replaced when Jeremy became earl.

What if Macrath didn't remember her? What if he never remembered when they held hands surreptitiously, or escaped to the terrace to talk? What if he didn't recall that she'd confessed her love for him in a breathy voice, nearly panicked at the admission?

She knew he wasn't married, thanks to Ceana's comments, but what if he was interested in another woman? Surely, his sister would have known?

She had to do this. Turning to Hannah, she forced a smile to her face, said, "I think we should advance, don't you?"

Hannah had not been told of the situation or the circumstances. Neither had she asked any questions about their journey. She would've thought the girl would be curious, if nothing else. Instead, the maid remained calm, her eyes flat, her smile thin.

Virginia wished she had one jot of Hannah's composure.

A shout, followed by a cloud of smoke, suddenly punctuated the silent day.

She sat forward, looking past Hannah to a crofter's hut, the same kind that had dotted the landscape throughout their journey. This house was longer, with two doors rather than one, and four windows, not two. The thatch was burning and white smoke poured through a large hole in the middle of the roof.

As she watched, three people ran from the structure toward the road. The one in the lead stopped, turned, and regarded the crofter's hut from a safe distance. The other men reached him and stood on either side, all three surveying the burning house.

Watching from the carriage, the stench reached them, and she withdrew her black edged handkerchief, holding it to her nose.

Whatever were they doing?

The acrid smell was enough for her to give the signal to the coachman. Like it or not, she'd been provoked into courage.

She eased back against the seat, willing herself to relax. She could do this. She must do this. From what she'd gleaned from the conversation of older women, men were interested in bed sport, almost to the exclusion of common sense.

Surely, Macrath would be interested in bedding her.

Her heart was beating too fast and her breath was tight.

She remembered every stroke of his fingers on the back of her hand and on her exposed wrist. She recalled the sight of his smile, not as common as other men's, but more precious for its rarity. His eyes, those engaging blue eyes of his studied her so intently she had the impression he knew all her thoughts.

Whenever she was in Macrath's company, her cheeks were flushed and hot. Her mouth felt odd, her lips too full. A laugh always bubbled in her chest, but she wasn't amused as much as delighted, enlivened, or simply thrilled.

Now, she gripped her hands together tightly and prayed for composure. What if he denied her entrance? The thought came unexpectedly and abrasively. What if he didn't welcome her?

What if Ceana's whispered answer at the funeral was wrong? What if Macrath wasn't in Scotland? They'd be forced to retrace this interminable journey.

The carriage approached Drumvagen slowly, almost cautiously. She shielded her eyes from the sun staring down at her accusingly through the window. Now was the time to turn around and go back to London. Neither the coachman nor her maid would question her. Only Enid, and the look on her mother-in-law's face would be condemnation enough.

Had Poor Lawrence wanted them all desperate and panicked? What good did it do to speculate? Poor Lawrence was beyond anything but divine questioning.

She took a deep breath, then another. Her heart was still racing and her hands were cold inside her gloves.

What was she truly afraid of—Macrath's reception or her own weakness around him?

Seabirds soared overhead, their piercing shrieks almost a battle cry.

Perhaps this was a battle. One of her conscience against her desires.

Was it permissible to pray for a successful conclusion to this errand? Would God send a lightning bolt to strike her if she did? She wouldn't be guilty of adultery, since Poor Lawrence was dead, but certainly her behavior could be considered wanton. Was prostituting herself for a good cause any less prostitution?

Even if she were successful in seduction, there was no guarantee she'd become pregnant. If she did, she might bear a daughter. If so, they were back in the same situation, with one more mouth to feed.

The carriage wheels crunched on the oyster shells lining the circular drive. Dozens of windows stared down at them like curious eyes. Was she wrong in thinking people stood there, watching them and wondering at their presence? Or was that simply conjecture, something about which she'd been lectured all her life?

"Stop imagining the worst, Virginia. Try to think of something good rather than always being focused on what could go wrong."

At the moment, it was all she could think.

The coachman opened the carriage door and she was forced to release the strap above the window. She straightened her shoulders and managed a smile.

Who had written that courage was not the absence of fear but the conquering of it? She'd wager the author hadn't been pushed into acting the harlot.

London
A year earlier

Her father was determined that she was to be cultured. He had no interest in anything but business, so while he met with various solicitors, off she went in the company of her American maid and her English chaperone, a woman with whom she'd been saddled since arriving in London.

Mrs. Haverstock was as far from a chaperone as Virginia could imagine. The woman had been widowed, she said, for over five years, which meant she must have married as a child. She was only a few years older than her, with blond hair so pale it appeared almost white in a certain light. She smiled often and was delighted by almost everything she saw, even Virginia's father.

"Mr. Anderson," she once said, "is an amazing man to have accomplished all he's done as young as he is." From that day forward, Virginia watched Mrs. Haverstock with curiosity, wondering if she had dreams of becoming the second Mrs. Anderson.

A curious thing to contemplate because she'd never once considered that her father would remarry. That he didn't was probably due more to his consuming interest in business over amatory pursuits.

However, she would not have been surprised if Mrs. Haverstock was successful. She'd managed to convince him to hire her after only one interview, after all.

The woman was indefatigable. They visited St. Paul's Cathedral one day and Covent Garden Market the next. One whole afternoon was spent at London Bridge, followed by a short and fragrant journey down the Thames.

Virginia would never forget how horrified she'd been by Madame Tussaud's Waxworks. She couldn't imagine her father approving that expedition so she never told him of it, or the nightmares that came for two days afterward at the thought of all those wax statues coming alive.

At Westminster Abbey, she was horrified to discover other tourists gouging their names into the royal tombs. When she said as much to her chaperone, Mrs. Haverstock just waved her comment away.

"They've done the same to the pyramids, my dear."

Mrs. Haverstock adored museums, and Virginia might have as well had she not been dragged to every one of them in London. The East Indian Museum was regrettably boring, but the British Museum was most impressive.

The concentric circles and curved shelves of the Round Reading Room fascinated her. So, too, the various readers occupying the tables. Each claimed his space beneath the vaulted blue dome like it was his home. One reader had strung a rope between him and the nearest table and hung tracts from them, cautioning a visitor from speaking to him. Another had brochures of anti-papal literature arrayed in front of him.

She was walking quietly from one shelf to another,

grateful to have momentarily lost Mrs. Haverstock to a conversation with an unexpectedly encountered friend, when she saw him.

Macrath leaned against a bookshelf and smiled at her.

Her heart was leaping in her chest like a child promised a candy.

"What are you doing here?" she whispered.

Looking around, she couldn't see Mrs. Haverstock. She grabbed Macrath's sleeve and disappeared in front of one of the curved shelves with him, well aware that, if seen, this infraction of decorum was sure to be reported to her father.

"What are you doing here?" she asked again.

"I could say that I visit the British Museum often," he said.

"Do you?"

"It's only my second time here."

For a month they'd seen each other at balls and dinners, and found a way to slip away from the crowd. More than once he'd asked for her reticule and she'd handed it to him, amused when he slipped a few broadsides inside.

"There, you won't have to lie. You didn't buy them."

Whenever he did that, she'd take out the broadsides later, smoothing her hands over the rough paper, not caring about what tales they told as much as that Macrath had touched them.

"You told Ceana you'd be here," he said, smiling.

She had occasion to meet Ceana one night, and the two became fast friends, each watching for the other at various events.

But it was Macrath who changed her life.

If Macrath was in a room, her eyes sought him out. If he laughed, her ears heard it. She could even tell if he spoke in a crowd because his Scottish accent was so distinctive.

"I came to see you," he said now. "I couldn't wait for tonight."

"You couldn't?"

Her heart had ascended to the base of her throat and something odd was happening in her eyes. She couldn't hold all the emotions she was feeling inside, and they had to be expressed as tears.

When she'd first entered the Round Reading Room, she was surprised at the number of people there. Now it seemed like they were all eavesdropping.

Macrath reached out and plucked a book from the shelf, appearing engrossed in the text.

She raised the book to see the binding, smiling when she read it. "I've always loved Tennyson," she said. "I was required to memorize some of his work."

"Were you?"

She nodded.

> *"Come into the garden, Maud,*
> *For the black bat night has flown.*
> *Come into the garden, Maud,*
> *I'm here at the gate alone."*

"Hardly proper reading for a young girl," he said, smiling. "It's been made into a song, you know."

She shook her head, surprised. "No, I didn't."

He leaned close to her and began to sing the words softly.

His breath smelled of mint, brushing against her temple. He was entirely too close for propriety, but she didn't move away, merely closed her eyes to savor his presence.

"Virginia," he said softly.

She took a deep breath and forced herself to open her eyes.

"Have you never heard of Robert Burns?" he asked, replacing the volume of Tennyson poems. "A much better poet by far."

Once again she shook her head.

He started searching the books. A moment later he found what he was looking for, and thumbed through the volume.

Unsmiling, he held the book out to her, pointing to a poem.

"You should read 'A Red, Red Rose,'" he said.

She took the book from him.

> O my Luve's like a red, red rose
> That's newly sprung in June;
> O my Luve's like the melodie
> That's sweetly played in tune.
> As fair art thou, my bonnie lass,
> So deep in luve am I;
> And I will luve thee still, my dear,
> Till a' the seas gang dry.

She glanced up at him, something sweet and hot racing through her body.

"Oh, Macrath."

Here, where there was a hushed reverence for the written word, she felt the same for him. In his piercing blue eyes she saw a reflection of someone she'd never known herself to be, a woman who was captivating and fascinating and brave. Being loved by Macrath made everything possible, even her transformation.

She knew she shouldn't put her hand on his chest. Nor should he wipe away a tear from her cheek with such tenderness.

"Miss Anderson."

She didn't want to turn and see Mrs. Haverstock. She didn't want to answer any questions. Or try to explain something so private and perfect.

When the woman walked into her line of sight, she had no choice but to drop her hand and step away.

"Thank you, Mr. Sinclair," she said. "I'll make a point of reading Mr. Burns in the future."

She nodded to him and turned away, when what she truly wanted was to have him enfold her in his arms.

"Until tonight," he whispered.

It would have to be enough, but oh how could it be?

Drumvagen, Scotland
July, 1869

A stranger had come to Drumvagen. A stranger in an ornate ebony carriage pulled by four of the finest horses he'd seen in a while.

Macrath strode down the road, wishing he didn't smell of ammonia and the other chemicals in his laboratory. Jack and Sam broke away, heading for their own quarters to bathe and change. He would have liked to do the same, but the carriage was sitting in front of Drumvagen, the door being opened by a burly coachman.

He stopped, transfixed by the strangest notion that he was in the middle of a dream. A black shod foot emerged first, then a flurry of black petticoat peeping beneath a silk skirt, ebony to match the carriage. Her gloved hand on the coachman's arm, she lightly stepped from the vehicle, the black-ribboned bonnet shielding her face from his view.

He knew. Even before she glanced up at him, he knew. Only one woman had ever affected him the way she did, as if she gave off a signal his body recognized.

Virginia.

His blood was pounding, his heart beating as loudly as the drums of war. Inside, he shouted with exultant joy.

Virginia had come to Drumvagen.

When he'd first met her, she reminded him of a delicate bird, one at the mercy of air currents and tossed aloft to a strange and foreign land. She was almost preternaturally still, like she'd been poured from a mold, but her eyes were alive and watching everything.

Her face was oval, her eyes a clear blue, so light in color it seemed like he could see into the heart of her. Her hair was black and fine. Tendrils always escaped her careful hairstyle and surrounded her face. Her smile was quick and held a surprised air, as if her own joy startled her.

She wasn't smiling now.

Her eyes had lost their sparkle. A lock of hair brushed against her alabaster cheek, only slightly tinged with a blush. Her mouth opened to greet him, then closed and firmed without saying a word.

He couldn't breathe, but that could be the lingering effects of the explosion and the chemicals he'd inhaled. More likely it was simply Virginia.

She was wearing black.

Dear God, did she bring bad news?

He strode forward, wanting to shake the words from her. "Ceana?" he asked. "Is she well?"

Recognition dawned in Virginia's eyes. "I'm sorry. I didn't think. Yes, she's well." She glanced down at her gloved hands. "It's Lawrence," she said, her voice vibrating with emotion. "He's dead."

He schooled his features to show nothing, not even a trace of gladness.

"My condolences," he said.

Why was she here?

The question thrummed between them. Her maid, and the interested glances from her coachman, kept him silent.

He turned and strode in the other direction, and she, as he'd hoped, followed him. He hesitated at the entrance to the drive, staring out at the expanse of sea and sky, one mirroring the other.

Boiling black clouds on the horizon promised a storm by nightfall. Drumvagen was a secure and comforting refuge in the midst of lightning and thunder. On another night he might have settled in front of the fire, sipping whiskey from a tankard belonging to his father. His thoughts would have returned to London and the woman who now stood silently beside him.

"Why have you come, Virginia? To tell me of your widowhood?"

She didn't answer. Her silence caused him to turn and look at her.

"Was it a happy marriage?"

She hesitated. When she nodded, he didn't believe her.

"A short one," she added.

Didn't she realize he knew how long it had been? He'd gotten drunk the day of her wedding, the first time he'd ever allowed himself to do so.

He wanted to embrace her, hold her close to him. He wanted to fall to his knees, wrap his arms around her hips, keep her there until he accepted she was truly at Drumvagen.

"Why are you here, Virginia?" he asked, his mind racing in a dozen directions at once.

She reached out one gloved hand and placed it on his shirted chest. His pulse raced at her touch, as if she had the power to burrow into his skin, stroke the heart beneath and quicken its beat.

"Let me rest," she said. "Feed me a meal or two, and

perhaps a glass of wine." She glanced away, then back at him, as if daring herself. "Then I'll tell you."

Turning, he looked at his home, taking in Drumvagen's sprawling glory. He would put her in the suite he'd prepared for her.

He held out his arm. She placed her hand on it, and he accompanied her up the drive and then the steps, much as he had thought of doing from the moment he met her.

What did she think of Drumvagen? Her eyes were wide as she took in the broad double doors. He'd ordered them from Italy and had to wait nearly a year for them to be finished.

Like a boy, he wanted to tell her about building Drumvagen, how he'd found it an unfinished shell and knew it was his home from the beginning. He wanted to brag about each of the furnishings, tell her the story of how he'd found the chandeliers, the carved doors, and the mirrored walls.

He kept silent, watching her, noting the delicate blush appearing on her cheeks and wondering at its cause.

This woman was the source of his greatest pain.

He should send her away, tell her about the inn only a few miles distant. He should send Jack or Sam as an outrider, to ensure she got to her destination and didn't think about circling back to Drumvagen. He should keep men at intervals along the road to guard the approach, to keep her from it.

Instead, he pushed open the door and stood aside for her to enter his home.

Chapter 6

Macrath hadn't changed. He was the same as he had been, a magnificent specimen of man. The only thing different was the strange smell surrounding him like a cloud.

She wished Hannah wasn't right behind her. She would've studied Macrath, from the top of his head all the way down his body. She felt his arm beneath her hand and wondered if he knew she was trembling.

He led her to a small parlor with windows overlooking the ocean with its wind tossed waves. The storm that had been threatening for the last hour was advancing. The face the clouds showed was gray and flat, the edges detailed and brightly limned by a sun she couldn't see. She heard thunder, but lightning hid like a cowardly mastiff.

The parlor was shadowed by the approaching storm, a cozy place to watch nature's display.

She glanced toward the white marble fireplace, the burgundy upholstered settee faced by two matching chairs and a mahogany table. Before she had time to remark it was a lovely room, or question the identity of the portraits along the fireplace wall, a woman joined them.

Virginia had been trained by her governesses never to show her emotions, especially in social situations. If she were surprised or taken aback, she must never allow anyone else to know.

The woman Macrath introduced as his housekeeper, however, almost jolted her out of her restraint.

Her face was broad and square, her nose narrow and long. Her hair, brown threaded with gray, was arranged at the back of her head in a severe bun. Perhaps she normally wore a genial expression, but at the moment, twin vertical lines appeared between her deep set brown eyes, and her square lips were thin.

She was nearly Macrath's height and sturdily built, dressed in a plaid skirt, a white bodice, and a length of the same plaid tossed over her shoulder and fastened with an oversized pin festooned with feathers. Virginia wondered if the woman was one of those affected to Highland dress. She'd been told that ever since the Queen first expressed her love of Scotland, all things Scottish were in vogue.

"This is Brianag," he said. "She'll show you to your rooms." Turning to the housekeeper, he said, "The Rose Room, Brianag,"

Once more he glanced at Virginia. "If you'll excuse me, I'll ensure I'm acceptable to present company. Otherwise, I'm going to smell of ammonia."

"Is that what it is?" she asked, smiling.

"We were experimenting with combining chemicals," he said.

"It wasn't dangerous, was it?"

After a quick glance at his housekeeper and Hannah, he only shook his head. A moment later he was gone, leaving the three of them standing there.

Without a word, Brianag turned and left the room. Virginia glanced at Hannah.

"Are we to follow her?"

"I don't know, your ladyship."

What a strange woman. Rather than wonder, she trailed after Brianag. A wise impulse, because the housekeeper was waiting at the base of the sweeping steps. She nodded at Virginia's appearance, grabbed her plaid skirt with one fist and stomped up the steps.

With one more quick glance at Hannah, Virginia followed, the two of them climbing to the second floor. In the middle of the hallway, the housekeeper opened a door and entered. Evidently, she expected them to follow her inside, if the impatient look she gave them was any indication.

Virginia stood at the doorway of a sitting room papered in pale pink silk. A settee, upholstered in a rose pattern, was arranged in front of the carved black fireplace, and next to it a table and chair with a needlepoint footstool. On the far wall was a secretary, and several thriving plants in black urns. The room was so spacious there was ample room to walk, to swing one's skirt, even perform a solitary waltz. She didn't doubt the bedroom was as comfortable.

"The room is lovely," she said. "But I haven't put anyone out, have I? It looks like it's been readied for an occupant."

"At Drumvagen there's a suite for the master and one for the mistress. This is the one set aside for the mistress. Himself had it decorated for his bride."

Virginia stood silent for a moment, deciphering that news, Hannah at her side.

"He didn't marry after all," the woman added, frowning darkly at her.

Turning to survey the room again, she wondered if Macrath had created this suite for her. Was she the bride he hadn't married?

How strange to feel so sad about it now.

Had he thought about her when he had the room furnished with rose patterned upholstery? Had he remembered her love of roses, her fondness for the shade of dark pink? Had he remembered she liked music boxes? Was that why the display case to her left was filled with seven of them? Had he, too, remembered her frustration about not being able to grow anything? Was that why the plants had been so lovingly tended they seemed to welcome her?

"You'll be comfortable enough here," the housekeeper said in a tone daring her to argue.

"Thank you, Mrs. . . ." Her words trailed away.

"My name is Brianag," the woman said.

"Yes, well . . ." Virginia felt flustered and not a little confused. Was she supposed to address her as Brianag? "Is it a Scottish name?" she asked.

"Would you be thinking it anything else? Welsh?"

Brianag did not approve of her.

"Will you be staying long?"

She hadn't expected the question, especially from Brianag.

"It's no matter of mine," the housekeeper said before she could answer. "Ti keep a calm souch."

"I beg your pardon?"

"Ti keep a calm souch," Brianag repeated.

Repeating something did not make it understandable.

She was then given an explanation about the bells for meals and told that a maid would escort her to the dining room. She smiled in response, which had no effect on the woman's scowl. When she closed the door behind Brianag, she sagged against it in relief.

At least she was here. She'd done that much. Macrath hadn't turned her away. The next step was going to be so much more difficult, however.

Perhaps she'd do as her mother-in-law implied—let Macrath know she was willing, and let him do the rest.

London
A year earlier

Whenever she saw Macrath, Virginia felt lighter, some-how. Any worries or cares simply drifted away. With him, she could do anything. Nothing was too great an obstacle to overcome.

When he left her, it was as if the sun suddenly dimmed and the cloud stayed in place until the next time she saw him again.

The day following the meeting in the British Museum, Macrath had simply disappeared. An entire week went by in which the days seemed as dark as night. Neither he nor Ceana had been to any of the endless entertainments she'd been forced to attend.

Had they returned to Scotland?

When she and Mrs. Haverstock visited the Victoria and Albert Museum and then the Science Museum, she kept hoping Macrath would appear. He hadn't, but she'd grown heartily tired of education.

If she never saw another sight in London, she'd be pleased.

"Miss."

Virginia put her finger in her book to mark her place, listening.

"Miss."

No, she hadn't imagined it. Someone was whispering to her. She peered around the chair and saw Bessie, the undercook, standing in the doorway.

Why on earth didn't the girl come toward her?

Evidently, something was capturing her attention, be-cause she looked to her left, then at Virginia, and to her left again.

"Quick, miss," she said. "Before anyone sees I'm gone."

"What is the matter?" she asked, standing and approaching the door.

The girl rarely left the kitchen. To find her in the corridor outside the parlor was odd, but not as odd as what Bessie did next.

She raced up to Virginia and whispered, "He said I was to give a message to Maud. I told him there was no Maud in our household, but he said there was, and it was you. A pet name, miss?"

"What did he say, Bessie?" she asked, desperate to know.

"You're to come to the garden, Maud," the girl said, then flew down the corridor to the kitchen.

Her smile reached her heart before traveling to her lips. Macrath.

He was here. He was here in the garden.

She straightened her skirt, wishing she'd worn one of her new dresses today, but she didn't want to take the time to change.

Skirts swinging, she took the same path Bessie had, avoiding the kitchen for the garden door, stepping down into the long rectangular lawn with heart beating and her breath coming too tight.

He wasn't there.

Had she misunderstood? Had he given Bessie a message that the girl hadn't understood? Was he waiting for her somewhere else?

The door to the shed at the end of the garden suddenly creaked open. She grabbed her skirts in both hands and flew down the flagstone path.

Suddenly, he was there, tall and handsome, his eyes twinkling. By his presence, he forever changed the garden into an enchanted place.

"You're here," she said, feeling foolish and too young.

"At last," he said.

"Were you away?" she asked.

"Yes," he said. "I had to travel to Edinburgh on business."

"I hope it went well," she said. How inane she sounded. Perhaps it was better than saying what was truly on her mind.

Don't go away again without warning me. Let me know when you'll be gone, so I'll know how many days to prepare myself for sorrow.

"I've missed you," he said, and her heart tripped over itself. In violation of every societal rule she'd been taught, she placed her hands on his arms. She stood too close. She leaned toward him.

"I've missed you as well. Every day has been a month long."

He didn't speak, and neither did she. They were comfortable in each other's silences, and it was so restful to be with him in one way and so tumultuous in another.

He made her feel things she'd never felt.

She wanted to be kissed. She wanted to be held. She wanted to know if an embrace was as wondrous as all the poets said it was. She wanted to know, most especially, what happened afterward.

Would kissing him ease this uncomfortable ache? Would it rid her of this craving to touch him, to stroke her hands over his broad shoulders and down his arms to measure the incredible breadth of him? She wanted to lay her cheek against his chest, marvel at the beating of his heart, thanking God all the while He had sent Macrath into her life.

"I turned to look every time someone entered a room," she said.

"I stored away a dozen stories I heard, thinking you would want to know what was happening in that part of the world."

"I wanted to talk to you about Gladstone's speech."

They smiled at each other.

"Will you be going back to Scotland soon?" she asked, her earlier fear returning.

"I think so, yes."

She tried to remain calm but the pain bit through her composure.

He'd never come out and said the words, but he'd given her to think he loved her. How could he now speak of leaving her?

"You would like Scotland, I think."

She only nodded, feeling numb.

"Will you come with me to Drumvagen, Virginia?" he asked, catching hold of her hand and drawing her back to him. "Will you be my wife and love me as I love you?"

Her heart was beating out of her chest. In a moment it would fly away like a suddenly released bird.

"I would be very amenable," she said.

Why was she being so coy? There must be no mistake. He must know exactly how she felt.

"Yes, Macrath, yes. With my whole heart. I love you so."

He leaned close, pressing his lips against her forehead.

"You'll talk to my father?" she asked, the words feeling too heavy to be spoken.

"Today if he'll see me."

She had never done anything as shocking as what she did next. She placed her hand on his chest and slowly stood on her tiptoes.

"Kiss me," she said. "Please."

"Virginia," he said, pulling back, "this isn't wise."

But, oh, she had been wise for so long, and he was such a temptation.

Suddenly, his arms were around her and his mouth on

hers. He angled his head to deepen the kiss. Every thought disappeared and every sensation vanished but for wonder and excitement.

She'd known he'd be direct, perhaps a little impatient, and he was. She'd suspected she would be eager and she was.

His lips were soft, his body hard beneath her hands. His tongue touched hers, darted back, and teased her again,

She linked her hands behind his neck and held on, allowing herself to sink into the deliciousness of his mouth.

Her heart fluttered. Her breath and pulse raced. Something dark, heavy, and a little frightening arced between them.

He was right in cautioning her. She never wanted to move from his arms.

When they finally parted, she moved back, touching her lips with her fingertips.

If someone saw her, she would be lectured for hours about deportment and how she'd failed to give the impression she'd been reared correctly.

But any punishment was worth it for one of Macrath's kisses.

Chapter 7

Drumvagen, Scotland
July, 1869

Freshly bathed and changed, Macrath sat in what had been designed as the Clan Hall by the architect. Stretching the width of the main section of Drumvagen, the room was supposed to be used as a gathering place. Exposed beams hinted at a history much older than the twenty years since Drumvagen had been started. He wondered, not for the first time, if some of the older features of his house had been taken from the crumbling structures dotting this area of Scotland.

The brick of Drumvagen was new, the gray tint purposely selected to blend in with the landscape. The house was a black pearl nestled in a bed of trees.

Virginia was here.

Virginia was at Drumvagen.

"You wanted to see me?"

His housekeeper stood at the doorway, frowning at him.

Brianag had a reputation as a healer. She was intuitive to a frightening degree, and known for being able to foretell the future, a talent she steadfastly refused to acknowledge.

She was also a termagant, frightened the servants and the inhabitants of Kinloch Village, and had no hesitation in telling him when he'd used ill judgment—according to her opinion.

She was only a few inches shorter than he was, with broad shoulders and a build hinting at masculinity. Her normal stance was to plant her large feet wide, fold her arms in front of her, and scowl down in judgment over the penitent.

God help the man who got on her bad side.

A great many people petitioned Brianag, and it might either be fear or their belief in her abilities. Many mornings he'd come downstairs only to be told his housekeeper had been summoned to the village to treat a broken bone or another injury.

According to Brianag, the villagers had nicknamed him the Devil of Drumvagen. He'd learned that interesting bit of nonsense a few years ago when she pinned him down in this same room.

"Why?" he asked. "I've never done anything to earn such an idiotic name."

"You'll find you don't have to, here at Drumvagen," she said matter-of-factly. "It's enough you look like Old Nick."

"What do you mean?"

She folded her arms and tilted her head a little, studying him.

"You've got the black hair and blue eyes, and a wicked grin when you're not all somber. I've heard tell in the village the girls were warned away from you. Maybe they're thinking you'd lure them here to have your wicked way with them."

He frowned. "Where would they get such an idea?"

She shrugged. "Still, it makes for a good tale. And it gives the village mothers something to use with their children."

Startled, he could only stare at his housekeeper. "You mean as a warning? Be good or the Devil of Drumvagen will get you?"

She smiled. "I think the devil part is because you expect people to jump to your bidding quickly, with no questions asked."

He regarded her in astonishment. He was unfailingly polite to his staff, including her, even though there were times when he was annoyed or irritated.

"I've never heard anything more ridiculous."

She thrust one imperial finger at him. "That's the reason," she said, "right there. You've a temper about you."

"And you, Brianag. I've heard you shouting at the maids."

Her frown was an imposing sight, with her bushy eyebrows coming together in a single line.

He suspected she agreed to work for him because of curiosity. Working here was a way to discover what he was doing at Drumvagen. Over the last five years she'd created a fiefdom, one she ruled with an iron hand.

"Is she settled?" he asked now.

"In the room you made for her," Brianag said.

How the hell had she known that? He'd given instructions for the rooms to be redecorated shortly after he met Virginia. The furniture was to be French, upholstered in a rose pattern. The curtains and wallpaper were to be the softest pink, her favorite shade. Pots were to be filled with the most priceless rose potpourri. He'd worried about the timetable of getting everything perfect for Virginia before their wedding.

The wedding that had never happened.

"How long will she be staying?"

He wasn't about to tell her he didn't know. Hell, he didn't even know why Virginia was here.

He was not going to question Providence at the moment, however.

"You'll see to her maid and the driver as well?"

When his housekeeper just raised one eyebrow, he amended his statement. "Of course you will. And dinner, too. Something special, I think."

The second eyebrow joined the first. Her mouth thinned and her arms remained folded in front of her.

Brianag's annoyance wasn't as important as another fact, startling, confusing, and a blessing.

Virginia was at Drumvagen.

Brianag tapped her foot impatiently. Who employed whom?

"Is there anything else?"

"You might try smiling once in awhile," he said. "Or stop looking so ferocious. Or try remembering I'm your employer. A simple 'sir' wouldn't be amiss from time to time."

"Is that all? Sir?"

He nodded, and she left the room, mumbling something in her indecipherable Scots.

Macrath had been born and raised in Edinburgh. He considered himself a Scot through and through. Yet the people of Kinloch spoke with such a thick accent he had a hard time understanding them. He'd heard Brianag in the kitchen, talking to the maids, and it might as well be a foreign tongue. When she noticed him, she always switched to a more understandable Scottish English, one not requiring interpretation.

When she was irritated, however, she spoke whatever she wanted.

He eased back in his chair, staring at the carved ceiling. Reaching inside his jacket, he plucked out the note he'd kept with him for a year. A handy piece of remembrance, a morality tale in a few sentences. Something to keep him sane—and probably bitter—for all these months. A reminder that he shouldn't be so overjoyed to see her now, or not until certain questions were resolved.

He read it again although he could see the words whenever he closed his eyes. A moment later he tucked it away again.

What explanation would she give him for both the note and her arrival at Drumvagen?

The last time he'd seen her, Virginia had been walking away from him with a smile, heading toward her father.

A man to whom he'd taken an instant dislike, a confession he'd never made to her.

"My daughter tells me you own a newspaper," Anderson had said on that first meeting. They'd both been sipping whiskey offered in one of the rooms set aside for bored spouses and male escorts.

Of average height, Anderson had black hair and blue eyes that were cold and flat, without one ounce of warmth. The only time he appeared remotely approachable was when he talked about his empire, how many shares of stock in railroads he owned, his cotton mills, and ships. Evidently, the recent war in America had only expanded his holdings.

A curiosity—not once did Anderson mention his daughter.

"The newspaper is a family business," Macrath told him. "I've since branched out into other fields. I've invented an ice machine."

"An inventor, eh? One of those fellas who tinker with things, then try to convince the rest of us to give them money for it. Is that it?"

"I suppose it is," Macrath said.

The American had just described, in unflattering terms,

what he'd done to get funding for his first machine. He'd come up with the idea, created a prototype, then solicited investors to whom he proved it would be a good risk. After the first flurry of sales of the Sinclair Ice Machine, having made five men richer than they'd been, he declined any further investments.

When he explained this to Virginia's father, the man didn't look impressed. Instead, Anderson studied him with a sour expression on his face.

"I've heard tales about Scotland. How you all prance about in kilts, showing your bare asses. I'm surprised there are any of you left, what with you beating each other over the head with swords for hundreds of years."

"Perhaps I'll get a chance to show you the real Scotland," he said, hoping such an occasion never happened. He couldn't imagine being trapped in a railroad car or carriage with Anderson for longer than a minute or two.

The man flicked his hand at him, as if to dismiss Scotland and Macrath. In the next moment he'd wandered off, leaving Macrath staring after him and trying to imagine the man as an in-law.

However, he'd been willing to put aside his feelings for Virginia's sake.

Evidently, Virginia had put aside hers as well. For him.

Why was she here? Should he even care? She was here, and that was all that mattered.

Virginia studied her reflection in the pier glass as Hannah fluffed her hem and straightened her hoop.

"It's a good thing you're one of those women who look handsome in black," her mother-in-law had said. "But you needn't wear those nightgowns edged in black, I think."

She had closed her eyes on that comment, not wishing to discuss her nightgowns with Enid.

Did she look her best in black?

Her eyes seemed to sparkle with unshed tears, looking bluer than normal. Even so, they were not as arresting as Macrath's eyes.

If she could be only half as attractive a woman as he was a man, she would be beautiful indeed. Once, a maid had told her she had all the qualities of beauty save one: the confidence.

Now she was trembling, and when she clenched her hands into fists, the tremors crept inside.

She was caught on a fulcrum, one side of her grateful she was here because it was the one place on earth she most wanted to be, while the other desperately wanted to be away from this place. It was almost like being split into two—angel and sinner—and each side warring with the other.

The storm had struck since she'd seen Macrath. Rain sheeted the windows, and gusts of wind occasionally caused the panes to shiver in their frames. Should she be worried about the rolling thunder? Was it a sign of disapproval from God? This was not the first time she'd sinned, but the only time she'd done so egregiously, with premeditation and not as much regret as she should have felt.

"Have you been given your quarters, Hannah?" she asked.

"Yes, your ladyship. I have an acceptable room with a window overlooking the sea. I can smell it and hear the birds as well. No doubt they'll wake me up in the mornings. Better than the maids arguing or carriage wheels on the cobbles, I'm thinking."

"Good," she said, wishing she had something to say to the girl. She and Hannah had never conversed much, but now it felt almost uncomfortable not to do so.

Or was she trying to think of anything but her upcoming dinner with Macrath?

Her gaze fixed on the massive four poster bed. Had Macrath imagined her here, too?

"Is there anything else I can do, your ladyship?"

Talk me out of this. Keep me from leaving this room. Instill some sense of decorum if not morality in me.

She only shook her head in response.

When Hannah answered the soft knock on the door, Virginia gave herself one last look in the mirror.

God help her, but she was running full tilt toward sin.

Chapter 8

The dining room was shrouded, lit only by a pair of silver candelabra on the long mahogany table and one on the sideboard. Shadows lingered in the corners as if wishing to reach out and snare her.

She was seeing threats that weren't there. If anything, she should be afraid of her own actions, not ghosts in a Scottish house.

"Perhaps it would be better if your maid joined you."

She started, clasped her hands tightly together, and turned to the sound of his voice. He emerged from the darkness like Satan given human form.

If ever a devil tempted a woman, Macrath Sinclair did.

"Do I need a chaperone?"

"Perhaps it would be best if you had one," he said. "You might be safer."

Her skin pebbled at the sound of his voice, almost like he had drawn a cold finger along her skin. And the heat bubbling inside? Where did that come from? Her own thoughts? Her recollections of a stolen kiss in London? Or from warm, forbidden dreams after her wedding?

No, this wasn't a safe place to be. This entire journey had been unsafe. Standing here, without an answer for him, was even more dangerous.

He came to the table, and drew out a chair. She nodded and sat, thanking him. He took his place at the head of the table, an expanse of at least six feet between them.

"Tell me about your marriage," he said.

She placed her napkin on her lap, rearranged her fork and spoon, moved the wineglass an inch to the left, then to the right.

"What do you want to know?" she finally asked. "My day-to-day routine?"

"I would like you to tell me about your marriage."

"It was a marriage," she said with as much equanimity as she could muster. "He was not much interested in me."

"Were you interested in him?"

She stared down at the plate, wondering at the pattern of the thistles along the edge. There was movement from the shadows, approaching the table. Then one girl served her a steaming bowl of turtle soup while another offered a dish of oyster pâté. She thanked them both.

In the next few minutes the courses started and she didn't have a chance to answer him. Or did he expect her to speak in front of the servants?

She was given a plate piled with slices of roast venison, accompanied by French mustard, eggs in aspic, slices of duck, and a concoction of peas mixed with mayonnaise.

When the servants melted back into the shadows, he said, "They're gone."

In other words, he expected an answer.

"I didn't like Lawrence," she said. "I don't think it mattered to anyone whether or not we liked each other. My father simply wanted something to show for all his money. A title he could brag about."

She forced herself to pick up the fork and taste the venison. He took a sip of his wine, but otherwise wasn't eating.

"And you, you wanted the title as well."

She smiled. "I didn't care," she said.

The food was excellent, and when she said as much, he only nodded, as if he expected no less. Was he always surrounded by effortless luxury simply because he was Macrath Sinclair?

He took another sip of wine, the gesture graceful and unhurried.

She'd never been afraid of him, but she feared this meeting, these questions. She might reveal too much.

Silence stretched thin, the only sound her fork as she rested it against the plate. How could she hope to eat when her heart was in her throat?

"Why are you here, only days after you're made a widow?"

"How did you know?"

"Your coachman."

"So, you plied Hosking with drink and managed to extricate from him information I would've given you gladly had you asked."

"I didn't ply him with drink," he said with a smile. "I asked a question and he answered it. Which is more than you're doing."

She took a deep breath, staring down at her plate.

"Almost a year has passed," he said.

She didn't raise her head. "Yes."

"A year in which you went from being an American heiress to a countess. Have you changed, Virginia?"

Had she changed?

What would he say if she told him the truth? She'd changed so drastically she expected to see a different person in the mirror. Someone with more experience in her gaze, her mouth thinned, her face tight with dread.

"What did you expect me to be like?"

"A society matron, perhaps. Someone who had fashion on her mind."

She could only smile. Had he forgotten the conversations between them, when she confessed to having no love or care whatsoever about what she wore?

"I haven't changed that much," she said.

"How do you find being a countess, then?"

"It's a comfortable life."

"Are you comfortable in it?" he asked.

What would he say to learn the truth? She decided to test him on it.

"I am not as hopeful as I once was," she said softly. "I don't anticipate the arrival of every morning with delight. I rarely laugh."

"Why is that?"

She shrugged.

"Was he kind to you, Virginia?"

She'd never thought this would be so difficult. Or that he would peel the veneer away from the truth so easily.

"No," she said. "He resented me, and you rarely treat those you resent with kindness."

His goblet came down on the table so hard she glanced at him.

His face was expressionless, but his eyes were heated.

She studied her plate again, a much easier sight than Macrath. The plate didn't peer into her soul or make her tremble.

"Then damn him," Macrath said softly. "May his soul rot cheerfully in Hell."

Shocked, she looked at him. "You shouldn't say such things."

"Why, to keep my soul from shriveling? Of the two of us, I think your earl has more to answer for."

He mustn't be protective of her. She didn't deserve it.

She twisted her napkin in her lap until it was a ball of damp linen, wishing he would say something else, lighten the mood between them.

Evidently, she was going to have to change the tenor of conversation. Should she speak about the storm still pounding Drumvagen? Was it God, voicing his displeasure in ways other people would note?

"Your sister is well," she said.

"Yes, I know. She speaks of you in her letters. I'm grateful for your friendship."

What had Ceana told him? Did he ask about her? Did Ceana keep her confidences?

She wanted to retreat to her lavish borrowed suite and pray for guidance. Or would God, having washed His hands of her, give her only thunder and lightning in return?

"Why are you here?"

There, an answer from God himself. She was not going to be allowed to retreat easily.

"I wanted to see you," she said. That wasn't a lie but it might be a sin. She shouldn't betray herself with words. "I wanted to see if you were well and happy."

"I am well," he said.

"Are you happy?"

"Are you?"

"You haven't married." Not a question, but he answered nonetheless.

"The woman I wanted went to another," he said.

She warmed at his words. "Not because she wished it."

"I think you could've fought harder had you wanted."

So said a man who was the king of his kingdom. A man, even in the semidarkness, who exuded power and confidence.

"I had a choice," she said. "To marry Lawrence, or be taken home to America in disgrace."

"I would've found you there," he said.

She stared into the candle flame, trying not to allow his words to affect her. He would have come after her, she was certain of it. The wedding night she'd so dreaded would have been with him and not Lawrence.

"You never protested?"

Yes, she had, but what good did it do to tell him? She'd been afraid, but she'd pleaded anyway. She'd begged. She'd offered logic and reason. Her father had never heard her.

Two reasons spared her from punishment, and neither was due to kindness or affection. Her father had no one to administer a beating to her and was no doubt loath to do it himself. Plus, since she was promised to the earl, he didn't want her to go damaged to her bridegroom.

Macrath didn't know about that, either.

She was suddenly angry. Why did he spear her with questions now?

"If you'd cared so much," she asked, "why did you give up so easily? It's easy now to say you would have gone to America. A year later."

He stared at her for long minutes while the fire crackled and the wind pushed against the windowpanes. She was not going to be the first to break the brittle silence.

"I never gave up," he said. "I went to your house many times and was turned away each time. I wrote you a dozen times. I never stopped until I got your letter."

She couldn't breathe. Had Hannah laced her too tightly?

"I never received one letter from you," she said. "Nor did I ever write you."

She'd been guarded so well she might have been able to compose a letter but never to post it.

He abruptly stood, striding toward her.

Reaching into his jacket, he pulled something out, placing it on the table beside her without a word.

Slowly, she picked up a much folded paper, unfolded it and read:

Macrath,

I am to be married. I know you will understand that it would be foolish of me not to agree to a union with the Earl of Barrett.

Please don't write me again.

I wish you great success in your future.

How could he think she would write something so impersonal and almost flippant to him?

"That isn't my handwriting," she said.

"Look at the signature."

She hadn't paid it any attention, but at his words, she did, feeling her heart sink to her toes.

Maud.

Of course he would think it was from her, from their meeting in the British Museum. The jest only the two of them had shared from that day forward.

"Mrs. Haverstock," she said.

Her chaperone had to have heard them that day. Or had Bessie told her? Had the woman also known about their meeting in the garden, when they'd kissed?

He returned to his chair as she placed the letter on the table between them.

He'd been as wounded as she.

She wasn't close to seducing Macrath. He was looking at her like she was a stranger, as if all those weeks they'd spent together had never happened. Had he tamped down the pleasant memories in favor of those that made him angry?

Easing back in the chair, she calmly straightened her napkin, smoothing out the wrinkles and folding it into fourths.

"I didn't write that letter, Macrath. But that hardly matters now, does it?"

"Why are you here, Virginia?"

She had always liked the way he'd said her name, the *r*'s rolling in a Scottish burr. She loved the way he spoke, even about commonsense things, the weather, the scent of flowers, or the sunset.

"I can't tell you," she said finally, in answer to his question. "I should tell you," she added, "but I can't. The words won't come." Then she took the truth and wrapped it in a lie, leading him to think this visit was the result of need and longing more than survival. "I just knew I had to see you."

His gaze settled on her breasts.

She warmed from the inside out, her breath coming too tightly. A year ago he'd always been a gentleman, treating her with respect and care.

Would he be the same now?

He stood and, with a scrape of the chair against the wooden floor, strode the length of the table to reach her. She tensed, but he turned her chair as if she weighed no more than a feather, lifting her from it.

He pulled her into his arms in a gentle embrace that surprised and comforted her. She closed her eyes, pressed her cheek against the fine wool of his jacket and took a deep breath of relief.

If he banished her tomorrow, she would at least have these moments of memory.

He pressed his cheek against her hair, stood there for long, treasured, minutes. Finally, he drew back and kissed her temple, such a gentle sweet kiss it brought tears to her eyes.

Slowly, she extended her arms around his waist, leaned her forehead against his chest. She needed courage now more than at any time in her life.

"Virginia," he said softly.

How strange to envision seduction in a bedchamber and

have it occur in a dining room. Or to have him kiss her tenderly on her cheek and summon her tears.

They'd kissed once, and the experience had been one of the most shocking and sensual she'd ever known. She wanted another one of his kisses, and now he was spurring her on without a word spoken.

She opened her eyes and tilted her head back, wanting him to know, in this at least, she wasn't lying.

He must kiss her. He must ease this need that had been fervently growing for over a year.

Each night, she'd pressed her fingertips to her lips and said a prayer in thought of him. Each night, she'd recalled the touch of his lips against hers, the whisper of his voice against her mouth. Each night, she had longed for him, and now he was here and this was no dream.

She had come to him and the kiss waited, payment for her patience.

"You tempt me," he said in a low burr. "I told myself I should find someone else."

"Did you?" she asked in a thin voice.

"They all sounded Scottish," he said. "Or English. None of them had your odd American and English accent."

She smiled in earnest. "Anyone might say you're the one who sounds odd, Macrath Sinclair."

She reached up and gripped the fabric of his jacket, one hand sliding beneath to touch the fine linen of his shirt. The pounding of his heart beneath her palm was as rapid as her own.

"I should leave now, Virginia. Tomorrow, you should go."

"Do not send me away," she said, her voice barely more than a breath. "Not tomorrow." She took as deep a breath as she could manage. "Not tomorrow," she repeated. "Not tonight."

He studied her in the faint glow of the candles.

In this, she must not fail. But need trumped desperation

in this silent moment. Her lips felt too full. Her heart beat too rapidly, and her legs trembled so badly she might fall any moment.

"Why have you come, Virginia?" he asked.

"I want to know what love is like between a man and a woman. Not simply what it felt like to be a frightened miss alone with an angry husband."

"Was he angry?" he asked.

"It seemed so." When he didn't speak, she said, "He took my virtue, Macrath, not my heart. Never my heart."

He pulled her close slowly, so slowly she might have turned her head or escaped from him easily. She didn't, only tilted back her head, praying for a kiss.

Softly, he placed his lips on hers. A kiss to reacquaint, an expression of remembrance, and a silent hello, one that didn't prepare her for the surge of feeling.

The kiss deepened, becoming something she'd never felt, as if their combined need created a maelstrom between them. She was left gasping for breath, but when he would've pulled away, she gripped his shirt with both hands and pulled him back to her.

"Teach me," she whispered. Before the words had totally left her lips, she was airborne, caught up in his arms.

She hadn't expected this. She'd thought they might escape to his room or her lovely chamber, tiptoeing through this magnificent home like thieves. She'd never thought he would brazenly carry her through the corridors like a drunken bridegroom.

She closed her eyes, hoping none of his servants saw them. Hoping, too, if they did, she didn't see them.

Her hands still clutched his shirt and she couldn't release them. Where their bodies touched there was such heat she was warned. This night would not be like her wedding night.

When dawn broke, she wouldn't be the same woman.

Chapter 9

Macrath wanted to resurrect the Earl of Barrett and ensure his death was agonizing.

Virginia had said the words in such a soft tone, it had taken a moment for them to register. The earl had been an angry husband? He'd show the bastard what anger was.

Regrettably, he wouldn't have the chance. All he could do was hold Virginia close and ensure those memories were pushed to the background.

Taking her to his chamber seemed oddly right, especially since it was patently wrong. She was his guest, a lone woman who should be protected and held safe.

He didn't stop to reconsider his actions. He didn't want to think at the moment, only feel, and even that was nearly overwhelming, like he'd breathed too much ammonia.

When he stopped in front of his door, he lowered her feet to the floor, holding her hand in case she wanted to escape. He wouldn't allow it. Not after the year of torture he'd endured.

Even so, he would have escorted her to her suite, said good-night and left her alone. But she'd uttered those words: "I want to know what love is like between a man and a woman."

The world, circumstances, fate, any damn thing you wanted to call it, owed them these moments, this time, this night. All hell could visit them tomorrow. For tonight, they'd have everything they'd once wanted.

He looked down at her and it all fell away. All the anger, all the longing, everything but Virginia.

Her face was pale, as if he'd shocked her by carrying her through his house. He held her in the safety of his arms, bent down and pressed a kiss to her hair. He smelled roses, which made him smile.

"Forgive me," he said. "I've rushed you. I've been a fool."

"You haven't," she said. "I was always foolish around you and about you."

"Do you want this, Virginia?"

She pulled back and gazed up at him. "Yes. For the last year, I haven't been able to forget you. Yours is the face I saw before I slept. I prayed for you when I should have been praying for my own husband. Perhaps if I had, I wouldn't be here now."

"Then we'll go to perdition together," he said, "because I can't be sorry for your husband's death."

He pulled her inside his suite, closing the door firmly behind him, striding through the sitting room and into the bedroom to stand beside his bed.

He'd left the lamp on in the sitting room and considered lighting the one on the table beside the bed, dismissing the thought instantly. That would take too long, and he was impatient enough as it was.

He removed her garments one by one, gently set them aside, revealing her like she was a present lovingly wrapped for his delectation. The bow was, perhaps, her bodice with its jet buttons and full sleeves. The paper was her corset cover and the corset he unlaced with deft fingers.

The package was her skirt, shift, and pantaloons, until

she stood in front of him naked with only her shoes and black garters holding up her silk stockings.

The contrast of her black stockings against her white skin was yet another present.

He held out his hand and she placed hers on it for balance. Bending, he removed her shoes then her stockings with such speed he was amazed at his own dexterity.

He stood studying her like she was one of his ice machines. He expected her to cover her breasts with her arms. Or shield the curls at the juncture of her thighs. She did neither, merely stood with her hands at her sides, letting him look his fill.

Now he wished he'd lit another lamp.

"You're as beautiful as I always thought you'd be," he said.

"You imagined me naked?" Her voice sounded surprised.

He smiled. "Endlessly."

He had never touched her breasts, never stroked her skin with fingertips that were rough and tender at once. Yet it felt like he had, as if he knew her like he knew himself.

Still, some innate caution whispered at him to pay attention; there was more here than he could see. She trembled, but was it from fear or eagerness?

The girl he'd known had acquiesced only too easily to her father's plans. Or did he judge her too harshly? Perhaps she had been a girl, and a woman stood before him now.

"Why are you here?" he asked, trailing a finger down her nose, then tracing the shape of her mouth.

Her full lips curved at the touch of his finger.

"For this," she said, another gift, this one of words. "To have you kiss me endlessly, until I grow tired of kisses. To have you love me until I'm exhausted from it."

"Virginia," he said, that one word uttered harshly.

The need for her slammed up against his self-control. He warned himself not to be too eager, but the message didn't reach his cock, straining against his trousers.

He was as hard as he'd ever been and as improvident: a man's body with a boy's excitement. He wasn't wise or cautious at this moment. Only desperate to feel her, touch every inch of her, and have her sob in his arms.

The room was quiet, while outside the storm pounded Drumvagen, the wind batting against the windows, throwing the drops of rain against the panes in a child's tantrum.

She vaguely noted the surroundings lit faintly by a lamp in the sitting room: a massive four poster bed, large enough for Macrath to stretch in any direction, a dresser, two armoires. The carpet beneath her feet was patterned, but in the semidarkness it was only black and gray.

Her breasts were full, the tips straining toward him. Desire thrummed through her body, extending even to her toes, showing her that passion could fill every pore. She wanted him to hurry, to be as naked as she, his skin rubbing against hers.

How did she say such a thing?

He bent to kiss her shoulder. "Virginia," he murmured against her skin. She cupped his cheek with her hands, hoping he didn't question her further.

Not now, not when she wanted this feeling to linger. Should she tell him how she felt? Should she mention the heat inside her body, or the trembling that had begun the moment he'd carried her to this room?

He'd been her dream lover for nearly a year, living in her dreams each night. Now he was here and real.

The timid girl she'd always been whispered to take

care, use caution. The woman she wanted to be stepped forward, eager and needy.

He stripped his clothes off in seconds. What a pity not to have more light so she could see him. Her fingers would be her eyes. Slowly, tenderly, gently, she would smooth her hands over him, learning him.

Should she feel sinful at this moment? Or guilty, if nothing else? Instead, she wanted to smile, or shout with joy, or lift her eyes to a storm-filled sky and say, "Thank you, God, for this moment." For him. For being alive. For being a woman he desired.

He picked up her hand, extending kisses along the back of it to her wrist, traveling slowly up to the crook of her elbow, then to her shoulder.

She smiled until he traced a path to her collarbone. Her smile faded when he placed a hand on either side of her breasts, plumping them together so he could kiss both at the same time.

He dropped his head, mouthing a nipple.

When he drew the tip into his mouth, she gasped aloud, prompting him to do it again.

She leaned forward, kissed his shoulder, tasting his skin. He smelled of Macrath, soap and something else, a scent reminding her of clean linen and spices. Something his housekeeper used to store with his clothes?

When he tumbled her back on the bed, she was startled. In the next moment all she could think was how he made her feel. Her skin was too tight, her body too hot.

She'd thought this seduction would be quick and easy. Instead it was dangerous, pulling her down into the darkness and the deep.

He brushed her lips with the tips of his fingers, then kissed her mouth lightly. With his next kiss the world vanished. Nothing mattered but the touch of his hands on her skin, his lips as he coaxed her mouth open. She inhaled his breath, gave him hers, wrapped her arms around his shoulders, her excitement mounting.

His fingers danced across her skin, in hidden folds, coaxing even more heat from her. When his finger entered her, she shivered.

She grabbed at his shoulders, turning toward him, urging him in a way that was foreign and new. She wanted the completeness, the feeling of being joined to him. She wanted to feel him inside her, her legs wrapped around his, her lips pressed against his throat.

As he poised above her, she had a moment to be alarmed. Then he slipped inside, filling and claiming her in that instant.

She'd remember this night for the rest of her life.

Macrath raised himself over her, gently pulled out, and surged into her again. Surprise had her gasping and grabbing his arms so tightly she gouged him with her nails.

Don't stop. Please don't stop.

All she could do was wrap her arms around his neck and breathe against his skin.

He was too slow, too measured, too careful of her. She beat a tattoo on his shoulders with the heels of her hands. A moment later she was gripping his buttocks, pulling him to her.

If this was seduction, the word was not expansive enough. It couldn't fully describe this battle of passion. He lunged; she submitted. He withdrew; she chased after him.

She never imagined the dreams she had of him were pale substitutions for what he made her feel now.

This was bliss stretched into a net, catching all the stars, and pouring them into her body. This was a thrumming awareness of every part of her, skin and muscle, blood and bone.

He chuckled as her fingernails dug into his backside to pull him closer. Her legs widened, her hips arched. She wanted to be savage and unrestrained, and so she was, nipping at his bottom lip, fingers curved and raking his back. He grabbed handfuls of her hair, held her still as he trailed kisses along her throat.

She moaned, and he murmured against her skin. Words that were cautionary or calming, she wasn't sure which. They had no effect on the rise of excitement, the flames licking at her from the inside out. Only he could ease this trembling ache, this need consuming her.

She might have screamed. She thought she did. She'd no choice. How could anyone live with such joy? It must be manifested in some way, expressed, and forever remembered.

He awakened Virginia at dawn with a kiss. With her eyes still closed, she smiled.

The seabirds cried outside his window, a call to be about the day. For now he was content to remain where he was, in his bed with Virginia.

With one finger, he traced a path from her ear, down her jaw to her chin, marveling at the softness of her skin.

She wrinkled her nose with her eyes still closed.

"You're bonnie in the morning, Countess," he said. "Most women aren't."

She opened her eyes and frowned at him. "Do you have much experience with women in the morning?"

He wasn't foolish enough to answer that question fully. He grinned at her. "My sisters. My cousin."

She held up her hand as if to forestall a recitation of other women.

"I must get back to my room," she said softly. "Otherwise, I'm bound to shock your servants."

"Every single one of them is loyal to me," he said. "You've nothing to fear from them."

"I can't say the same about my own maid. If I'm not back in my chamber before she arrives, Hannah's tongue might begin to wag."

For a moment he was content to simply study her, note her pink cheeks and sparkling eyes. Passion became her. So did sleeping in his arms.

"The look of sadness is gone," he said.

She reached up and cupped his face.

"I thought it was because of your husband," he said, turning his head and kissing her palm. "But it's gone."

"Is it?" she asked, smiling.

"Do you like being a countess?"

"Why would you ask that?"

He needed to know. How fond was she of a title? Enough to remain in London? Or would she be willing to give it up?

"If I never knew you before, I wouldn't have approached you now," he said, offering her a strange truth.

Her smile was gentle.

"You can't tell me, Macrath, that you would've been put off by a title."

"No," he said. "You wouldn't have interested me because you belong to a certain class of people I normally ignore."

"Why? Because you think them arrogant? Aren't you guilty of the same?"

He had the feeling he was walking close to the edge of a cliff, and took a cautious step back.

"It's been my experience that a great many people with titles feel they are better than others because of their birth. They're singled out as being special, when they're not, in truth. They're simply the sons or grandsons of men who did something."

"Since I don't know many people with titles, I can't argue with you."

"You didn't associate with people of your rank?"

"I didn't associate with people at all," she said, surprising him again. "I spent my time at home, with Lawrence's sisters or with my mother-in-law."

He kissed her again, simply because he wanted to. No, he had to.

"What did you write me?" she asked. "Those dozen letters you wrote, what did you say?"

"The ramblings of a man in love," he softly said. "Foolish, unwise comments, no doubt. How much I loved you. How much I longed for you. How much I wanted to spend the rest of my life with you."

"Oh, Macrath."

She always skewered him when she said his name in that tone, with that look of wonder in her eyes. He wanted to be the man she thought him, powerful and without sin or blemish.

He'd take her to his cottage and show her his first ice machine, introduce her to Jack and Sam. He'd show her the rest of Drumvagen, so she'd be suitably impressed about his home, enough to stay. He'd convince her to remain in Scotland, coax her into not returning to London at all and marry her with indecent haste.

People would gossip about the two of them, how he'd acted like a border reiver and how she'd been willing to give up everything in England for him. They'd call him a devil, perhaps, for abducting her, for convincing her to stay.

And her? What would they call her? A wild American, a woman in love.

Before he allowed her to leave him, he loved her again, cherishing her moans as he teased her to pleasure.

He thrust into her, impatient, desperate to last. He wanted this moment to be elongated, stretched until pleasure was a skein wrapping around and forever joining them. He wanted to please her while he pleased himself. As he erupted into her, it was with the knowledge that he was lost, his spirit and body shrunken, his heart once more given to Virginia.

Chapter 10

Virginia returned to her room a scant ten minutes before Hannah, ducking into the bathing chamber to wash and change.

Twice, Hannah asked if she needed any assistance, and twice she assured the maid she didn't. A personal maid was more a hindrance than a help. She didn't like someone underfoot all the time, but when she said that to her mother-in-law, Enid had only laughed gaily and said her penchant for privacy was one of her Americanisms.

Perhaps it was true. In America she wasn't given a maid until the last year, and the girl had been more independent and less intent on her tasks. Hannah saw nothing wrong in overseeing her bath, or walking in on her when she'd much rather be alone. It had taken months for her to accept that privacy was one of those things she'd sacrificed by becoming a countess.

The title had pleased her father a great deal more than her.

"Did you sleep well?" Virginia asked as she exited the bath chamber.

Another thing she shouldn't do—care about the servants, ask them personal questions, or be curious about their lives.

As usual, Hannah smiled at the question, ducked her head and answered, "Yes, your ladyship, thank you."

She would never know if Hannah tossed and turned or spent a sleepless night. Hannah would never tell her. Hannah was a more perfect servant than she was a mistress.

Perhaps if there had not been so much propriety between them, she might have confessed to Hannah about the night she spent in Macrath's arms. No, the memory was for her alone to savor. She couldn't imagine sharing it with anyone else.

Did she look different to Hannah? Could the maid tell, just by glancing at her, that she was not the same woman who'd left London only a few days earlier? Her lips were full, almost swollen from being kissed all night. On her shoulder and her left breast were faint pink marks from Macrath's morning beard. Her body still thrummed with bliss, each muscle loose, every inch of skin touched by Macrath.

Dressed only in her wrapper, she walked to the window, drawing open the drapes to see a bright fresh morning the storm had given them. To her surprise, this room faced the approach to Drumvagen, so she was spared the sight of the sea.

She cranked open the pane, breathing in the clean air. How different Drumvagen was from London. Not only was there no fog, but it was quieter, without the ever present traffic. Only the seabirds' faint call, and the breeze reaching in to toss the ends of her hair.

Hillocks hid the crofter's cottage she'd seen yesterday. The earth undulated like a rumpled carpet until it reached a forest of tall trees. To her right she could see the glint of the sun on the water. Was it the river they'd crossed just before reaching Drumvagen?

There, like a tiny gray ribbon, was the road they'd traveled just yesterday, a lifetime ago.

She should return to London now, she thought, before she became more ensnared. Seduction wasn't as simple a task as she'd imagined. If she remained at Drumvagen for long, leaving him would be nearly impossible. Then where would they be?

But she'd been right to think that last night would change her.

She wanted to be with Macrath. She wanted to take his hand and hold it in hers, talk to him and share her thoughts. She wanted to pull him into a secluded area and kiss him senseless. He'd fascinated her even before she bedded him. Now? Words were flimsy things and not constructed to hold the weight of all she felt.

London
July, 1869

Enid, Dowager Countess of Barrett, stared down at the columns of figures in front of her, wishing she was like so many of her acquaintances and totally ignorant of the facts of life. Her father, however, the nephew of a duke, had insisted his five children be well educated in the basics, even the females. So she was proficient in mathematics, and could balance her own household books. A good thing, as it turned out, because they had been skirting the edge of penury for years.

An American had saved them.

Virginia Anderson might save them once again.

An ancestor had fought against the Americans in the war of their independence. She apologized to the man in her thoughts and hoped he'd understand. One must do what one must, however difficult it might be.

At least Virginia had understood duty.

What a pity Lawrence hadn't. She'd failed by not properly instilling that value in him.

She put down her pencil, leaned back in her chair and pinched the area above her nose. Perhaps she should investigate getting some spectacles. The numbers occasionally floated on the page. If she glanced away periodically, she didn't get a headache. But she must focus on the numbers, the better to get this onerous chore done.

Just like her long-dead husband, she rarely used the library. The room, filled with bookcases and framed portraits of Traylor men, was always in shadow, even on a bright morning. Decorated with a dark patterned carpet and hunter green walls, it was an oppressive room, one giving her the impression of walking into a forest cave.

Here was where she disciplined servants, meted out merit raises, went over the household accounts, and wrote the business correspondence that made her slightly nauseous. She despised those letters of an official nature, such as the one to her solicitor, asking to be informed of the exact state of their finances and her return reply when the news had been received.

Their fates were in the hands of a timid girl, willing enough to traipse off to Scotland. Whether Virginia would be able to seduce a Scotsman was another thing. Enid had heard they were fierce creatures, dressing in kilts with nothing beneath them. She honestly hadn't believed the story until a dear friend assured her it was true.

Perhaps the Scotsman in question would be so worked up by the wool rubbing against his member he'd toss Virginia to the ground the minute she arrived and have his way with her.

She could only pray something of the sort would happen.

She put down her pencil, rubbed at the blister forming on her middle finger. Tallying the sums again would not help her. On paper, the family was wealthy because of the rent and profit from the farms. But once the title went to Jeremy, so did all the income from the entailed property. They would be dependent on charity.

Enid doubted Jeremy would take them in as poor relatives. All these years, they'd managed a cordial relationship, but a distant one. He was a good enough man, tall, thin, with a receding chin and hairline, teeth regrettably turning brown, and a cringeworthy laugh.

His wife was his match in every way. Her hairline didn't recede as much as her chin, but her laugh was as obnoxious. Her only saving grace was that she wasn't amused often.

Their children, shockingly, were all attractive, but were very noisy and intrusive creatures.

No, she couldn't imagine living with Jeremy, sitting in the corner knitting scarves for the children.

Eudora could possibly marry, but she needed a new wardrobe and some money before sending her out into the marriage mart again. Ellice was still too young, but only by a year or two. By the time she was ready for a season, they would be lucky to have a roof over their heads.

She heard Ellice laugh, followed by Eudora's calm voice. Every day since Virginia had been gone, they'd asked about her. Was she well at her friend's house? Would she return soon? Of course, they understood she needed to escape London for a bit. Being here constantly brought Lawrence to mind.

It had been a silly excuse for Virginia's absence, but Ellice and Eudora accepted it because they were soft-hearted and genuinely lovely people. How could Lawrence have thought to punish his sisters so? What would happen to her darling girls?

She had no relatives to speak of. Only an ancient aunt who couldn't accommodate the four of them along with their staff, or what staff she could still retain. She would have to dismiss most of the servants, which meant they'd have to do without much help. That fact, more than any other, brought home the disaster of their situation. Neither of her daughters had ever washed a pot or their own clothing.

Poverty would ensure they learned quickly. They'd lose the ability to buy a book or a bottle of perfume. They'd never marry. What kind of mother would she be if that happened?

She frowned down at the column of figures again. She needed to start austerity measures. She'd look at all the cuts of meat Cook ordered herself, inform the merchants that she was to approve all expenses.

Could they go another year without new uniforms?

Cook was baking bread, and the smell of it wafted into the room. How well were they being fed? Couldn't they cut down somewhere? Did they need to eat all those sweets? Were there more economical meals Cook could prepare?

A sound caused her to glance up. Paul stood there.

Although he'd been Lawrence's attendant, she hadn't had the heart to dismiss him after her son's death. Indeed, Paul had been useful in a great many ways. Besides, she owed him some gratitude for alerting them to what Lawrence was doing. Pity that they couldn't have prevented him from spending all the money.

Unfortunately, Paul would have to be one of those she let go, but she wasn't in the mood to do it right this minute.

"If you wish to meet with me," she said, "I'll see you in a few hours. Until then, if you don't mind, Paul, I would like some privacy."

She expected him to leave the room soundlessly in that way he had. Glancing up, it was to find him still there and smiling at her.

"What is it, Paul?"

"I require a few minutes of your time, your ladyship," he said. "It's important."

Annoyed, she sat back in the chair. "I don't wish to be disturbed right now. Whatever it is can wait, I'm sure."

"Perhaps Lawrence's cousin will be interested, then."

She put down her pencil, folded one hand over the other and composed her expression.

"What are you talking about?"

He settled into one of the chairs in front of the desk.

"You've sent her off to Scotland, your ladyship. If she returns with child, your problems are over, aren't they?"

Ice coated the inside of her stomach. What did he know? Nothing, unless she verified it for him.

He was an attractive man, but one of those men who was well aware of his looks. Perhaps not vain as much as brash, certain of himself. In this situation, he could not be allowed to get the upper hand.

She forced her lips to curve into a half smile, the same expression she used when communicating with her solicitor. The dowager countess smile indicating she was the equal of any news he could impart.

"I don't believe I understand what you're talking about, Paul."

He smiled. "Oh I think you do, Countess. I think you know exactly what I'm talking about." He settled back in the chair and crossed one leg over the other, a relaxed and confident pose.

She should have dismissed him the day after Lawrence's death.

"You sent your daughter-in-law off to seduce a man. I heard you myself."

"I don't know what you heard, Paul, but whatever it was has confused you. Virginia is merely visiting with friends. She wanted to get away from London."

"Scotland, Countess?"

Her fingertips were like ice and her lips were numb. In the next minute she might begin to drool.

This odious man was not going to make her lose her composure.

"I don't know why you're so concerned where her ladyship is, Paul. It's none of your concern."

"I'm not greedy, Countess. A few pounds every Friday night would go a long way to making me happy. Or being released from some of my new duties, perhaps?"

"Do you have any duties?" she asked.

"Albert has found a few for me to do. Shall I furnish you a list?"

She stared down at the column of figures, seeing nothing but his smiling face.

If he went to Jeremy, they were ruined. The plan was doomed before it began. Not that it was a guarantee, but it was the only chance they had.

"I want my servants to be happy," she heard herself saying. How calm she sounded, a result of years of schooling her features to be pleasant in the midst of chaos.

This was most definitely chaos.

"I'll speak to Albert," she said. A word to the majordomo and Paul would be freed of most of his duties. "I'm certain we can find a few pounds to offer you in payment for your loyalty." She'd sell her dresses if she had to.

"I'm happy we had this conversation," he said, standing and going to the door. "I look forward to many more."

As soon as the door closed behind him, she expelled a breath.

Oh dear, what was she to do about Paul?

Drumvagen, Scotland
July, 1869

"Would you like to select a dress, your ladyship?"

Virginia waved a hand in Hannah's direction. "Pick anything you like," she said. "They're all the same anyway. Black is black."

"In no time at all, your ladyship, you'll be able to wear white on your collar and cuffs."

Who made up all these rules? She was certain if she posed that question to Hannah the maid would be shocked, so she remained silent.

Virginia turned and faced the armoire, frowning at the sea of black silk. It seemed like she'd worn nothing but mourning for years. First, for her father, and now Lawrence.

Her father had been such a distant figure in her life, she could readily imagine him still alive. As far as Lawrence, how did she pretend to mourn a man she'd never truly known?

Hannah was still standing there, patiently waiting.

"I'm not feeling well," she abruptly said. She turned and walked toward the bed. "I believe I'll rest. I didn't sleep well last night." Her face flamed.

"You do look feverish, your ladyship," Hannah said, concerned.

She perched on the edge of the mattress and nodded.

"I think I'll spend most of the day sleeping. I'm fatigued from the events of the previous week."

She was, after all, a new widow.

The maid closed the armoire door and came to stand at the foot of the bed.

"Would you like me to fetch you some tea, your ladyship?"

"No," she said, lying back against the pillows. "I would just like to be alone. Consider yourself off duty today, Hannah. Perhaps you can make friends among the staff."

The expression of surprise on Hannah's face was so fleeting that Virginia almost didn't catch it.

"You needn't call on me for the rest of the day," she said firmly. "I'll ring when I need you again."

There, she'd used such a direct and forceful tone that Hannah could not help but obey her. The maid nodded, stepping away from the bed and moving toward the door.

"If you're certain, your ladyship," she said, glancing back once more.

"I am," Virginia said. "I'll be sleeping the day away."

A few minutes later she heard the sitting room door close.

In a flash she was off the bed and donning one of the hated black dresses. Granted, she could have done so more easily with Hannah's help, but then how would she have explained her plans?

If she hurried, perhaps she might catch Macrath in his chambers. She pulled on the bellpull, hoping against hope that Hannah didn't respond to her summons. The maid who appeared at the door five minutes later was a stranger. The poor girl was out of breath, a sign of how quickly she'd raced up the stairs.

Virginia pressed the note she'd written into the maid's hand. "Would you convey this note to Mr. Sinclair?"

"Yes, your ladyship." The girl dropped a curtsy and disappeared without another word, racing down the corridor.

Virginia closed the door and leaned against it. Was she being the most foolish woman alive?

If she was, it felt wonderful. This whole day, from now until dinnertime, when she was certain Hannah would come to check on her, was hers. For these hours she could do as she wished. She didn't have to be Virginia Anderson, daughter of Harold Anderson or the Countess of Barrett, wife to Lawrence Traylor, the tenth Earl of Barrett.

The bright sunny morning called to her. The blue sky beckoned her to come and explore. Let the breeze play with her hair, make her eyes water. She'd inhale her fill of it, glorying in Scotland. She'd hold Macrath's hand, feeling the calluses of his large fingers and knowing just how tender they could be on her skin.

She wanted to eat something Scottish again. She wanted to taste the salmon she didn't properly appreciate last night. She wanted to hear bagpipes she'd only heard in a ceremony in London. She wanted to smell the flowers lining the road.

Give her a taste of this land of Macrath's.

She studied her reflection. Her bright pink cheeks truly did look feverish. What explanation could she give for her sparkling eyes and her smile? A smile had never come so naturally to her face or been so difficult to subdue.

Braiding her hair was an easy task. She tucked her braid at the back of her head, pinning it tightly, then loosened a few tendrils at her temple.

Until today she honestly doubted when people called her attractive. Her father's money meant most people were blind to her flaws. Now, however, her pink cheeks accentuated the odd paleness of her eyes and the fullness of her lips. She looked like she held a delicious secret, one that amused her.

Dusting off her black leather shoes, she slipped them on and laced them, feeling her excitement mount.

For the first time in her life she was going to do what she truly wished and not what someone had planned for her.

Chapter 11

When the knock came, Virginia thought it was the maid returning with an answer. But when she opened the door, Macrath stood there, smiling at her.

"I was sorry to hear you were taken ill," he said, holding out his hand for her.

"It was a sudden thing."

"I, too, have a need to rest."

"Have you?"

"It's come upon me suddenly."

"Perhaps it's contagious," she said.

"I suspect it is, but limited only to us."

They smiled at each other in perfect accord.

"I haven't taken you from your experiments, have I?"

"They'll always be there," he said. "You won't."

She pushed that thought away as she placed her hand in his.

Would it be untoward to tell him how wonderful she felt? She was aware of herself in a way she'd never before been. Her breasts were sensitive; she was conscious of the contours of her lips. She remembered every single spot he'd kissed, praised, and worshiped with his fingers, and gloried in all of it.

Reaching up, she pressed her fingers against his cheek, her thumb tracing the edge of his bottom lip.

"I would not trade last night and this morning for anything. I want to thank you for it," she said.

He grabbed her hand, curving the fingers inward toward the palm, and kissed her knuckles.

"Virginia," he said softly. Just her name, spoken with such tenderness that she felt her heart expand.

How could he nearly bring her to tears with a glance?

Shame enveloped her, pushed her to confess. The minute she said the words, he'd send her away, she knew that well enough. But she'd already transgressed. What was wrong with another sin, one of omission?

"Come with me," he said.

"Where are we going?"

"If we're supposedly ill, I think we should avoid my staff, don't you? Perhaps we'll explore the woods or walk in the tide. I've so many things I want to show you."

With that twinkle in his eye, she would go anywhere with him.

"Lead on, MacDuff," she said, smiling brightly at him.

His laughter warmed her heart. "*Macbeth*?"

"My father insisted on a varied curriculum. I can even operate a sextant, a compass, and I know how to build the fire."

"The perfect companion," he said, tugging on her hand.

Where were they going? She wasn't dressed for exploration. The silk of her skirts would no doubt be torn by the brambles and branches. Her fine leather shoes were polished and would probably be scratched by the undergrowth. Then, too, she was supposed to be a proper widow. She shouldn't be gamboling about in the woods with Macrath, playing the hoyden.

A sign of her foolishness, that she didn't ask. Nor did she care.

Reaching behind her, he closed the door, grabbed her hand, and they were suddenly away, laughing like children as they raced along the corridor and down the stairs. With each successive footfall the years fell away, and they were boy and girl. She could imagine that they were children of nature with no obligations other than to explore the world outside. They might spy a bird's nest on an upper branch, watch the wind dance along the moor, or smile at the sight of a squirrel chittering angrily at them.

But Macrath didn't lead her out of Drumvagen for the woods or the ocean. Instead, he turned left, strode down a hall and entered a library.

She only had time for a quick impression of bookcases, fireplace, two chairs, and a large desk before he went to the side of the room and pulled a sconce on the wall. A moment later a crack appeared behind one of the book-cases.

"A secret passage?" she asked, fascinated. "It's like something out of a book."

"Not just a passage. Something even better."

Now was the time to remind him that she wasn't exces-sively courageous. But it seemed like she was, especially with him.

"Would you like to see one of my favorite places at Drumvagen?" he asked.

She would do anything with him. Didn't he know that? Hadn't last night and this morning proved that?

Her face flushed as she nodded.

He lit a small lantern, held it aloft with one hand, and, turning back to her, held out his other hand. With no hesi-tation, she allowed him to pull her into the passage and close the door behind them.

"You know your way, I hope."

"Else we are doomed to spend the rest of eternity wandering through Drumvagen," he said, humor in his voice.

In the next moment it felt like the two of them were on a great adventure. As they descended shallow stone steps, a briny smell wafted up from below.

"Will you tell me where we're going?" she asked, fervently hoping they weren't heading toward the ocean.

"No," he said. "It would spoil the surprise."

"Not even a hint?"

"No hints."

"Are you normally this stubborn?"

"Yes," he said, although he didn't sound the least apologetic about such a character flaw. "I like to get my way."

As they descended into the darkness, she said, "Perhaps you're Hades and I am Persephone."

"I've no pomegranate seeds," he said. "Besides, I've already had my way with you."

"Should a gentleman say such a thing?" she asked, uncertain whether to be amused or affronted.

"I'm not a gentleman with you," he said. "I'm not the owner of Drumvagen. I'm only Macrath. And you are not a countess, an American, or a widow. You are simply Virginia."

Warmth traveled through her at his words. He was right. If he hadn't been, she wouldn't have lied to Hannah, pretending illness and fatigue. She wouldn't be here now, clutching her skirts with one hand and his hand with the other, descending into blackness, the lantern giving off only a small circle of yellow light.

The air grew cooler as they descended. Sounds faded until their breathing was loud in the silence. A brine-tasting breeze sought them out, urging them forward. Sand crunched beneath their feet.

The staircase expanded, the passage becoming larger and lighter. He stopped, extinguished the lantern and placed it on the ground. Taking her hand again, he led her down into a sunlit room of stone, the shape reminding her of a mushroom. At the top was an opening allowing sunlight to stream inside the space. Even more amazing was the window on one wall. A wide arch had been cut out of the rock, so perfectly created that it possessed a sill. Here someone could sit and draw up his legs, staring off into the distance where the ocean met the horizon.

"It's a grotto," she said, amazed. Her voice echoed back at her.

He smiled. "It's an effect of the stone," he said.

He dropped her hand as she turned in a circle to see everything. The room was almost perfectly round. Besides the window and the chimney hole, there was another opening in the other curved wall.

"Where does that lead?" she asked.

"The beach."

"I can imagine why it's your favorite place at Drumvagen. Did you come here as a boy?" she asked.

"The only place I knew as a boy was Edinburgh," he said. "I purchased Drumvagen five years ago."

Surprised, she glanced at him.

"I wasn't always wealthy," he said. "It's a recent event for me."

Wealth was not a subject of polite conversation. Either you had it and everyone knew it, or you pretended you had it, and everyone allowed you the pretense. But it was never openly discussed.

When had they ever ascribed to societal rules when it came to what they talked about? No topic was considered off limits between them.

"My father was like you," she said. "I don't think he had much respect for people who inherited their money."

He smiled slightly. "I don't think your father had much respect for anyone except himself."

His comment startled a laugh from her.

"Why did he settle on Lawrence?"

"I think he was impressed by my mother-in-law. She can be very persuasive."

"At least your father got the title he wanted," he said.

"He didn't have long to enjoy it." She glanced at him. "But you don't know. He died two months after my marriage." Poor Mrs. Haverstock had never had a chance to charm him, since she'd been dismissed just before Virginia's wedding, along with her American maid.

"My own parents have been gone many years," he said. "But my sisters and cousin have tried to make up for the lack."

"Have they succeeded?"

"As far as they're concerned," he said. "If your father had approved my suit, they would have swooped down to London to look you over before our wedding."

"And if they hadn't approved of me?"

He smiled. "I would have sent them back to Edinburgh," he said. "They would've remained silent, only because I contribute to their household in a significant fashion."

"In other words, you would have bribed them."

"Which is what your father did," he reminded her.

"It was easier being Virginia Anderson from America. As an American, I was expected to be a little odd. 'Those Americans, what can you expect from them? They come from the colonies, after all.' "

He laughed at her perfect British accent.

"As a countess, I have a whole other set of rules to follow."

"You would like my sister, Mairi," he said. "She cherishes being a little odd."

She turned to him. She only knew Ceana, who always seemed a conformable type of person.

"Mairi's determined to run the printing company. So far, she's making a success of it."

"You're proud of her," she said, surprised.

"Why wouldn't I be?"

Her father had never been proud of any of her achievements, not that there were many to laud. Nor had Lawrence ever cared enough to ask what she'd done or even wished to do.

Suddenly, she wanted Macrath to be proud of her. She could hardly do that on this journey to Scotland, could she? What she was doing was wrong in so many ways, she owed him an apology now. Or perhaps an explanation.

"I think it's easier for a man to create his own destiny. Like you," she said, nearly desperate to stop her thoughts. She'd much rather talk about him than think about what she was doing.

He moved to the window and she followed. Leaning against the sill nature had created, he stretched out his legs, smiling into the distance "I had it in my mind to create an empire so that people would always know about my achievements."

"They would revere you," she teased. "They might even bow down in front of your picture."

"I need to get my portrait painted," he said. "In order for them to do that, of course."

"Of course," she said, smiling. "However, I think they'll remember you even if you never get your portrait painted. You're an unforgettable man."

Without looking at her, he stretched out his hand. She took it, threading her fingers with his. What a wonderful person he was, and how quickly he'd become lodged in her heart again.

She looked around. "Is it a secret? Does everyone know about the grotto?"

"I would imagine a great many people know," he said. "After all, Drumvagen stood empty for years."

"Did it?"

He nodded. "Evidently, the first Earl of Pembarton and the architect argued about money. The house was unfinished, open to the elements, and nearly a ruin."

"Until you came along," she said. "Perhaps it was meant to be. Drumvagen needed an owner, and you needed a house."

"I was looking for a castle," he said.

Startled, she glanced at him. Rather than meeting her eyes, he looked away, almost like he was embarrassed.

"When I was a boy in Edinburgh," he said, "I always thought it would be a wonderful thing to own a castle. To start my own clan. Perhaps I thought of myself as the Sinclair, laird of all he surveyed."

"A clan?"

"Who doesn't want to leave some part of himself behind? My father was much beloved in Edinburgh. I think I wanted the same, but in my place, on my terms."

She looked around. "I think you made a better choice," she said. "A castle would be drafty and cold. Drumvagen is not only magnificent, but it's a comfortable place to live, even being so close to the ocean."

"You don't like the ocean?"

"I don't like the ocean."

He stared out the window. "The ocean makes you feel as small as a grain of sand. I worry about the factory in Glasgow, or how sales will go on the Continent, only to look at the ocean and realize all my cares and concerns aren't important."

"While I look at the ocean and think of all the people who died."

He glanced at her.

"My father owned several ships. I happened across a manifest one day," she explained, deciding not to tell him she had broken a rule by being in her father's office. But she'd wanted to leave him a note, someplace where he could not overlook it. A note he would have to read. She didn't want to go to England, but he'd been stubbornly refusing to hear her pleas.

"One of his captains reported there had been seven births and twelve deaths aboard ship during the voyage."

She glanced down at the sand laden floor and fluffed her skirts. "He listed all their names, how old they were, and how they'd died." She folded her arms then unfolded them. "They'd been buried at sea. I remember the manifest when I look at the ocean."

He did not, thankfully, utter any platitudes about life or death. Nor did he try to cajole her out of her thoughts. He merely listened, which was such an oddity in her life, she marked each conversation with him as special.

He straightened and strode to the far right-hand side of the window, staring toward an outcropping of rock.

"I own a ship," he said. "One of my first major purchases before Drumvagen. Her name was originally the *Sally Ryan,* but I changed it."

His eyes sparkled and his grin was so wide she could only ask, "What did you change it to?"

"The *Princess,*" he said smiling at her. "The figurehead was redone as well. It resembles you."

"Me?"

He didn't answer, merely raised his hand.

She followed where he pointed. Above the rocks in the distance stretched a series of tall poles or denuded tree trunks. No, the longer she stared, the more she was able to tell they were masts.

"It's Kinloch Harbor," he said. "Where the *Princess* is berthed. If you look to the right, you can see her mast. It's one of the tallest."

Had he named his ship for her? Is that how he thought of her? A princess? Many people had once held a similar opinion. They saw her father's wealth and it blinded them to anything else. She should tell him the wealth was all gone, translated into houses, farms, and land to go to Jeremy.

Above all, she should tell him why she was here. Would he understand? Or only be angry at her duplicity? Whatever his reaction, it might be easier to live with herself if she were honest.

Being in London and thinking of him was easier and simpler than standing so close to him. After last night, she felt like a traitor, the worst kind of manipulator. She drew back, the words on the tip of her tongue.

"I wanted to show you this place," he said, silencing her confession. "The moment I met you, I wanted to show you Drumvagen."

"Was the house built where it was because of the grotto?" she asked, trailing her fingers over the stone of the sill. How smooth it felt, almost like glass beneath her fingers.

"I don't know," he said, glancing at her. "I never spoke to the original owner or architect. But I would have built a house here because of it, I think."

"For nefarious purposes? Like smuggling?"

He glanced around. "It seems the place for it, doesn't it? Perhaps patriots used it to hide arms during the last rebellion."

She knew little Scottish history, and when she admitted that to him, his chuckle caught her unawares.

"I think the history of America and that of Scotland are similar. Not on the same timeline, but in our craving for freedom from England."

"Yet we Americans now gravitate to England," she said. "Is it the same with you Scots?"

"Perhaps it is," he said. "Or else I would not have given Ceana a season in London. We would have remained in Edinburgh."

She would never have seen him, never known him, and wouldn't be standing here now. She'd never been one to give much credence to fate, but she couldn't help but wonder if there was something to it.

No other man had ever made her feel the way he had. She couldn't imagine giving herself to someone else. Or experiencing such freedom and joy in the act.

"You didn't seem enamored of London society," she said.

He'd been different from the beginning, a little rougher, a little less refined. No, that wasn't it. The other men she'd met in London had been too effeminate, too caring about how long their tea was steeped or the cut of their coat and the shine on their shoes. He was a man among men. A man with an accent and a separateness that marked him as unusual.

Did all Scots have that sense of independence?

He'd stood on the sidelines and watched others with a light in his eyes that told her he found most of what he saw to be ridiculous. A half smile played around his mouth; his stance was relaxed.

He'd never tried to belong in the drawing rooms of London. He rarely spoke to others, aloof and somewhat detached. He did not join the rest of the men in their entertainments. He was polite for his sister's sake, and present so that Ceana could have her season.

"You were a magnificent dancer," she said. "I was surprised."

His laughter echoed through the grotto.

"That's because you were my partner," he said. "I don't remember dancing with anyone as effortlessly."

How strange to feel jealousy for that person she'd been, innocent and more than a little naive.

"Did you dance with many women?"

He smiled at her like he knew how foolish she was being and wanted to reassure her.

"I never imagined a place like this as a boy," he said, blessedly changing the subject from London. "Besides, I was too busy worrying about earning enough money to eat."

"Yet you still dreamed," she said.

He nodded. "You always have time for dreams." He stared off into the distance, and she wondered if he was recalling those years in Edinburgh.

"Was it an awful childhood?" she asked, then realized the question was unbearably rude.

"At times," he said, before she could call back the question. "After my father died, I remember being afraid all the time. A friend of my father's loaned me the money to bury him." He glanced over at her. "That was the first debt I paid."

She settled onto the ledge beneath the arched window, uncaring about the damage to her skirt, hoping he would continue to speak about his childhood and worried that doing so would trouble him.

"I couldn't let the girls know how desperate we were, so I worked harder than I ever had before." He smiled. "I sold broadsides for hours every day, then went back to the office and worked with Mairi to write them for the next day. Being out on the street helped me, because I heard what interested people, what worried them, what angered them."

She pulled up her skirt and, she hoped, with a ladylike grace, scooted into a more comfortable position.

"How did you go from being a printer to inventing an ice machine?"

He grinned at her, such a charming expression that she couldn't help but smile back.

"I used to clean the typeface with ether. Every time I did, it got cold. That fascinated me. I wondered if there was a way to get the air cold."

"Was there?" she asked, fascinated.

"As a side effect," he said. "But I also discovered I could create ice."

"And your sisters never again had to worry about their meals."

"Add another mouth," he said. "My cousin, Fenella. Mairi invited her to live with us when her parents died."

"Do they ever come to Drumvagen?"

He leaned against the stone wall. "They do. Mairi's only two years older than me, but she thinks she's my mother." He glanced over at her. "Fenella occasionally accompanies her. Ceana hasn't come back to Scotland after her marriage, but I think it's probably only a matter of time."

"Did you never wish for a brother, rather than all those females?"

He laughed. "My life was filled with relatives. I can't say I wanted another."

"I wanted a brother or a sister," she said, giving him a confession of her own. "Maybe my childhood would've been easier. My father would not have cared so much about my studies. Or maybe he would have visited me more than twice a year."

"While I think being an only child could be a blessing," he said. "Mairi always wants to know why I haven't married. She harangues me constantly about my plans for the paper. She gets into arguments with Brianag."

Before she could comment that Brianag was a formidable figure, he moved to stand in front of her.

"See, you've changed this place already," he said. "The

grotto will forever smell of roses, and I'll be able to close my eyes and say to myself, Virginia was here. I'll mark the exact date and time."

He mustn't do that to her. He mustn't cause her to want to weep simply with words.

Or perhaps that was her conscience rearing its head.

She moved her skirt aside so he could sit.

"What will you be thinking when you come here?" A foolish question, and one she should not have asked. His smile gently chided her, but he answered nonetheless.

"I'll be wondering why you came to me on a stormy day. Why you stayed until the weather was fair. Why I know, even as you sit here, that you're planning to leave again."

She reached out and touched his cheek with the tips of her fingers.

"What would you say if I told you that I came all this way for what happened last night?"

A comment that was too close to the truth.

"Or a kiss?" he asked. He bent his head down as he spoke, his voice a little rough, accented Scottish. Her breath hitched at the sound of it, at the feel of his breath against her temple.

He kissed his way to her lips, hovered over them.

"A memory I might be able to summon any moment of any day."

He kissed her softly, gently, his lips barely there. Suddenly, he clasped his hands behind her head, keeping her prisoner as he deepened the kiss, their tongues tangling, heat erupting between them.

She felt like her clothes might melt.

"I've never been able to forget you," she said long minutes later, when the kiss was done. How would he respond to that confession?

He didn't say anything, merely took her hand and kissed the tip of each finger.

"While I sat and brooded," he said.

She smiled gently at him. "I doubt you brooded all that much. Ceana said that you've been very successful. People crave your attention all over the world."

"It was easier to travel," he said, "then sit and remember you."

Perhaps this wasn't the best topic. When she returned to London, she would not be able to easily forget this interlude. That's all it was. For now, however, she didn't want to waste one moment.

She slipped off the rock sill and stood in front of him.

"Did you ever think of taking me here?" she asked, wondering at her own daring. The girl she'd been, the woman she was, would never have considered saying such a thing. But for now, Virginia the mouse had become someone else, a shocking woman with an edge of desperation.

Not because she needed a child, but because she needed him.

His smile faded, his look growing even more intense, as if he were judging the limits of her courage.

Slowly, his hands reached out and gripped her shoulders, pulling her toward him. Before she could ask what he was about, he'd lifted her. Then she was on his lap, her knees on either side of his legs. Such a position opened her, made a mockery of any hint of modesty in her pantaloons.

She gripped his shoulders as he moved back, bracing himself with both arms.

"Never dare a Scotsman," he said.

Chapter 12

Her hands clutched his shoulders; her whole body bending toward him. One of his hands twisted in her hair. He thrust the other beneath her skirt.

He smiled at her look of surprise, watched as her eyes changed, turning soft. He leaned forward and kissed her, sinking against Virginia's lips with a feeling of coming home.

Somehow, he had to convince her to remain with him. Life at Drumvagen would not be the same without her. He could promise her the world. He didn't remain in Scotland year-round. She could travel with him. He was due in Australia in a few months, and she would enjoy the voyage. She would be at his side, someone who could listen to his thoughts, who could reason with him, someone who would believe in him.

He had to convince her to stay.

He held his hand over hers, conscious of the delicacy of her fingers. She had nearly unmanned him last night with this delicate hand. She had clenched him to her, had held him between her palms, had expressed such genuine delight he'd wanted to take her again and again until the newness of his conquest had worn off. Except, after their loving at dawn, he realized it wasn't the novelty of Virginia ensnaring him, but her smile, the sparkle in her eyes and the tenderness of her touch.

She was the woman he'd loved for more than a year and thought lost to him.

The day could not be more wonderful. But it wasn't the sparkle in the air after the storm or the blue, cloudless skies. Even if snow had fallen, followed by a monsoon, he would never feel this day was anything but miraculous.

She had come to him. Not only yesterday, but last night. She had come to him. All those nights of sitting and staring at the fire, wondering if she had found bliss in her husband's arms—all those questions had been answered. Another miracle—she was nearly a virgin. She'd moaned in wonder and disbelief, and he had been the one to bring her those sensations, to gift her with satisfaction.

He pressed his cheek against hers, synchronized his breathing to hers, pressed his hand against the small of her back, wanting to know her more intimately than any other person.

"You've been in my dreams for so long," he said, giving her the truth. "I wanted to know what it was like to touch you. Now that I know, I'll never forget."

A moment later he pulled back. "Are you crying, Virginia?"

She buried her face against his chest.

"Is that a no?" he asked when she sighed. "Or a yes?"

"You mustn't keep doing that," she said. "You bring me to tears with your words, Macrath."

He enfolded her in his arms again, pressed her cheek against his chest, feeling a burst of tenderness for her.

"What a terrible woman I am to be in another man's arms."

"Newly widowed."

"Yes," she said.

His conscience, restrained until now, shook free of its ropes. "And I should release you."

Neither moved.

Long moments went by before he reached up and pulled free the tantalizing braid she wore, starting to unplait it.

"Another dream of mine," he said as she rested acquiescent in his arms. "To see your hair around your shoulders."

She remained still, encapsulated by sunlight, a radiant woman with flushed cheeks and full lips.

Gulls serenaded them, the tide adding a layer of soft sound.

The desire coursing through him was a languid thing. He didn't need instant completion as much as simply to touch her, breathe in her air.

"Are you seducing me?" she asked, reaching up to press her lips against his throat.

"Is it working?"

He felt her lips curve against his skin.

"Have you had a great many lovers?" she asked, sounding more British than American at the moment.

"Not all that many," he said.

She stiffened and he called himself ten times a fool.

"But there were some?"

What kind of idiot discusses his past while holding the woman he loves in his arms?

Pulling back, she peered into his face. "Did they all seduce you? All those women? Or did you seduce them?"

He didn't get the chance to answer. Her hands came up and pressed against the back of his neck, forcing his head down. She kissed him, not the soft and gentle kisses she'd given him before.

Her mouth opened, her tongue explored his, measuring the contours of his lips.

This moment, this time, with the sound of the sea and the tide and the bright glare of the sunlight warming his back, was unique. A memory he would recall forever.

To his surprise and delight, she unfastened the buttons of his shirt, spread her hands wide over his chest, her fingernails raking his skin.

She made a sound, a soft moan giving voice to desire.

He wanted to make her scream.

When her fingers trailed lower to fumble at his buttons, he bit back a strangled oath and placed his hand on hers.

"I call quarter," he said. "Would you unman me?"

"I would mount you," she said, her voice a mere whisper.

He moved his hands away, holding them up in a gesture of surrender.

"Then do your worst, I'm your slave."

Her lips were full and slightly swollen. He wanted to kiss her again, but when he leaned forward, she gently pushed him back, grabbing the silk of her skirts and moving them to the side so she could see. One by one she unfastened the buttons of his trousers, and when he was free, grabbed him with both hands.

He wanted to sing hosannas when her heated palms and fingers explored the length of him.

"You are so beautiful," she said, her head bowed to study him.

She was the beautiful one, her cheeks flushed pink, her hair flowing around her shoulders.

"Stay with me," he said, softly against her temple. He kissed her there, noting her shiver. Was she as attuned to him as he was to her?

He knew when she trembled, when her excitement was at its peak. He knew what pleased her, from soft kisses on the inside of her wrist to long strokes of his fingertips from her ankle to her hip.

He wanted her beneath him, wanted to press his forehead between her breasts, inhale her scent and feel himself home at last.

She was his harbor, and the thought warmed him. He knew he could tell her his secrets, his fears, and she'd keep them safe.

"Stay with me," he said again. "Stay at Drumvagen." He hadn't expected to be this direct. But once he said the words, he smiled into her face. "Don't be the Countess of Barrett," he said. "Be the American Virginia Anderson."

Instead of answering him, she raised up on her knees, holding onto his shoulders for balance. After some rearranging of her skirts, she slowly, so slowly he ached to pull her down, lowered herself on him. Her eyes were closed, an expression of such intensity on her face he couldn't look away. Finally, she was seated, sitting astride him as easily as if he were a saddle.

Let her mount him, then. He would give her the ride of her life.

She opened her eyes, blinked at him, a smile curving her lips. Her face was flushed, and he knew he would never forget the sight of her at that moment.

She pressed her hands against his chest, her fingers splayed to tease his nipples. He surged upward. Her eyes fluttered shut, her smile fading.

"Not too fast," she said. "Make it slow. Make it last."

"I'm not sure I can," he said. "You feel so damn good."

Her smile was back. "So do you. But I like this," she said. "So much."

She was going to kill him. He was certain of it. But he didn't move. Instead, he concentrated on the row of buttons down the front of her bodice.

He wanted her breasts. He wanted her nipples in his mouth. There, a task he could give himself to forget how hot and tight she felt around him.

The buttons done, he unfastened the busk at the front of her corset, pushed it away from her rib cage and stared at the black lace trimmed shift. With a murmured apology, he tore the edge of it until he could reach her breasts. His thumbs abraded her nipples while she was driving him mad by rocking on him.

He might not survive this.

He lowered his head until he could mouth one nipple, surging upward as he sucked on her. She gasped, gripping his chest with nails as sharp as talons.

She slowly rose up on her knees until he was nearly out of her, then lowered herself again.

Pleasure pierced him. "I'm not going to last if you keep doing that," he said.

"I don't want you to last," she said. She smiled at him, a creature poised between innocence and knowledge. "I like seducing you."

"You're too expert at this."

She shook her head slowly from side to side.

He pressed down on her hips, seating her on him. All he could think was: how much longer did she want this to last?

She slowed her movements, up and down, a little to the side, then raising up on her knees to tease him once more.

He bent his attention to her other breast, praying his stamina would last. If he could withstand the next few moments, perhaps he'd be the one to drive her mad and not vice versa. Either way, they'd both be delighted.

His hands clenched on her waist. He wished she was naked so he could feel every inch of her. Kissing her neck, he tasted the dampness of her skin, the heat of it. Her heart beat in a fierce rhythm and her breath came in gasps to equal his.

Now, it must be now. He couldn't last any longer.

"Come with me, Virginia," he whispered against her ear. "Come with me."

She moaned against his lips as she climaxed. A second later he was with her, the world graying as his body shuddered.

Hannah knocked softly on the door, waited a moment, then opened it slowly.

She tiptoed through the sitting room. No doubt the silence meant the countess was asleep. She hoped it was not a fever or anything contagious.

When she reached the bedroom, she peered inside only to find the bed empty.

Opening the doors of the armoire, she surveyed the dresses. One was missing.

The room smelled of the rose scent the countess favored. Turning, Hannah faced the bed again.

The dowager countess would be pleased about these developments.

Yet the situation was also worrisome. Macrath Sinclair was not the type of man one tricked. Nor was Virginia, the Countess of Barrett, the kind of woman who could take advantage of someone with impunity.

Still, it was none of her concern, was it? The countess and her mother-in-law wouldn't be the first women to take matters into their own hands. That thought did not ease her fears about the future.

A feeling of foreboding swamped her as she closed the armoire doors slowly, then left the room.

Long minutes later Virginia pulled back, her expression a combination of embarrassment and incredulity.

He stroked his knuckles over her heated cheeks, feeling his heart expand. He was happy, and the feeling buoyed him, expanded through him like air into a balloon.

For years he'd been willing to do almost anything to succeed, and he had. Until now he hadn't realized he'd neglected a vital part of life. He hadn't thought about his own happiness. Now it seemed of paramount importance.

In a day his life had changed course. One single day and suddenly his focus was different.

How did he retain this feeling of elation? He suspected the answer was absurdly simple—by keeping Virginia with him.

How did he coax her into loving him? Not with wealth, because she'd always been wealthy. He doubted he could pretty up his speech enough for it to be considered poetry. What could convince her to love him?

He'd always been able to find answers for his problems, either from correspondence with men more learned than he or by seeking out answers through trial and error. Who, though, did he go to for advice about love?

Brianag? Perhaps she could furnish him a potion to use, if she didn't strike him for hinting she had powers of witchcraft. He would have paid the devil a ransom if Virginia remained with him.

She got to her knees and moved to his side. She rearranged her skirts and buttoned her bodice while he made himself presentable.

"Stay here. Don't return to London," he said.

She didn't answer, only stared down at her clasped hands. A moment later she shook her head.

"I cannot," she said. "How could you ask that of me?"

Had he been wrong? Did she value her title that much?

"I'm expected back in London," she said faintly.

"You're expected back in London," he repeated.

She wouldn't look at him, slipped from the ledge and turned her back. Her hair was floating about her shoulders in a cloud, enticing him. He wanted to thrust his hands into it, tilt her head back and watch her try to avoid him then.

"We're not in London, Virginia," he said. "We're far enough away the gossips wouldn't know you're here. Or care. Stay with me. If you insist on mourning your earl, we'll marry after enough time has passed."

She turned toward him, her eyes widening, her face so pale she looked like she might faint.

"Oh, Macrath." She walked closer and stretched out her hand, cupping his jaw in her palm. "Dearest Macrath." Her voice sounded teary, but her eyes were dry.

"You won't stay?"

"I can't." She dropped her head, staring at the stone floor.

Silence stretched between them. Not the expectant kind that allows for anticipation, but something darker and more troubling. This silence was one of unvoiced truths, hidden meanings, and lies.

The ocean-born breeze sighed through the opening to the beach. The gulls cried aloud in joyous triumph over a school of fish. The tide rolled onto the sand as the sun poured in through the hole at the top of the grotto. Life went on, even though he was as cold as ice.

He buttoned his shirt, each movement of his fingers allowing his frozen thoughts to thaw.

She started to braid her hair, her fingers flying expertly over the tresses.

"Didn't your husband's family think it an odd journey for you to take so soon? What did you tell them?"

"I needed to get away," she said. "To escape London. And maybe myself," she added.

"Or for a bit of entertainment? You had an itch and decided to scratch it?"

She glanced at him. He had never seen her complexion as pale as it was now. She bit at her bottom lip.

"No, Macrath," she said, stretching out her hand to him. "I can't stay with you, however much I may want to. To do so would be to thrust Lawrence's family into the center of controversy and scandal."

"Then why come to Scotland days after you became a widow?"

"Because I needed to see you," she said, her voice sounding like she pushed back tears. "Because I wanted to see you."

"I feel the same. Stay with me."

But, damn her, she didn't speak. She only inspected her clothing, fluffed up her skirts and strolled toward the passage. He followed her, grabbed her arm, and turned her before she could escape.

"Like it or not," she said softly before he could speak, "I am the Countess of Barrett. I have people depending on me, just like your sisters are dependent on you."

A few minutes ago they'd been as close as any two people could be. Now a continent separated them.

"I think, perhaps," he said, speaking the words with remarkably little emotion, "it would be best if you left Drumvagen as quickly as possible."

He should've guarded his heart with greater care. He should have remembered she'd wounded him before, but that injury had not been at her hands.

This was one was.

Chapter 13

The sun slipped behind gray clouds, the diffused light giving the moor almost a pastoral appearance. Seabirds swooped overhead, soaring on air currents preceding another storm.

Macrath stood at the window watching as Virginia Traylor, Countess of Barrett, departed Drumvagen. She didn't stop, didn't ask the coachman to pull the carriage to the side of the road or look for a wider place to turn around to come back to him.

I am the Countess of Barrett. I have people depending on me, just like your sisters are dependent on you.

She hid behind her title when it suited her and dismissed it at other times.

The girl he'd known had vanished. Where was the Virginia who delighted in the news of the day, whose eyes had sparkled with mischief? Where was the girl who talked politics with him, who whispered of the latest broadsheets in an excited voice? In her place was a woman who fascinated him but remained a stranger even now.

He knew her body well, but did he know her mind? Who was Virginia?

He'd been a silly, lovestruck idiot a year ago, and he

wasn't going to long for her again. Perhaps there was one woman in every man's life who showed him to be a fool, who turned his stomach inside out and made pudding of his mind. If that were true, he'd just banished his.

He wouldn't think of her any longer. He wouldn't return to the grotto until the image of their loving had faded, until she was no more than a ghost. He wouldn't come back to the suite where he now stood until all hint of her perfume had dissipated. Open up the windows, air out the rooms, banish her scent.

Could he erase his memories? If so, he'd wipe out the whole last day along with the joy, the lilting happiness he'd felt in her presence.

"She's gone, then?"

He didn't turn at Brianag's words. He only nodded.

"You'll be better off, I'm thinking."

"Are you a soothsayer now, Brianag?"

"Some say I have the gift."

He glanced over his shoulder. "But you don't," he said. "Because that would be too much like witchcraft."

When she smiled, her face looked odd, almost like it wasn't prepared for amusement. Scowls suited her better.

"She wasn't for the likes of you, her with her maid and her airs."

He turned back to the window. "I don't think Virginia has airs," he said. One sin he couldn't lay at her feet.

"Well, it doesn't matter now, does it?" Brianag said. "She's gone and she won't be back."

"No," he said, feeling something inside twist with the realization. "She won't be back."

After she left, he strode into the bedroom, flinging open the doors of the armoire. The space was empty. What had he expected to find? Something he could use as a talisman, a reminder? Something he'd tuck into his pocket? He never wanted to forget Virginia Anderson Traylor, Countess of Barrett. She was a walking, living, breathing lesson.

He opened the bureau drawers. Nothing there, either, showing her maid was exceptionally conscientious.

No, he didn't need anything to help him recall her. She was there, etched in his mind like acid.

Why hadn't she stayed with him? Had she come to Scotland to resurrect a lost love, only to find that it had died just like her husband?

Once, she'd loved him, he was certain of it. And now?

Evidently not enough to remain in Scotland with him.

Walking to the bed, he placed his hand on the pillow, half expecting the smooth linen to be warm. The faint depression suggested she'd lain there, but not for long. Last night she'd been in his arms, and this morning they'd awakened each other with passion.

How quickly passion had turned to anger. Or perhaps his rage was merely a shield, a camouflage behind which his true emotions hid.

He'd lost, and failure didn't come easily to him, but that wasn't the reason he clenched his hand into a fist and left the room, slamming the door behind him.

London
July, 1869

Returning home, if London could ever be considered that, took forever. Virginia survived the journey by not once thinking of Macrath. Whenever he came into her thoughts, she caught herself and immediately started to think of something else, anything but him.

Once they reached London, traffic was horrendous, as usual. She could probably walk to their town house faster than the carriage would arrive. She'd already broken so many of society's edicts, she didn't dare do such a thing. One look at her, in her attire, and people would start gossiping about the Walking Widow.

She was tired of mourning, and yet she had another year and a half of it. In truth, she didn't mourn Lawrence as much as she mourned Macrath.

No, she would not think of him.

"It looks to rain again, your ladyship," Hannah said, peering behind the leather shade.

She didn't care, but she mustered a smile for the maid's benefits. "Isn't it always raining in London?"

"Was it ever so at your home? In America?"

She clasped her hands together tidily in her lap, sent her mind back to those days of her childhood, to the estate overlooking the Hudson River. She'd run and tumbled over acres of lush green grass, laughed with abandon, and hid from those instructed to care for her behind the great oaks bordering the property.

"I don't remember it raining much," she said, as images of deep blue skies came to mind. "But when it did, we had pounding thunderstorms that felt like God was shaking his fist at us."

She'd had a privileged childhood, if a lonely one. She rarely associated with children her own age. Most of her companions were adults. She'd been reared to be silent rather than vocal, unobtrusive rather than to step forward, timid rather than courageous.

She had enjoyed growing up at Cliff House, loved everything about her life until the day she'd been told to prepare for her English debut.

"I'll be damned if you'll marry a common man, Virginia," her father told her. "I'll get a title for myself. I've always liked the idea of being a duchess's father."

But he was unable to find a likely duke. The only available one had been a nearly deaf octogenarian.

"He smells bad," was the one and only comment her father ever made about the Duke of Marbleton. To her everlasting gratitude, the man had annoyed him.

Harold Anderson was a man of varied opinions and obstinate viewpoint. When he took umbrage to someone, there was no changing his mind. For that reason, he'd never truly considered Macrath's suit. Macrath had not groveled enough for her father. He wasn't impressed by her father's consequence.

He had only loved her.

No, she would not think about Macrath.

Oh, but she would long for him in earnest now. She would gaze at herself in her bath and remember when he'd praised her breasts, lifting one, then the other, saluting their shape with a kiss to each nipple.

Her knees would not simply be knees from now on, but marvels of creation, objects of his kisses and the teasing touch of his fingers behind them, to see if she was ticklish there.

Not one spot on her body was left untouched, bereft of a stroke or comment. Not one inch had been left unaltered.

Would he remember her touch as well?

Her fingers seemed to retain the memory of his hard chest, the curve of his muscular buttocks, the tantalizing shape of his manhood. He'd urged her to learn him and she had. Even now she could feel him, hard and heavy against her palms.

She closed her eyes, wishing she could return in time. He'd loved her three times, and each had been a memory that would last all her life. What she experienced with him had been unlike what she'd imagined love to be.

No, she would not think of Macrath.

How could she help but think of him? Regret colored each thought.

The seduction had been accomplished then, her mission performed. But, oh, it had been so much more than that. He'd changed her with his loving, and she wasn't the same woman who'd left London.

He wanted her to stay with him and had offered her marriage. She would tuck that memory into a box called Impossible Wishes. Being with Macrath would guarantee her future, but what about Enid and her daughters?

How much was she to sacrifice for them?

Even now she ached to be in Scotland.

No, it was much better not to think of Macrath.

She and Hannah sat, waiting for one of the advertising vans to move. Everyone was trying to sell something in London, from the sandwich men who plodded back and forth on the street to the vans slowing traffic everywhere.

She didn't like the city, but she'd never realized how much until just this moment.

When it wasn't raining, the fog was so thick she felt like she was swallowing air more than breathing it. On some days the only way to get to the carriage was with a handkerchief pressed against her nose and mouth, her mind on something other than the sulfurous stench.

She didn't have much affection for society, either, and all the rules she still didn't understand. Odd little things about greeting people in the order of their importance, of always appearing apologetic, of being self-deprecating to the point of absurdity.

Also, no one had warned her she'd have to spend a few months learning how Londoners spoke. The upper classes elongated their speech, each word followed by a pause, like they were too weary to finish a thought. After a time the affectation started to wear on her. More than once she'd had to stop herself from demanding the speaker simply get on with it and say what he meant to say, for heaven's sake.

She understood the Scottish easier than a titled Londoner.

When the carriage finally rolled to a stop in front of their town house, she felt a great sense of relief, tempered as it was with reluctance.

The house was in a prosperous square, surrounded by other, identical, homes. The reddish brick was still sharp on its corners, the town houses having been built only a decade or so ago. The windowsills were painted white, the doors black, and brass fixtures and lamps of wrought iron adorned each residence. A small fenced yard sat in front of each house, and in the rear was a similarly small garden. It was, however, a pleasant enough place to live, and probably much better than their future accommodations.

A week ago their circumstances had been dire enough. Now they seemed doubly so. Going to Scotland hadn't done anything but give her a feeling of such shame she wanted to scrub it from her skin.

Would she ever feel clean?

She left the carriage, thanking Hosking, and mounted the steps, Hannah behind her.

Rather than Albert, the majordomo, greeting them at the door, Paul was there, his appraising glance sweeping from the tips of her shoes to her bonnet.

What was he thinking with that sharp gaze? She didn't want to know. She didn't care.

He didn't look like he was going to step aside. She glanced back at Hosking, who hadn't driven the carriage around to the stables. Instead, he stood there impassively, watching the other man with the same dislike she, too, felt.

"We've missed you, your ladyship," Paul said.

She started to wiggle her fingers free of her gloves.

Must she remove them and her bonnet on the steps of the town house?

"Will you allow me inside?" she asked.

His eyes flattened and his lips thinned, worrisome signs of temper. Who was Paul Henderson to be angry at her?

"Of course, your ladyship," he said, bowing slightly and moving to the side. She and Hannah entered the house and immediately went upstairs. Perhaps she should speak to Enid about the man without delay.

She had many things to do, but she didn't feel capable of any of them right now. Being so close to tears didn't help, either.

Chapter 14

Drumvagen, Scotland
September, 1869

"It's too far away, Macrath," his sister said.

Since Mairi was prone to issuing edicts, he only waited. She would finish in a moment, marshaling her arguments as she always did.

She was, save for being female, perfectly suited to manage the Sinclair Printing Company. To the world that paid attention to such things, he owned the company, inheriting its assets and liabilities from his father. Mairi, however, ran Sinclair Printing, signing his name without hesitation to those documents she couldn't execute on her own.

When she had to transact business in person, she did so. Only rarely did she encounter an obstinate male who refused to deal with a woman. When that happened, Mairi simply retreated and corresponded with the gentleman, using his name.

"It's entirely too far away, Macrath."

"I've been to Australia before," he said.

"Yes, but when you left home, you'd a date in mind to return. Now you don't." She frowned at him.

He smiled and drank his whiskey, the glass cold against his fingers. He wished he could appreciate the taste of the single malt in solitude, but his sister and cousin had descended on him last night, having received his letter that he was leaving for Australia and determined to change his mind.

If he'd delayed sending the letter by one day, he would've been aboard the *Princess* and out to sea by the time they arrived at Drumvagen.

Now, however, he sat in the Clan Hall with the two of them, wondering how long this harangue would last.

The room smelled of heather, a scent he normally didn't notice. Was it because he was leaving? Brianag was forever bringing in blooms of some sort or another and sticking them in ornamental vases to dry.

"At least give me a date when you'll return," Mairi said.

After all these years, his sister hadn't yet realized he was as stubborn as she, although not as militant about it

"Mairi's right," Fenella said.

His cousin thought anything Mairi did was right, perhaps because Mairi had welcomed Fenella into their home when their cousin was newly orphaned. At the time, one more mouth to feed had been a burden. Or an incentive for him, not that he needed one, to succeed at his invention.

"It's a long way away, Macrath. Must you go?"

He smiled reassuringly at her. "I must."

"Are you coming back?" Mairi asked, frowning at him.

"Why would you think I wouldn't?"

"Which isn't an answer, Macrath."

She stood, marched to the sideboard and poured a measure of whiskey. His only response was to watch his sister sip cautiously, then take her glass and return to her chair. He noted she didn't continue drinking the whiskey but finished her tea instead.

That whole demonstration was an example of his sister's character.

"There are fires aboard ship," Fenella said. "And scurvy."

"Not to mention boredom," Mairi said.

"You didn't say anything about pirates or cholera," he added.

The two women frowned at him.

Anyone looking at them wouldn't have known they were related. Fenella had wispy blond hair and hazel eyes leaning toward green. Mairi, on the other hand, had dark brown hair and the Sinclair blue eyes just like his younger sister, Ceana. Fenella was, perhaps, prettier, but people tended to remember Mairi with her high cheekbones and stubborn chin.

Her personality was forceful and her temper wasn't to be underestimated. He'd seen grown men quail before her. He wasn't, however, one of them.

"Can't you conduct your business here?" Fenella asked. "Must you go all that way?"

"Fenella's right," his sister said. "You don't have to go halfway around the world."

"I do if I want to assure the Australians I can bring their meat to market in England."

"I don't see why you have to go there, Macrath."

"You needn't worry about me so much, Mairi," he said.

"Still," she said, her voice trailing away.

"It's important to be in a position to expand the business."

"Are we running out of money, Sinclair?" Fenella asked.

The question was so out of character, he and Mairi turned to look at her.

Her pale cheeks blazed with color. "I only meant there are certain economies we can practice. I purchased three dresses this quarter and I didn't need them."

"Nonsense," Mairi said, turning her frown on him again.

While Mairi ran the Sinclair Printing Company, Fenella acted as her assistant and managed her household. The two of them lived in the Edinburgh house, a residence he'd purchased when the first ice machine made a profit. He only wished his parents had lived in such splendor.

He'd wanted Mairi and Fenella to move to Drumvagen, but Mairi was insistent on keeping the printing company. Fenella, just as he'd expected, dug in her heels as well, and he had no choice but to accede.

However, he'd arranged for their protection, since single women were not safe living alone. He'd installed two men in their household. James was their driver, reporting to him. Robert was a second cousin and perfect chaperone since he was old enough to be their grandfather and was as proper as an archbishop. Robert also did the accounting for the printing company.

"You could sell Drumvagen," Mairi said, looking around her. "Finishing the house must have cost you a fortune."

He put down the glass and held up both hands in surrender, before Mairi could launch another salvo against Drumvagen. She didn't like his house, didn't understand his need to create something of his own, and frankly didn't comprehend why Edinburgh had become too crowded and stifling to him. Yet when she came to Drumvagen, she seemed to enjoy herself immensely.

He hoped he could convince her to leave before him. Mairi and Brianag being here together without him was not wise. The two women clashed.

Twice now he'd watched as Brianag had stomped across the doorway, just to make sure he knew she was there. Pots clanged and banged, maids whispered, and buckets of water were dragged across the stone floor.

"We're doing fine financially," he said. "We've more money than we could spend in two lifetimes. That doesn't mean, however, I'll quit trying to earn more."

"Are you still set on establishing a lineage, Macrath? If so, you need to find a woman to marry."

His smile was a little more forced.

"I could say the same to you, Mairi. Emulate Ceana. She's happily married."

If she kept frowning like that, her face would be permanently marred.

"I'm not Ceana," she said.

His two sisters were as different from each other in temperament and personality as Mairi and Fenella were in appearance.

"I've disassembled my new machine," he said, "and it's in the hold of my ship, my trunks are packed, and I'm leaving tomorrow."

His words didn't seem to make an impact on his sister's frown.

"I want away for a while," he said, hoping the truth would stop Mairi from asking any more questions.

Her eyes widened at his comment, or perhaps it was the tone in which he uttered it.

She leaned forward. "Has something happened, Macrath? Something you need to tell me?"

His smile was easier; the words were difficult. "Nothing has happened, Mairi. I just need to explore a bit."

She settled back in the chair, eyeing him with some disfavor. "Why do I feel you are not telling me the whole truth?"

Because some truths could not be voiced. Virginia's face suddenly appeared, seeping out of the vault where he'd put her.

"Why is it that women are so perfidious, Mairi?" he asked, sipping at his whiskey.

She folded her arms. "I might ask the same of you, Macrath, only about men."

"He wasn't worth you," he said, speaking of the suitor she'd had a few years earlier. The man had rejected her, and although she'd never said the words, he knew she'd been hurt. "You shouldn't judge all men by one."

"Again, I might say the same to you."

"Why do you think a woman is on my mind?"

"Because you're acting the same way you did last year. You're my brother, Macrath. A younger brother, granted," she added, frowning at him as if daring him to mention her age. "A foolish brother, perhaps."

She held up her hand when he would've spoken. "You can be brilliant with your machines," she said. "But you are lacking knowledge when it comes to women."

He stifled his smile. "Why would you say that?"

"Because it's obvious you're pining for one now. It's why you're off to Australia. It's just about as far as you can get from Scotland."

"She has nothing to do with this."

"There," she said, satisfied. "I knew it was a woman."

How did she do it? She was like an irritating sound repeated over and over and over, until you would do almost anything to get it to stop.

But she was right about one thing—the farther he went, the faster he went, the better.

London
September, 1869

Virginia lay on her bed with a pillow over her face, wishing Eudora would go away.

"Are you certain I can't pour you some tea?" Eudora asked.

She closed her eyes, prayed her stomach would settle, and took several deep breaths.

"I'm sure," she said. Ever since she'd returned from Scotland, Eudora and Ellice hadn't left her alone for a moment, probably fearing grief would swamp her if she had any time to herself.

Between her sisters-in-law and Enid, she didn't have a moment alone all day.

Perhaps it was just as well, since their constant companionship kept her from remembering. Macrath remained in Scotland and not in her thoughts.

"Could you please put the tray outside?" she asked, nearly done in by the revolting smell of kippered herrings. How could anyone eat such a thing first thing in the morning? Just seeing the jug was enough to bring back her nausea.

"Are you sure? You need to eat something."

Not kippered herrings. Not rashers. Maybe toast, later, but nothing now.

She pulled the pillow off her face to find Eudora still standing over her, now fanning the air with the magazine she'd been reading.

This morning she wasn't in the mood for company. She was exceedingly tired and wanted to go back to sleep. She could barely stay awake.

She'd felt this way once before, when they were traveling to England. She'd been exhausted then, too.

"You're sad, that's what it is," her maid at the time had said. "It's to be expected, leaving your home and all."

Poor girl, she'd been dismissed a few days before her marriage to Lawrence, replaced by Hannah, who, her mother-in-law had said, was the perfect English maid.

Perhaps she was sad after all.

She closed her eyes as the door opened again. *Please*

don't let Ellice be bringing something else to eat. Her stomach could not tolerate any more food odors.

"Are you sure, Virginia? There's enough tea in the pot. I can add a bit of lemon to it. Or cream if you prefer. Perhaps it would settle you."

Her stomach was rebelling once again. She waved her hand in the air, hoping Eudora would take the gesture as a request not to mention food or drink.

"I'm not feeling well, Eudora," she said. "Would you mind leaving me alone?"

Please, go away.

"Yes, dear, go and find Ellice. We'll go off to the market in a few minutes. For now, I want to visit with Virginia."

She slitted open an eye, to find her mother-in-law now occupying Eudora's chair. She didn't have the strength to face Enid without a fortifying cup of tea, thoughts of which caused her stomach to reel again.

The moment the door closed behind Eudora, Enid started to smile.

"Oh dear Virginia," she said. "I thought you'd failed in your task. I thought I had sent a girl to do a woman's duty. But you've succeeded beyond my wildest expectations."

Virginia held the corner of the pillow aloft, staring at her mother-in-law.

Enid positively exuded joy.

She let the pillow drop, wishing Enid would depart in the haste with which she'd arrived.

"Oh my dear, don't you see? The chambermaid told me you were ill. That you were retching again this morning. Isn't it the most marvelous thing?"

Once more she slid the pillow away, frowning up at Enid.

"You are with child!"

Virginia closed her eyes. "It's something I ate," she said.

"One morning, perhaps," Enid said cheerfully. "But you've been sick for the last four days. Of course you're with child. And I've seen you falling asleep over your needlework at night."

Her stomach clenched and for the first time in days it wasn't nausea. She opened her eyes to find Enid had moved the straight-back chair closer to the side of the bed and was now sitting there patting her fingertips together.

"I know the symptoms, my dear. I've delivered three children."

She didn't know what to say. Evidently, however, her mother-in-law didn't mind that she was a mute participant in this conversation.

"Tell me, my dear, did he enter you from behind? Did you copulate standing up?"

She stared at Enid.

"All these positions are guarantees of a male, my dear. There's something to be said for the man lowering himself to you. But there's a greater chance for an heir if he entered you from behind."

Had her mother-in-law lost her mind? She had no intention of discussing Macrath's manhood or any position they might've assumed.

But, dear God, what if Enid were right? What if this passing sickness wasn't sickness after all?

She counted back. Six weeks had passed since she'd traveled to Scotland. Could such a thing be true? She clenched her hands into the pillow, keeping her eyes shut so as not to see Enid's triumphant smile.

"Oh my dear, we're saved."

She slitted open one eye, determined to bring her mother-in-law back to some form of sanity. It wasn't to be. Enid was still smiling as she leaned forward, grabbed her hand and patted it enthusiastically.

"It could be a girl," Virginia said.

Was it true? Was she going to be a mother? She pressed her hand against her midriff. A child, growing inside her. A child. She'd been unable to forget one minute of that enchanted day at Drumvagen. Could it be true? Could their lovemaking had given her the greatest gift of all?

Macrath's child. A son or his daughter, she didn't care.

"Even so, we've been given a respite," Enid said. "The attorneys will not be able to advance their case until you're delivered, my dear. You must take great care. I will not allow you to tax yourself in any way. I shall hire another maid to care for you along with Hannah."

"We can't afford another maid, Enid."

"Nonsense. I will petition the solicitor this morning. He will surely advance us the rents to maintain the household until you deliver. After all, you might well carry the heir to the earldom."

She stared at Enid, unable to think of a thing to say to counter her excitement.

Drumvagen, Scotland
September, 1869

"The last of the equipment's loaded, sir," Jack said. "I've my trunk and Sam has his, but that's all."

"My sister isn't planted in front of the carriage?" Macrath asked, fastening the last strap on his valise. He glanced over at his assistant with a smile. "No last minute protestations?"

Jack grinned at him. "No, sir."

He'd plucked Jack from the Edinburgh streets where the boy had been working for Sinclair Printing. Jack had been a hawker, collecting pennies for the broadsides the company printed three times a week. Macrath knew the job well, since he'd done it since he was eight.

Short, with brown eyes and hair, Jack might be nonde-script in appearance but he made up for it in other ways. His sense of humor kept Macrath chuckling, and Jack's wish to make a success of his life was second only to his own ambitions.

After four years of working for him, Jack was nearly as adept as he was at repairing an ice machine. If Jack ever decided to leave his employ, the man would easily be hired by one of the mills in England. He could repair almost anything, and as he did, he crooned to it, like a man would to a woman he was seducing.

"There you go, you sweet thing. Go right in there for me. Good for you, you beauty."

Sam, his other assistant, was quieter.

A Kinloch man, with a Kinloch accent, he was tall and thin, despite always eating. His black hair was long, falling over hazel eyes that watched and took in everything. His face was narrow, marked with a burgundy scar running the length of his jaw. When Macrath had asked about it, Sam said something Brianag had to translate, meaning he'd had the scar since birth.

Either he was getting more adept at deciphering the Kinloch accent, or Sam was getting better at speaking like an Edinburgh man, because they rarely had difficulties un-derstanding each other lately.

Sam remembered details Macrath had forgotten, in-cluding measurements he could recall off the top of his head. Not content with fishing for a living like the men of Kinloch, he was never happier than when learning some-thing new.

This voyage to Australia was the highlight of his life. Macrath would bet the man was already seated in the car-riage, impatiently waiting for the trip to Kinloch Harbor to board the *Princess*.

Jack grabbed his valise and left. Macrath followed with one last look around his bedroom. The scent of roses came to him along with the ghostly echoes of throaty laughter. A woman's face smiling up at him was obscured by a mist, not formed of time, but determination.

He wasn't going to think of Virginia.

Brianag stood at the base of the stairs waiting for him.

"I'll leave Drumvagen to your care, then," he said, smiling.

Brianag looked him in the eye. "It's a big responsibility you've given me," she said.

"One you can handle better than anyone. There were days when I didn't pay any attention to Drumvagen. Yet, because of you, everything went smoothly."

"So, you'll be wanting me to be called the Devil of Drumvagen now. Or maybe the crone?" She surprised him with a grin, one he couldn't help but answer in kind.

"Mairi won't be staying long," he said. "But if you need anything, be sure and tell her."

"And what would I be needing? You've left enough money for me to set up my own castle, furnish it with kilted lads in bagpipes, and enough whiskey to keep me satisfied until the Second Coming."

He stared at her, uncertain if she was kidding. The image of Brianag consorting with kilted lads was not one he wanted to have in his mind.

She strode to him, poked him in the chest with one finger. "I've had a dream, Macrath Sinclair, of a ship."

He waited, certain she wasn't finished.

"A ship sitting on dry land."

"I suppose that means something," he said.

She frowned at him. "It means I'll be seeing a coffin soon."

"Not the words a man wants to hear when he's leaving on a voyage, Brianag."

"You'll be taking care, then?"

"I will," he said.

"Then go on with you. We'll be fine. But you should worry about us a little and come home quickly."

"A Scotsman's never as much a Scotsman as when he's abroad, Brianag."

"I've no knowledge of that. All I do know is Drumvagen will not be the same without you. Aince awa, aye awa."

He wasn't given to demonstrations of affection, but he leaned forward and put his arms around Brianag, who stiffened first, then reached up and patted his cheek.

A strong woman of long bones and firm muscles, she smelled of spices. And maybe Scotland, with hints of fresh wind and heather. Damn if he wasn't going to miss their confrontations.

Drawing back, he said, "I'll be back before you start to miss me."

"You're a good man, Macrath Sinclair. It's guid ti hae yir cog out whan it rains kail." When he looked at her, she translated: "You go, make the most of your opportunities. We'll be here, waiting for you."

He said farewell to the rest of the staff and found Mairi and Fenella standing by the carriage. Glancing back at his home, he marveled, once again, at the beauty of Drumvagen.

When he'd first seen the house, half done and abandoned, he couldn't imagine how anyone could have walked away from the majesty being built. Yet here he was, doing the same. Not for the sake of his purse as much as his well-being. Perhaps once aboard the *Princess,* he'd be able to sleep at night. He'd be about creating his future and living his life.

Perhaps he'd even forget about a certain countess.

Chapter 15

London
March, 1870

If the weather were better, Virginia could have escaped to the garden. But the March morning was cold and wet, hinting that spring would be delayed this year. She settled for retreating to the conservatory.

Over the last year, Eudora had ordered topiary bushes to be placed around the fence, and they hid the carriage house and drying yard from sight. The honeysuckle vines were just starting to flourish after the winter, further shielding Virginia from the curious looks of her neighbors.

She was, after all, in the last stages of her pregnancy and not to be seen.

In her condition, she was expected to be invisible. Hardly possible since she was so large she could barely walk or lever herself out of a chair. But she didn't want to be confined to her bedroom. Nor was she going to sit in the parlor and be conversed to death.

She'd never realized how much her in-laws liked to talk.

Laying her hand on the protruding mound of her stomach, she said, "Soon, my son." From the beginning, she'd known this child was a boy.

Ever since midnight she'd been feeling uncomfortable. Her child, as if knowing, had ceased moving. Her back ached and from time to time she got twinges across her stomach, signs that her time was near.

She wanted her son to be born yet she knew the moment he was he'd be whisked from her and belong to others. Enid would ensure the world thought her a doting grandmother and Lawrence's sisters warm and loving aunts. As his mother, however, she would be ignored from then on, her main task having been performed, providing the heir.

She stared longingly at the garden, sighed, and sank into the settee in the middle of the conservatory, the book of poetry Ellice had purchased for her in her hand.

Eudora possessed an uncanny ability for growing things. The lush plants surrounding her were deeply green and vibrant, smelling of fecund earth. Three plants had already begun to bloom, white peppery blossoms reminding her of spring.

Once again she lay her hand on her stomach. How fitting her son would be born in the season of renewal, the winter having passed.

For a few minutes she simply enjoyed the oasis of silence in a house of sound. She hoped the respite would last, that no one would suddenly say, "Oh, where is Virginia? She mustn't be alone."

She opened the book, thumbed through the sonnets, and started to read.

> *I love thee to the level of everyday's*
> *Most quiet need, by sun and candlelight.*
> *I love thee freely, as men strive for Right;*
> *I love thee purely, as they turn from*
> *   Praise.*
> *I love thee with a passion put to use*

> *In my old griefs, and with my child-*
> *hood's faith.*

A few minutes later she closed the book and hugged it to her chest.

Poetry was, perhaps, not the best choice of reading matter. Even now she couldn't bear to read Tennyson or Burns. Soft words and romantic notions made her think about things she would be better off not remembering. Above all, she should not recall Macrath, the quirk of his smile, the way he stood as firm and unmovable as a pillar, his legs braced apart, his arms folded, like he dared someone to try to move him.

She should not think about the time when they'd been entwined with each other, still flush from loving, their hearts gradually slowing from the race to passion.

"I could get lost in your eyes," he had said. "They're so pale a blue they're almost like clouds."

"I never knew you had a penchant for poetry," she said.

"I don't, unless it's around you. I love the color of your hair, for example," he continued, twirling a lock around his finger. "I love how it's so black it shines with its own kind of light. I love how your cheeks always turn pink when I compliment you."

What had she said in return? She couldn't remember. She'd probably kissed him and held him, eyes closed against the wonder of Macrath.

She skimmed the rest of the book, selecting another poem.

> *"Yes," I answered you last night;*
> *"No," this morning, sir, I say.*
> *Colors seen by candlelight,*
> *Will not look the same by day.*

Was everything going to remind her of Macrath?

No, poetry wasn't wise. Poetry glorified the highs and lows of emotion. The authors were either rapturous with joy or immobile from grief.

She felt the same being with child. The fatigue and nausea had blessedly disappeared, to be replaced by emotions she couldn't control. The sight of clouds overhead could summon tears. The sweet and warm scent of the honeysuckle caused her to weep. But she was just as easily annoyed, which was why she had found a quiet place in the conservatory rather than listening to the eternal chatter inside the parlor.

Perhaps she should read an adventure like *Ivanhoe*. Or something that would elevate her mind. She did not want to feel the pain of love lost or the joy of love found.

Would Macrath ever know of his son? For this ruse to work, he mustn't. Yet she wanted to tell him, and the compulsion to do so was growing each day. He needed to know, even if in doing so she condemned herself to poverty.

But she didn't wish that for her son.

For the sake of her child she had to remain silent.

"There you are."

Virginia bit back a sigh, and wondered if there was anyplace she could truly escape. Was there anyplace Paul wasn't?

He didn't seem to do much during the day except walk around and watch everyone. When she'd suggested to Enid they might want to consider dismissing him, her mother-in-law said something vague in reply, avoiding an answer. Twice, she'd brought up the subject, and twice Enid deflected the question.

Evidently, keeping Lawrence's attendant also kept Lawrence's memory alive. Virginia had stopped commenting about Paul, but she also avoided him when she could.

She pointedly returned to her book, hoping he would get the hint and simply go away.

Instead, he took the chair opposite her.

Was he going to force her to be rude?

He regarded her with the intensity of a hawk, a habit of his that bothered her.

She didn't look up but continued to read, staring at the words on the page.

"You're looking lovely today," he said, breaking the silence.

Please go away.

She would have to take her courage in hand and talk to Enid again. This time she would insist on Paul's dismissal. She'd tell her mother-in-law about all the times she turned to find Paul watching her. Not only was he always underfoot, but he questioned Hannah at length about their visit to Drumvagen.

She turned the page, hoping her silence would give him a hint she didn't wish to be disturbed.

"I've heard that women who are with child look exceptionally lovely."

She would not look up.

"It's not much longer, is it? I wonder who the child will look like?"

Before she could frame an answer to his effrontery, Hannah came to the door.

"Your ladyship," she said. "You've a visitor. Mrs. Montgomery. Do you wish to see her?"

She nodded. Not only was Ceana a friend, but her arrival would mean Paul would be forced to leave.

"Yes," she said. "Ask her if she minds coming to the conservatory." The alternative was she had to stand and waddle her way into the parlor. At least this way their conversation could be private.

Hannah turned and looked pointedly at Paul. He stood and without another word left the room.

"Was he bothering you, your ladyship?" Hannah asked, her eyes too sharp.

"What does he do all day?" Virginia asked, her eyes remaining on the doorway.

Hannah shrugged. "No good, I think. Are you certain you're up for a visit?"

"Yes," she said. "I'm certain."

She wiggled into the corner of the settee, piling the needlework around her. Not a good distraction, as it turned out, simply because she was so large.

Had Macrath's mother been as huge?

She clasped her hands together, a gesture that was becoming difficult over the mound of her stomach. She'd told Hannah, more than once, that she truly didn't need a tray on which to rest her tea things. Her stomach was more than capable of doing the job.

Ceana entered the room in a rush, handing her bonnet to Hannah. Macrath's sister stopped a foot from the settee, staring at her.

"Good heavens, Virginia. No wonder I haven't seen you lately. Are you feeling well?"

"Very well," she said, not trying to hide her amusement. She stared down at herself. "I am large, aren't I?"

"As a horse," Ceana said, then covered her mouth with her gloved hand. "That's hardly a compliment, is it? I shouldn't say it, should I?"

Had Ceana always been so voluble and excited?

Her friend settled into the adjoining chair, pulling off her gloves and beaming at her all the while. Her hair was mussed from her bonnet, but she didn't seem to care. Her eyes, so similar to Macrath's, made Virginia wonder if her son would have the same shade.

"I just couldn't wait. I wanted to tell someone. I've told Peter, of course, and he's beyond overjoyed. I've written Mairi, but she's in Scotland. I've written Macrath, but heaven knows when the letter will reach him. I wanted to tell you."

What did she mean? She bit back her question about Macrath in favor of Ceana's news.

"I'm going to have a child," Ceana said, her smile as bright as a summer day. "Is it as marvelous as I think it must be?"

"After the first three months, it was for me," she said. "Before that, I felt seasick all the time." She wished she could lean forward, grab her friend's hand or wrap her in a hug. In her position and as difficult as it was to rise, all she could do was smile at Ceana.

"You'll be a wonderful mother," she said. "I'm so happy for you."

"Peter wants the baby to be born at Iverclaire," Ceana said. "We're leaving for Ireland tomorrow." She sighed. "Which means I'll be alone, with none of my family around. I wouldn't mind but Macrath is so far away." Looking directly at Virginia, she asked, "Does he know?"

For a hideous moment she thought Ceana had penetrated her masquerade.

"You asked for his address. I can only think you wished to communicate with him. Does he know about Lawrence?"

Dear God, she was so grateful Hannah wasn't in the room.

Would the rest of her life be filled with moments like this one? Or, once her child was born, would everyone forget everything but the fact he was the eleventh Earl of Barrett?

"Does he know about your child?"

She shook her head.

"We really should have been sisters," Ceana said.

For the blink of an eye Lawrence lingered between them, disembodied and ghostly.

How difficult it was to talk. She could barely push the words past the lump in her throat. "Macrath's away?"

There, that sounded dispassionate enough. She didn't reveal anything, did she?

"He's in Australia. He's been there for months and months. My Peter thinks he should be gone more, but then, he's a bit intimidated by Macrath. Which he shouldn't be. Peter is a paragon in his own right."

Ceana's husband was the younger son of an Irish duke, and a financial genius, from what she'd heard. He managed the family's considerable fortune, increasing their wealth each year. Although he was several inches shorter than Ceana, her friend obviously adored him, as he did her.

"I think he should come home, but when he does he'll probably bring a wife. How do you think an Australian wife will fare in Scotland?"

"As well as an American in England," Virginia said.

Ceana was still talking. "I do hope our child will take after my family and not Peter's. Two of his brothers have bright red hair."

"Is he due back anytime soon?"

"Peter? Oh, you mean Macrath. We don't know. When he left, he wouldn't tell us when he was coming back. Perhaps there's a reason he's lingered. A woman might have kept him there."

Would she stop saying that?

"Did he know?" Ceana asked.

For a second her mind would simply not focus.

Ceana's smile faded as her eyes softened. "Dear Lawrence. Did he know he was going to be a father? How utterly sad, if so."

She hadn't considered the question and didn't know how to respond now. She looked away, and a moment later one of the maids entered the room bearing a tea tray. Ceana served them, her concentration on the task releasing Virginia from having to tell another falsehood.

The maids knew to serve her only a special kind of green tea, one Enid had decreed would be good for her digestion. Thankfully, she had grown to like the vegetal taste, and sipped it now, grateful it gave her an excuse not to talk.

She hadn't thought how difficult it would be to lie. Nor had she considered the questions people might ask. For the last several months she'd been a hermit at home, kept from society not only because of her mourning but her condition.

The rest of the conversation was blessedly Macrath free. They spoke of things maternal, including their wishes and hopes and dreams, all the while skirting over the topic of giving birth. Other matrons were more than happy to convey what a hideous experience it would be, how much pain they'd personally endured, and how fortunate each woman was to have survived it.

Listening to these stories seemed to be part of the entrance fee to a select and secret sisterhood.

Neither she nor Ceana mentioned the delivery, but it was on her mind as she bid her friend good-bye.

Was it easier to endure what was coming when a husband waited, anxious for news of an heir or a daughter? Did a husband's love and affection mitigate everything a woman had to go through? She doubted Lawrence would have feigned any care or concern.

And Macrath? She could see him at her side, holding her hand, speaking softly, trying to take her mind from the pain.

How odd that she'd thought him at Drumvagen all these months and he'd not been there. He'd been fixed in her mind as walking the moors, working in his ice laboratory, striding from room to room, and all this time he'd been in Australia.

She should have known somehow. She should have felt him gone.

Pain suddenly stretched across her stomach like a fierce band. She gasped, wondering when it would ease. She was being broken in two. Closing her eyes, she clenched her hands on her skirt. All she had to do was endure it. From what Enid said, the pain came in waves.

This wasn't a wave. This was a celestial hand squeezing her belly.

Gradually, the pain eased. She sat against the back of the settee, weakened.

Perhaps it was all those thoughts of Macrath, but her son was suddenly anxious to be born. She had to tell Enid her time had come.

Paul stood outside in the garden, watching the conservatory.

She was ignoring him. Despite his solicitude, Virginia rarely paid him any attention.

Didn't she understand what it was like to see her round with another man's child? When the whelp was born she would devote all her attention to the infant.

His mother had been the same. She kept them clean, as much as she was able, and as fed as she could manage. She patted his cheek with his palm, sent him off after his father every morning with a look in her eye that said she'd do it differently if she could.

A son of his would never have to do what he had. A daughter would be feted like any countess.

He knew the baby wasn't Lawrence's. Did she truly think people would believe such a thing? Lawrence hated her. He had more occasion to know what Lawrence felt than anyone else.

Her friend left and she sat there for a while, her gaze turned inward. He was about to move away when he realized something was wrong.

Through the glass of the conservatory, he could see Virginia leaning back, her face etched in pain.

He left the garden, entering the house, and reached her side.

"Enid," she said, her voice quavering. "Tell Enid."

Despite her objections, he gently scooped her up in his arms. The feeling of her so close nearly unmanned him. Did she remember? Did she long for him like he had for her?

She clenched his shirt, moaning in pain. He wanted to ease her somehow, tell her it was going to be all right and it would soon be over. Since his mother had borne three children after him and only two survived, he wasn't sure it would be the truth.

As he made his way up the stairs to her bedchamber, a thought came to him. It wouldn't be the worst thing in the world for the Scottish whelp to die being born.

Chapter 16

Paul was carrying her. She was in Paul's arms and despite her protests he wouldn't put her down, insisting on taking her to her room on the second floor. Perhaps she should remain silent. How would she manage the stairs otherwise?

But he mustn't get the wrong idea. He mustn't think she accepted such behavior, or even tolerated him.

The pain was suddenly a red hued monster, holding her in its mouth. She couldn't speak or move for fear it would bite down and crush her.

Paul lay her gently on her bed, shouting for Hannah.

How considerate he was being. So much nicer than when he asked who her child would resemble.

She waited until the monster had turned its head before trying to speak.

"Enid," she said, but one word was all she could manage before the rolling pain came again. Should it be so soon?

She thought he left the room but wasn't sure. When Enid came, she'd be shuffled off to the room prepared for her on the third floor. The mattress had been covered, the room swept and draped. The sheets had been stripped from the mattress, and a heavy quilt laid over it. Two more sheets were tied to the bed frame, so she could pull on them.

There was nothing comforting about the room, but Enid had assured her that she had borne all her children in a similarly equipped chamber.

Her back ached so badly it felt like it was breaking. Was such a thing normal? Pain stretched across the width of her stomach, as if to wake her quiescent son. Had he been quiet in the last few hours to store up energy for his birth?

According to Enid, someone would sit with her during a long night, no doubt read the Bible. Were there any uplifting verses in the Bible? Was there something about the joy of childbirth? Or must she be told all those depressing stories?

Would she be brave? Would she be silent and stoic? She rather doubted it. When she was a little girl and cut herself, or fell down the steps, she wanted people to know she hurt.

What if she screamed? Perhaps she should, if for no other reason than to take advantage of this perfect opportunity to be less than demure and restrained. She could voice all the anger she had for Lawrence and all the grief about Macrath.

She wished Macrath were here. If he sat with her, holding her hand, she would be brave. She would be silent and stoic.

The pain tightened around her, threatening to cut her in two.

"Your ladyship."

Thank God Hannah was here. She opened her eyes and tried to smile.

"I think it's time, Hannah."

Her maid said something but she couldn't hear anything, her attention focused on the pain.

Now she was in the belly of the beast and its roaring took away her hearing and the crimson walls stripped everything from her sight. Even her child, the cause of this tearing, ripping agony, was secondary to this. She bowed down before it, gave it obeisance, allowed it to claim dominion over her, and when it retreated she lay gasping.

"Oh my dear girl," Enid said from beyond the pain. "You've hours more of this."

She wouldn't be able to bear it.

Her mother-in-law sat beside the bed, patting Virginia's hand, which meant she was being conciliatory and otherwise ignoring her.

"You don't understand, Enid," she said, trying to concentrate on the words above the pain. "I believe the child will be born soon." With great difficulty she focused on her mother-in-law's face.

"Nonsense, Virginia," Enid said, her round face softening. "You can look forward to a day or more of labor. With Eudora, it was nearly three days for me."

Was she supposed to endure this for three days? It didn't seem possible that any woman could survive that.

"You must submit to my greater knowledge, Virginia. I've given birth three times."

She nodded as another wave of pain sliced her in two, taking her breath and her thoughts.

"It's hours before we need to fetch the midwife." Enid stood, looking down at her. "We should get you to the third floor, though." Glancing at Hannah, she said, "You'll help your mistress."

Hannah nodded.

Virginia kept silent, recognizing Enid's stubbornness. Whatever her mother-in-law wanted she normally got, by sheer dint of her will and personality.

In this matter, however, Enid was wrong.

Her mother had died in childbirth. Would she, too? Would Macrath miss her?

Did he ever think of her?

She was about to bring the eleventh Earl of Barrett into

the world, but his true father was on the other side of the earth. Would Macrath know, somehow, that an event of momentous import was about to happen?

Sydney, Australia
March, 1870

"**A**re you going to participate in the race, Mr. Sinclair?"

Macrath turned at the question, forcing a smile for the benefit of the young lady who stood there.

The daughter of his host, she was a charming creature with blond hair and warm brown eyes. Her smile flashed and he'd heard her tinkling laugh all evening.

"Yes I am, Miss McDermott," he said.

"My father says Scottish inventors are the best," she said, smiling winsomely at him. "Is the contest really between you and Mr. McAdams?"

"Perhaps it would be better if I didn't brag," he said. "However, I believe my newest modifications mean a better machine."

"Just think, Mr. Sinclair, what it would be like to ship things all over the world and keep them fresh until they've reached their destination."

"I believe your Australian ranchers hope that's the case," he said.

The race was simple. Four steamships would be equipped with whatever modifications the individual inventors wished. They'd start the journey from Sydney, with the destination London. Whoever arrived in London first with a consumable cargo won the race. The prize was a lucrative contract with Hamish McDermott and his consortium of ranchers.

The proceeds could add substantially to the Sinclair

empire, not to mention the reputation of the Sinclair Ice Company.

"It's a pity American canned meat has taken over the market, Mr. Sinclair. It strips us of our ability to compete. Even Canada has outsold us, because we aren't frozen most of the year like they are."

Surprised, he could only stare at the woman. Evidently, she was well versed in her father's business.

"Are you interested in reading the newspaper, Miss McDermott?" he asked.

She tilted her head, her eyes softening as she smiled. "Why, yes, I am, Mr. Sinclair. Is that an attribute in your sight? Or a detriment?"

"Merely a curiosity," he said, smiling back at her.

She was an attractive woman, one still in the first blush of youth, without the shyness and insecurity of a girl right out of the schoolroom. She had more poise and confidence about her than Virginia had when he met her. He couldn't imagine Miss McDermott coming to him and holding out broadsides with trembling fingers.

Nor could he imagine Miss McDermott ever being surprised when someone told her she was beautiful.

He watched as she moved away, smelling of oranges and tea. He'd have to ask for the name of her perfume. She greeted one guest after another. Later, she'd herd them into dinner like a sheepdog, nipping at their heels with a delicate mixture of a smile and a guiding hand.

Three times now he'd been invited to the McDermott home. After the first occasion he'd figured out that the smiles from his host were due more to his status as a rich, unmarried man than to his ice machine.

He sipped at the drink he'd been given, something tasting vaguely like champagne mixed with lemonade, but not as awful as the orange mixture he'd once tasted in London. Nor had he seen any fog for as long as he'd been there.

He'd traveled through Australia, impressed by the hardy people who reminded him of his fellow Scots, the awe-inspiring scenery nearly as beautiful but lacking the majesty of Scotland, and the capacity for making a fortune. That, more than anything, recommended Australia to him.

But he'd never emigrate. He'd miss his family and his homeland. Even now, Scotland called to him. He'd been gone too long. Brianag had taken to writing him once a month. Thanks to her stewardship, he didn't worry about Drumvagen, but there was other business needing to be handled.

His empire was growing.

His family was, too. His younger sister was going to give birth to her first child, another reminder he needed to be about building his clan.

He needed to find a wife.

What good did it do to think of Virginia?

Months had passed, yet she was still in his thoughts. He'd started to write her a half dozen times and each time stopped himself. Her role as countess interested her more than anything he might be able to offer her.

Instead, he should give some thought to replacing her in his mind and in his life. Miss McDermott, with her full lips, bright blond hair, and warm brown eyes would be an asset to Drumvagen.

He'd been wrong, before, to allow a woman to tie him in knots. Perhaps his pick of a wife was a decision better served by logic. On the face of it, Miss McDermott would be a more than adequate candidate for marriage.

Her father's business interests could pair with his. There, he'd done two things—intertwined his desire for an empire along with his wish for a clan.

"May I escort you to dinner, Miss McDermott?" he asked when she circled back around to him.

"You may, Mr. Sinclair," she said, placing her hand on

his arm. He could feel the warmth of her palm through the
wool of his coat.

This time when he courted a woman, he would do so
without involving his emotions. He would be kind, atten-
tive, and polite, but would extend his hand rather than his
heart.

London
March, 1870

Her mother-in-law was barely out of the room before a
sweeping pain started at the base of Virginia's spine, coil-
ing around her body and nipping wherever it touched.

Thankfully, Hannah was there.

"We don't have time to get to the third floor," she said.

"My mother had eight children. As the eldest, I know
what to do, your ladyship."

"Then I suggest we do it now. And quickly."

In less than three minutes her clothing was removed.
She donned the nightgown she'd selected for the birth and
Hannah stripped the top sheet and coverlet from the bed,
placing a blanket across the mattress.

"How long have you been having pains, your ladyship?"
Hannah asked, helping her up the steps to the mattress.

"Since last night. They were barely noticeable." Her
smile was forced. "Not what I'm feeling now."

"You might be one of the lucky ones," Hannah said.
"I've heard, for some women, birth is easy."

"This doesn't feel easy," she said.

"But it hasn't been days."

"No, thank God."

Hannah went into the bathing chamber, poured some
water into a bowl and returned, placing it beside the bed.

She folded a bit of toweling and placed it beside the bowl, then put the remaining toweling on top of the blanket.

The eleventh Earl of Barrett was born less than an hour later.

She didn't have time to scream. The urge to push came first, then this amazing sense of pressure building and being released. Hannah held up her son, placing him between her breasts. "He's the most perfectly formed child I've ever seen. I think it's because your labor was so short."

Virginia closed her eyes against the pinch of another pain.

"I can only imagine what it's like when it goes on for days," she said when she could speak again.

Hannah smiled. "I don't think you'll have any difficulty, your ladyship. They say the second child comes in half the time as the first."

"Since I'm a widow," she said, "there won't be a second child."

They met each other's eyes, and Virginia was the first to look away. There, another lie to solidify her child's heritage.

Hannah bathed her son next to the bed, commenting on the baby's attributes.

"Just look how long his fingers are, your ladyship. And his feet. They're perfect. His skin is so soft and his features are beautiful." She glanced at Virginia. "He's a beautiful child."

When he was wrapped in a diaper and blanket, Hannah placed him in her arms.

His hair, black as Macrath's, covered the top of his head in a downy fuzz. His eyes, clenched shut most of the time, were blue. He didn't cry, however, which bothered her at first. But perhaps that was because he was too busy gnawing on his fist.

His name was out of her control. A long and illustrious family history was attached to the name he'd been given before he was born. Elliot. Another name starting with E, pleasing her mother-in-law.

Perhaps now was the time to tell Enid her middle name was Elizabeth. Or ask why Lawrence had somehow escaped the E fixation.

She was remarkably energized. When she asked Hannah if such a thing was normal, the other woman smiled and shook her head.

"Most women are exhausted, your ladyship. But you had a short labor."

She could barely remember the pain as she held Elliot close to her breasts. A knock disturbed the perfect peace of the moment.

She whispered to Hannah, "Tell her anything, but please get rid of her."

Enid was banished by the simple expediency of another lie: Virginia was sleeping.

"A good thing I didn't listen to her, but to my own instinct," Enid said to Hannah at the door, sounding annoyed. "I told the girl it was too soon."

When she had left, Hannah returned to the bed, smiling down at Elliot. He started to fuss, tiny sounds of distress that were somehow, Virginia thought, connected to her heart. He thrust his hands into the air, wrinkled his face and pursed his lips.

"We need to get him to the wet nurse," Hannah said.

Another point of contention, one in which Virginia had remained silent. Enid assumed a wet nurse would be hired. Virginia wanted to tend to her child herself.

"I'm not giving him to a wet nurse," she said now. "I'm feeding him." She opened her nightgown and put her son to her breast.

Hannah didn't say anything, but silence didn't mean acceptance.

"I know it isn't done," she said, meeting the maid's eyes. "But I'm doing it."

Hannah surprised her by smiling. "Then we'd best be about it, shouldn't we?"

Elliot Traylor, eleventh Earl of Barrett made a mewling sound before he started to suckle.

Chapter 17

London
June, 1870

The garden was lovely on this pleasant June afternoon. Eudora had coaxed the most wonderful blossoms from the plants in the corner. They smelled of roses although they didn't look similar. Combined with the scent of the honeysuckle, it was a perfect scented breeze, almost enough to counter the smells of London.

The sun warmed the bench where Virginia sat near a topiary bush. Elliot lay in her arms, asleep, his face twitching from time to time. Did he dream baby dreams? Or was he getting ready to awaken, hungry again?

Carefully, so as not to wake him, she tenderly adjusted the blanket below his chin with her fingers.

When Hannah had gone to fetch tea, she'd escaped to the garden, cherishing the moments alone with her son.

No one could have been as sweet or kind as Eudora and Ellice. Eudora had sewn all the clothes Elliot could possibly need, while Ellice added new lace to Lawrence's christening gown for the ceremony scheduled next month.

Most of the time, one of her sisters-in-law hovered

around her son, commenting on his every movement, his surprising black hair when no one in the family had a similar shade, or how much his nose resembled Lawrence's.

Truly, such slavish adoration could not be good for the child. Look at Lawrence. Everyone in his family had treated him the same way.

Enid remained silent, except for praising the rate at which Elliot was growing. Only she and Enid knew he was a few weeks early. To the rest of the family, he had been born on time.

His lips twitched in sleep.

When she made the comment that she loved his smile, Enid shook her head. "He's much too young to smile. He merely has stomach distress."

Elliot woke and gurgled at her, his deep blue eyes fixed on her face. Suddenly, Macrath was in her thoughts so sharply she could almost see him.

She wasn't going to wonder how long the voyage to Australia was or how dangerous. It would be foolish to worry about him getting sick. He was strong and healthy, not a newborn babe or a sickly mother. He would return. Would he come back with a wife?

If so, it was none of her concern.

She should forget him, but how did she do that, especially with his son looking more like him each day? How did she smile into Elliot's face and pretend his father was dead?

Above all, how did she rid herself of this feeling of guilt? How did she live with herself for the rest of her life?

Should she write him? Should she put pen to paper and somehow find the words?

Dearest Macrath, you are a father of a son, born on a wet and rainy March day in a burst of energy. He's a darling child, handsome and intelligent. I see great things in his future.

Perhaps, rather than writing him, she would keep a journal. She'd record Elliot's accomplishments. She'd tell him what she thought when their child smiled at her, and how her heart ached to think he would never see and never know of Elliot.

When Macrath married, she'd find a way to be glad about his happiness. She wouldn't think of them living at Drumvagen, a jewel of a house mirroring Macrath's hopes for a clan. Soon, he'd have children, Elliot's half sisters and half brothers.

Elliot would never know his father, and the knowledge rested on her soul like a huge black stone.

Macrath married was the same as Macrath in Australia, out of sight and out of her life. Not entirely, however, with his son's face looking back at her every day.

If she did keep a daily journal, what would she write?

Today, our child turned four months old. He is growing faster than I would have thought possible in size and knowledge. He knows my face as I lean over him and reaches for me.

He reminds me of you, dearest Macrath. Not only because of his intent look, but his smile. It seems to have been taken from your face.

Elliot's nose wrinkled and his face started to turn red. His cries were full blown in seconds. She propped him on her shoulder and rubbed his back, hating to hear him whimper.

"I think he's hungry," Ellice said, coming into the garden followed by Eudora. Ellice was carrying a tea tray and Eudora another plant that she placed near the bench were Virginia was sitting.

They each wore summery dresses of black silk with white cuffs and collar. Eudora looked well in black but it washed out Ellice's coloring.

"You're right," she said, standing and cradling Elliot in her arms. "If you'll excuse us, I'll go and feed him."

The girls look startled, just as they did every time she reminded them she was rearing Elliot in a forbidden way. Granted, she'd allowed Enid to hire a nursemaid, a sweet young girl named Mary who cared for Elliot at night. Even so, she still nursed him.

Enid had lectured her almost every day that such behavior was not done in London society. She had stood firm, however, refusing to be swayed. Every day, she simply walked away, taking Elliot to a secluded corner where she could feed him in peace.

As she left the garden, she looked down into his face. "You're going to be such a handsome man, aren't you?"

His mouth twisted.

"Will you break a woman's heart? Just like your father? Please don't do such a thing," she told Elliot, placing him against her shoulder and rubbing his back.

His head bobbed against her cheek, and she placed a kiss on his delicate ear.

"Do not let a woman yearn for you. Find one you can love, and make her yours, even if you have to spirit her away."

What would've happened if she'd stayed in Scotland with Macrath? A selfish act, and one that would have pleased her but put Enid, Eudora, and Ellice in peril.

Now their future was assured. Their present was protected. All she had to worry about was forgetting the past.

Someone should warn Virginia that sitting in the sunlight would cause her skin to darken and look more common.

Paul watched her caring for the child, the spawn of the Scotsman, like he was the eleventh Earl of Barrett in truth.

He admired her for the courage of the ruse, for daring to do something few of her contemporaries would do, even as he loathed her for it.

She could have chosen him. Together, they could have raised their child as the earl. He would even have stayed in the background, allowing her to be portrayed as the earl's widowed countess, content to be her lover by night and her servant by day.

She'd never given him the chance.

He supposed the child was comely. Children had never interested him.

Each of these titled brats boasted a better future than the one he'd been granted. Without doing one thing, they would be feted and applauded, supported and praised. They would, simply by drawing breath, be congratulated.

He didn't hate the rich and the titled. He hated that they never saw anyone beneath their aristocratic noses. They believed they were touched by divine providence and were special. They saw themselves as different people than the masses, graced by privilege and deserving of it.

Virginia was unique, however. First, she wasn't born to the peerage but had come from America. Second, she noticed people around her, often conversed with the maids, thanked Cook for a lovely meal, and never considered anyone beneath her. She'd even been kind to Lawrence, who didn't deserve her consideration.

Did she know what else Lawrence had done besides spending her father's fortune?

He doubted it.

The only person she wasn't considerate of was him, the one individual who deserved her notice and appreciation. He'd protected her. He'd done what he could to ease her life. He'd carried her to her room when she was in labor and she'd not once mentioned it.

He'd never forgotten the feel of her in his arms.

Now, her sisters-in-law joined her, the sound of their laughter carrying across the lawn like crystal chimes.

He was glad she was happy, even if he wasn't the source of it. For now, he was content to watch.

When it was time, he would go to her and tell her everything. She'd welcome him. She'd open her arms to him, seeing him for who he was, a man of great ambition and talent, who would provide for her for the rest of her life.

Perhaps they'd go to America together. He'd leave the spawn of the Scotsman here and take her away. There, they'd be alone, and when she bore another child, it would be his.

He watched as she stood and entered the house, then walked around to the kitchen entrance.

Someone spoke to him, but he ignored the summons, intent on intercepting her. There she was, at the base of the stairs.

"Have you quit the garden, your ladyship?"

She turned her head and regarded him. Did she think he was handsome? The maids did, and Ellice thought so as well. Eudora was curiously indifferent to him.

He placed one hand on the banister, the other on the wall, trapping her.

The scent of roses trailed after her, marking the air as special. Did she wear it for him? He doubted it. She didn't yet notice him.

One day she would look at him differently. One day she'd seek him out wherever he was.

"Yes," she said, starting up the staircase and cooing to the baby in her arms.

He followed her slowly, mounting the steps behind her.

"He's a lovely boy," he said. "All hale and robust. Not at all like his father, is he? He doesn't have Lawrence's heart problems?"

She stopped on the steps but didn't turn. "No. He's very healthy."

"He doesn't look like him, though, does he?"

She kept her gaze on her son's face. "I believe he looks a great deal like my father," she said.

"Pity no one remembers what your father looked like. Were his eyes that shade of blue?"

She gripped the banister tightly with one hand until her knuckles whitened.

No, she didn't like that comment at all, did she?

She half turned, gazed down at him.

"Why do you care, Paul?"

He smiled. "I am but curious, your ladyship."

"Is curiosity a wise emotion in a servant?"

He kept his smile anchored with difficulty.

"You'll never find a man more devoted than I, your ladyship."

He bowed slightly, not above such gestures in her presence. He would have knelt at her feet if it would have done any good. No, time was what he needed, and time was on his side.

Smiling, he descended the steps, patient for the day when she realized who he was.

Virginia watched as Paul descended the stairs, taking the first deep breath since seeing him.

Wasn't there any way to prevent him from approaching her?

If they'd still employed a majordomo, she would have gone to him with her complaints about Paul. But Albert had left their household two weeks ago, citing illness in the family.

Someone needed to take Paul in hand. He laughed

with too much abandon with Ellice. The girl's excuse was
that she was sixteen. He complimented Eudora outland-
ishly and the elder girl smiled, accepting the words as
her due.

How dare he question Elliot's health? Nor did she care
for his examination of her son, almost like he was matching physical features and coloring with his memories of
Lawrence.

What did he know? What he might suspect was an entirely different thing, however.

Perhaps she should think of retiring to one of the other
properties Lawrence had purchased with her father's
money. Surely the girls and Enid would be willing to quit
London for a while.

Lawrence had spent a goodly sum on a house in Cornwall. From what she'd heard of the region, the winds were
fast and chilled. Although too close to the sea, at least they
wouldn't be subjected to the odor of London's sewers.

She would go and try to talk Enid into Cornwall, and
while she was with her mother-in-law, she would bring up
the subject of dismissing Paul Henderson.

A few minutes later she put Elliot in his crib, bid the
nursemaid to watch over him, and went in search of Enid.

She found her in the library.

"I'll come back," she said when she realized Enid was
going over menu plans with Cook.

"Nonsense," Enid said, motioning to the other woman.
"We're done."

Cook stood, bobbed a little curtsy to both of them, and
left the room, shutting the door behind her. Cook always
smelled of bread and the scent was a pleasant one.

"The price of beef is so dear today, we have to conserve
where we can."

Virginia nodded, but her attention was on what she was

about to say or perhaps how to say it. She eased into the chair in front of the desk.

"We need to dismiss Paul Henderson," she said, a little more bluntly than she intended.

Enid settled back, her eyes on the papers in front of her. "Do we?"

"Yes," she said firmly. "We do. He does not act appropriately with either Ellice or Eudora. Nor does he seem to do anything except watch people."

She smoothed her hand over the curved edge of the mahogany desk. How long had it been in the Traylor family? Was it, too, another possession that must pass from heir to heir?

"I know he reminds you of Lawrence," she said.

"Don't be foolish."

Startled, she glanced at Enid. Her mother-in-law stared back at her, eyes steady. Her lips were clamped together, plumping her face in an unattractive way, until she bore a striking resemblance to an angry bulldog.

"He knows about your trip to Scotland," Enid said. "He's intimated Elliot is not Lawrence's child. I've kept him on because if I don't, he'll go to Jeremy."

Virginia clenched her hands together. "Oh."

"Indeed."

Beyond the door were normal sounds. Ellice laughed. Eudora said something to one of the maids, who answered with a lilting voice.

"What are we going to do?" she asked, all thoughts of Cornwall pushed to the back of her mind.

Enid picked up the pen in front of her, studied it, then let it slide from her fingers.

"What can we do?"

When she didn't answer, Enid continued. "Employ him for the rest of his life or ours. Ensure he's happy."

If she told Enid that Paul looked at her oddly, would Enid do anything about the situation?

Her mother-in-law couldn't dismiss him, for all their sakes. The minute she did, Paul would go to Jeremy. This elaborate ruse they'd concocted would come falling down.

As she folded her hands tidily on her lap, a stanza from Sir Walter Scott came to mind:

> *Oh what a tangled web we weave,*
> *When first we practice to deceive!*

She couldn't help but think that Enid and Paul were spiders on either side of an elaborate web, while she was in the middle, trapped like a fly.

Chapter 18

Virginia knew something was wrong because of the silence. Eudora and Ellice were not chattering at each other. Ellice was not picking up her skirts and flying down the hall, violating at least three of her mother's tenets. The maids weren't congregating at the stairwell engaged in gossip.

Even the day was quiet. The garden was perfectly still, without a gentle breeze.

She found Enid in the doorway of her eldest daughter's room. Her mother-in-law was pale, perspiration dotting her upper lip and forehead. Before she could ask what was wrong, Enid shut the bedroom door and leaned back against it.

"Where is Elliot?" Enid asked, her voice quavering.

"In the nursery. I've put him down for a nap. Mary's watching him."

Enid nodded. "Good. Good."

"What is it, Enid?" she asked, taking a few steps back from the doorway.

"You need to keep him on the third floor."

"Why?"

"I've only seen it once before," Enid said, "and I hope my memory is false. If not, my darling Eudora is very ill."

"Enid, what is it?" She pressed her fingers against the brooch at her neck. A gift from Enid, it contained a lock of Lawrence's hair.

"Smallpox." Enid pressed a hand to her chest as if uttering the word had caused her heart to flutter.

"I was never vaccinated," Virginia said. Her hands were cold, panic stiffening her spine.

"We were," Enid said. "But somehow, my darling Eudora is still ill."

Virginia wanted to gather up her child right this moment, leave her belongings behind and simply race away from this house. They'd go to Cornwall, or America, or even Scotland. Somewhere safe, where the hint of disease couldn't touch them.

Was any place safe in the world?

She grabbed her left wrist with her right hand, holding on so she didn't fly to pieces.

"Do not be around Elliot, Virginia," Enid said, leaning her head back against the door. "Keep Mary and only Mary with him. She doesn't mingle with the rest of the staff."

She nodded. "What if he becomes ill?" she asked, giving voice to her worst fear.

"Then we'll have to be as prayerful as we can, Virginia. Starting now, I think. Say a prayer for Eudora."

She turned away from Eudora's bedroom, but not before she heard Enid's softly spoken words. "And a prayer for the rest of us, too."

Virginia took the stairs to the nursery, her heart pounding so rapidly she thought she might faint. Standing at the door, she called out to Mary, but when the girl would have opened the nursery door, Virginia held onto the latch.

"Do not open the door to anyone, Mary," she said. "Not even me."

She was giving the care of her child over to another child, but she had no other choice.

After she explained the situation to the young girl, she said, "Every day, Hannah will come and ask about Elliot." She placed her hand flat against the door. "Tell her if you need anything. I'll arrange for your meals to be placed on a table in the hallway."

They would have to get a wet nurse, a woman from outside the house. Someone safe, who could feed her son.

Pressing her hand against her aching breasts, she gave Mary further instructions, all the while distracted by a growing fear.

Maybe Enid was wrong. Maybe she'd been mistaken. A hope that lasted until the doctor attended Eudora.

A week later he returned to the house to treat Enid, but not for smallpox.

Eudora, lovely and talented Eudora, had died of pneumonia, and Enid was inconsolable. At her shocking and rapid death, Enid had simply collapsed in on herself, retreating to her bedroom much like Lawrence had, leaving instructions she was not to be disturbed.

When a scullery maid died four days after that, her family took possession of the body, the transfer done at midnight at the rear of the town house. She was a sweet girl, with a gap-toothed smile and pleasant disposition.

Virginia had been left the task of conveying their condolences to the parents. A difficult task when she could not seem to keep from crying herself. Grief over Eudora and fear for Elliot made her weep incessantly.

After three more days she thought she might be as exempt from illness as Enid, Ellice, and the rest of the staff seemed to be. When they got word that Albert, too, had died, one mystery was solved: how they had been exposed to the disease in the first place. The majordomo's family had been infected, and he'd unknowingly carried it to the town house.

Every day, Hannah relayed news of Elliot's health. Every day, she sat in her bedroom, afraid to be with the other people for fear she would either catch the disease or pass it on.

One morning she awoke with an ache in her temples and a feeling of growing discomfort, like she was coming down with a cold. The small of her back hurt, reminding her of when she was laboring with Elliot.

When the maid delivered her breakfast tea, she kept her outside.

"Are you ill, your ladyship?" the girl asked, her voice fearful.

Virginia was panicked as she stood on the other side of the door, leaning her forehead against the panel.

"Yes," she said, "I'm ill."

Would the maids refuse to serve her? In all honesty, she couldn't blame them.

She stared down at the palms of her hands. A painful rash had appeared there this morning and on the soles of her feet. Her mouth was sore, her tongue swollen, and the taste at the back of her throat was something she'd never experienced before, almost like she'd eaten something made of metal.

Five minutes later Hannah entered her room.

"You should leave," she told her.

Hannah only shook her head. "I'll stay, your ladyship."

She was so grateful that tears sprang to her eyes. Above all, she didn't want to be alone when she died.

Hannah coaxed her back to bed and closed the draperies. She brought in several brown glass bottles, set them on the chest, and started unrolling long strips of material.

"What are those?" Virginia asked. "They look like bandages."

"You'll have some pustules in the worst of it," Hannah said, matter-of-factly. "You'll want to scratch at them, but if you do, you'll scar."

"I'm not concerned about scarring."

Hannah didn't say anything, merely unstoppered one of the bottles. A pleasant minty odor emerged as she poured the contents onto a bandage then began to wrap it around one of Virginia's hands.

She stared down at her hand, more afraid than she'd ever been. Was this punishment for her actions? She had grievously sinned, but Elliot needed her. She didn't want her son to grow up without his mother, as she had.

Hannah regarded her somberly for a moment, then finally smiled. "You aren't going to die, your ladyship."

"Eudora did," she said, looking at her. She could no longer blink back her tears. Dear God, she was so afraid. "So did the scullery maid."

Hannah nodded. "They didn't have me caring for them, now did they?"

Virginia wiped at her cheeks with the back of her hand, closed her eyes and said her prayers, like a child again in upstate New York, the only child of a rich and powerful man. Except this time the prayer was absurdly simple and didn't mention her father, her governess, or her dog.

Please, God, protect my child. Please don't let me die.

Between Sydney and London
July, 1870

The air was heavy on his skin, pressing in on him. Macrath could do without sea spray in his face, coating his hair and stiffening his clothes. He was tired of the ocean. Tired of the endless noise of his own ice machine. Tired, too, of traveling. He wanted to be home at Drumvagen. Home in Scotland where he didn't have to eternally explain that, no, he wasn't immigrating to Australia like so many Scots he'd met.

He'd met more Scots in Australia than in London.

"Congratulations, Mr. Sinclair," Captain Allen called out, motioning him to his side.

Macrath moved to stand next to the captain on the bridge.

Allen reminded him of a Highland bull, with the mop of his hair falling down on his brow and his wide, blunt nose. Even the captain's beard, trimmed to a point, fit the picture.

"The *Crown* threw their cargo overboard this morning," Allen said with a grin. "Rancid meat, most like." He pointed to a dark horizon. "They may be faster than we are," he said. "But their ice room isn't better than yours."

"They chose insulation and nothing else," Macrath said. "They've no machine on board."

"All is well with yours, I trust?"

The Sinclair Ice Company had provided the machinery for Captain Allen's ship. Macrath's model worked on air compression and expansion. Installing it on the *Fortitude* required it be powered by the main boiler. He and Jack had insulated the refrigeration room with charcoal and wool batting. The frozen beef, mutton, lamb, and butter were wrapped in wool and the surrounding air withdrawn, cooled, and expanded back into the chamber. To spare the machinery, he turned it off for hours at a time, but monitored the temperature in the chamber before and after doing so, to ensure the cargo remained frozen.

"The temperature is well within acceptable ranges," he said now.

"You think, then, that we'll reach London with the cargo safe?"

"Ready to be eaten by the good citizens of England," Macrath said.

"It's about time the world tasted Australian beef," the other man said.

He grinned at the captain, who smiled back. Together, the two of them stood to win not only a large purse for this contest between ships, but bragging rights as well.

"Your achievement is remarkable, Macrath," Allen said. "I didn't think I'd be impressed but damned if I'm not."

Macrath smiled. He liked this Australian. "It's a good design," he said. "The ice room holds in the cold as well."

"I would never have thought of using wool for insulation. Nor did I expect you to have the machine running clear across the ocean."

Two of his three competitors had opted to build a cold room, while the third chose to use ether as a refrigerant. Macrath had built a cold room as well, along with a protective shed for the latest version of his ice machine. He and Jack had spent most of the voyage wiping the machinery down, keeping it clean of salt spray, and praying it lasted the duration of the voyage.

The *Fortitude* was powered by steam and had cut the trip between Sydney and London to about sixty days, a savings of almost half the time of a clipper. He'd sent Sam home aboard the *Princess,* and they might reach Scotland before him.

The *Grafton* had started dumping its cargo two weeks out of Sydney. With the news that the *Crown* was out of the running, too, the *Magellan* was their only competition.

"We've a fortnight till London," the captain said, "but I've a wager you'll win."

"A wager you've made with the other captains?"

"Aye," the man said, grinning at him. "We'll have one of those haunches of beef you're cooling for us."

They spoke of the voyage for a few more minutes before Macrath turned back to his machine. Tending it all these days had been wearing, but not if he won the wager.

In a fortnight he'd be in the city where she lived.

He'd tried not to think of her, the second time he'd attempted to wipe his memory clean. He'd given a valiant effort to eradicate all thoughts of loving her, of that time in the grotto, of her kisses, her whispers, the sound she made when she found pleasure in his arms.

In the process, he'd been willing to admit he was only human and some memories were not easily forgotten.

Even now he could summon her simply by closing his eyes. He could feel her, pliant in his arms, her breasts overflowing his hands, her laughter echoing in his ears. She trembled the first time he'd kissed her. In Scotland she'd done the same, but without the intrusion of prying eyes he was able to hold her close until she was the impatient one. Until she reached up and kissed him back.

How the hell could he forget that memory?

He wasn't a man who confided his feelings to others, but on nights like these, when the stars peered down at him like a million interested eyes, he wished there was someone to whom he could say, "I was a fool not to court Miss McDermott. It wasn't her fault she didn't possess a throaty laugh or eyes reminding me of clouds. Nor was she to blame for my being unable to get Virginia's face from my mind."

If he were honest he might have said, "I should hate her for leaving me. For choosing a title over me."

Despite her protestations, being the Countess of Barrett had meant more to her than anything else. More than staying in Scotland with him. More than his feelings for her. More than his love.

The stars, winking above a black sea, were silent.

London
July, 1870

In her delirium, Virginia was a girl again, racing through
the woods near Cliff House, laughing. In the next instant
she was standing on the bluff overlooking the Hudson
River shining blue-gray and bearded by strips of forest.
Her father owned most of the land she saw, but he rarely
seemed pleased about his possessions. Or her, for that
matter.

Then she was swinging, her skirts in the air, her stomach plummeting as she soared, her nurse fussing at her to
be less of a hoyden and more of a young lady.

Her dog, Patches, was barking beside her as she ran
from the porch of Cliff House across the wide expanse
of lawn to the woods. She loved the woods bordering the
white painted house above the Hudson, loved the smell of
the rich, loamy soil, and the sweet scent of the purplish
white flowers growing in wild abandon.

Suddenly she was in the ballroom, having to walk a
straight line from one side of the room to the other, turn
and walk back over the parquet floor to the other wall while
maintaining a rigid posture, her chin level, an insipid smile
painted on her face. The voices of her governesses, three
in all because they'd each failed in some way to please her
father, rang in her ears. The dancing master despaired of
her, but she was good at balancing a book on her head,
keeping her two feet parallel to each other, and pretending she was walking on a train track. There were so many
rules to learn. More rules than countries and capital cities.

Her skirts must not sway. She must, above all, know the
names of the guests attending her father's annual summer
party. She must be seen but never heard, unless her father

asked her a question, and then she must reply as quickly as possible with the right answer so as not to embarrass him.

Her governess was rarely pleased with her, unless it came to spelling or geography. She was good at both, less competent at mathematics, and not at all interested in French or Italian.

"Why can't I just speak English?" she asked in her fevered dream.

Her governess sharply rapped her knuckles for that question.

"I have a child," she said, pulling the ruler from the governess's grasp. "He's the most wonderful child in the world," she added in perfect Italian. "Have you any children? Has any man loved you?"

The scene shifted yet again and she was standing beside Lawrence's coffin. In the way of delirium and dreams, she knew some of what she was experiencing had been true. She felt the sleek mahogany of the coffin top and remembered touching it and the brass nameplate there.

Then she was standing inside the burial plot, and the caretaker lowered Lawrence's coffin to her. She perched atop it, her hoop billowing around her waist, as they piled dirt on top of her. Her pantaloons were covered in dirt and she was missing one shoe.

Abruptly, it was no longer Lawrence's coffin but Eudora's. Poor Eudora was screaming in disbelief. Ellice was pointing at her and giggling.

None of the mourners seemed to think anything was amiss as both of them were buried alive. Not one person said anything, even Macrath, who stood at the end of the burial plot, looking down at her with a severe expression.

"Will you help me?" she asked, stretching up one hand.

His fingertips touched hers, and just when she thought he would grip her hand, he pulled back.

"Why didn't you tell me you loved Lawrence?"

"I didn't. It was you, Macrath. I always loved you."

She called out for him and only heard Hannah's voice. "Hush, your ladyship. Someone will hear you."

Abruptly, she was a child again, being told to be quieter. "You'll wake the dead with your laughter, Virginia Elizabeth."

Mommy? Where was Mommy?

"Your mother died at your birth, Virginia. It's a hard lesson for a little girl to learn, but learn it you must."

Enid rapped her on the knuckles with a ruler. "You should never have married Lawrence. You can't speak French."

She was running in the rain. She loved the rain, storms, and thunder. Cliff House was always secure and safe, perched as it was above the Hudson, the home of a man who'd become wealthy by being ruthless.

Cliff House magically became Drumvagen. She was happy there. So much delight filled her that she was nearly weak with joy. She wanted to hug everyone she saw, or kiss them on the cheek in gratitude for sharing this day with her. They'd come from so far away to celebrate with her.

She was dressed in white, her long veil trailing behind her. She approached the altar in Drumvagen's chapel. Macrath slowly turned and smiled at her.

In the next instant Macrath changed, becoming Lawrence, but not the sickly husband she'd known. Instead, he was a grinning corpse who held out a skeletal hand. Repulsed, she pulled away, just as he became Paul, leering at her.

She glanced around for Macrath but he was nowhere to be seen. She was no longer at Drumvagen. Instead, she was in London again.

The world faded to gray, then black, as she descended into nothingness with relief.

Chapter 19

London
July, 1870

They'd arrived in London yesterday and were directed to their quay at dawn. Now Macrath could hear conversations and cursing in a dozen different languages. The noise of creaking winches vied with the rumble of wheels against the cobbles as a procession of empty wagons appeared on the pier.

Masts of sleek clippers stood next to iron hulled steamers, each one at the end of a voyage starting a world away, bringing spices, cloth, china, and mail from such places as Shanghai, Foochow, Zebu, and Yokohama.

Granaries and warehouses edged nose to tail on the quay alongside the offices set aside for business. Captains would meet with shipowners or their factors, produce their logbooks, and give an accounting before signing over their cargo.

"It's a fair day, Mr. Sinclair," Captain Allen said from behind him. "A good day to win, I'm thinking."

Macrath turned and greeted the man. The tip of Captain Allen's beard was being blown upward by the breeze, calling attention to the man's grin.

"It's a good day, Captain Allen."

They were the last of the four ships to reach the East India Dock, but the only one with a frozen cargo. Forty tons of it, which meant the *Fortitude*—and the Sinclair Ice Company—had won the race from Australia to England.

He wasn't celebrating just yet. Politics could come into play. Two of his rivals were Australian, and their nationality might factor into the awarding of the contract. Or it might not, since his competitors had to jettison their cargo.

Regardless of the ultimate outcome, he still had bragging rights, and he would ensure that men who'd been tentative about purchasing one of his machines knew who had won this race.

He liked being able to plan something on paper, develop it, build it, and have it work the way he'd seen it in his mind. If he built a flywheel to turn clockwise, it didn't suddenly decide to rotate counterclockwise.

Maybe he should only deal with machines and leave humans alone.

"Will you be going home to Scotland now, Mr. Sinclair? Or is it back to Australia for you?"

"I think it's home, Captain," he said.

Drumvagen called to him. So did being able to work on a new version of his ice machine, a new design that had come to him on the voyage.

Jack, too, was anxious to return to Scotland. The other man was visiting Edinburgh first before returning to Drumvagen.

"While you're here, you should see something of our city. London is like no other place on earth."

"I know London well," he said, telling him of Ceana's season.

"Then you'll be off reacquainting yourself with old

friends." Allen lifted a hand in a signal to his first mate. "Let me know where you're staying," he said as he walked away, "and I'll buy you a tankard or two in the way of thanks."

Macrath turned back to his place along the rail, watching as the *Fortitude*'s frozen cargo was wheeled out of his ice room with Jack directing the activity.

Nearby, pepper was being offloaded. He could taste it in the back of his throat. Crates of tea were being stacked at the end of the pier. As he stood there, a factor approached, met with two other men and started counting.

What friends did he have in London? A few businessmen with whom he had a nodding relationship. A solicitor he'd employed to look over some of his English contracts.

Virginia.

If he sought Virginia out, it would be tantamount to admitting to her and the world how much he'd missed her, how much she was in his thoughts.

She'd turned her back on him. She walked away when he asked her to stay. All he'd gotten in return was the scent of roses and memories relentlessly haunting him.

Where was his pride? Caught and captured by an American lass with a lilting laugh.

For someone who called herself fearful, she was remarkably courageous. Why else would she come to Scotland only days after being widowed? To test him? Had she come to him to see if he felt the same about her as she did about him?

Had he failed her test somehow?

What had he done wrong? For that matter, what could he have done to keep her in Scotland?

Whenever he worked on a machine, the ultimate design began as a plan, but evolved as a prototype. What might have looked functional when he started might be tossed in the manufacturing process. Give and take, trial and error, they were all vital to a successful finished product.

He had the inkling that the same process would work in relationships, especially this relationship. They were drawn to each other by strong emotions and pulled apart by circumstances, first of her father's making, and then because she was the Countess of Barrett, newly widowed.

Enough time had passed that she wouldn't shock the world by marrying now.

Nor would he be guided by his pride when he might find happiness.

"**I** can't work like this, Mr. Paul," the maid said, sniffing into the corner of her apron.

If it hadn't already been stained with the polish she'd spilled earlier, he would have demanded she find a handkerchief instead.

"With her looking out of the corner of her eye at me like she's waiting for me to make a mistake."

"Cook is overworked like the rest of us," he said, hoping to calm the girl. "I doubt she cares as much about what you're doing as long as it doesn't affect her workload."

"She wants me to clean the pots. I'm no scullery maid," she said.

Did she know she stunk of onions, so strongly that the library reeked?

He smiled, an expression that had always caused the maids to flutter their eyelashes and giggle. In the last month, however, his smile had no effect on the female staff at all.

The household was in shambles, but he was trying to muster everyone together. He was the de facto majordomo since Albert had left and the position was vacant. Eudora had died, the dowager countess had taken to her rooms, Virginia was ill, and Ellice was too young to assume any command. He alone was there to mitigate the disagreements and hear the whines and complaints from the ten staff members.

The maids listened better than the men. He had fired the stable master for insubordination, but the man was refusing to leave.

"I don't take my orders from you," he said. "When the dowager countess fires me, I'll consider myself gone. But not by you."

The stable master's mutiny had been joined by the coachman. Hosking was another one he'd fire when he got the power.

"All the downstairs maids are taking turns," he said to the girl now. "You can't expect Cook to fix all the meals and scrub all the dishes."

She sniffled again. He took a deep breath, trying to keep his temper in check.

"Do it today," he said, smiling at the maid. "Just today, and I'll find a schedule to accommodate everyone."

She wiped the corner of one eye, sighed dejectedly, and took herself off to the kitchen. No doubt she would whine about her new chore for as long as she had to do it.

What did she expect him to do? Lavina hadn't died solely to upset her schedule. Trying to find a replacement for the scullery maid had been difficult. Once likely candidates learned Lavina had died of smallpox and the household was still battling the disease, they weren't in any hurry to work at the Countess of Barrett's home.

Virginia would survive. He'd been at her door many times over the past week, engaged in a battle with her maid.

Hannah wouldn't allow him to see her. No matter what

he promised or threatened, she refused to let him inside the room.

All he had was Hannah's word that Virginia hadn't been damaged by the disease.

"She only has one or two scars on her face, Paul."

"You're sure?"

Perhaps he should dismiss Hannah as well. The girl didn't know her place, witness her frown just before she'd closed the door in his face.

He settled back, surveying the library, his palms smoothing over the polished arms of the chair. The desk was an attractive piece of furniture, conveying substance and power. He liked being in charge, liked the control. He'd been the force behind Lawrence, but most people hadn't realized it.

Had he erred in suggesting Lawrence spend as much of Virginia's fortune as possible? He'd let loose a streak of anger in Lawrence, one that had manifested in odd and disturbing ways. Even he hadn't realized the degree of Lawrence's retaliation until the solicitor visited the dowager countess.

Lawrence hadn't been the agreeable invalid everyone thought. Virginia wasn't the downcast and malleable woman people expected.

Nor was he the loyal servant.

"**H**ow is she, Hannah?" Ellice asked.

The young girl stood outside the door of Virginia's bedroom, just as Hannah had instructed. No one was to enter the countess's chamber for fear of being infected. Ellice, however, came every morning to ask about her sister-in-law, standing just as she was now, draped in black, her hands twisted in front of her, her face white with worry.

"She's the same," Hannah said.

When Ellice seemed to pale even further, Hannah reached out and patted her arm in a violation of all she'd been taught. If one was in service, one did not touch an employer.

"That's not a bad thing," Hannah said. "You mustn't think it such. She's not worsened. She's no fever, and she's been able to take some broth."

Ellice nodded, seeming to take some comfort from Hannah's words. "Mary says Elliot seems fine," she said. "He shows no sign of the disease."

"I've heard the same," Hannah said.

Ellice had aged substantially in the last two weeks. Perhaps it was the strain of being the head of the household while her mother was incapacitated, or grief for Eudora. Regardless of the reason, she had taken on a maturity greater than her sixteen years.

"Is she truly getting better?" Ellice asked. "You're not just saying it to keep me calm, Hannah?"

"No, I'm not," she said. "The countess hasn't had any new pustules for four days now."

"You haven't been away from her side since she became ill. I know my mother would join me in thanking you for your diligence."

"There's no need," Hannah said, feeling her face warm. She didn't like caring for the ill, but the Countess of Barrett was a different story. Not because she was any less ill, or more delicate in her sickness. But simply because she seemed so alone and friendless that Hannah could not turn her back on the woman.

How on earth did she tell Ellice the truth?

Besides, in her delirium, the countess had said too many things that would've caused the servants to gossip. Better she had been there, than one of the other silly girls who would've repeated her ramblings to anyone with ears.

"Regardless," Ellice said, "thank you. I can only hope I inspire as much devotion as Virginia does, or someone in my service is as kind as you."

Hannah was tired of this room, of sickness, and worrying about Virginia, the only reason why tears spiked her eyes.

Looking down at the floor, she said, "Thank you."

"I'll come every day, then, and let you know about Elliot," Ellice said. "Would it be all right?"

As she studied the other girl, Hannah realized Ellice was feeling as lonely and as afraid as the rest of them. She at least had some reassurance, having had the disease a dozen years earlier and survived. The chances of her contracting smallpox again was low, if not impossible.

Ellice must be worrying about her own health as well as her mother's. Also, she was grieving for her sister. Eudora had been the stronger personality in this house.

The girl needed something to do, some way to feel valuable.

"I'd appreciate knowing about Elliot," Hannah said. "It would save me the trip to the nursery."

Slowly, she closed the door, leaned back against it and studied the bedroom. When the earl died, his mother had taken his suite of rooms, leaving the countess only this small chamber. Hannah was heartily sick of the place.

Thanks to the countess's potpourri, all she could smell was the scent of roses. She'd opened the windows, but there wasn't a breeze, only hot air. The room felt even more closed-in and suffocating. Hay had been put down on the street to muffle the sound of carriage wheels. But with so many black wreaths in this part of the city, there weren't many visitors. Those who didn't have to come to this affluent area stayed away. Even the residents remained inside their houses.

Still, she was better off than a great many people, even her own family. She wasn't sick, she had a roof over her head, and a living.

For now, she was a nurse. Virginia was weak, so she had become her guardian against the staff, all of whom were acting like children crying for their mother. She'd also stood between Virginia and Paul Henderson, whose eyes lit in a strange way when he talked of the countess. Her skin crawled in the man's presence.

Virginia would have to get well. The countess was going to have to protect herself, not only against enemies inside this house, but those outside as well.

Or did she think to escape the consequences of her actions?

Life had never been that simple.

Chapter 20

The hired carriage had seen rough use. The sagging leather seats needed to be reupholstered. Two of the window shades were missing, and the floor bore some stains he didn't want to contemplate. But the driver had been available, and for a sum probably twice the amount he should have paid, was willing to cross London.

Half the country had moved to the city it seemed, and the result was a congestion of people, carriages, and horses.

When the vehicle abruptly stopped in the middle of the street, Macrath waited, thinking traffic delayed them. When they didn't move, he opened the door and descended the steps.

"What's wrong?" he asked the driver.

"There's hay in the street," the man said. "Someone be sick there. And there's a black wreath." With the handle of his whip, he pointed to a door across the street.

"People get ill all the time," he said.

"Not like this. I'll not get smallpox no matter how high the fare."

"Smallpox?"

The man gazed at him with narrowed eyes. "You're new to London, then? You've not heard of the sickness?"

He shook his head.

"Aye, rich and poor alike this year. It looks like one of the rich ones got it this time."

He paid the man the remainder of the fare. "I'll walk the rest of the way," he said.

"Then God go with you, and I hope the errand isn't worth the death of you."

He didn't bother telling the man he'd had cowpox as a boy, and such a thing seemed to carry with it some sort of immunity.

The next block was even more worrisome, if he judged his surroundings by the driver's fear. Three of the town houses were decorated with black wreaths.

He stood at the base of the steps leading up to the address his solicitor had given him. This door, too, held a wreath. Dread was the father of the fear traveling from his feet to lodge in his throat. Someone had died in this house.

It couldn't be Virginia. He refused to believe it.

He removed his hat, scraped a hand through his hair and replaced it. With the fingers of one hand, he tested the folds of his cravat, while the other smoothed down the front of his coat.

Glancing down, he inspected the toes of his shoes. They were still shiny despite the dust from the hay.

His knock was answered by a man in his shirtsleeves. "What do you want?"

"Is this the home of the Countess of Barrett?" he asked, wondering if his solicitor had gotten the information wrong.

"Why would you be wanting to know?"

Macrath didn't like making instant judgments about people, but he took an immediate dislike to the man who stood in the doorway, blocking his entrance.

"I'd like to see her," he said, withdrawing his card.

The other man read the card, frowning. "A Scot," he said, his tone leaving no doubt of his contempt.

Macrath bit back his annoyance. He didn't care what the idiot thought of him. He needed to see Virginia.

"Tell her Macrath Sinclair is here to see her."

"She's ill."

Time slowed, each minute freezing in slow motion.

"She's ill?" He glanced at the wreath on the door. "Is it smallpox?"

"It's none of your concern," the man said, and tried to close the door in his face. Macrath slapped his hand on the door, pushed it open and entered. He was half a foot taller than the other man and angrier.

"I want to see her. Now."

"She'll not see you. She's not seeing anyone."

"I'm not leaving until I make sure of that myself," he said. He was going to find her if he had to knock on every door in this house.

If she was sick, she'd be in her room. He strode toward the staircase, but before he could reach it, the other man grabbed his arm. He shook it off and took the steps two at a time.

"Virginia!"

On the second floor, a maid at the far end of the corridor door turned and stared at him, clutching toweling to her chest.

Before he could reach her, the idiot attacked him.

Hannah heard the shouts, and her first thought was someone else had died. Her second was that Paul had lost his mind, shouting the way he was. The third, immediately on its heels, was that retribution had come, today of all days.

She glanced at her patient. Virginia was asleep, but this morning she'd eaten her first solid food in two weeks and perched on the edge of the bed, dangling her feet. Tomorrow, she would get her up and let her sit in the chair by the window, for a change of scenery if nothing else.

Now, however, the wrath of Scotland was upon them.

She hurried to the door, pressing her ear against the wood.

Macrath turned and struck out, hearing a satisfying crack as his fist slammed into the man's chin.

The bastard fell, and he went after him, straddling the man's chest, pulling him up by his collarless shirt and shaking the man until his eyes opened.

"Where is she?" he asked, enunciating each word.

The man rebounded like a cat, striking out with his feet and connecting behind Macrath's knee. He stumbled, catching himself at the last moment. Enough time for the man to get to his feet, come after him like a bull and butt him in the stomach.

The air left him in a whoosh, but he wasn't done yet.

He hadn't learned how to fight by the Marquess of Queensberry rules. Instead, he'd learned from the boys in Edinburgh who'd shown him a few dirty tricks. What they hadn't known about fighting was a waste of time anyway.

He turned his back, and when the bastard rushed him, used leverage to force him off his feet and over his shoulder. As he flew past, Macrath dug his elbow into the man's midsection. This time when he landed, he didn't get up fast. Instead, he slowly shook like a wet dog, rising to his hands and knees.

Macrath planted his boot in the middle of his arse and shoved.

"Where is she?" he repeated.

The maid, who hadn't moved, dropped her toweling and pointed to a door.

He stepped over the man's body. Feeling his ankle

gripped, Macrath kicked out and freed his foot, going to the door.

Two knocks later Virginia's maid opened it, and upon seeing him, immediately closed it again. He heard the lock engage and shook his head.

Nothing could be easy today, could it?

What was her name? Sally. Sarah. Hannah.

He knocked on the door again. "If you don't open it, Hannah," he said, his voice deliberately mild, "I'll just have to break it down."

Seeing movement from the corner of his eye, he turned just in time to get punched in the head. A bright red flash filled his vision just before the pain hit, traveling across his forehead and down the back of his neck.

He was getting tired of this.

He balled up his fist, connecting with the other man's nose, lifting him in an almost graceful arc before he crashed to the floor.

Macrath stood there a moment, shaking his hand, wondering if the idiot was going to get up again.

Satisfied, he stumbled back to the door.

"Hannah, open the door."

A second later he heard the key turn in the lock, but she only cracked open the door a bit.

"It's not safe for you, sir. My mistress is ill."

"Is it smallpox?" he asked, hoping the answer was negative.

"Yes, sir," Hannah said. "She's had a hard time of it, but she'll live."

Bracing his hands on either side of the door, he wondered what would convince her to allow him to see Virginia.

Before he could speak, she said, "You needn't worry about the child, sir. We've all been very careful. He isn't sick, and there's no sign of illness."

"The child?" he asked slowly.

He'd evidently been hit too hard. The words made no sense.

Hannah nodded. "We check on him every day, sir. He's a sturdy little mite."

He placed his hand flat against the panel of the door. "Where is he?"

"He's in his nursery, sir. Upstairs, on the third floor."

He looked back the way he came. The stairs ended at the second floor. He turned to the young maid who was still standing frozen at the end of the corridor.

"Take me to the nursery," he said. She only nodded repeatedly. Was he that alarming?

A moan from the man on the floor answered that question.

He wasn't going to think. He wasn't going to say anything. He wasn't going to feel anything. He refused to render judgment until he had additional information.

He felt encased in stone as he climbed the stairs behind the silent, trembling girl.

On the third floor she stopped in the middle of the hall and pointed to a white painted door. She didn't look at him, merely clutched her apron with both hands, staring at the floor.

"Thank you," he said.

She nodded, stepping away. He didn't try to stop her as he opened the door.

He saw the girl first. A young thing, merely a child, with dark brown hair caught up in a bun, she was dressed in a blue uniform with a white apron. The other woman was taller, older, and had the largest bosom he'd ever seen. She sat in a large chair and in her arms was an infant.

"Are you the doctor?" the young girl asked.

"No."

"Then you shouldn't be here," the older woman said.

He entered the nursery, closing the door behind him,

taking time with each task. A curious odor of vinegar and spices scented the air, coming from squat white pots placed throughout the room, one of which was close to the door.

Was this their way of keeping smallpox away?

With measured footsteps, he advanced closer, his attention not on the woman but the infant she held. Her eyes never moved from his face, almost like she thought she would stop him by a look alone.

God Himself couldn't stop him at this moment.

"He's asleep, sir."

The sound of her voice woke the child. His hands were abruptly raised in protest. A second later he gnawed on one fist, his eyes opening as he stared balefully at Macrath.

In that instant he knew. This child was his. A son, a little boy who scowled at him with a face so like his own.

Could you hate a woman you loved? Could the two emotions live side by side?

"How old is he?" he asked softly.

"Five months and a few days," the nursemaid said.

He reached out one bloodied finger and touched the infant's cheek. How could skin be that soft?

The baby turned his head, blue eyes fixed on Macrath.

His next question was to the older woman. "What's your position here?"

She looked like she didn't want to answer him, but after a quick glance at his bloody hands, evidently changed her mind.

"I'm the wet nurse. Mary's the nursemaid."

He nodded, turning to the girl. "How old are you?" he asked.

"Twelve, sir."

"I can offer you each a salary double what you earn here. But you need to choose now."

Each female looked at him wide-eyed.

"I'm leaving for Scotland with the child. Come with me."

"Are you stealing him?" Mary asked in a tiny voice.

"I'm a friend of the countess," he said. "I'm taking him somewhere safe, where there's no disease. If you want to come with me, tell me now."

"Well," the wet nurse said, "I'd be a fool to say no, wouldn't I? What with the countess still sick."

"Elliot will need us," Mary said. "I'll go as well. We'll come back when everyone is healthy, won't we?"

He smiled, willing to lie if necessary. Once they were in Scotland, he'd decide whether to send them back to England and hire his own staff or keep them on. For now, he needed them.

How could Virginia do such a thing? How could she hide their child from him?

Macrath looked down at his son and found another dimension, another part of him he'd never known existed. This is why his sisters wanted him to marry. Why they fussed at him to find someone to love. Not for the companionship. Not solely for the joy of being in love.

But for bringing a child into the world, for carrying on his lineage, for starting his clan.

He was no longer angry. Instead, wonder mushroomed inside him, burning away every other emotion.

He would protect this child with his life. He would do everything in his power to ensure his son was happy and the world bowed down before him.

Even if it meant taking him from his mother.

Was she crying in her dream?

Virginia raised her hand and touched her face. She wasn't crying and she couldn't remember the dream. If she wept, she didn't know why.

A sound came from just beyond the bed. She wasn't crying but someone else was.

Blinking her eyes open, she concentrated on the tester above her head, gradually focusing on the pattern embroidered there before looking around the room.

Hannah huddled in the chair beside her bed, her hands covering her face, her shoulders hunched. No doubt the girl was trying to weep soundlessly, but she was doing a poor job of it.

She stretched out a hand to her maid, patting her on the arm.

"Hannah?"

Was it Elliot? Please let him be all right. Please don't let them have lost another member of the family. Please don't let the doctor have given her bad news.

Would the epidemic never stop?

"Is it Elliot?" she asked. "Is he sick?"

Hannah dropped her hands, but rather than meeting Virginia's eyes, she turned her head.

"Hannah," she said again, using her elbows to raise herself on the bed. "Is he sick?"

"Oh, no, your ladyship. it's so much worse than that."

What could possibly be worse than smallpox?

Hannah's mouth turned down, her face slack, her eyes dull and red-rimmed. Slowly, she shook her head from side to side.

Virginia's heart thundered in desperation.

"He's gone and it's all my fault."

She didn't understand. All she could do was watch Hannah, who stared down at her clenched hands.

"Elliot's gone?" The words didn't even make sense. "Is he dead?"

"No, your ladyship. He isn't ill. He doesn't have smallpox."

"Thank God," she said, settling back against the pillow. Hannah shocked her by bursting into tears.

"It's my fault, your ladyship. It's all my fault. Oh, your ladyship, I'm so sorry. I didn't know he didn't know."

"I don't understand," she said, wanting to scream at the girl to explain. "What has happened?"

"Mr. Sinclair, your ladyship. He took Elliot."

Chapter 21

On the way to Drumvagen, Scotland
July, 1870

On the journey back to Drumvagen, Macrath was grateful he'd amassed a fortune. He hired a private train car so his son wouldn't be exposed to strangers, and arranged for meals and beverages to be stocked.

He estimated Elliot weighed less than one of the handles on his ice machine, which made the situation all the more amazing. Besides costing his father a fortune, he had three adults at his beck and call.

By the time they got to the border between Scotland and England, Macrath had gained a hearty respect for the young girl who tended to his son. She didn't get flustered when the baby started to scream. She merely placed Elliot on her shoulder, patted his well-diapered bottom, and commanded him to "Hush, right now, just hush."

She rocked back and forth on the seat so much, Macrath was almost seasick, but it was a movement evidently pleasing his son because every time she did it, Elliot fell asleep.

The wet nurse, not to be outdone in her care of his son, appeared triumphant when she unbuttoned her dress and put Elliot—what kind of name was that?—to her breast. His son immediately stopped fussing and started to gurgle appreciatively.

Wise beyond his months.

The eleventh Earl of Barrett, my ass.

He was not going to surrender his son to anyone, not even to the nobility of England. If Virginia thought the world would be fooled, all they had to do was look at the two of them together.

She had lied to him. Or, if she were only guilty of the sin of omission, it was a pretty damn big omission.

How could she not have told him about their child?

He settled back against the seat, surveying his companions.

Agatha, the wet nurse, had a round face with cheeks as red as her rosebud mouth. She smelled of warmth and his son, a fact that might be linked to her plenteous bosom, about which she seemed unduly proud. Her breasts preceded her out of a room and into one, a fact for which he was grateful, since Agatha was the source of his son's nourishment.

If Agatha had any worries, they didn't appear to concern her. She thought everything was amusing, her smile showing several missing teeth.

"Is he all right?" he asked a few hours later. Elliot had spent half the night in sleep, only to awaken with a cry that clawed its way up Macrath's spine to settle at the base of his neck.

"Oh, yes sir," the wet nurse had said, hauling out her breasts again. "He's just a growing boy and he's hungry."

"Is it normal for him to cry like that?" Whenever Elliot screwed up his face, it was a warning. In a moment the ungodly, bansheelike shriek would fill the car.

"Oh, yes sir," the wet nurse said again, this time giving

him a pitying look. Did she save the look for all males, or just him?

Even Mary, a serious little birdlike child, smiled, the same expression she'd no doubt give a half-wit.

The private car allowed him to be intimate with his son's needs. The first time Mary changed his diaper, he stared out the window and focused on the passing scenery, the shape of the clouds, the gorse blowing stiff-necked in the breeze, anything but the odor now filling the space.

How could anything as small produce something that foul?

The next time Mary changed his diaper, he'd only been wet, and Macrath had taken the opportunity to inspect his son surreptitiously. Yes, Elliot was definitely his offspring.

Once back at Drumvagen, Brianag confounded him. She took one look at his son and said, "Ach, he's an ugly one, he is."

When he instantly disagreed, she frowned at him. "Hauld yir tung, or ye'll forespyke the bairn."

As he was to learn, his child had to be guarded by a series of rituals he found not only odd but superstitious to the extreme. To keep Brianag calm, however, he agreed to as many as he could.

He was never to say anything complimentary about Elliot, for fear he would be cursed, or forespoken.

A brooch in the shape of a heart was pinned to the back of Elliot's petticoat. No one could place him back in his cradle—an old one borrowed from Brianag's sister-in-law—without speaking the words, "God be with you."

After she instructed Mary that every time Elliot was dressed he was to be turned over, heels over head, then shaken with his head downward, Macrath reached his limit. He waited until Brianag left the room before turning to Mary.

"I'll dismiss you on the spot if you treat my son that way."

The nursemaid only nodded, and he caught a glint of humor in her eyes. Maybe she thought him being cautious around his housekeeper was amusing. What wasn't funny was feeling like he had to protect Elliot constantly. When he said as much to little Mary, she shook her head at him, a gesture mirrored by Agatha.

"It's what a mother does, sir," she said, her soft little bird voice flailing him with the truth. "If you've taken him from his mother, you'll have to be both now, won't you?"

He could only stare at her in silence, wondering how a girl of twelve had more sense than he possessed.

London
July, 1870

Virginia perched on the edge of the bed, feeling the room spin around her.

She focused on the far window, willing the dizziness to pass. When the world was finally stable again, she stood, gained her balance, and made her way to the door of her bedroom.

"Please, your ladyship," Hannah said. "You can't do this. Please, don't hurt yourself. You're not strong enough."

She didn't answer, concentrating on reaching the staircase to the nursery.

Hannah sighed but thankfully put an arm around her waist. If she hadn't supported her, Virginia wasn't at all sure she could make it up the stairs.

The last few steps, she nearly had to pull herself up the stairs with both hands. At the top, drenched in sweat, she was so weak she wanted to collapse.

"You need to rest, your ladyship."

Virginia only nodded.

At the doorway, she stopped, staring into the nursery.

The room was empty, the silence stark.

Elliot was truly gone.

Mary wasn't there. Nor was the wet nurse she'd never met. Nothing was in any of the bureau drawers or the armoire. Elliot's empty cradle rested in the corner of the room. She went to stand over it, stroking her fingers over the carving at the top, feeling every indentation and curve.

His pillow was still here, the lavender inside it perfuming the air. Why hadn't they taken his pillow?

"How long?" she asked. "How long have they been gone?"

"This afternoon, your ladyship."

Why hadn't Hannah alerted her earlier?

"Tell Hosking to ready the carriage," she said, sinking into the chair by the door. Somehow, she would have to get to Scotland.

"I don't think this is wise, your ladyship," Hannah said. "You haven't yet healed."

Virginia took a deep breath. "I can't simply remain here."

"Then rest a day, or two at the most, your ladyship."

She shook her head, got dizzy, and waited a moment. When she stood, Hannah held her arm, and she smiled in thanks, closed her eyes and prayed for the strength to do what she had to do. Leaving the nursery, she steadied herself at the top of the steps. Had the staircase always been this steep?

"He has Elliot, and I can't remain in England while my son's in Scotland."

"You know where he's gone," Hannah said. "Two days, that's all I ask. You look like you could collapse if someone looked cross at you."

For the first time in days, Virginia felt a tinge of amusement. "I'll have to ensure someone doesn't look cross at me."

She would also have to prepare to face Macrath.

"The worst of the scabs have not yet fallen off."

"You mean people will be frightened of me?" Virginia asked.

"They'll think you're still contagious."

She glanced at the maid. "The doctor says I'm not. I wouldn't put Elliot in jeopardy." She held up a trembling hand. "I won't be swayed, Hannah. I must go after him, don't you see? He's my son."

"We can't leave at night, your ladyship. We can leave at first light."

Glancing at the window, she realized Hannah was right. Darkness had fallen. Ever since she'd become ill, time passed so quickly. Whole days were gone before she realized.

"Tomorrow, then," she said. "First thing in the morning."

How could Macrath have taken Elliot? How could he have done something so unconscionable and cruel? She could almost hear his voice now. *How could you have hidden my own son from me?*

How was she to answer that question? If she were wise, she'd start marshaling her arguments now for the confrontation with Macrath.

Even if she'd been wrong, she was not going to remain meekly here and let Macrath steal her child.

"I'm coming with you," Hannah said.

She hesitated, looking at her maid, a woman who'd become so much more than a servant over the past months.

"I should tell you no," Virginia said. "Enid could use your help here."

According to what Hannah had told her, the whole of the household was in shambles. Meals were late, the bells never rang, two footmen had quit. Several of the maids were still recovering from smallpox. Paul was acting as the head of the house, and that, more than anything else, was symptomatic of how disruptive their lives had become.

Hannah shook her head. "I'm not staying here while you travel to Scotland alone."

Slowly, Virginia started to descend the steps. She managed a smile for Hannah's benefit. "And I don't think I could make it to Scotland without you."

The next morning Virginia still felt weak but was determined to make the journey to Scotland. Because she was still in the process of healing, she decided it would be safer not to travel by train. Even heavily veiled, someone might see her scabs and wrongly deduce she was still contagious. She didn't want to cause panic. They would travel by carriage, the same way they had before, in the same manner. She would be as surreptitious as she'd been as a new widow.

After drinking her morning tea, she went through the laborious process of dressing. Twice, she almost collapsed, and twice waved away Hannah's concern.

"I'll be in a carriage," she said. "I won't be doing anything but sitting."

After descending the stairs, she leaned against the wall, willing her stomach to calm and her heartbeat to slow.

Before she left, she was going to visit with Ellice, an encounter she didn't anticipate. Hannah left her at the door with another concerned glance. She pasted a determined smile on her face and entered the parlor.

Ellice sat in her favorite chair, staring down into a cup of tea like the answers to all the problems of the world were to be found there.

Every time Virginia came into the room, she remembered the dawn when she'd kept vigil with Lawrence's casket and arranged a deceit.

The room still smelled of death. Flower arrangements placed there for Eudora hadn't been removed and sat on the mantel and side tables, dropping their petals over the floor.

Dearest Eudora. How empty the house was without her presence.

The sun heated the room, showing the streaks left on the windows by careless maids. Enid wouldn't have tolerated such slovenliness in normal times.

Virginia eased into the chair beside Ellice in a spot usually occupied by her mother-in-law. For a moment they sat in silence, the ticking of the mantel clock the only sound.

"You're really leaving?" Ellice asked.

"I wouldn't go, but it's Elliot," she said, reaching out and placing her hand atop her sister-in-law's.

Ellice nodded. "I understand."

She met Ellice's eyes. So much was left unsaid, most of it centering around Enid. She'd yet to come out of her room.

"I'm sure it will be fine," Ellice said. "I'll see to Mother. And everyone is recuperating. We've no other cases."

She put her cup on the table in front of her and studied Virginia.

"Why did Mr. Sinclair take Elliot? I don't understand."

She almost told Ellice the truth, then decided she'd already burdened the girl enough.

"I don't know, but I'm going to bring him home."

Ellice didn't respond, but her lips were pursed and a frown marred her lovely features.

"I don't anticipate the journey to be a long one," Virginia said. She handed Ellice a sheet of correspondence on which she'd written Macrath's address. In case anything else happened, Ellice needed to know where she'd gone.

Please God, don't let anything else happen.

She was going to leave him. She was going back to the bastard who'd impregnated her, the Scot who'd taken her child.

Her pallor worried him. So, too, her slow steps to the stable door. A journey to Scotland would tax her strength.

He couldn't allow it. He had to keep her here.

Paul followed her, waiting until her maid went around to the other side of the carriage. Virginia placed a hand against the vehicle to steady herself.

That's when he knew he had to do anything to stop her, even to telling her the truth if needed.

"I don't want you to leave," he said.

She glanced at him, her eyes widening.

His nose was broken; both eyes blackened and a purple and greenish bruise covering the right side of his face. His bottom lip was cut, his jawline swollen, and he held one hand against his side. He'd suspected a few ribs were cracked when a footman bandaged him.

Let her look her fill. This is what her lover had done, the same man who stole her child.

"I'll be fine," she said. "There's no need to worry about me. I would care for yourself."

When she opened the carriage door, he reached out and slammed it shut.

"You're not going to Scotland."

She stepped away. "Who are you to dictate my movements?"

If she knew the truth, it would change everything. She'd realize, finally, how he felt about her.

"I was the first man to have you," he said. "You were a virgin, your ladyship, when I bedded you."

"What are you talking about?" she asked softly. But he saw the dawning awareness in her eyes. "You were Lawrence's attendant in all ways, is that it, Paul? When he didn't wish to perform his marital duties, you took up the task?"

He smiled at her, and she recoiled, moving closer to the carriage.

"Hannah!"

"You don't have to call your maid," he said. "I'll take your things back to the house."

"Hannah!"

"Yes, your ladyship?"

Hannah came around the back of the carriage.

"Summon Hosking, please," Virginia said, never moving her gaze from his face.

"You're making a mistake," he said when the maid disappeared to do her bidding.

She didn't say a word.

Didn't she realize? She was his.

Hosking was a tall man with burly arms, and a grin that reminded her of Macrath's charm. He wore a cap and always forgot about it. Most of the maids were fond of him and always had to remind him to remove it. His face was round and pleasant, and no doubt one day would become a mass of fleshy wrinkles.

He seemed a happy sort of person, one who loved his horses and cared for the carriages like they belonged to him. Except he wasn't looking happy now.

"Are you all right, your ladyship?" he asked, scowling down at Paul.

"No, Hosking. Mr. Henderson is in my way. Perhaps you can convince him to step aside."

The coachman approached Paul until they were standing nearly nose-to-nose.

"I'm sure Mr. Henderson will be leaving," he said. "And let you be about your business, your ladyship."

Paul looked at the three of them, adopted a cool smile and shrugged.

"At least you know now. You also know what a fool you were not to have chosen me. I would have given you a child. I would have even let you keep it."

After climbing into the carriage, Virginia lay her head back against the seat, fighting a wave of dizziness.

"I have never liked him," Hannah said, sitting opposite her. "There is something not right about Paul."

Surprised, she opened her eyes to face the maid. "I've felt the same," she said, a confession she wouldn't have made a few weeks ago.

Hannah didn't ask what Paul had meant. Was it because she had no curiosity? Or because she'd known, all along, that Elliot was Macrath's child?

Paul had touched her. He'd been her lover.

Her skin crawled.

Nausea swamped her. Whether from the effort of walking from the house to the stable or from Paul's admission, she didn't know or care. Grabbing the strap above the window, she held on, even though the carriage had not yet begun to move.

She must continue this journey, no matter how sick she was.

Had the trip to Scotland been difficult for Elliot? At least Macrath had the sense to take his wet nurse and nursemaid with him.

The plan that had been so foolhardy all those months ago seemed even more idiotic now, and cruel as well.

She'd trade a thousand fortunes for Elliot.

Did her actions equal or surpass Macrath's? If she hadn't plotted to become pregnant from him, he wouldn't have stolen her child. In this instance, she was the greater sinner.

She lay her head back against the seat, feeling the rumble of the carriage wheels through her bones.

Thousands of people had died in the epidemic, that much she knew from the physician. She was lucky not to be one of them.

She was so tired it was a burden to remain upright. Her skin pulled at her, weighing her down. Her bones wanted to bend. She was will and stubbornness, nothing more at this moment.

"Your ladyship, are you sure you want to do this?"

She didn't open her eyes, merely licked her lips and answered Hannah.

"Yes," she said, even that short word an effort.

She had to get to Scotland and convince Macrath to give her back her son.

Drumvagen, Scotland
July, 1870

The carriage entered Drumvagen's drive, just as it had a year and a half ago. This time, however, Macrath stood at the head of the steps, his legs braced apart, his arms folded, and his face expressionless.

He would send her back to London. He wouldn't even give her a chance to rest and recuperate from the journey. She was a dangerous woman, and he knew it only too well. She was the only person in his life to cause him pain.

The door opened and the maid was the first to descend. She looked around her, at the commanding staircases of Drumvagen, and saw him standing at the top.

She trudged up the stairs, frowning at him. The coachman descended from his seat, opened the door and entered the carriage.

Hannah reached him just as the coachman emerged from the interior of the carriage with Virginia in his arms.

Macrath pushed back a surge of alarm. He told himself he didn't care what happened to Virginia, Countess of Barrett.

"She's sick," Hannah said bluntly. "I told her she was still too ill to travel here, but she was all for coming after her son." She planted her fists on her hips and glared at him. "Well?"

He had the impression that while he might be a mastiff and she a kitten, the maid was not adverse to challenging him.

"Well what?"

"Summon a physician! Do something!" She took a deep breath and closed her eyes, then seemed to compose herself. "Or do you want her to die?"

"She'll not bring smallpox to my home," he said. "I have a child to care for. There's too much danger with her here."

Hannah's eyes widened. "Then where do you suggest we go?"

"There's a crofter's hut not far from here. I used it as a laboratory. I'll send bedding for you and I'll have meals delivered. The minute she's well enough to travel, you'll leave Drumvagen."

With that, he turned and left her.

Chapter 22

Macrath made his way to the room he'd designated as his son's nursery. Located just a few doors down from his own suite, it was close enough that he could check on his son. Last night he'd been awakened by the baby's cry, only to be reassured by a sleepy Mary that Elliot was only hungry and Agatha was already seeing to him.

Now he entered the room quietly, closing the door behind him. His son had only been here for two days, and the atmosphere of Drumvagen was altered. Or perhaps he was the one who'd been changed. He found his mood immediately lightened when he heard his son's gurgling laughter.

"No, they aren't to be eaten, you silly boy."

Mary was leaning over the cradle. When she heard him, she glanced over her shoulder. "He's nibbling on his feet, sir. He thinks his toes are grand things, don't you, silly?"

He hesitated in the middle of the room, his glance encompassing Agatha and Mary.

"His mother is here," he said. "She isn't to see him, under any conditions."

"Is she still sick, sir?" Mary asked.

"She might be. I don't know."

She'd been foolhardy, coming after them so quickly. Anyone with a modicum of sense would have waited until she was well. Was that a sign of a mother's devotion? Or her desperation?

Would there ever come a time when he judged Virginia simply, without looking for a dual purpose?

Mary frowned at him. "If she isn't, sir, why shouldn't she see him? She's his mother. She's the Countess of Barrett," Mary added as if he didn't know. "And Elliot is the eleventh Earl of Barrett."

The wet nurse, being older and wiser, didn't speak.

He looked at Mary. "She isn't to see him."

At the door, he turned. "Oh, and another thing. His name, from now on, is Alistair. Not Elliot."

Her eyes widened but she didn't say a word.

Fine, let her believe he was a despot. He didn't care.

Brianag was in the kitchen garden, picking herbs. He almost asked if it was for one of her potions before he came to his senses. He didn't need to alienate his housekeeper now.

The garden was a new addition to Drumvagen, something Brianag had insisted on when she came to work for him. He'd given her the latitude and the manpower, and the result was a neat square of hedges. Inside, protected from the ocean winds, were paths and herb beds. Nothing was labeled but she somehow knew which plant was which.

"We have a visitor, Brianag," he said when she straightened. "She's ill. Will you treat her?"

"The widow?" she asked, arranging the herbs in her basket.

Maybe he was wrong and she wasn't picking just herbs. Something smelled of onion and lemon, twin odors surprisingly compatible.

"Do you know everything happening at Drumvagen?"

"What's needed to know. The rest I just ignore."

"She's recovering from smallpox," he said, amazed at the calmness with which he said those words.

"Has she any rash?"

"I don't know. I didn't see her."

After the first glance, he hadn't looked in her direction. The coachman, however, hadn't had any qualms about carrying her. When he said as much to Brianag, she nodded.

"She's probably through the worst of it." She eyed him. "You're worried she's brought the sickness to Drumvagen."

He nodded.

"You're also worried about her."

He frowned at her but didn't refute her comment.

"You'll be sending her home as soon as she's well?"

"She doesn't belong here."

She smiled. "There were those who said the same about you, an Edinburgh man all for buying himself Drumvagen."

"Do they still say that?" he asked.

"Oh, you fit in well enough now," she said, smiling.

"Even with the name of Devil?"

"The name didn't matter once I came to work for you."

He wasn't certain what to say. Brianag's arrogance was occasionally grating, and this was one of those times.

"So it was you and nothing I did?"

None of his contributions toward village events mattered? His paying for the new altar at the church counted for nothing?

She shrugged, which annoyed him further.

"If I hadn't come, no one from the village would work here. Drumvagen was getting a reputation for being haunted."

He folded his arms and regarded her. "Do you believe in ghosts?"

Her smile broadened. "There are people who do," she said. "They need to be humored. I figure the dead have better things to do than bother with the living. But we living like to think we're important enough to be visited from time to time."

"So you let people think you've deghosted Drumvagen?"

She frowned at him. "I'm not a witch. It was enough I was here. No ghost would dare haunt me."

How had they gotten on the subject of ghosts?

"Will you see to her?"

Her nod was a jerk of the chin. "I'll see to your countess," she said. "And to your child."

He wanted to explain, then realized she probably understood the whole of it. Turning, he left the garden before she could annoy him further.

The cottage they'd been directed to was longer than it was wide, furnished with a square table and two chairs, a small area she took to be a sleeping alcove separated from the rest of the space by a half wall, and a kitchen that held a small stove. There was no bathing chamber, but a small lean-to had been built along the back wall and could be used for their intimate needs.

Within a quarter hour four men arrived, two carrying bedding, another a large chest. The fourth man carried a steaming kettle he set by the door.

Virginia sat in one of the chairs at the table, noting that none of the four came close to her. She couldn't blame them. For all they knew, she carried pestilence.

"Our cook sent this for you," one of the men said.

Whatever it was, it smelled delicious. Her stomach grumbled at the scent of onions and chicken broth. The man reached forward and put a loaf of bread on the table before quickly retracting his hand.

"Where is my son?" she asked, the words coming with difficulty. She was so weak she could have slept for days. First, however, she had to make sure Elliot was well and being cared for properly.

Two of the men left the cottage, probably reasoning if they left, they couldn't be commanded to answer.

The man who'd carried the food looked back, but when he spoke, it was to Hannah.

"You've not had the disease?" he asked.

Hannah shook her head.

"The Sinclair says you can come, then, and see the boy is provided for."

Hannah turned to look at her. Virginia nodded, and her maid left the cottage.

Before the last man left, she glanced at Hosking standing at the door.

"Can you find accommodation for my coachman?" He'd been her loyal protector against Paul, and she wouldn't have him sleep on the bare ground.

The young man nodded at her. "I'll see he gets quarters."

In a matter of moments she was alone in the cottage.

Two cots rested in the corner with bedding atop them. To Macrath's credit, the mattresses appeared plump. She should organize the cottage so it was habitable. She should fix their beds, if nothing else. Even the idea exhausted her.

She lay her head down on her folded arms, closed her eyes and would have fallen asleep had not the door of the cottage flown open at that moment.

"I've come to see to you," Brianag said, her voice as loud as thunder.

Macrath's housekeeper hadn't made a secret of her dislike when Virginia had visited Drumvagen the first time. She could only imagine what Brianag had to say now.

"I'm fine," she said. "I don't need your help."

"I'm the wise woman of Kinloch Village and Drumvagen," Brianag said. "I'll see to you."

"You're a witch?" she asked faintly.

"I'm not a witch," the woman said, putting a covered basket on the table and coming around to Virginia's side. "I'm a good Presbyterian."

She leaned closer, peering into Virginia's eyes.

"Have the scabs fallen off?" she asked. When she didn't answer, Brianag folded her arms across her ample chest. "Do I have to tell the Sinclair you wouldn't let me see to you?"

She didn't want to subject herself to an inspection, but it might be the only way Macrath would allow her to see Elliot. For that reason, she nodded.

"Most of them," she said. "Except for two on my arm."

"Show me," the woman demanded.

She hesitated, then finally unbuttoned her cuff, rolling up her sleeve to show her left arm.

"I would not have brought smallpox to Drumvagen," she said.

"We don't know for sure, now do we?" Brianag said, holding Virginia's arm and touching each scab. Her hands, while large and swollen with arthritis, were gentle. "I'm thinking you're in such a hurry to find your son you didn't think about the rest of the world."

Since that comment was too close to the truth, she remained silent.

"My maid told me I'm no longer contagious," she finally said.

"Oh, your maid, is it? Perhaps I should have her look at some of the injuries in the village. Old Man MacPherson is having some problems remembering his kin. Perhaps she can help with him as well."

"There's no reason to be disagreeable," Virginia said.

The woman looked startled. A moment later her face

melted into a smile. She pulled up a chair and sat so close their knees met.

"Any fever?"

Virginia shook her head. "Not for a few days."

"Are you fatigued?"

"Yes," she said, "I imagine it's to be expected."

"You're as weak as a newborn lamb. Good thing we've no wolves."

She didn't know what to say to that, so she kept mute.

Brianag placed a palm on her forehead. "You're cool to the touch. Not clammy, either."

"I'm feeling much better."

The other woman didn't respond.

Instead, she leaned forward, peering into Virginia's eyes again.

"Any headaches?"

"Not now."

"Delusions?"

"Unless believing Macrath would be reasonable could be considered a delusion."

Brianag raised one eyebrow and said something that had her staring at the woman.

"I beg your pardon?"

Brianag smiled. "You'll need to learn the way of speaking if you're to remain here," she said. "I told you biting and scratching is Scots folk's wooing."

"Well, I have no intention of wooing Macrath and I know for sure he isn't wooing me."

The other woman merely smiled.

Finally, Brianag settled back, nodded once, then reached into her basket. "You'll use this twice a day on the remaining scabs," she said, pointing to a jar. She held up a brown bottle. "And this once a day after you bathe your face and neck. The scars won't show as much."

"What will you tell him?" Virginia asked. "That I'm well, I hope. And I should be allowed to see my son."

For a moment she thought Brianag wouldn't answer her.

"I'm thinking you should wait for a few days. A week, maybe."

"And after that?"

Brianag smiled again. "The tree doesn't always fall at the first stroke."

She stared at the door long after the woman left.

Hannah took one look at Mary and Agatha and stopped in the doorway. Folding her arms, she glared at both of them.

"And what would you be doing here?" she asked. "Did he pay you enough to forget about your loyalty, then?"

"He paid us enough to remember it's the babe who needed us," Agatha said.

"Leave them alone," Macrath said, coming out of the shadows.

Startled, she dropped her arms and forced herself to stare back at him. Macrath's hard eyes judged her like he was a hungry eagle and she was a rodent scampering up a hillside.

She'd faced him down once, she could do it again.

"I'm here on behalf of my mistress," she said. "To ensure Elliot is being cared for."

"My son is well," he said.

Mary glanced out the window, while Agatha pretended great interest in the buttons of her bodice.

"Tell her nothing will convince me to allow my son to leave Drumvagen," he said.

The three women looked at each other.

Elliot uttered a short, sharp cry, but before any of the women could go to his side, Macrath was at the cradle, reaching down and picking up the child.

Surprised, Hannah regarded him as he tucked Elliot into the crook of his arm, smiling down into a face so like his.

Now what did she do?

"You can see Alistair is doing fine."

"Alistair?"

"His name is Alistair," he said. "It was my father's name and now it belongs to him."

Oh dear, her ladyship was not going to be pleased.

At least the countess would be happy about her report on Elliot. The child appeared to have gained a stone, his little cheeks pink and plump. His eyes sparkled with delight as he waved his hands, contacting with his father's chin.

Macrath didn't do anything but smile and grip his son's flailing fists with one large hand.

"Alistair is not leaving Drumvagen. Not now. Not ever."

"Can she see the boy?" she asked softly.

The other two women stared at her, no doubt in surprise at her daring. She stood her ground, her hands clasped behind her, wondering if Macrath would be so annoyed at her that he banished her from Drumvagen.

He regarded her in silence, as if measuring her courage.

"She has survived much, sir," she said in defense of Virginia. "Her fever was so high I feared she would die, but she rallied."

Macrath smiled at her, such a beguiling expression Hannah knew, suddenly, how devastatingly charming he could be when he tried.

"I'll let her see him," he said. "The day she leaves Drumvagen."

Virginia stared at her maid, every emotion, along with every single thought, flying from her mind.

She couldn't formulate a sentence. She couldn't string two words together.

Macrath expected her to leave?

"Your ladyship?"

The title was amusing since they were sitting in a cottage in the midst of a Highland thunderstorm, the torrential downpour having found four holes in the thatch roof. The hard dirt floor was liquefying beneath their feet. She breathed in the scent of mud and motioned Hannah to one of the chairs at the table.

"The man's lost his senses," she said as Hannah moved around the worst of the puddles to take a seat. "You knew all along, didn't you?"

Hannah didn't answer, merely made a point of tucking her skirts up so the hem wouldn't get wet.

"I don't doubt there are many situations in society similar to yours, your ladyship," she finally said.

Surprised, she regarded the other woman. "Do you truly think so?"

Hannah smiled and nodded. "There are simply too many convenient births, your ladyship. Society merely nods, and as long as everyone is discreet, life goes on the way it's meant to. Titles are kept in the family, along with any property and money."

"Are you aware of what my husband did?"

To her surprise, Hannah nodded again. "Servants aren't invisible, your ladyship, as much as people would like them to be. We know most of what goes on in the houses where we work. People do talk, you know. Servants hear everything, and there are more than a few of us who like to gossip as well."

"Did you gossip about me?" When Hannah looked away, she said, "It's all right. I think I would've talked about me, too. Here comes this American girl, knowing nothing about society. She thinks to be the Countess of Barrett, just because her father's wealthy."

"We never said anything bad about you, your ladyship. We all felt sorry for you. You were so afraid of everything."

She nodded, unable to deny those truths.

"I daresay that this journey to Scotland and the one before it were the most courageous things you've ever done."

How odd to see the look of approval on Hannah's face.

"You don't think he means to give up Elliot," she said.

"No, your ladyship." After a moment she spoke again. "He's changed Elliot's name. He's calling him Alistair."

She nodded. Another comment for which she didn't have a response.

"And Elliot? He looks well?"

"Very well, your ladyship." Hannah smiled. "He seemed to like being in his father's arms."

Virginia looked down at the floor, watching the raindrops hit the mud.

"Shall I alert Hosking?" Hannah asked.

Surprised, Virginia glanced at her. "Why?"

"To prepare the carriage for the return to London."

"If you feel you must return, Hannah, I can't forbid you from doing so. But I'm not leaving Drumvagen without my child."

Hannah looked at her wide-eyed. As well she might, because in her timid mouse way, Virginia had just declared war on Macrath Sinclair.

Chapter 23

For the first week after arriving in Scotland, Virginia slept most of the time. As she began to recuperate, two thoughts played in her mind: How could she convince Macrath to relinquish her child, and had Lawrence truly done that to her?

Had he paid Paul to bed her? Or was it Paul's idea? What was the influence Paul had over Lawrence? All these months, they'd thought it was the opposite, that Lawrence had been the Machiavellian one. Now she wondered if they'd been wrong all this time.

She couldn't go back and remake the past. If she could, she'd save dear Eudora. She'd certainly find a way to prevent her own marriage to Lawrence.

Macrath steadfastly ignored her, refusing to visit the cottage. Brianag checked on her daily, but the housekeeper was taciturn and about as communicative as a stone.

During the second week, Virginia started making battle plans.

First, she had to regain her strength. Every morning she practiced lifting a bucket of water with her right arm, then her left. She bent and stretched, intent on conquering the dizziness she occasionally experienced. As she perched on the edge of the cot, she lifted one leg then the other until she could feel her muscles pull, then trudged through the cottage until she was steadier on her feet.

A few days ago she'd asked Hannah for a mirror, and the maid had come back to the cottage with a small hand mirror. Before she looked, however, she asked Hannah for the truth.

"Is it bad?" she asked.

"No, your ladyship," Hannah said, studying her. "There are a few marks on your forehead and two near your right eye, but that's all. Your arms and shoulders took the brunt of it."

She nodded, having seen the scars there.

Courage seemed far away as she lifted the hand mirror, only to see it tremble in her grip. She lowered it, sat there composing herself.

She had never thought she was beautiful. A few scars would not alter her appearance.

Resolutely, she raised the mirror again and stared at her reflection.

How strange. The color was the same, but there was a world of knowledge in her eyes. She blinked at herself. What other changes would she find?

Two more scars Hannah hadn't mentioned sat near her hairline. Her face was thinner, her chin and nose more pronounced. Her mouth seemed larger. But it was the change in her eyes that fascinated her. She looked worldly. Experienced. Like she'd seen the suffering of the world and understood it.

Had smallpox done that to her? Or had giving birth changed her in some way?

Slowly, she lowered the mirror.

"I'm different, aren't I?" she asked.

Hannah smiled. "You've been sick, your ladyship. That's what you see."

"No one could be a more diligent nurse," she said. "Or a more caring one."

"You were a good patient. Except when you were going off on a journey just when you were making a turn for the better."

She gave Hannah a rueful smile. "It might look foolish, but I couldn't do anything else."

"I know, your ladyship. But if you injure yourself, Elliot will be without a mother."

Virginia smiled. "You're very wise, Hannah."

"My mother used to say I had an old soul. She also said I was a bossy thing, forever giving people orders, even as a child."

"It must've been difficult for you to go into service."

"Why would that be, your ladyship?" Hannah asked, frowning.

"You didn't find it so?"

"We were all trained to go into service. What else were we to do? Oh, we could have gone to work in one of the mills, but I think it's a better position to be your maid then to stand for eighteen hours in a dusty factory."

She'd never once considered that going into service might be something to be preferred. Nor had she ever had to worry about food or housing—at least until Lawrence died.

The morning of her assault on Drumvagen, Virginia sat at the table as Hannah prepared to leave, as she did every day. She hadn't told the other woman of her intent, and now watched her fill an earthenware container with heather, the scent perfuming the air.

"Do you think he'll change his mind today?" she asked her maid.

Hannah only glanced at her and shrugged.

Each day, through Hannah, she'd sent word to Macrath that she had recuperated and would like to see her son. Each time, he'd sent back a note with only four words on it: *When you leave Drumvagen.*

At least he'd not starved them. Every morning and evening a wagon appeared in front of the cottage. Hannah would come back inside with a large stew pot filled with something smelling wonderful. She'd be accompanied by either a maid or a young man bearing a small crate filled with other items like tea, pudding, jars of preserves, and a loaf of bread.

Hannah kept the small stove at the end of the cottage fueled with firewood delivered every few days. Now, on the fateful morning she would make her assault on Drumvagen, Hannah placed a cup of hot tea in front of her.

"You'll be drinking it," she said. "And I've some hot broth with chicken."

"Are there no end to your abilities?" Virginia smiled at her. "You can deliver babies, be a nurse, and now you cook."

"I try to be of use," Hannah said, turning away, but not before she saw the flush on the maid's cheeks.

"You have been," she said, sipping her tea. "What would I have done without you?"

Besides her other capacities, Hannah acted as intermediary with Macrath, who allowed her to check on Elliot and speak with Mary and Agatha. Each day when Hannah returned, Virginia asked the same questions and Hannah dutifully answered. Had he grown? Was he well? Did he smile? Has he learned anything new? Did Mary or Agatha express any concerns?

She hated having anyone be proxy for her, even dear Hannah.

Every day for the past two weeks Hannah had gone to Drumvagen and was allowed into the nursery, a converted guest room on the second floor. Evidently, Macrath did not want his son relegated to an upper floor. That was the first thing that surprised Virginia. The second was that Macrath was in the nursery every day, either supervising his son's care or simply being with him.

"He looks at him, your ladyship," Hannah had told her, "like he can't believe Elliot is there and half expects him to disappear any moment."

She knew the feeling well, having experienced it herself in the weeks after Elliot's birth.

How was she to know Macrath would be as captivated by their son as she? His affection only complicated the situation.

Macrath must understand Elliot was the eleventh Earl of Barrett. The world recognized him as such. His future was assured.

"How can I convince him if he won't meet with me?" she asked Hannah now, just as she had every day. Her maid only shook her head, as always.

"Give my little boy a kiss for me," she said.

Her maid smiled. "Yes, your ladyship."

She watched Hannah leave the cottage, close the door behind her, then she moved to one of the cottage windows to track her progress.

Hannah sauntered with a bounce in her step, nodding at the flowers lining the road. Was she happy here?

Drumvagen was almost an enchanted place, silent but for the branches of the trees swaying in the gusty breeze. The whispering sounded like the trees were talking, discussing the day and the weather.

White filmy clouds skittered across the sky while the horizon was gray, the color of Drumvagen's bricks. They'd had their share of storms lately. The morning after, however, the air sparkled like it was touched by magic.

Virginia knew she needed a bit of magic now, and prayers wouldn't hurt, although she wasn't certain petitioning the Almighty was a wise thing to do. After all, she'd sinned in many egregious ways.

If God couldn't forgive her, how could she expect Macrath to do so? But God wasn't an unyielding Scot like the owner of Drumvagen.

She left the cottage then, closing the door behind her. For a moment she simply stood on the path, hands clasped in front of her, looking down the road to Drumvagen. To her left, Drumvagen Wood hid the river from view. To her right was the ocean. Straight ahead was the house that held her son—and Macrath.

The day was cool, hinting at chilly, and she didn't have a shawl. In London, planning this journey, they'd thought it would take a few days at the most. Neither she nor Hannah had expected to be in Scotland for more than a fortnight.

At least Hannah had made friends with the laundress at Drumvagen, which meant their clothing and bedding were clean.

Of all the decisions Enid had forced on her, hiring Hannah had been the best. What would she have done without the woman? Hannah was courageous and kind, and had become much more than a servant.

Virginia had dispensed with a hoop that morning and worn only one petticoat, which meant her skirts dragged on the ground. Resolutely, she grabbed her skirt with one hand and started walking.

She knew, well enough, that if she went up the broad staircase to the front doors of Drumvagen, Macrath would refuse her admittance. Even though Brianag had pronounced her free of disease, he'd been adamant about not letting her see Elliot.

Would her son even remember her?

She could petition Macrath once more. The result would be one more terse note: *When you leave Drumvagen*.

Did he think she would walk away from her child? If so, he was even more mistaken than she had been. Yes, she'd sinned. Yes, she'd taken advantage of him. Yes, what she'd done was wrong. Whatever he wanted to say about her was probably true.

She was not, however, going to desert Elliot.

Even if Macrath thought she was the most venal woman to have ever lived, she wasn't going to abandon her son.

In America, she'd been left at Cliff House for years at a time, her father only visiting at Christmas and once in the summer when he brought friends to party. Even with the full staff and her governess, she was alone, a privileged, wealthy orphan.

Elliot would always know she loved him. There would never be a doubt in his mind about how she felt. He wasn't an impediment. He wasn't an inconvenience. He wasn't someone about whom she thought periodically, then dismissed.

He was her darling little boy, and she wasn't leaving Scotland without him.

She would have liked Macrath's understanding, but that might be too much to expect. She was heartily sorry for what she had done. She regretted using him. She should have, somehow, communicated with him, even if he was on the other side of the world.

But she could never regret Elliot.

She wiped her palms against her dress, straightened her shoulders, and kept walking, intent on finding a way into Drumvagen. In the last two weeks, she'd devised a plan, one she hoped would work.

The sun glittered off the ocean, nearly blinding her. Several stubborn late summer flowers bobbed their heads at her. At another time she would have marveled at their bright yellow color or the sweet scent accompanying her walk. Now, however, she was intent on her plan.

Drumvagen hugged the coastline, perched on the edge of a cliff overlooking the sea. There must be a way to reach the beach, get into the grotto, and from there climb the passage into the house.

Now, she saw to her surprise a few outbuildings north of Drumvagen, structures she hadn't noticed or known about on her earlier visit.

As she approached, she saw a large stable, three other buildings, and a structure that looked like a barn except taller. They sat between Drumvagen and the road she was on. At least a dozen people were working, and several gave her curious glances. She smiled in greeting, pretending she belonged there, and passed them, intent on finding a way down to the beach.

A quarter hour later she found a spot that looked well traveled, tiptoed to the edge and peered over the side. A narrow path led from the road down to a crescent-shaped beach. The descent was dangerously steep. She drew back, fighting a sudden wave of dizziness.

She could stand here being afraid or simply ignore the feeling and go on with her plan.

She grabbed her skirt in one hand, the other outstretched to give her balance.

Did Drumvagen boast mountain goats? If so, this path was created by them, going in one direction then abruptly turning in another, forming a Z on the face of the cliff.

Halfway down, sand covered the rocks, the narrow path becoming even more treacherous. Twice she almost fell and caught herself by gripping clumps of gorse. Each time she uttered a quick and fervent prayer, hoping God would forgive all her previous transgressions in favor of saving her now.

Her heart was pounding and her breath coming in sharp pants. She could only concentrate on her footing, not the ocean's nearness or the tide.

She jumped the last foot or so, landing on the beach. Glancing back the way she came, she knew she'd have to find the grotto. She wouldn't be able to retrace her steps up the steep incline.

Never would she have thought she'd do something as adventurous as climb down a cliff. But then, since Lawrence's funeral she'd done a great many things she would never have imagined. She'd seduced a man, borne a child, survived smallpox. Now she was trying to gain entrance into Macrath Sinclair's home.

Hardly the behavior of a countess. She could almost hear the rumormongers whispering. "Have you heard? The Countess of Barrett was seen clambering down a cliff! Have you ever?"

Thank heavens she was far away from the drawing rooms of London. She could only imagine what would happen if they discovered the greater scandal.

"My dear, he isn't Lawrence's son, didn't you know? Some Scot, I hear."

That wasn't going to happen. Somehow she would protect Elliot, even from his father if necessary.

She grabbed her skirts with one hand and picked her way across the sand. When she rounded an outcropping of rock, she almost sagged in relief, seeing the arched window of the grotto.

A few minutes later she was below the window, dismayed to realize it stretched a good distance above her. Even the large shelf of black stone that looked like a windowsill was out of her reach.

Turning back, she searched the ground for what she needed. At the narrowest part of the beach she finally located a rock large enough to stand on. The journey back to the window took several minutes because she had to stop, put the heavy rock down, rest, and a moment later pick it up again.

Placing the rock beneath the window, she stood on it and stretched her hand upward. The ledge was still several inches out of her grasp.

For the next few minutes she gathered up stones, setting them on the larger rock already below the window. One by one she added the smaller stones, each big enough to stand on. When she was finally done, she stood on the rock platform and could finally place her palm on the ledge.

She'd simply have to climb the rest of the way.

She glanced down at her silk skirt. In London, before leaving for Drumvagen, they'd only packed two dresses. She would have to sacrifice this one for a greater purpose—getting to her son.

Balancing on the pile of stones, she found a foothold on the stone wall and pulled herself up. Placing her foot in another gap, she repeated the movement, climbing an inch at a time.

She should have thought to wear gloves. Her palms were badly abraded and her knuckles scraped raw.

After reaching the ledge, she lay there, exhausted. The realization that she'd accomplished half her goal was enough to impel her to swing her legs over and slide down into the grotto.

Memories immediately swirled around her.

She'd never been able to forget the way Macrath made her feel. How could she? She'd experienced joy wrapped in laughter, wonder coupled with a passion so overwhelming it stripped from her the lessons she'd been taught on deportment and manners.

Here, in this spot, she'd been the instigator in their loving. She'd seduced him, not because Enid ordered it, but because she wanted him.

Her cheeks flushed.

Had Macrath been able to forget?

If so, how? Perhaps he would share the secret of his patchy memory with her, and she could banish him from her mind as well. She wouldn't remember his kisses or his tenderness.

No, if she recalled anything, it should be that he'd stolen her child.

Chapter 24

Had the grotto always smelled of the sea? She hadn't noticed it before, probably because Macrath had been with her. Now it was ripe with the odor of fish and stone baked by the sun.

Seabirds circled and screamed overhead. Did they announce the incoming tide or simply fuss at her for invading this space?

Light spilled into the grotto from the window and the hole in the rock ceiling. Once she got to the stairs, however, she'd be in shadow. By the time she ascended the rough-hewn steps, there would only be darkness.

She had always tried to keep her dislike of the dark a secret. Mrs. Silverton, a governess, had been amused by her fear, extinguishing lamps when she could and locking Virginia in dark rooms. Her father had taken umbrage at the woman's disrespect—of him, not his child—and dismissed her, which is how Miss Flom, a genuinely kind person, had come into her life.

But having learned her lesson, from that day to this Virginia rarely spoke of her dislike to anyone.

The more people knew about you, the more weapons they had.

She inspected her dress. The fabric of her bodice and the front of her skirt was shredded where she'd slid across the stone. The hem of her skirt was coated with sand. Her hair was coming loose. Her shoes were filled with pebbles. Moisture was running down her back and beneath her arms.

She was not, however, about to quit.

At the base of the stairs she couldn't help but remember the last time she'd come this way. Macrath had been beside her. He'd kissed her tenderly on this step and this one.

"Stay with me," he'd said.

What had she said? Something, anything, hoping he wouldn't pressure her.

A year and a few months had changed everything.

Would she do the same now? Would she come to Scotland with thoughts of deception and duplicity? The answer came so quickly it didn't even require thought. Yes, if it meant, at the end of the regret and shame, she'd have Elliot.

Did that mean she was a vile person?

She would have to answer the question later. For now, the shadows at the top of the steps taunted her.

Why hadn't she thought to bring the lamp from the cottage? Or matches, if nothing else? She'd tried to plan so well, but had forgotten about the darkness.

Standing at the base of the steps, she stared up, her left hand gripping her skirt, her right flat against a stone. If she meant to do this, she must do it now. Otherwise she might as well curl into a little ball on the sand and let the ocean come and get her.

The flagstone floor was uneven, canting toward the left, then the right. She pushed away the thought of spiders and pressed one hand against the wall for balance.

Her stomach was in knots at the first step and she was nauseous by the second. She heard a buzzing sound in her ears by the third, and stopped at the fourth, taking a deep breath. There was nothing there. Mrs. Silverton was long gone from her life, and there would be no cackling laughter or cruel words.

Elliot was at the top of the steps. So was Macrath. She wanted to hold her child and talk to Macrath. She couldn't do either if she gave into fear.

Perhaps it would not be amiss to say a prayer. Or, if it would be unwise to call the Almighty's attention to her, perhaps she could recite the Psalms, which she'd been required to memorize. No, that would only summon Mrs. Silverton from the mist of her past.

If she thought of anyone, let it be Macrath.

He had bought this house and stamped his personality on it. She couldn't imagine Drumvagen belonging to anyone but Macrath.

There, she was nearly at the top and hardly trembling at all. The darkness was like a fog, however, enshrouding everything. The higher she advanced, the more it encompassed her, until she was certain she wouldn't be able to see the door to the library, let alone be able to figure out how to open it.

Providence, luck, or the hand of a merciful God, who pitied her not for her sins but for her stupidity, led her to a latch. She gripped it tightly with her right hand and pulled down on it.

Nothing happened.

She turned the latch in the opposite direction. Again, nothing happened, not even a protest of hinges.

Disheartened, she leaned against the door, and it abruptly opened, so suddenly she almost fell.

She froze, hoping Macrath was not in the library. If he saw her first, he'd prevent her from seeing Elliot, she was certain of it.

After a moment she dared to move, to take three steps into the room, closing the entrance to the passage.

His scent, something reminiscent of sandalwood, hung in the air. On the desk were several loose pages. Was he working on designs for a new ice making machine?

She crept to the door, opening it slowly. Seeing a passing maid, she closed it swiftly. After a moment she opened the door again, waiting, breath drawn, for the girl to reach the end of the corridor. Once she was certain no one was in sight, she raced toward the staircase and up the steps, her heartbeat keeping pace with her fear.

No one stopped her.

No one shouted for her to be thrown out of Drumvagen.

On the second floor, she hesitated only a minute. Thanks to Hannah, she knew where the nursery was.

"It's in a room between the suite you were in last year and his set of rooms, your ladyship. Elliot has a right little kingdom for himself there, with Mary and Agatha in the next room."

At least Macrath had the foresight to steal a wet nurse along with her child.

She opened a door halfway down the hall, only to find it empty. Had Macrath moved her son to hide him?

Fear crouched inside her chest, cold and patient.

She calmed herself. She simply had the wrong room, that was all. The second door she tried was the right one.

Mary sat in an overstuffed chair, staring at a bit of needlework, her lips twisted in concentration. Beside her was a cradle.

"Your ladyship," the girl said upon seeing her, standing and dropping the needlework to the floor.

"Is he all right?" Virginia asked, moving to the cradle.

Elliot lay on his back, asleep, his face turned away from

the faint light from a curtained window. His fist was in his mouth, his eyelids twitching in baby dreams.

The world fell away. Fear had caught at her heart for weeks. As she stood beside the cradle, she was suffused with happiness and at peace for the first time.

Gently, with trembling fingers, she placed her hand on Elliot's chest, just to feel his heartbeat. Just to know he was alive and well.

Had he suffered for their separation? Did he still remember her?

"Leave him," Macrath said from behind her.

She didn't move, her fingers remaining where they were.

Elliot blinked open his eyes and reached for her, the cry he uttered sweeping away any fear. She plucked him from the cradle and held him close, talking to him softly.

"There you are, my precious little darling," she whispered. "I've missed you so."

Slowly, she turned to face Macrath, recognizing the rage in his eyes.

The moment of reckoning was finally here. They stood silently looking at each other. Would he forgive her? Should she even try to plead her case?

What about the terror she'd felt on discovering Elliot was gone? Did he bear no responsibility for that?

"How could you take him from me? You had no right."

"I had every right, or do you deny he's my son?"

Beneath his rolling accent was anger, sharp and pitiless and not at all melodic.

She looked away, wishing he didn't seem so large standing there. Or wasn't as forbidding. His face was immobile, like he'd been hewn from rock.

She'd never been afraid of Macrath and she wasn't now. Perhaps she was most afraid of saying the words aloud, of admitting to him what she'd done.

Patting Elliot on his back, she listened to the sweet sound of his babbling at her.

"Yes," she said, the single word condemning her. "Yes, he's your son."

He didn't speak, didn't say a word. Instead, he stood there watching her like she was some loathsome creature that had crept across Drumvagen's threshold.

"**H**ow did you get here?" he asked.

"The grotto," Virginia said, surprising him.

He frowned. "There's no way to the grotto, unless you approach it by boat."

She shook her head. "I took the path down to the beach."

There was no path to the beach, only a channel of loose shale and stone carved out by the water when it rained. His chest tightened at the thought of her navigating that part of the cliff.

He pushed the thought away to investigate later. For now, there was a more important question.

"Have you come to say good-bye?"

She shook her head, attending to Alistair. She walked to the secretary, padded to act as his changing table, and lay him down on his back.

"Where are his nappies?" she asked.

Mary hastened to bring her one, but surprisingly, Virginia didn't turn Alistair over to the girl. Instead, she changed his son, crooning to him all the while. Alistair looked blissfully happy and crooned right back to her.

Macrath glanced at Mary and nodded toward the door. She bobbed a curtsy and left the room as quickly as humanly possible.

Smart child.

"You're adept at that," he said.

"And why shouldn't I be?" she asked. "He's my son."

"I didn't think countesses bothered with their children," he said.

"This one does." She finished with the nappy, lifted Alistair into her arms and returned to one of the chairs beside the window.

"I nursed him until I became ill," she said, smiling down into their son's face.

Another surprise, that she would do such a thing.

"Say good-bye to him, Virginia."

"How can you be so cruel? You were never cruel before, Macrath." Her eyes were filled with sadness.

"You never gave me reason, Virginia."

His son patted her face with his hands, much in the way Alistair did to him. Did he recognize his parents? Did he know his mother?

Her eyes swam with tears. He felt a curious tightening in his chest looking at her.

"I was just the rooster to your hen," he said, a comment that had her blinking at him.

"What an interesting way to put it. I suppose you were."

Not the response he expected.

"You cannot keep a child from his mother, Macrath."

"You cannot keep a child from his father, Virginia."

She looked away, facing the window. For a few moments she ignored him, speaking to their son in tones too low to be overheard. The gentleness of her movements didn't need speech, however, nor the quick act of brushing her face with one hand.

He'd thought of her at Drumvagen, knowing they would weather anything together. She would bear his children who would inherit his empire. When they spoke of him, which they surely must do, they would also speak of his great love for an American woman.

Except, of course, none of it had happened.

Her hair, black as a crow's belly, shone in the sun. Her eyes were such a pale blue they looked almost like clouds passing across a Scottish sky. Her face, oval and delicate, featured a nose at once aristocratic and pert, a mouth lush enough to fuel his dreams.

He didn't want to remember her long, long legs or those magnificent breasts right at the moment. Not when he was thinking she was a selfish bitch.

She faced him, her eyes direct and unflinching, yet her shoulders were too straight, her posture too rigid for true composure.

Did she think he was unaware of her tears?

She should leave this moment. He would escort her to the door himself, summon her coachman and send her fleeing from his property. She would no longer be able to look at him with those soft eyes of hers and her mouth trembling.

He could easily hate her for what she did. Easily despise her for how conflicted he felt in her presence. No one else had the ability she did to turn his world upside down, then smile at him in apology.

"I was always so careful in telling you the truth when you did nothing but lie to me. Why did you do it?"

Her smile seemed forced as she turned Alistair in her arms, patted his hands together, and leaned her head against his.

He would damn well stand here until the North Sea turned to ice, but he was going to get an answer.

"Why did you take Elliot?"

"His name is Alistair," he said. "My father's name. Not Elliot, which is too English. He isn't English, you know. He's half American and half Scot."

"The world doesn't see it that way. He's Lawrence's child. He's the eleventh Earl of Barrett."

"Then the world needs to be corrected," he said.

"And, in doing so, would you label your son a bastard?"

"I would label my son a Scot," he said.

She frowned at him. "You once admitted you were stubborn. Do you take pride in it?"

"Yes."

Her eyes widened.

"Did you expect me to lie to you?" he asked.

"I don't know what to expect from you," she said, and the words were said with such exasperation he suspected they were the truth.

"Don't expect anything. Just leave."

"I'm not going anywhere," she said. "Not as long as Elliot is here."

Their son started to fuss. She stood with him in her arms and began to walk back and forth in front of the window, patting his back as she did so.

She looked comfortable tending him.

"I received two letters from my sister while I was in Australia," he said. "Pity yours was lost."

She glanced at him. "It wasn't lost. I never wrote you."

"I know."

"I couldn't put something like that on paper," she said. "I couldn't take a chance someone else might read it."

"If they had, would the situation be any worse than it is now?" he asked.

She surprised him by smiling. "No, it wouldn't."

"You need to leave Drumvagen."

"I'm not going," she said, turning and facing him, their son now calm in her arms. "Not without my son."

The sight of her tears hit him with the force of a blow.

"Alistair is not going anywhere. His home is here."

"His name is Elliot," she said.

"I can starve you out. Refuse you food or water."

"I imagine there are berries to be found, and there's a river not far away."

The stone on his heart moved just a little, enough to allow a tendril of humor to enter.

"Who's stubborn now?"

She frowned at him. He much preferred her smiles.

"If you think living in your cottage these past weeks was a joyful experience, I beg to differ. Your roof leaks and the floor turns to mud. Not to mention you seem to have an abundance of insects on your moor."

He folded his arms. "I couldn't take the chance you would bring disease to Drumvagen."

She surprised him again by nodding. "I understand, Macrath, and I don't fault you for it. I mention it only to explain that refusing me food and water won't alter my living conditions appreciably."

"Enjoy your visit," he said, turning and walking to the door.

"Can I come again? By way of the front door this time?"

"You won't be here," he said, and without waiting to hear her response, left her, closing the door firmly behind him.

Chapter 25

For a week, Macrath had not made good his threat. He continued to send them food, water, and more than a few creature comforts, including workmen to repair the thatch roof.

A good thing, as it turned out, because another storm was approaching. Dark gray clouds skidded across the sky like puffs of smoke from a dragon's nose.

Hannah had taken their soiled clothing to Drumvagen earlier that morning, and Virginia was grateful the maid would not be alone in the cottage when the looming thunderstorm hit.

A Scottish storm was like no other. Rather than a gentle rain, the droplets were hurled from the clouds. Thunder reverberated over the hills, lightning speared from cloud to ground, and winds whipped up waves that crashed onto the shore.

She left the cottage for Drumvagen, anticipating seeing her son.

Elliot was a delight. He smiled, waved, and entertained her with conversations as unintelligible as Brianag's comments. He tried to eat everything, including her mourning brooch and her hair, when he wasn't thrusting his fist into his mouth and drooling around it. His gummy grin sparked her smile.

She'd expected the startling blue of his eyes to fade, but they hadn't. His black hair got curly, something she hadn't foreseen. His face, though, was a younger version of his father's, even down to the frown.

Her heart stuttered to look at him.

She'd gone to Drumvagen the day after her entrance from the grotto. Macrath had answered the door. Rather than forbidding her entrance, he'd stepped back, a word-less invitation.

As she passed him, he said, "It wasn't a path you took down the cliff, Virginia. Don't come that way again. I don't want to have to explain to Alistair how his foolish mother fell to her death."

She stopped and stared at him. "As I would hate to ex-plain to Elliot his idiotic father wouldn't allow me to enter through the front door."

The battle was joined.

Now, the rolling clouds were advancing on her, the lightning darting to the ground an impetus to hurry. She picked up her pace. With luck she could reach the house before it started to rain.

On the first day, she only stayed an hour or so. The second, her visit encompassed the whole morning. Over the last week, she'd remained in the nursery the entire day, playing with Elliot and talking to him about various things, even though Mary giggled at her conversations.

"Do you think he understands you, your ladyship?" she'd asked.

"I don't know, Mary, but it seems natural to speak to him, all the same."

The only time she grew quiet was when Macrath en-tered the room, took a chair beside hers, regarding her silently. He unnerved her when he did that. How could anyone remain still as long as he did? At least she had Agatha and Mary to talk to while he was there, as the other women directed their attention only at her, and avoided looking at Macrath. At those times, the topic was always Elliot, how much he'd grown, his recent achievements, or worry that he still didn't sleep through the night.

When Macrath stood and left, she let out a breath, both grateful and disappointed he was finally gone. With his absence, she could breathe easier. But with his presence, the world seemed more alive somehow.

Their uneasy truce—if it could be called that—was so fragile she didn't dare approach him about allowing her to return to England with Elliot.

Nor was she going to try to charm him.

Besides, it was dangerous to even look in his direction. His stare was too direct, too mesmerizing. He stripped her of speech with his slow, dawning smile.

Would he come to the nursery today? Would he sit there silently watching everything she did? She told herself it was foolish to anticipate such a thing. Unwise, also, to remember a time when they were friends and lovers rather than whatever they were now. Not enemies, but cautious about each other.

Would he come? Would he sit there smelling of sandalwood and looking so handsome her heart melted? Would he be thinking of other times?

Or would today be the day he banished her from Drumvagen?

Macrath stood at the window of the suite Virginia had occupied on her last visit to Drumvagen. From there, he could see the road to the cottage.

A few months ago he decided on a motto, one that would be passed down to future generations of Sinclairs. "Good fortune despite adversity." With any luck, his descendants would continue with the good fortune part, while the adversity faded away.

The source of his greatest adversity was approaching Drumvagen slowly.

Virginia was standing out in the open while a storm was approaching, the wind whipping her hair around her face. Whenever she stopped to remove a tendril of it from her cheek, he wanted to open the window and shout for her to run. Did she think herself exempt from a lightning strike?

Daft woman.

Daft man, to be standing here watching her as he had for the last week.

The knock came softly and he called out, turning when Hannah entered the room.

"Thank you for agreeing to talk with me."

"It's not like I had much choice," she said, frowning.

He bit back his smile. His wife's maid had never been cowed. Her loyalty to Virginia was admirable but still managed to be annoying.

"Was she very ill?" When Hannah's eyes narrowed, he added, "I want to know what it was like for her."

She relaxed her pursed lips long enough to say, "Begging your pardon, sir, but shouldn't you be asking her ladyship?"

"Yes," he said. "Under normal situations. This isn't a normal situation." He rubbed the back of his neck with one hand.

Hannah's brow furrowed. In a few years she would look as fierce as Brianag.

"Go, then," he said. "If you can't help me, then just leave."

He was turning back to the window when she spoke.

"I think she was ill with worry about Elliot first. Especially when Eudora died."

He turned to face her. "Eudora?"

"Her sister-in-law. Everyone was frightened after that."

"I didn't know," he said.

"There's a lot you don't know."

He speared a hand through his hair. "Then why don't you tell me?"

"Why, sir?"

"Because I need to understand," he said, answering her when he'd no intention of doing so. "Because I have to understand."

Just when he thought she was going to remain stubbornly silent, she started to speak. "She was very sick," Hannah said. "She called for you sometimes, in the worst of it."

How easily she said the words that went through him like a spear.

"Did she come to Scotland to get herself with child?" he asked, a suspicion that had been niggling at him since he'd entered the nursery to find he was a father.

Hannah moved to sit on the chair beside the window. A cheeky maid, but perhaps more than that. Virginia's protector. Her guardian when he'd not been there.

"Let me tell you about Enid," she said. "And the errand she sent the countess on a year ago."

When she was done, he asked, "Will you be telling her about my questions?"

Hannah looked as if she were considering the matter. Finally, she shook her head.

"It's none of my business, sir. I'll not be aiding your cause or taking away from it. The two of you need to find common ground without other people meddling any more than they have."

He dismissed Hannah finally, turning back to the window to find Virginia was no longer in sight.

If he were wise, he'd pretend she hadn't come to Drumvagen again. If he were truly astute, he'd avoid her while she was here, or shorten her visits so she didn't remain as long. Nor would he enter the nursery as long as she was there.

He'd seen Virginia's many emotions, but had never been as fascinated with her as when she cared for their son. Her soft crooning shouldn't have enthralled him as it did. Her laughter when Alistair patted her face should not make him want to lean over and kiss her soundly.

What kind of father was jealous of his own son? When she looked at Alistair, softness in her eyes, her lips curving in a smile, he wanted her to look at him like that.

She confused him, interested him, and he thought about her too much. He should have sent her back to London days ago. Why hadn't he?

Was it because of her tears when she'd held Alistair? Or her stubborn refusal to leave their son?

Or was it because he was still in love with her? If so, he was ten times a fool.

Even though she'd been on her sickbed, she traveled to Scotland.

She'd climbed down a damn cliff to be with their son.

Yes, but she wasn't above being duplicitous.

And so it went, two people living in his mind, each of them set on a certain viewpoint. One of them told him to dismiss her from Drumvagen as soon as possible. The other urged compassion and empathy.

Neither looked to be winning or losing the war.

Common ground? What was that?

He allowed Virginia to come to Drumvagen. When he heard the sound of her laughter, he smiled. Once, he'd entered the room to find her sitting on the edge of the chair, rocking back and forth, singing softly to their son. Rather than sleeping, Alistair had reached up and pressed his palm against her cheek in wonder.

Macrath had sent for a rocking chair that day.

When her daily visit was done, she returned to the cottage. He pretended she wasn't there on the moor. Until darkness fell and he came to this window to see if a light was lit in the cottage. He told himself she was far away, so she couldn't disturb his peace of mind, or what was left of it.

He wondered at her thoughts and what she was doing. Did she find it easy to sleep on the narrow cot? Did she once think of returning to London? Why had he never noticed the core of stubbornness in her?

Would he have done what she did? If he were facing poverty, would he have calculated to get a child to save a fortune?

The question was foolish, because he couldn't put himself in a woman's position. But he'd been familiar enough with being poor. As a boy growing up in Edinburgh, he'd known there were weeks when the income from the printing company was barely enough to support them all. He'd seen his father's worry. He'd known his own, when the support of his sisters and cousin had fallen on his shoulders. He'd been determined, then, to rise above his circumstances. He never again wanted to lay awake at night wondering if he could keep a roof over their heads or how he would be able to feed them all in the coming weeks.

That's why his threat to Virginia was so empty, because whatever she'd done to him, he wouldn't inflict on her the sense of desperation he'd felt as a boy.

He'd sold papers on the corner, bartered for the equipment for his first ice machine, drummed up investors who'd all chipped in a little for the promise of a good return. He'd earned a fortune for them, too, enough so they still clamored to be part of the empire he was building.

Virginia hadn't had the opportunities he'd had, so she'd survived the only way she could.

Had her desperation been the equal of his?

At least he hadn't lied to other people. He had never taken advantage of anyone. Nor had he treated someone he loved as badly as she had.

That was the thought keeping him awake. Perhaps she didn't feel anything for him. Perhaps he had simply been a means to an end.

It was plain she loved Alistair.

What did she feel for him?

Poverty didn't excuse Virginia from keeping the secret concerning their child. He understood the lure of a title, but his son wasn't the eleventh Earl of Barrett.

Alistair was a Scot, a damn sight better than being an earl.

Things had to change. He couldn't go on like this. He either had to banish her from Drumvagen or welcome her wholeheartedly.

He left the room to greet Virginia in the nursery, biting back a surge of excitement. Another sign of his idiocy, that he anticipated this moment.

His life would be a great deal less chaotic if he'd never met Virginia Anderson. But would he have felt as truly alive? Would he have learned the full measure of love, how miserable it could make him or how happy?

He needed a resolution, something more than this polite vacuum they were operating in, their emotions cooled to the point of ice.

He wasn't a machine and neither was she.

Did Virginia realize he didn't give a damn about what

the world said, but he wasn't giving up his son? If she loved him, she wouldn't ask it of him. Did she feel anything for him?

If she loved him, he'd fix this situation somehow.

If she didn't love him, well, he'd kill what he felt for her.

First, however, he'd find out which it was.

London
August, 1870

"**Y**ou've been ignoring me," Paul said, opening the door to her sitting room without knocking. "I told your maid, repeatedly, that I needed to speak with you."

Enid stared down at her clasped hands. "I don't wish to see anyone," she said, her voice sounding scratchy and unused. She raised her head and stared at him. "I especially do not wish to see you."

Despite her words, Paul entered the room, closing the door behind him.

Why hadn't she had the courage to dismiss this arrogant boor a few months earlier? Because she'd been afraid he would tell someone what he knew. Wasn't it strange how things could change in the interim? Her perspective was different. Life was different without her darling Eudora.

"We have to talk."

"I don't want to talk to you," she said.

Nothing was the same as it had been, and he didn't seem to realize it. She barely ate or slept. She rarely spoke. The pain at the back of her throat felt like her unshed tears had turned to acid.

She wasn't hungry; she didn't feel pain. She couldn't hear or see. She was enveloped in a black cloud.

His face altered. Gone was the perennial affable servant.

In its place was a scowling man with brown eyes flashing fury. His hands balled into fists as he strode toward the chair where she sat.

At another time, he would have frightened her.

She touched the locket at the base of her throat. Inside was a lock of Eudora's hair. The locket had become a talisman, a way of enduring one moment to the next.

She'd discovered something odd about grief. Grief was different depending on the person being mourned. She'd never thought about it before and now she couldn't think of anything else.

Her husband's death was unexpected, yet she'd mourned him with the devotion of a wife married twenty years. She anticipated Lawrence's death from the moment he'd been born with bluish lips. She'd watched him grow more frail with each passing year and worried about his death so much that his eventual demise had been almost a relief, God help her.

Eudora's death, however, had been shocking and unreal, the loss still twisting inside her like a knife wielded by God.

Her darling daughter was gone. The lovely child with her husky laughter would never tease her once more. Eudora, with her love of shopping, would never again be fascinated by the scents and spices imported from around the world. Eudora would have liked to travel. She would have written letters from the places she was visiting, sprinkling each with anecdotes about people she'd met.

Eudora couldn't be dead and yet she was. Enid dreamed of her when she finally slept, and when she awoke it was with tears on her lashes and a heaviness in her chest.

No, she didn't want to talk to Paul Henderson. Nothing he had to say would interest her.

"Virginia's been gone three weeks," Paul said. "You need to summon her home."

Even before Eudora's death, she would've taken umbrage to his tone. Now his words flailed her like a whip.

"How dare you speak to me in such a way?"

"I dare a great deal, Countess, since you've refused to leave your room. Don't you care about your household?"

No, she didn't. Nor did she care that she didn't care.

"Virginia needs to return to London."

"Are you dictating to me now?"

She leaned back in the chair and regarded him with steady eyes. He had threatened her a few months earlier. At the time, she'd thought it was simple greed, a case of him taking advantage of a situation he could manipulate to his benefit. Now, watching him, she was not so sure. There was a light in Paul's eyes she should have noticed. A ferocity to his expression she should have seen before now.

"Where the Countess of Barrett is, or what she does, is none of your concern."

He strode forward, putting his hands on either arm of her chair, trapping her. Leaning forward, he breathed into her face, his lips twisted in a cruel smile.

"If you don't summon her home, Countess, I'll be forced to tell the truth about Lawrence's heir. Tell me, does being thrown into the street appeal to you?"

Once, his threats might have mattered. How foolish of him not to realize everything had changed.

She was calm and strangely at peace when she smiled at him. "Do your worst, Henderson," she said, reaching up and patting him on the cheek. "I find I simply do not care."

Chapter 26

Drumvagen, Scotland
September, 1870

A week passed. A week of harmony, at least on the surface. Every morning, Virginia left the cottage for Drumvagen, returning only at the gloaming, as the Scots called it. Except for those times when he visited Elliot when she was there, she didn't see Macrath. They didn't converse. He didn't threaten, and she didn't try to convince him of anything.

He spent a lot of time in the nursery, however, and that was disconcerting.

When he smiled at her, she forgot what she was saying, her words stumbling to a halt. She stared at him and he looked oddly pleased, leaving her wishing he hadn't come to see Elliot.

"He loves the boy," Agatha said one day after Macrath left.

"That he does," Mary added. "Elliot smiles in a certain way when his father comes to tuck him in at night."

Anyone who saw them together could tell Macrath adored Elliot. He wasn't afraid to lift him from his cradle, carry him from place to place, and even play horse with him. His knee was the steed and Elliot squealed in delight when Macrath bounced him up and down.

Each time he placed Elliot back in the cradle, he said, "God be with you." She'd always look away and pretend she wasn't affected by his soft-voiced blessing.

Once, she glanced back to find Macrath watching her. At times like that she could almost convince herself he was feeling amiable about her.

Perhaps he would allow her to leave. If she worded her request in exactly the right way, he might see the reason in her argument.

Was she being naive to even think such a thing?

He didn't, however, bring up her leaving Drumvagen again. Nor did she, unwilling to face the impenetrable wall of Macrath's determination. The situation could not continue to exist as it was. Macrath was not the type of man to simply acquiesce to circumstances.

He manipulated them.

She returned to the cottage, annoyed that Macrath was able to bid Elliot good-night. He wasn't living in a cottage on the moor. He was only a few steps away from the nursery. He could straighten the covers, say a prayer over his child, and ensure he was ready for sleep.

Hannah wasn't in the cottage, and Virginia wondered if she'd walked to the village. Life in their small cottage was occasionally boring. Macrath employed a large staff at Drumvagen, easily fifty people, most of whom were men who lived in the village and didn't try to hide their appreciation of her maid.

Hannah didn't seem adverse to being noticed by the Scots, either. She'd yet to see one in a kilt, but Hannah said they wore them in the village.

What was it about Scottish men? Perhaps it was their

way of speaking, the rolling lilt of their voice sounding like warm cream.

When Macrath talked, she wanted to close her eyes and simply listen. He could be reading an atlas and make it sound delicious.

Or maybe it was the twinkle in his eyes. Did all Scottish men have it, or was it simply Macrath?

What woman could resist him?

She must.

After checking the stove to ensure the fire was still banked, she put on the kettle and returned to the table.

The cottage had changed from two weeks ago. She'd returned one day to find boards had been laid over the dirt floor and rugs atop them that had to be worth more than the whole cottage. There was china, too, easily the equal of what she'd used in London, and crystal that she thought better than Enid's.

Macrath was evidently determined to be a good host.

When the kettle started hissing, she moved it to a cool spot on the stove, poured the boiling water into the teapot and stood waiting for the tea to steep.

From her spot by the stove she could see a hint of one of Drumvagen's towers. The air was different at gloaming, diffuse and almost hazy, like nature couldn't bear the thought of night and submitted to it by degrees.

She felt the same tonight. Darkness was coming and with it loneliness.

Her son was safe, feted, and adored. His father was a man of principle, ambition, and wealth. If those were the only issues she had to deal with, life would be easy indeed.

A wagon lumbered down the road, but rather than passing the cottage, it stopped in front of it.

Curious, she craned her neck to see if it was one of

Macrath's men bringing supplies. Earlier that day they'd come with firewood, food, and two blankets, explaining the early autumn winds could be fierce.

The first inkling she had that something was wrong was Hannah storming into the cottage. The maid's lips were pursed, her eyes narrowed, and she halted in front of Virginia and folded her arms in a pugnacious stance. Her cheeks were bright red, and if that wasn't an inclination something was amiss, Hosking following on her heels certainly was.

"How nice to see you, Hosking," Virginia said, feeling the first tinge of anxiety. According to Hannah, her coachman had found occupation in Macrath's stables, caring for their horses and performing any other chores he might find.

Hosking nodded, looking like he'd rather be anywhere but there. Hannah nudged him, and he removed his hat, ducking his head.

Yes, something was definitely wrong. Otherwise, Hosking wouldn't have avoided her eyes.

She turned to Hannah, but before she could ask her what was happening, two other men entered the cottage.

Her anxiety mushroomed into panic.

Macrath was sending her packing. He wasn't going to let her take Elliot back to London. He wasn't going to listen to reason.

Would she ever be able to see her son again?

"Tell me," she said, waiting for the words.

Please God, please God, please God, let me find some way to stay here. Let me be able to convince him to let me stay. Or take Elliot back to London. Please don't let him banish me.

"The high and mighty Sinclair, the devil himself, wants you out of here," Hannah said.

She wasn't leaving Drumvagen without her son. She wasn't going back to England alone. She had to think of something to convince Macrath to let her stay.

"We're to bring all your things, and mine, to Drumvagen."

The words didn't make sense. She stared at Hannah, her heart beating so fiercely she could feel the pulse in the back of her throat.

"To Drumvagen? He's not sending us back to England?"

Hannah's eyes lost some of their heat. "No, your ladyship. He's all for us moving to the house."

"Is he?"

The surge of relief dizzied her. She sat at the small table, her fingers splayed across the wood. "Is he?" she repeated, staring down at its scarred surface.

She closed her eyes, took a deep breath.

"If you give him any trouble, Hosking is to carry you bodily back to Drumvagen. That's what he said. Otherwise, the devil himself will come and get you."

Opening her eyes, she said, "Will he?"

She couldn't live at Drumvagen. The realization collided with her earlier envy. Nothing made any sense, let alone her chaotic thoughts. She couldn't be close to Macrath.

She would want to touch him. Worse, she'd want him to touch her.

Rather than simply bearing his presence in the nursery, she'd see him in the hall, perhaps at meals. She'd smell the sandalwood perfuming his clothes, hear his voice, his laughter.

No, she couldn't live at Drumvagen. How foolish could he be?

Didn't he feel the attraction between them? What if he didn't? What if he felt nothing for her?

She covered her face in her hands. She couldn't even

think about living at Drumvagen. Besides, who was he to say where she lived? As long as he allowed her to see Elliot every day, the cottage would be fine for her needs.

Being so close to Macrath, seeing him constantly, would not be a good idea. Surely, he could see that? Or perhaps he didn't have the same reaction to her presence as she did to his. Perhaps he didn't remember the last time she was at Drumvagen. No, she was definitely not going to recall those memories, and living at Drumvagen would make it more difficult to keep them at bay. She was only human, and regrettably weak where Macrath was concerned.

Standing, she brushed down her skirt, straightened her shoulders, and addressed all of them.

"I will talk to him myself," she said. Turning to the two Drumvagen men, she added, "Nothing is to be moved until I return. I'll go resolve this misunderstanding."

"Our orders are to take your things to Drumvagen," one of the men said.

Were all Scots incredibly bullheaded?

"I don't care what your orders are," she said, "nothing's to be moved until I return."

The man didn't answer. Nor did he nod. Instead, he simply stood there with a bored, almost dismissive look while his companion looked the same.

She glanced at Hosking and Hannah. "Stay here until I come back," she said.

Hosking nodded. Hannah turned and glared at the two men as if daring them to move a muscle.

She left the cottage, heading for Drumvagen and another battle.

Night would be on them soon, but Macrath wanted to finish up the support for the massive flywheel before they quit.

"We need to ensure the flange is bolted down," he said. Jack nodded, intent on his task.

On the voyage from Australia he'd thought about a new design, one using rapidly expanding ammonia as a coolant. To do so, the ice machine would have to be larger. The frame of this machine, mounted on a brick base, was constructed of timbers. Once the equipment was installed, they'd cover the whole of it with a thin membrane of metal.

Because of its size, they had to construct the frame in the building he'd erected for it. The roof was tall enough to accommodate the main flywheel mounted on the outside of the machine to control the flow of ammonia.

The system of pulleys and gears was essential to the success of the new design, and for that he trusted Jack. Sam, on the other hand, had hands the size of hams, and with as much dexterity. He was an organizational genius, however. If they needed a part shipped from Edinburgh or London, Sam got it on time. He was also good at documenting everything they were doing.

Macrath considered their mistakes more important than their successes. He learned more from them. Errors were valuable. He just didn't want to repeat the same ones over and over again.

He wasn't going to repeat the same mistakes with Virginia, either.

He wasn't going to allow her to take Alistair from Drumvagen. Alistair was developing his own character. The boy laughed and clapped his hands when he made a face. When Macrath spoke Gaelic, it seemed to amuse his son.

He'd commissioned a few toys from one of the men in the village who was talented in woodworking. A wagon, a fire truck like those seen in Edinburgh, and a boat waited on the windowsill for Alistair to be old enough to play with them. Brianag had created a soft little doll she called a rabbit. At first he'd frowned at the object, uncertain whether it was masculine enough for his son. Alistair had stripped him of all criticism when he reached for it, clutching it to his chest with acquisitive glee.

From the time he was a young boy and realized people were different, Macrath had been suffused with a need to rise above his circumstances. He'd always wanted to be one of the wealthy ones. He wanted to own one of the black lacquered carriages carried by four matched horses. He wanted to wear fine clothes that had never been splattered by mud. He wanted to be able to buy anything he wished and to ensure his family never lacked for anything.

He never again wanted to see Ceana's face when another little girl had a new doll, or hear Mairi announce she didn't need any new dresses. Or worry about the cost of charity when Mairi had taken in their cousin. One more mouth to feed had seemed an insurmountable burden at the time.

He'd never craved respect from others as much as he'd wanted freedom, and early on he'd realized that money meant he could do what he wished on his own timetable. He would be beholden to no one. Nor would he have to explain himself.

The desire to achieve had been a drug to him, one dictating his life. He'd focused on only two things in the last decade: his ice machine and his family. The success of the former had allowed him to provide for his sisters and his cousin. Making a fortune had changed his life. Taking Ceana to London for her season had led him to Virginia, the one person to whom he'd gladly explain himself.

Now he felt another emotion, one as powerful as his need to be successful. He wanted to protect, to create as perfect world for Virginia and his son as he could imagine. He never wanted Virginia to be afraid again. If she disliked the ocean, he'd build another house, one farther inland.

He wanted Alistair to always feel safe, to never worry about where his next meal was to come from, or how he would support himself.

Life was not without risks and tribulations. He wanted Alistair to be challenged and learn from his successes and his failures. But Macrath wanted him to do so with a firm foundation, the knowledge that he would always have a home, his father would always believe in him, and he could achieve what he wanted as long as he had an idea and the will to accomplish it.

He had no intention of allowing Alistair to be taken from Scotland. Nor was he going to let Virginia return to London.

A boy needed his mother. Macrath knew he needed her, too.

She was a widow. She should be married. He was in need of a wife. What better solution than to have Alistair's parents marry?

Of course, that still didn't solve the problem of Alistair being the eleventh Earl of Barrett. He would have to dissuade Virginia from maintaining the ruse. His son could survive any lingering gossip about his birth. After all, he'd be reared in Scotland, away from petty English minds.

The screeching sound of metal against metal pulled him from his thoughts.

"That can't be right," he said, walking to Jack's side.

"I think the clearance is wrong. How much do we have on this side, sir?" Jack asked.

He retrieved his drawings and handed them to the other man.

At least Jack was intent on the job at hand. A change

from how he'd been for the past few weeks. He wondered if Jack suffered from the same malady bothering him—a woman.

What was it about Virginia? How did she, above all other women, have the power to change his mood? If she wept, he searched his mind for things he might have said to upset her. If she laughed, the outlook for his day was brightened.

No one should have that much control over his emotions. No one ever had before now.

Sam lit the first lamp by the door. Before he could light the second, Macrath stopped him.

"We'll have an early night tonight," he said.

His men were at the cottage, bringing Virginia and her belongings to Drumvagen. He suspected she wouldn't like it, which meant he had an opportunity to discuss the matter with her.

He would plead his case and convince her to remain at Drumvagen.

Jack put down the plans and glanced at him.

"You're sure, sir?"

He hadn't been sure about anything since meeting Virginia, but he wasn't about to admit that to anyone. He only nodded, left them to the business of straightening up, and strode to the house.

Chapter 27

How dare Macrath act in such a way?

Anger fueled Virginia's walk to Drumvagen. Still, the journey seemed twice as long as it normally did, only because she was aware of the passing minutes. She wouldn't put it past Macrath's men to start packing her things and bodily remove Hannah and Hosking.

Everyone went out of their way to satisfy Macrath's wishes.

Darkness had fallen by the time she arrived at the top of the grand steps. The lamps beside the door were lit, however, pushing back the shadows. For a moment she stood there, going through her arguments.

One never went into battle with Macrath without being fully prepared.

She would be more comfortable in the cottage. He didn't need to know she would feel safer as well if she were away from him and his influence on her.

How dare he just decide where she would live, snap his fingers, and expect it to be carried out just like that? What about asking her?

She straightened her shoulders, grabbed the ring in the dragon's mouth and let it fall.

The knocker echoed in the silence. Even the seabirds were quiet. Were they gone for the night? Or did they congregate somewhere, watching and anticipating this confrontation?

Macrath didn't open the door. Brianag did.

"Where is he?"

The housekeeper's eyebrows wiggled. "He's in the Clan Hall," she said, but didn't step aside.

"I need to see him."

"Do ye now? Fancy was a bonnie dog but fortune took the tail from it."

She truly wasn't in the mood for Brianag's Scottishisms, but she'd never been to the Clan Hall and didn't know where it was.

The woman seemed to know it, too, because a smile split open her craggy face. She turned and strode down a corridor to the left.

Virginia didn't have any other option but to follow, and hope the housekeeper wasn't leading her to the dungeon.

Brianag stopped, waving her toward an arch.

"Say but little and say it well," she said before walking away.

She stared after the woman. What did that mean? Did Brianag try to be confusing?

She walked into the Clan Hall, her anxiety fading in the face of such beauty. Here was the true heart of Drumvagen. High white walls covered in tapestries and paintings led to a ceiling timbered in dark wood beams. Two rose marble fireplaces, each as tall as Macrath and as wide as a settee, stood on opposite sides of the room. Narrow windows were cut high up in three walls, revealing a night sky sparkling with stars. During the day, light would flood into the room, touch the upholstered furniture arranged around mahogany tables, and illuminate even the darkest canvas.

Now, lamps scattered throughout the room colored the walls a pale yellow and beckoned her inside.

Had Macrath commissioned those portraits? Or were they from his family? Or had he simply purchased them because he liked the faces and the colors?

Questions she might ask him if they ever talked again like they had in London or those magical moments in the grotto.

Crystal bowls filled with cloves and other spices— Macrath's scent—rested on tables beside comfortable looking chairs. Shiny brass andirons shaped like dragons perched in the fireplaces, while ceramic vases painted blue and looking foreign rested on the hearth and mantel.

Rather than placed against the wall, the furniture was arranged in seating areas, encouraging a visitor to sit before the fire and talk. Each settee was upholstered in a fabric she'd never seen, colors resembling autumn leaves embroidered on an ivory background.

The room was blessedly uncluttered and spacious. A warm and inviting room she would be proud to call hers.

She froze.

Macrath was sitting near the cold fireplace in a high-back chair watching. The setting reminded her of London, enough that she wondered if he'd staged it that way.

His eyes were intent on her, his hands relaxed on the carved arms of the chair. He wore a white shirt and dark trousers, but there was no doubt he was the master of Drumvagen, its laird and its devil.

A worthy adversary, her father would have said.

She took a deep breath and entered the room, coming to his side and taking the chair next to him before he asked her to sit or even invited her to do so.

"Did you know Drumvagen has fifty-two rooms?"

She shook her head. "No."

"It has thirty-two fireplaces, ninety-six doors, two hundred fifty-six windows, and a total of twenty-two hundred panes of glass. That's only the main house, not the outbuildings."

"Did you memorize all that?"

"I own it. Don't you think I should know what I own?"

"You don't own me," she said, putting her knees together and placing one hand atop the other on her lap, a pose she'd been schooled in by all her governesses.

"I do not."

His tone was agreeable, but the sharp look in his eyes said something entirely different.

"I'm not leaving the cottage."

"Ah, but the cottage is not up to your standards."

"I don't recall saying that," she said.

A quirk of his lips irritated her. Had she amused him?

"Very well," she said, remembering the litany she'd leveled at him about the conditions of the cottage. "The roof is repaired, you've had planks placed across the floor. I'm comfortable there."

"Yes, but you're my son's mother. I would say you deserve the best."

"I don't want to move."

"But you have," he said, smiling lightly. "I expect the wagon to arrive momentarily with your possessions."

"I told them not to move anything until I returned."

"I told them to ignore anything you said."

She frowned at him. "Let me go back to London."

"Alistair needs his mother."

"Yes, he does," she said. "In London."

"He's not going anywhere. Nor are you."

"How do you expect to keep me here?"

He smiled. "Charm? Seduction? Cogent arguments?"

She didn't doubt all three would work, the first two faster than the third. Even now her heart was beating rapidly and her palms were sweaty. He had that effect on her. He seemed to know it, too, if his smile was any gauge.

"If I allow you to seduce me, will you let me leave?"

"With Alistair? No."

She'd known the answer to the question even before asking it.

"What if I seduced you?" She fixed a smile on her face, keeping it there by will alone.

His smile slipped a little but the expression in his eyes didn't cool by one degree.

Perhaps he was the devil, indeed. She was not, however, an angel.

"You did before, as I recall."

Her fingers curled against her palms. Looking down, she marveled at the perfection of the flagstones. How many maids labored here to make everything tidy and dust free, to keep all the brass polished? She had no doubt Brianag was a martinet.

"Virginia."

She would not look at him.

"You have a choice, Virginia. To occupy my room, or the suite across the hall."

Suddenly he was there, standing in front of her chair. He pulled her up to him, and in the next instant was leaning close, his lips against her temple.

"Please do not," she said, pulling away from him.

"Why? Have you developed a distaste for my kisses?"

She walked toward the fireplace. Perhaps she should grab a poker for protection.

"What good does it do to kiss you? To lose myself in your kisses? I'll surrender to you and you'll take me to your bed. In the morning there would be the same problems between us."

"At least we'll have the memory of pleasure," he said, taking a step toward her.

She glanced over her shoulder at him and shook her head.

"You don't understand," he said. "You're a temptation. A drug. You're whiskey."

She faced him. "You're foolish. Boyish. Rash."

"Perhaps all three," he said. "Being around you strips me of my sanity, my reason, and my age. I want to run with you, hand in hand. I want to laugh with you. I want to kiss you senseless and come in you until I'm satisfied."

"Stop."

"No," he said, reaching out and gripping her shoulders, gently pulling her toward him. "I don't seem to be able to stop where you're concerned. I tell myself I should still be enraged at you. I should remember you betrayed me in the worst way a woman can betray a man. You're likely to do it again. Then I remember the girl I met in London, the one who wanted desperately to talk of broadsides, murder, and politics."

"I'm no longer interested in any of those," she said, pulling away from him and putting several feet between them. "I'm not that girl."

Just like that, Paul was there, his words etched like crystal in the air. Just like that, the excitement of bantering with Macrath was gone.

"I'll take the suite," she said. "The one I occupied last year."

"My wife's rooms."

She turned and stared at him.

Before he could say another word, she gripped her skirts with her hands, leaving the Clan Hall like the devil was truly after her.

Macrath watched as his men arrived with Virginia's belongings. Since most of the items were those he'd furnished for the cottage, they weren't taken to her suite. Only two valises went to the rooms he'd created for her, and he suspected one of them belonged to Hannah.

Hannah frowned at him as she stomped up the steps.

He waited until she went up the servants' stairs before going to Virginia's suite. He didn't want another confrontation with the protective maid tonight.

He only wanted an answer. What had he done? What had he said? In a second Virginia's face had changed. Her eyes had dulled and she'd nearly run from him.

He wasn't going about this courting the right way.

Nothing worthwhile was easy, however, and he anticipated winning Virginia Anderson Traylor. He wouldn't have to go to her father, only her, and he wasn't above using every means at his disposal.

Did she want money? He was wealthy.

Did she want a title? More than one earl had been created because of his contributions to the Empire. He'd start making overtures, letting it be known he wouldn't be adverse to the Queen doing the same.

Did she want to travel? He'd show her the world.

Did she want to talk politics? He'd take her to Parliament.

Did she want freedom? As long as she stayed with him, she could do as she wished. She could smoke cigars, wear trousers, and swear like a sailor.

Anything she wanted he would give her.

He was going to make her enthusiastic about remaining in Scotland. Most of all, he wanted her to be eager about remaining with him.

He knocked on her door. When he heard her voice, he

entered the sitting room. He debated about leaving the door open, then decided it was too late to be circumspect now. Everyone in the house, and probably the village, knew Alistair was his son. They probably already assumed he and Virginia were lovers again.

The room smelled of roses, like she'd never left it.

Virginia stood at the window, the fingertips of one hand pressed against the glass. Beyond her, stars winked behind riffling clouds. Another storm was coming. Would there be a matching storm in this room?

"Are you settled in?"

"Yes," she said. Just that and nothing more.

He would have to pry the words from her mouth.

Annoyed, he advanced on her.

"What did I do?"

She glanced at him. "What did you do? Except refuse to release my son and keep me prisoner?"

He'd seen Virginia's many emotions, but never anger. She'd been contrite, sad, amused, and fiercely protective of their son. He had never seen her cloud-colored eyes flashing their own kind of lightning until tonight.

"Are you a prisoner?"

She walked away from the window, marking each object in the room with a delicate touch of her fingertips. Her palm swept across the front molding of the bureau. At the secretary, she halted to straighten the blotter and a journal.

Returning to the window, she stood there for a long moment before finally turning to face him.

"It's a luxurious prison, but it's a prison all the same, Macrath."

"You're an honored guest," he said.

Her slight smile was mocking. She'd never been derisive before.

When had she become so adept at putting him on the defensive?

"Have you come to seduce me, Macrath? Charm me into remaining at Drumvagen."

"If I have?" He planted his feet apart, gripping his hands behind his back.

She was no longer the girl he'd known in London. Marriage hadn't changed her as much as motherhood. He'd seen what she was willing to do for Alistair. The kitten had become a lioness.

Strange, she was only more fascinating.

"My marriage was never consummated," she said, turning back to the window.

He remained silent, waiting.

"Lawrence paid his servant to bed me," she said. She quickly glanced over at him and away.

"Did he?" How calm he sounded when he wasn't feeling especially calm. The image of Lawrence in her bed hadn't been one he wanted to contemplate, yet here she was, giving him another vision to lay over the first.

She turned and smiled at him faintly. "You know him well. Paul Henderson."

The man he'd fought in her London town house. He should have killed the bastard.

"Does it matter?" he asked. "I didn't come to our bed a virgin, either."

Her eyes widened.

"I grew up in the streets of Edinburgh," he said, annoyed again. "If you expect me to be as delicate as a London dandy, you'll be disappointed."

"You always sound very Scottish when you're angry."

"You don't belong to him. You didn't belong to Traylor, either."

"Who do I belong to, then? You?"

He smiled. "I'd prefer that to the other, wouldn't you?"

"I'd prefer to belong to myself."

She didn't smile, merely kept her gaze on him. He realized, then, she'd not told him the whole of it. She hated that Henderson had touched her as much as he did.

He walked toward her slowly, giving her a chance to stop him. When he stood in front of her, he reached out, tucking a tendril of hair behind her ear.

"I could love you tonight," he said. "Burn away the memory of anyone but me."

She remained silent.

"But I won't keep you here by passion, Virginia."

She bowed her head. He extended his arms around her, pressing a kiss to the top of her head.

"I could kiss you until you forget everything but my kisses. I could love you until you only remember my name, my touch."

"Macrath," she said, but he pulled back, pressed a finger against her lips.

Perhaps they talked too much. He leaned down and placed his lips on hers, gently at first. Angling his head, he deepened the kiss, her mouth opening beneath his.

She made a sound in the back of her throat. One of awareness or surrender, he wasn't sure which. He pulled her deeper into his arms, until a thought couldn't come between them.

Her hand reached up, fingers touching his throat. Long moments later he pulled back to find her watching him.

He smiled as he dropped his arms. "But you were right," he said. "In the morning, we'd have the same problems between us."

He strode to the door, turned and watched her. Did she realize leaving her was one of the hardest things he'd ever done?

Her eyes were wide, her face pale. She gripped the fabric of her skirts with both hands.

"Good night, Virginia," he said, forcing a smile to his face.

Sleep would be a long time coming.

Chapter 28

Virginia half expected Macrath to return to her room. When he didn't, she wasn't disappointed. That's what she told herself in the soft, filtered light of a gray Scottish morning.

Hannah, despite her anger at Macrath, was overjoyed to be back in the house, with water running hot from the boiler and a bathing chamber available. Her maid was positively giddy this morning, commenting on how lovely the day was—it wasn't. Hannah also commented on the welcome she'd received from Brianag—which Virginia doubted. The one blessing in moving to Drumvagen was that she was able to visit the nursery without a long walk.

She'd tucked Elliot in herself last night.

"I'm glad you're happy," Virginia said, staring at her reflection in the mirror. Her hair was perfect, if a little too styled for this raw day. She didn't care about the loops of braids or the intricate bun. "But you mustn't think we're staying much longer."

Hannah's eyes met hers in the mirror.

"We've been gone for weeks already," Virginia said. "My aim was not to remain in Scotland. Merely to get Elliot and return to London."

Hannah bent and retrieved a hairpin, studying it like she'd never seen one before today.

"Do you think he will, your ladyship? Let Elliot go, I mean?"

"Not now," she said. "But there must be something I can do. Or say."

Once her hair was done, she stood, walking to the window. The brisk wind on the moor called to her. So did the sight of Macrath standing there, solitary and still, like he waited for her.

"I wish we'd packed my cloak," she said.

"You can't be thinking of going out in this," Hannah said. "It's blowing near a gale out there, your ladyship. Another storm is coming."

"I've a chance to beard the lion in his den," she said.

Without another word she left the room.

At the first rise she stopped, waiting for Macrath to turn and see her. When he did, she still didn't move. Instead, she stood waiting for a sign, an encouragement. When he started walking toward her, she picked up her skirts and approached him.

The girl she'd been two years ago would have raced toward him, her laughter as free as a soap bubble. He would have held his arms open, catching her with his hands on her waist, twirling her around.

The woman she'd been, newly widowed, would have felt her heart expand at the sight of him. She would have joined him, held his hand, and let him lead her where he wished.

This Virginia was a bit more cautious, sadder, and more burdened.

For a moment neither of them spoke.

"I was coming to see you," he said.

"Were you?"

He nodded. "I wondered if you would like to see the rest of Drumvagen."

Surprised, she nodded. "I would."

He reached into his pocket. "I've a present for you," he said, extending a small book to her.

"Thank you," she said, a little bemused. "It's Tennyson."

Did he mean her to recall their meeting in the Round Reading Room?

"Come and meet Jack and Sam," he said, taking her hand.

They approached the tall building she'd seen before. When she asked him why it was so large, he grinned, looking like a boy.

"To hold my new invention," he said. "The flywheel is sixteen feet high. It's designed to make ice at a faster pace than anything I've invented," he added. "Plus, it uses ammonia."

He went on to explain the process and she tried to respond intelligently while vowing to read something about Macrath's inventions.

Jack and Sam turned out to be young men who regarded Macrath as if he were godlike, asking questions and waiting respectfully for his answers.

She realized she'd never seen this side of Macrath before. Here was the man in charge of a growing empire, an employer, a task master, someone who noted the height of a massive wheel with a quick eye and asked a question about ratios beyond her understanding.

Sam greeted her with a shy smile. Jack, however, waited until Macrath and Sam were speaking to address her.

"Hannah is well, then?"

Surprised, she answered him. "Yes, she's well. You know her?"

He nodded. "She came to visit with the laundress a few times. I met her then."

She wanted to ask more questions but was constrained by the presence of the other men. But she did take the opportunity to give him a warning.

"She's a good person, Jack," she whispered. "I would not have her hurt."

His face flushed. "I would never hurt her, miss. Ma'am. Your ladyship."

She nodded and walked away, standing at the wide door. From there she could see the ocean glittering in the morning sun, and the rear of the house bathed by the same light.

"What was that all about?" Macrath asked, stepping close to her.

"Love, I'm afraid," she said.

Macrath surprised her by not asking any further questions. Instead, he extended his arm and she put her hand on it, allowing him to lead her through the rest of Drumvagen.

He told her of the trials of finishing the house, pointing out where they'd found stones from a keep probably built hundreds of years earlier.

His stables were magnificent, built of the same brick as the house.

"Good Scottish stone," he said with a smile. "Everything I could buy from Scotland, I did. What I couldn't, I found in France or England. The chandelier in the hall, for example, is from France."

"As is the furniture in my suite," she said, then verbally retraced her steps. "In the suite I'm currently occupying."

He only smiled at her mistake, led her to a stall and introduced her to a pretty little mare named Empress.

When she once confided she'd never been a great

horsewoman, he hadn't tried to convince her to try riding again. He had never tried to change her, a fact she appreciated.

They visited the barn and enclosures, where she admired one of the black-faced ewes heavy with lamb.

"Most lambs are born in the spring," he explained. "She found herself in this predicament, no doubt from too much frolicking."

The remark was meant to be joking, but it cut too close to their own situation. Frolicking, indeed.

Was that why he hadn't visited her room, because he was cautious about frolicking?

The question never left her lips.

The sun appeared through a rip in the clouds, promising a bright and sparkling afternoon. But when she begged off from any more exploration, he didn't object, merely nodded.

"I need to return to the nursery," she said.

He only smiled, an expression that had her wanting to reach up and place her fingers over his lips. He mustn't try to charm her as he'd done all morning. He really shouldn't smile at her in such a way.

She took her book of poetry and returned to the house, feeling more than a little cowardly for escaping.

Macrath fascinated her too much.

She had to remember why she was here, and why she needed to leave. Daily, however, he was making it more difficult, and she couldn't help but wonder if he'd planned it that way.

Paul smiled and plunked down the coins for the drinks on the table. With a bit more ale, maybe he'd be able to understand his companions better.

He'd never held an antipathy for the Scots, at least until meeting Macrath Sinclair. Now every single Scot he met reminded him of the man.

Money, a perennial lubricant, aided him in his quest for information. By the second day in Kinloch Village, spent in one of the wharf-side taverns, he'd loosened enough tongues to get directions to Sinclair's house.

He'd even had the good fortune of talking to several lads employed at Drumvagen. Now he had enough information to draw a map of the place.

The harbor town proved beneficial in another way. Two ships were leaving soon, one of them the *Oregon*, bound for America. He hadn't hesitated in booking passage for two.

He shook his head when William would have downed the contents of his tankard. The man looked disappointed but put the tankard down. William needed to pace himself or he'd be a liability.

A beggar worked harder than a man used to eating. Before he left London, he'd hired William, who willingly confessed to being a snakesman when Paul had asked. A past they'd shared, although he hadn't confided in the man that he, too, had been a burglar before he got too large to crawl into some of the windows.

William was tall and gaunt, like he'd never eaten his fill. His hair, black and stringy, was queued at the back of his neck, revealing features that could do with a bit of a wash.

Paul was careful never to remain downwind of William for long. His hints about the man's aversion to bathing had fallen on deaf ears, as did his caution about drink. William liked his ale and whiskey almost as much as he disliked soap and water.

One thing he did do about the man's appearance, and

marginally his odor, was to send William off to a used clothing mart to replace his stained shirt and trousers. William had returned looking much the same but smelling better.

Amazing what a decade could do. Ten years ago he'd been just like William, a sour stench clinging to him, his clothes as dirty and soiled. He'd wanted better and had set about changing. He'd learned to speak like the toffs, to bathe and smell good, to eat with the right utensils, to rid himself of the habits clearly labeling him as lower class.

In the task he'd hired William for, appearance didn't matter. Still, he didn't want him to attract undo attention. Luckily, the smell of fish was so strong that it easily overcame William's body odor.

He'd told William a tale, one of a woman who needed to be rescued. William was just young enough to believe it, and old enough to cast himself in the role of good Samaritan or a prince rescuing a princess.

He took a sip from his tankard and nodded when William glanced at him. William drank deep, settled back in the chair with a satisfied sigh and belched loud and long.

The other men laughed. Paul smiled and ordered another round. Leaning forward, he said, "Now, tell me more about this grotto."

Virginia sat in Macrath's library, a room so like him she could almost feel him there with her.

The fireplace on the far wall was surrounded by white marble. In the winter it would burn brightly, warming a room now pleasantly cool.

The large desk stretched nearly the length of the room,

a leather chair sitting behind it. Lining the walls were shelves of books, most of them having to do with electricity or inventions of sorts.

She'd brought the book of poetry he'd given her, picked one of the leather wing chairs, and propped her feet on a footstool. For the last hour she'd been half involved with the book, and the other half engaged in thoughts of Macrath.

She'd been his guest, if she could call herself that, for a week now. Each day, he'd been charming and polite. Every night as she retired, she expected a knock on her door.

They should be lovers, he'd say. After all, they'd already been lovers. Why were they trying to deny themselves the pleasure each felt?

Except he'd never come.

In all these nights, he'd not once kissed her or teased her into passion. He'd not seduced her or driven her mad with his touch.

Instead, he'd done things that surprised her.

A rocking chair had recently been brought to the nursery, followed by another delivery the following day. A larger cradle was carried in by two burly men. To her horror, a live hen was tied inside it. She'd been told by Brianag, who seemed to have endless knowledge of such things, that it was unlucky otherwise. Nor could the cradle touch the ground before it was put in its permanent place.

Brianag also cautioned her that she shouldn't talk to Elliot.

"He'll learn to talk before he walks," she warned. "He'll be a liar for sure."

Being unfamiliar with Scottish customs, Virginia would have liked to ask Macrath about some of them, but he'd disappeared. He not only avoided coming to her room, but rarely made a visit to the nursery in the last week. At least, he'd not come when she was there.

If she hadn't been afraid the answer was yes, she might have found the courage to ask him if he was avoiding her. Was it because of Paul? Was he adverse to touching her because of what she'd told him?

Suddenly, like she'd conjured him up from a wish, Macrath was there, standing in the doorway. He entered the room like a gust of fresh wind. As she did every time she saw him after an absence of a few moments or hours, she marveled at her reaction. Her pulse raced and her chest tightened.

"I went looking for you," he said. "I couldn't find you, and for a moment I felt almost as panicked as a grandmother."

She closed the book slowly.

"A panicked grandmother? The only grandmother at Drumvagen is Brianag, and I can't imagine her in a panic. Ever."

He grinned. "She likes you, you know," he said, coming to sit beside her on the companion chair. He reached over and held her hand loosely, the first time they'd touched in days.

"Does she? I like her as well. Once," she added, "I realized she wasn't nearly as frightening as she first appeared."

His laugh brightened the room. "She struck me that way, too. I wondered why she had such high recommendations. All she did was scowl at me, demand to know what I was going to do with Drumvagen, and then dictate terms of her hire."

"She's very intimidating, but no more so than you." She moved her feet over so he could put his foot up on the stool. He nudged her foot playfully, then rested his shoe next to hers.

He raised one eyebrow.

"You're very forbidding when you wish to be, Macrath Sinclair. You stand just so with your legs braced apart, and when you look at someone, it's like you're trying to see all the way inside them."

He grinned at her. "I had no idea you noted my appearance with such interest, your ladyship."

She glanced away.

Macrath stood and pulled her to her feet. He walked to the bookcase and pulled on the sconce, pulling the bookcase away from the wall.

"I've a yen to see the grotto," he said, his smile boyish and without shame. "Can I lure you to my lair?"

Holding out his hand, he smiled at her.

The last thing she needed to do was go to the grotto with Macrath. He'd be able to easily seduce her then. She'd might even seduce him first. No, the very idea was foolish.

She took a step back, shaking her head.

"Come with me," he said, his voice low.

She was prevented from answering by Hannah's appearance.

The maid halted at the doorway. "A secret passage, sir?"

Macrath glanced from her to Hannah, evidently understanding the moment had passed. Or perhaps it had never truly come.

"Yes," he said, closing the bookcase door. Giving Virginia a rueful smile, he bent and kissed her on the cheek.

"I'm to tell you the package has arrived, sir," Hannah said, placing the tray on the table between the two chairs with great concentration. She gave the task more attention than it required, meaning she felt as embarrassed at interrupting them as Virginia.

She'd almost gone to the grotto with Macrath. Surely she shouldn't be feeling so excited.

Without another word, Macrath left the room.

She and Hannah looked at each other.

"A package?"

The maid nodded. "Brianag was most determined I should say package. Not crate or present."

The mystery deepened when Macrath and Jack reappeared a few moments later, the two of them carrying a large wooden crate. She smiled at the young man, but his attention was on Hannah. Macrath called him back to the task, and Jack helped set the box down on one side of the library.

When they were done, he stood there smiling at Hannah, who smiled back.

Virginia bit back her sigh.

"I have a present for you," Macrath said after Hannah and Jack left the room. "I remembered how much you like to read broadsides."

"I could tell you it was to educate my mind," she said. "But you and I know such is not always the case."

"You were interested in the Atlantic cable."

She nodded. "I'm afraid that was the exception to the rule. I was fascinated with the most gruesome stories."

"Then you will love these," he said, using a small iron bar to open the top of the crate. "I had my sister send the last few months of broadsides."

She went to the corner, peering inside the crate. There, stacked in neat little bundles, were all sorts of broadsides and what her father would've called scandal sheets.

Macrath had done this for her.

"I always wondered," she said, picking up one of the stacks, "if the reason my father refused to consider you as a suitor was because you owned a newspaper."

"I take it he was not in favor of them."

"He was excoriated by reporters. When he became interested in politics, they held him to account more strictly than he'd expected. They were always asking questions, and he was always trying to avoid them."

"He was the only man I was willing to beg."

She glanced at him, feeling her chest tighten.

"I never got the chance," he said.

She looked away, occupying herself by trying to untie the rope binding one bundle. She didn't want to weep today. She didn't want to think of the girl she'd been a few years ago. Had it only been a few years? Why, then, did it feel like a lifetime?

"Perhaps if he'd agreed and you and I had married," she said, "we would have become disinterested with each other."

"I can't imagine that happening, can you?"

"It isn't wise to want to change the past."

"No," he said, "but perhaps wishes can change the future."

She looked over at him. He was smiling at her, his gaze intent.

Their time was coming to an end. Surely he knew it as well.

Her absence from London could be explained by the fact she was recuperating from smallpox. But if she were gone too many more weeks, people would start to wonder, to speculate among themselves. Even as reclusive as she'd been, she was still the Countess of Barrett and people talked.

She wasn't concerned as much about society as she was Lawrence's cousin. He would not hesitate to question her remaining in Scotland. Perhaps he'd even demand to see Elliot.

"Thank you," she said. "For the broadsides."

He nodded, placing his hand atop hers.

"Virginia—" he began.

She shook her head, so close to tears at the moment that she wouldn't be able to remain composed, regardless of what he said.

She stood on her tiptoes, kissed him softly on the cheek, then turned and left the room before he could stop her.

Chapter 29

Virginia returned from the nursery to find another gift in her sitting room.

Not content with giving her a crate of broadsides, Macrath had sent her a shawl yesterday, along with a note saying he'd purchased it from a woman in Kinloch Village renowned for her skill with the soft wool from Drumvagen sheep. The day before that it was a bouquet of heather and other late summer flowers, bunched together with pine sprigs and oak leaves. *To remind you of Drumvagen Woods,* he'd written.

This gift, however, was a rolled paper, tied with a simple string.

"Was there a note?" she asked.

Hannah sat in the chair beside the window, intent on adding white cuffs and collars to all Virginia's mourning dresses. She bit off the thread with her teeth and shook her head.

Slowly, Virginia unrolled the paper to find it was a design. She traced the lines, realizing it was a plan for something at Drumvagen, to be built directly behind the house.

"It's for the rose garden," Hannah said, startling her.

The maid had come to stand beside her and was peering at the plans.

"How do you know that?" she asked.

Hannah's cheeks grew pink. "Someone told me," she said.

"A rose garden?"

"Macrath knows you like roses," Hannah said.

They were standing in a room specifically decorated with her in mind. Roses were prolific in the upholstery fabric, not to mention the potpourri scenting the air.

He'd gone too far. Entirely too far. He couldn't keep doing such things, reducing her almost to tears with a simple gesture.

She rolled up the plans and tied them with the string, leaving them on the round table in the middle of the room.

Instead of returning to the nursery, she headed for the stairs.

The last two nights had been fitful ones, with Elliot waking every hour. She'd been desperate to calm him but nothing had worked. Not a warm bath or walking him, or even singing to him.

Brianag had been summoned by either Mary or Agatha, she wasn't sure which. The housekeeper had taken one look at her son, nodded with a jerk of her chin and pronounced the child needing a teethin' bannock. An hour later Brianag returned, producing a biscuit in the shape of a ring. When Virginia started to ask about it, Brianag placed her finger on her lips and shook her head.

The four of them watched as Elliot reached out, grabbed the ring and started to gnaw on it. When it was broken, Brianag gave her a piece, then shared the other pieces with Mary and Agatha. They all ate their pieces under Brianag's watchful eye. The taste reminded Virginia of oatmeal cooked too long.

"He'll sleep now," Brianag said, watching as Elliot gummed the last of the treat. "The bannock takes away the pain of teething."

To Virginia's surprise, Elliot did sleep, which was why, rather than returning to the nursery, she escaped outside for a little fresh air and solitude.

Drumvagen was unique, being sandwiched between the coast, a river, and woodland. She'd made it as far as the river, but this time she climbed to the top of the hill, standing on its crest and surveying the view framed by tall sycamores.

From there she could see Kinloch Village and its houses clinging like baby possums to the hills overlooking the harbor.

Below was the river, stretching wide and blue, undulating through the glen. At the base of the hill was a gate leading to an arched stone bridge weathered green and gray.

The storm of the night before had washed the world clean. Sunlight shone like lace through the emerald leaves, danced along the river, and glimmered on the ocean waves.

For years she'd lived in a city, missing the land and forest around Cliff House. As a child she heard the sigh of the wind through the branches at night. During the day she went into the woods and sat silent, listening to the life around her. At times she'd even escaped from her governesses, pretending not to hear their annoyed calling.

How had she tolerated London all this time?

The bridge appeared to have been carved from one large piece of stone. She strolled across, hesitating at the arched top, staring down into the rushing waters below. What an enchanting place this was. What a glorious kingdom Macrath was creating.

Elliot was part of his family, and yet he was—as far

as the world was concerned—the eleventh Earl of Barrett, with all its rights and privileges.

He'd be schooled in how to behave, how to act in every situation. He'd memorize ranks, learn Lawrence's family history, become the head of the family. One day he'd be compelled to marry, just as Lawrence had, to protect a title.

Elliot was only an infant, but she could almost see him in the various stages of his life. A boy, educated by a tutor who was a great deal kinder than any of her governesses had been. Later, he'd go away to school, to Lawrence's alma mater. How would she bear the separation? He'd be tall, with black hair and blue eyes, and all the girls would look at him when he entered a room.

He'd never know anything of Scotland.

He'd be as regimented as she'd been in England, without ever having experienced the freedom of being unnoticed at Cliff House.

He'd never know his father was a unique man, one who'd created his own life rather than being handed a title he inherited. He'd never know he was the scion of a clan, the heir to an empire, one crafted from intelligence, determination, and a little luck.

He'd never realize his father's eyes lit up on seeing him, that Macrath often held Elliot in his arms, staring down into his face with wonder.

Perhaps she could find a way to bring him back to Scotland periodically.

Macrath would never agree to losing his son for any length of time.

She turned back to Drumvagen, the beautiful day doing nothing for her sudden disheartened mood. As she walked, she glimpsed a flash of white through the trees. Curious, she followed the sight.

The sounds of birds faded, but other noises took their

place: her soft footfalls, the crunch of leaves blanketing the ground. Beneath the leaves was moist earth, the scent of it heavy in the air. Mushrooms clung to the trunks of the lichen-draped trees.

The air grew cooler, the light more filtered.

Suddenly, she was in a clearing. A gazebo stood there, painted white with delicate frescoes carved on its sides, a bronze statue of a stag mounted atop its cupola.

She could imagine such a lovely structure at Cliff House, or even a park in London, but not here in the Scottish countryside, surrounded by towering trees and the silence of Drumvagen Wood.

Was it used for hunting? Or simply to lure a forest visitor to rest and reflect on the surrounding beauty?

She climbed the three steps and perched on one of the cunning ledges built into the structure. Here was the perfect place for contemplation and reverie. Here she could sit and wonder at the complications of her life, most of them caused by her own actions.

She was the architect of her own misery.

She heard a rustling sound, almost like something walking through the thick undergrowth of leaves.

Standing, she waited, and when Macrath appeared, she almost laughed.

"I thought you a stag," she said, "and I was right."

"Were you, now?" he asked, smiling at her. "You found the gazebo."

"Did you build it?" she asked.

"No, it was one of the few structures finished before the owner abandoned Drumvagen."

"Was it always called Drumvagen or did you rename it like you did your ship?" she asked, sitting again.

"The name is several centuries old, I understand." He took the steps, looking around him.

"Are you taking a break from your work?"

He sat beside her.

"I was," he said. "We had a small issue with the fly-wheel. I thought it was going to come off and roll right into the ocean."

She reached out and touched his arm, stroking the fabric of his shirt, feeling the muscles beneath.

"You will be careful, won't you?"

He studied her, his look so strange she wondered if she'd done something wrong.

"I can't remember the last time someone worried about me."

"Surely that's not true. What about your sisters? I know Ceana was very concerned about your voyage to Australia."

He smiled. "It's a different kind of concern," he said. "With Mairi, it's her unquenchable need to run my life. In Ceana's case, she's always been a mother hen." He smiled. "She'll make a wonderful mother."

The most recent letter from Ceana had come with the news she'd given birth to a healthy baby girl. Elliot had a cousin, one he could never recognize.

"Perhaps my worry is warranted," she said, forcing her thoughts away from their dilemma. "The first time I came to Drumvagen, there were puffs of smoke coming from the cottage."

"It wasn't intentional," he said with a smile. "Why are you here? Are you communing with the badgers and the foxes?"

"Actually, I haven't seen any animals. I should like to see a fox, I think. We used to have foxes near Cliff House. I don't believe I've ever been close to a badger, though."

"That's a good thing," he said, stretching out his legs. "They're not at all sociable, especially when they feel cornered."

"Like Brianag."

His laughter caused some nearby birds to suddenly abandon their perch and fly skyward.

"Do I have problems in my household?"

"No, you don't," she said. "I'm a guest. I wouldn't dare to offer a suggestion or a criticism."

He looked away to where the forest deepened in color until it was nearly a solid wall of emerald green.

"You know that you, above all other people, have the power to say anything. Or do anything," he added.

She didn't want the power. She didn't, above all, deserve it.

"Have I ever told you how much I love your voice?" She looked at him, holding his intent gaze. "It's your Scottish accent."

His smile dawned slowly, became a wondrous thing lighting something inside her.

"Sic as ye gie, sic wull ye get."

She frowned. "What did you just say?"

"It's the dialect around here," he said. "I'm still learning it, good Edinburgh lad as I am. I said you only get out of life what you put in, one of Brianag's homilies. And there's always 'muckle wad aye hae mair.' Those who have a lot always want more. I hear that one a great deal."

"Say something else," she said, smiling.

"I could speak the Gaelic, but I'll tell you things I learned in Edinburgh," he said. "I was a precocious youngster."

"I can imagine the girls discovered you early," she said.

Would he have noticed her if she had grown up in Edinburgh with him? Would they have been fast friends? Would she have believed in him? She thought the answer was yes to all those questions.

"I learned, too, 'Never marry for money. You can borrow it cheaper.'"

"Wise advice," she said as he leaned forward to kiss her cheek.

She should stop him now. They should be reasonable about this. They shouldn't be kissing, especially when he had a teasing look in his eye.

She placed her hands on either side of his face. "Macrath," she said. Just his name, but it was warning enough.

He placed his hands atop hers and smiled down at her.

At that moment she knew she was lost.

"'They talk of my drinking but never my thirst.'"

Like she thirsted for him? No, she wouldn't say such a thing aloud.

"'Be slow in choosing a friend, but slower in changing him,'" he said, unfastening the top button of her bodice.

She slapped his hand. "Macrath Sinclair, we're in the middle of the woods."

"Ah, but we're in the middle of the woods alone," he said. "'Fools look to tomorrow. Wise men use today.'"

"Still, is it entirely proper?"

He tipped his head back and laughed.

She was too aware of him, each separate nerve and muscle attuned to his presence. Her skin was tight. Her heart beat so rapidly it felt like a drum inside her chest. Her palms dampened while her mouth was too dry. She wanted to weep while she danced for joy, and wasn't that ridiculous?

She was going to catch fire if he kept looking at her. He crooked a finger and she leaned toward him, surrendering her mouth to his. He kissed her slowly. Extending his tongue, he touched the tip of hers then withdrew, teasing her, taking her breath and causing her heart to race.

The warmth inside her suddenly swelled, becoming a tide of need.

"'Willful waste makes woeful want.'"

"We shouldn't be wasteful," she said, barely able to speak.

A noise startled her. She froze, her hands on his shoulders. "What was that?"

"A fox or badger," he said, trailing kisses down her throat.

She pulled back. It wasn't a fox or a badger. Instead, it had sounded like footsteps on leaves.

She pressed her hand against his chest.

"Would you like me to go see?" he asked. "Just to reassure you?"

She nodded. "It's probably not necessary," she said, feeling foolish.

He smoothed his knuckles over her cheek. "I don't want you worried," he said.

He bent and kissed the tip of her nose.

"I'll be right back," he said.

She watched him walk away. How could a man be as attractive from the rear as he was facing her? His shoulders were broad beneath the white shirt, his back tapering to a lean waist, long legs, and beautiful derriere. His neck fascinated her, as did the shape of his head, his arms, even his large hands. What didn't intrigue her about Macrath Sinclair?

He had such energy. Surely everyone knew he was a different sort of person the minute he walked into a room. Macrath was a magical being, someone who'd decided on his course in life and would do everything in his power to reach his goals.

Macrath Sinclair was not a normal man or an average one.

Who was she to think she could resist him?

Because he would have stepped away the moment she asked. He would have kissed her cheek and left her. He would have smiled and walked away.

Why was it so impossible to refuse him?

How much easier when they remembered their hurt rather than the passion between them.

She should stand right now, leave this place and return to Drumvagen. Instead, what she truly wanted was for him to love her. Perhaps for the last time.

If he had any sense at all, he wouldn't have sought her out, knowing what happened when he got too close to Virginia. Macrath's mind simply relinquished any will to his body. He wanted her desperately, and all the pent-up celibacy of the last year strained to be released.

The fact he hadn't bedded her in the last week was a damn miracle. Right now he was tired of being superhuman.

"There's nothing there," he said, returning to the gazebo. "Perhaps a curious hawk. Or a rabbit, hiding in the leaves."

Her smile was a beautiful thing, moving him to place a kiss on her forehead. He wished he could stop time, freeze them both in tender foreplay.

She pulled away. Before he could marshal his arguments why he should continue to kiss her, she startled him by walking to the back of the gazebo, sitting, and starting to unfasten the rest of the buttons on her bodice.

He came and sat beside her, replacing her hands with his.

She didn't speak or dissuade him, for which he was grateful. Instead, she smiled at him again, making him dumbstruck with acute lust and love at the sight of her.

Lowering his head, he placed a kiss at the base of her throat, then trailed a line of kisses down to the top of her black edged shift.

She shivered in response, another reaction for which he was thankful.

He possessed a mechanical mind, but the busk of her corset almost defeated him. Finally, it separated, allowing him to see her shift, and below, the shadow of her glorious breasts.

"I remember loving you in the middle of the day," he said. "In the bright sunlight."

She looked away, and he turned her face with a finger to her chin.

"There's nothing to be embarrassed about, Virginia. I thought you were magnificent. It's one of my favorite memories."

Her cheeks bloomed with color. "I like to think Elliot was conceived then."

Bending, he placed his lips around one nipple, gently sucking.

"They're larger," he said, drawing one fingertip over the slope of a breast and down to the nipple.

"An effect of bearing your son," she said.

Such a comment should not have had the effect of hardening him even further, but strangely, it did. He wanted her now. He wanted to simply widen her legs, loosen his confining trousers, and enter her. He'd hold her, looking into her eyes as he buried himself to the hilt.

Instead, he bit back his impatience and looked away, concentrating on the thick growth of trees until he could control the lust surging through his body.

Her fingers danced along his jaw, traced the edge of his bottom lip, teasing until he looked at her.

"Won't you kiss me?"

"I'm trying to be restrained," he said.

She leaned forward. "Don't," she whispered. She smiled at him almost pityingly and placed her fingers against the placket of his trousers, pressing gently.

"Not as restrained as you think," she said. "I feel the same, only my desire doesn't show."

His smile answered hers. "Not true," he said, reaching out and gently flicking an aroused nipple. "It just shows in different ways. Shall I show you where else?"

Her eyes widened.

Spreading her legs, he moved between them, a hand on each stockinged knee.

He reached in to the slit of her pantaloons, palming her. "You're damp," he said.

She nodded, her smile having vanished a few seconds earlier.

"If I were to move my fingers just so," he said, pairing the action to the words, "I'd find you swollen and sensitive."

She licked her lips.

One finger trailed through her intimate folds to the opening, stroking softly. She closed her eyes, biting her lips. He coaxed a kiss from her, inhaled her breathy sighs, and spoke into her mouth.

"If I were to enter you now," he said, gently inserting a finger into her, "you might gasp aloud. Or feel a surge of lust."

Her eyes flew open. "Do you feel lust for me?"

How could she ask that question?

"Endlessly," he said. "Eternally. When I was sailing to Australia, when I was sailing home."

"But not in Australia?"

The question startled a laugh from him.

"Perhaps I met an attractive aborigine," he said, "and she caused all thoughts of you fly from my mind."

She drew back, frowning at him again. "What's an aborigine? And why have you given me such a conundrum?"

"Why are we talking?" he countered. "When I could be inside you?"

Her face flamed brighter but her eyes sparkled.

"What conundrum?" he asked.

Her answer was breathless. "I wonder why you weren't

lusting after me in Australia, while I should be grateful you weren't. After all, I'm not entirely certain I should want you lusting after me."

"What a pity," he said, words nearly beyond him at the moment. "When it's evident to a blind man I do."

She kissed him without any further talk of aborigines or the propriety of lust.

Then, even thoughts faded beneath the sheer bliss of loving Virginia. When she moaned, he stood with her in his arms. Sweeping the leaves away with his foot, he placed her on the floor of the gazebo. Perhaps this wasn't the best place for a tryst, in the middle of the woods, but it was too far to Drumvagen.

He needed her now.

He wasn't certain whose moan indicated fulfillment first. All he knew was the world dimmed and receded. For a time there was only her and the knowledge he couldn't live without Virginia.

Stretching his legs out before him, Paul peered up at the canopy of leaves. Pity he'd never learned about trees. He'd no idea if he rested beneath an oak or a pine.

He'd picked a place not far from Drumvagen to have the carriage and coachman wait, but the day was too lovely not to take advantage of the sun and the solitude.

He leaned back against the trunk, closed his eyes and let himself drift off on a cloud of thought. He was waiting for William to return, and until he did, he would simply enjoy the sunny Scottish day.

"Begging your pardon, sir," William said, waking him from his semidoze.

He blinked open his eyes to find the younger man standing there, twisting his hat between his hands.

"Ah, you're back. What have you discovered? Any signs of the grotto?"

From what he'd learned in Kinloch Village, the grotto led directly into Drumvagen.

"No, sir. I couldn't get close enough to the beach. There were people around."

He nodded, not showing his surprise or displeasure.

Difficulty did not deter him.

Paul was under no illusion Virginia would want to come with him. He'd been right in front of her and she'd never seen him. After a month or two at sea, however, she'd understand he was the right man for her. At first she wouldn't be so compliant.

William looked away, his mouth twisting. "There's something, sir."

He stood. "Well, what is it?"

"The lady?"

"What about her?" Paul asked, adopting a disinterested air as he brushed the leaves from his trousers. He glanced at the younger man, surprised to see William's face was flushed.

"Well, what is it? If you have something to say, say it."

"I saw a lady like you talked about. Strange blue eyes and black hair."

"Yes?"

"She's a bit of an itch, isn't she?"

Paul stared at him. "Why would you say that?'

"She's dabbing it up with the toff, ain't she? Acting like a Judy, she was, out in the open and all."

"Was she?"

William's speech took Paul back to his youth and a host of unpleasant memories.

"Him putting his Nebuchadnezzar out to grass right there where anyone could see."

"Where was this?"

"In the woods. They've got a little building there and I saw 'em."

"Thank you, William," he said, keeping his voice calm.

"You still set on her, sir?"

He was still set on her. But if it was Virginia who William had seen, she'd have to be taught she didn't cheat on him. Not with the Scotsman. Not with anyone.

"We'll come back tomorrow," he said. He would return every day for the rest of his life if he needed. He'd find this damn grotto and a way into Drumvagen. He'd find a way to get to her.

She was his, and he'd prove it to her.

Chapter 30

Brianag's distinctive voice came through the door, followed by a maid's laugh. Despite the housekeeper's glower, laughter was a common sound at Drumvagen.

Virginia was in Macrath's library, a room she'd visited every day since the arrival of the crate of broadsides. When she wasn't in the nursery, she was here, at least as long as Macrath was occupied with his new ice machine.

When she questioned him about why he worked so hard, he smiled at her, reached over, kissed her, and said, "I'm creating an empire."

She only nodded, remembering their conversations in London. He'd told her about Drumvagen then, but in her mind she'd seen it as a black fortress, a formidable stronghold. Instead, it was a palatial estate set in a storybook setting.

The last few days had been enchanted ones. She pretended she belonged at Drumvagen, that it was her home. Her son, as its heir, was cosseted, and she, his mother, treated almost the same. Even Brianag had stopped grumbling around her and sent her a gap-toothed grin from time to time.

Macrath was the most enchanted part of it all, a prince

in this castle. He made her laugh, and brought her to tears with his tenderness. They slept close to each other, and when she woke in the middle of the night, he was there when she wanted to touch him.

At dawn he loved her until the sky grew pink and the seabirds started their morning squawk.

This morning she'd been visited by her monthlies, which meant she'd escaped the consequences of this hedonistic week. No doubt this time of the month was the reason she was also so tearful. She could weep at the mention of the weather, a smile from Mary, or a question from Brianag.

Hannah noted her mood, but except for a quick look from time to time, hadn't questioned her.

After cutting the rope binding the next bundle of broadsides, she grabbed half the stack and returned to her chair. How much easier to forget about her own life and read about the terrible story of the midwife who confessed, on her deathbed, to killing a dozen babies. Or the song written about the murder of poor Bessie Smith.

She started to read, caught up in the story.

> Come all false hearted young men and
> 　　listen to my song.
> It's of a dreadful murder that lately has
> 　　been done;
> On the body of a damsel fair, the truth I
> 　　will unfold,
> The bare relation of this deed will make
> 　　your blood run cold.

The poor girl had gone into service and been courted by a young gentleman. On discovering she was with child, he'd lured her to a grove and killed her despite her pleas of mercy for their unborn baby. The young gentleman had slit her throat and now awaited hanging for the crime.

Saddened for the girl, she placed the broadside face-down on the table.

What would Macrath have done if she'd written him while he was in Australia? If he'd discovered she was with child, he would have whisked her from London and installed her here in Drumvagen as his wife.

Yet he'd never once mentioned marriage to her in all the weeks she'd been here.

Did he still distrust her?

There was so much left unsaid between them. She had never once told him how much she loved him. He had never said the words to her.

They lived in the *now* of their moments, afraid to recall the past, and with the future so uncertain neither mentioned it.

She lay her head against the back of the chair. Did it matter what he felt about her? Even if he confessed he adored her, what difference did it make?

Right or wrong, she'd created a birthright for Elliot. He was the eleventh Earl of Barrett, with all its attendant rights and honors. He could sit in the House of Lords. He would have her father's fortune at his command.

Could she strip it from him?

He's a Scot. Better a Scot than an earl. She could almost hear Macrath's voice.

She smiled. How arrogant Macrath was. How certain he was right in all things. Yet he'd had to be hadn't he? From the time he was a boy, he'd had to help support his family. He'd done that and more.

He wanted a clan, the Sinclair Clan, known throughout Scotland for their achievements.

Elliot was Macrath's firstborn son. How could she take

the child away from the man? Look how he was with Elliot. He consulted with her and Brianag about his diet, was concerned if Elliot sneezed, and delighted in his every smile.

How could she be faced with this choice? Why hadn't she thought about this moment, this predicament?

If Cliff House hadn't been sold after her father's death, she would have retreated there, taking Elliot with her. For a few years she would have hidden from the world, or at least from society.

She couldn't remain at Drumvagen. Worse, Macrath hadn't asked her to stay. As far as he was concerned, she could leave today as long as she didn't take Elliot.

A soft knock on the door blessedly interrupted her thoughts. She called out, and Hannah entered, a silver salver in her hand.

"Your ladyship," she said, "they've returned from Kinloch with the post. There's a letter for you."

Hannah presented the salver, bobbing a curtsy as if to remind her she was the Countess of Barrett. She felt less like a countess and more of a sham, a fraud, a cheat, and a liar.

The black-bordered letter rested on the tray, daring her to pick it up and open it.

What would Hannah say if she told her to take it away and destroy it? She didn't want to open it. She recognized Ellice's handwriting, but rather than anticipation she only felt a cold prickle of dread.

How could she possibly cope with any more bad news?

Slowly, she reached out her hand and picked up the letter, thanking Hannah. The other woman glanced at her curiously but didn't say anything as she turned and left the room.

For a minute, maybe two, she stared at the front of the

envelope before opening the letter and smoothing her fingers over the paper.

> *Dearest Sister,*
>
> *I trust this letter will find you in good health and recovering. We have heard so little from you of late it is with misgiving I write you now.*
>
> *Will you be returning to London soon? Or has your health worsened? Is my dearest nephew well?*
>
> *Could you write and let me know when you'll return? I know our mother's cares would be eased by your presence. She has taken to sitting in the garden on a fine day, staring off into the distance. She will not hear talk of Eudora, not even to gently recall her. I worry about her so, and have no one to talk to of my concerns.*
>
> *Lawrence's cousin has visited, but Mother will not see him. She will not see anyone, I fear.*
>
> *The staff seemed subdued by our loss. I have tried to remember all Mother's lessons on economy, but she has not looked at the household accounts for weeks now. Without Albert here, I feel myself inadequate to the task. I would appeal for help from Paul, but he left us unexpectedly recently, having come into a fortune. Hosking is much missed here, as is Hannah.*
>
> *Please, dearest Virginia, come home. I do so need someone to talk to, and I miss you and dear Elliot.*
>
> > *Your sister,*
> > *Ellice*

Tears filmed Virginia's vision. Lifting her head, she defied them to fall.

She hadn't mourned Eudora properly. She'd never once thought of Ellice's plight, or her mother-in-law's deep grief. Instead, she'd been too immersed in her own misery to see the needs of anyone else.

She felt so sorry for her sister-in-law. Enid was evidently still grieving for Eudora, to the extent of forgetting about her other child.

Ellice's comments about Jeremy, Lawrence's cousin, disturbed her as well. What could he want? What could he suspect, for that matter?

She had to return to London. Somehow she had to make this right.

What could she possibly say to Macrath?

"I love you. I love you and I'm going to hurt you. More than I hurt you before. I'm going to turn my back on Drumvagen and you, and I won't be back again. I beg you not to acknowledge Elliot as your heir. I beg you to let this ruse go on. Find someone else to love. Find the woman who will help you reach your dreams, Macrath. Be happy, my darling."

No, she couldn't imagine giving him that speech or leaving Elliot at Drumvagen. She wanted Macrath to love her. She wanted to remain here with him. She wanted Elliot to laugh, run, and explore the woods. She wanted him to point out a buzzard to Macrath and demand an answer for what it was. Why was the sky blue? Why was the grass the same shade as the trees in the forest?

She wanted to laugh with Macrath, discuss politics, read broadsides from Edinburgh, and argue over whatever came to mind. She wanted to share his big, wide bed, feel his arms around her at night, and know, somehow, that around him she was a different woman. One who was courageous, daring, and never afraid.

Was it too terrible to want to live her life with him?

Yet she had to leave. She had to leave Drumvagen and return to London with Elliot.

Her only recourse was to involve the authorities. Elliot was her son and Macrath had no legal right to keep him here. Perhaps being the Countess of Barrett would come in useful for the first time.

Involving the authorities, however, would put a wedge between her and Macrath, one that would never be removed.

Standing, she went to the bellpull and tugged on it. She would give Hannah instructions to pack their belongings, and tell Mary and Agatha it was time to return to London.

Only then would she go to Macrath and tell him of her decision. A conversation she dreaded but one that had to happen if she ever hoped to be free.

Paul stood on a hill overlooking the ocean. All around him were clumps of tall green and brown grasses clinging to the edge. Below him the earth was scooped out as if by a giant spoon. At the base were rocks, gradually giving way to toast-colored sand.

"Are you certain you understood?" he asked, looking down at the beach.

"Yes, sir," William said. "The grotto's to the left. Down that bit."

He was doubtful the other man had gotten the directions correctly. The beach was more rock than sand, ending in a formation of stone covered by lichen on one end and an outcropping of rock at the other.

"How do we get down?" Paul asked.

William shook his head.

Not a font of information, was he?

Was he supposed to slide down?

He turned to ask William if he'd thought to bring a rope and saw he'd moved a few feet away. "Here, sir," William said, pointing to a divot in the earth.

Paul peered over the edge. Not as bad a descent as he'd feared.

"You stay here. Lower the basket once I'm on the beach," he said, afraid the bottle inside might break during his descent.

William nodded and squatted on the edge of the grass, the basket in his hands.

Paul disliked nature, or perhaps it was simply the absence of civilization. He was a city man, born and bred.

He slid down the hill, annoyed it was the only way to reach the beach. Once on the rocks, he called up to William, who lowered the basket to him.

Now, to find Virginia.

"We're leaving?" Hannah asked, her eyes wide. "We're returning to London?"

Hannah had never questioned her instructions.

Virginia folded the letter, placed it on the table, and studied her maid's thinned lips and slumped shoulders.

"Have you developed a fondness for Scotland, Hannah?"

"Drumvagen is a very pretty place," her maid said. "Although I've been told the winters can be fierce."

"You knew we weren't going to remain here."

Hannah nodded slowly, staring down at the floor.

"Is there a reason you don't want to leave?"

"No, your ladyship," Hannah said softly.

"You and I have gone through a great deal together."

Hannah glanced at her, then away.

"You know my secrets, Hannah, and I trust them with you."

Hannah nodded.

"I can't stay at Drumvagen, but there's no reason why you should not if you wish."

Hannah took a deep breath, exhaled it on a sigh. "No, your ladyship. My place is with you."

"Then we will both miss Drumvagen," she said. And the men who lived here. "If you'll also inform Hosking," she added when Hannah turned to leave.

The maid nodded, hesitating beside the bookshelf. "Is there really a secret passage?" she asked.

Macrath himself had said there was no secrecy about the grotto. Otherwise, she would have deflected Hannah's curiosity.

Virginia walked to where she stood. "Would you like to see it?"

She went to the door, opened it by pulling the sconce straight down. Once the bookcase was ajar, she and Hannah pushed it open.

"I've never seen anything like it," Hannah said, peering inside.

Virginia grabbed the lantern from the hook inside the passage, lit it and held it aloft. "Would you like to see where it leads?" she asked, daring herself.

Hannah smiled. "I would. It will be a grand adventure."

"Our last at Drumvagen," she said.

She was grateful for Hannah's company traveling down the long passageway. The last time she was here, she'd been desperate with fear.

"Oh, your ladyship, it's magnificent!" Hannah said when they reached the opening to the grotto.

The bright afternoon was the perfect time to first view the stone room. Sun poured in through the chimney hole. The arched window revealed a view of a sparkling sea and glittering sand.

Virginia extinguished the lantern, set it on the stone

floor and glanced away from the window embrasure. She didn't want to recall those moments with Macrath. Not now, when she was leaving him.

Leaving Hannah to wonder at the marvel of nature, and strolled to the other entrance. She'd never been there before, had never thought to explore this short passageway. From there, she could see the beach, and beyond, the endless water.

The ocean was a patient predator, waiting, always waiting. The tide rolled in like a hungry tongue, licking at the sand, tasting the toes of her shoes. She backed away from the foam. The sea had a voice, or maybe it was the wind, tasting of salt, flicking her hair into her eyes. She pulled the loose strands away, tucked them behind her ear while staring out at the gray green Moray Firth, and beyond to the North Sea.

Macrath had said the ocean made him feel insignificant in comparison. How could he ever think that? He was the Sinclair, the Devil of Drumvagen, the taskmaster and genius who had vowed to create an empire when he was sixteen and done so by the time he was thirty.

Macrath was an entity to himself, a man who had created his life out of an idea, a dream. How foolish she was to think he would simply do what she wished because she wished it.

She didn't want to summon the authorities. She didn't want to appear before a magistrate, or whatever the Scots called their judiciary. She especially didn't want to cause a scandal, one that would reverberate to England.

Hopefully, the threat of what she was willing to do would be enough to convince Macrath to release Elliot.

The tide was like a heartbeat, the sound of it rhythmic and almost hypnotizing. Gripping her skirts, she turned to the right, daring herself to step out over the sand, as close to the ocean as she'd ever been. Here, there was no vessel beneath her feet, only the tide lapping at her shoes.

She felt almost nauseous as she kept walking, hating the fact she was afraid of the ocean. Hating, too, the coming confrontation with Macrath.

Who was she to dare the ocean? What did she expect would happen, that the seas would part, the tide would roll back and allow her to walk on dry sand?

Who was she to dare Macrath?

At the end of the narrow beach was a rough black and brown arch, created by centuries of battering by the waves and tinged green where lichen clung to it in dramatic defiance. She headed toward it, her footsteps soundless on the sand.

When she could walk no farther, she turned to head back, congratulating herself on this small demonstration of courage.

"How fortunate I'm a patient man, even though my patience was wearing thin. I'd almost decided to lay siege to Drumvagen. But here you are, coming to me."

Chapter 31

Virginia froze, then forced herself to turn.

Paul Henderson stood there, his face made even more attractive with his smile. Anyone looking at him would think he was a genial man, unless you looked in his eyes and realized there was no humor there.

"What are you doing here?" she asked.

"I've come to rescue you."

She frowned. "I don't need to be rescued."

"I think you do."

Paul took a couple of steps toward her, which was when she realized there was nowhere to escape. The outcropping of rock was behind her. The sea was to her right. A tall embankment was to her left. He was between her and the grotto, and it didn't look like he was going to give way.

"I've come to take you away from this place, Virginia. I've booked passage to America."

She took a step back. "I'm not going anywhere with you and certainly not America."

Even though they weren't far from the house, she was still alone with him. She most definitely didn't want to be alone with Paul Henderson.

"I planned this out carefully," he said. "By the time we get to America, you'll have changed your mind. You'll be with child, and grateful to be my wife."

"Your ladyship?"

She glanced beyond him to see Hannah standing there, halfway between Paul and the grotto entrance. Before Virginia could shout a warning to her maid, Paul was after her. With the back of his hand, he struck Hannah, knocking her to the sand. She was up in the next instant, and he hit her again, this time with his fist.

Virginia launched herself at Paul then, beating him on the back and screaming at him to stop.

He easily flicked her away as he struck Hannah once more. When the maid didn't rise, Paul grabbed Virginia by the arm, swinging her around until her back was against his chest.

"How protective you are, Virginia," he said, his breath rasping against her ear. "I can only hope you'll feel the same for me and for our children."

He dragged her closer to the base of the hill, bent down and opened a basket she hadn't seen until now. Throwing her to the sand, he knelt atop her chest. She struggled but was no match for his strength. When she would have screamed, he pressed a rag over her mouth and nose. She tossed her head from side to side, but he easily held her as he unstoppered a brown bottle and poured the contents on the cloth. The sickening sweet odor made her stomach roll.

He released her and stood. She told herself to move, to run, but she was suddenly adrift in a pleasant and frightening lassitude.

The last thing she noted was regret—that she hadn't been able to save Hannah or herself.

The flywheel of Macrath's new ice machine laboriously turned, gaining speed.

Jack and Sam's jubilation was vocal and well-deserved. They'd all put in long hours to get the design to work. The steam engine powering the flywheel was loud, and they'd thrown open the doors both in front and back. The noise, if not their celebration, was attracting Drumvagen's staff.

Macrath would have gladly celebrated with them had he not had something else on his mind.

How did he ask a woman to marry him when he was afraid her answer would be no? Twice, he'd come up with an appeal, and twice rejected it.

Perhaps he should simply fall back on the truth. She couldn't leave him. He couldn't allow it. He'd send Hosking back to London. Everyone in Kinloch Village would know not to give her aid or provide transportation. In other words, kidnap her and keep her here against her will.

He had not yet resorted to that. But he might, if he couldn't convince her otherwise.

Wasn't love supposed to make the world a better place?

His world had narrowed, compressed to two people—Virginia and Alistair. He didn't care about going to France or traveling to India. He didn't want to leave Drumvagen. If he had to travel, he'd take them with him.

Wasn't love supposed to make him happier?

Wasn't he supposed to be convivial? He didn't want to talk to Jack or Sam. He didn't want to hear Brianag's concerns or questions. He didn't want to greet a maid in the hallway or one of the young men he employed at Drumvagen. He felt like a thundercloud followed him wherever he went. He had never, even as a boy in the throes of poverty, been as gloomy a person as he was now.

He wanted to be with Virginia, talk to her, explain his

new ideas to her. He wanted to tell her about his plans for Drumvagen, for finishing the third floor. Did they need a ballroom? Did she want a conservatory?

Was love supposed to enhance the senses?

He could smell Virginia's perfume across the house. He could hear her soft footfalls on the upstairs carpet runner or the swish of her skirts as she slowly came down the stairs. Her throaty laughter lingered in his mind. He could feel her soft skin on his fingertips. He could too easily see her smile and the beauty of her eyes.

Except for those sensations, love made him miserable. Or perhaps the reason for his foul mood was the thought of living without the two of them. He could not consider life at Drumvagen without Virginia and Alistair. He couldn't foresee the rest of his life, stretching out over years and decades, without the woman he loved beside him. Or being with the child who sparked amazement and an over-whelming protectiveness in him.

All his life he'd been accused of being stubborn, and he had readily admitted it. But allowing Virginia to leave him wouldn't be obstinacy as much as stupidity. Somehow, he had to convince her to stay.

He couldn't keep her prisoner here, and that's what he was doing by refusing to allow her to take Alistair back to England.

Did he have the courage to offer her the freedom to choose? What if she chose to return to England? What if she left this afternoon, or tomorrow? He would have to take the chance. Otherwise, love became only a collection of letters, a word meaning nothing at all.

He'd have to be his most persuasive. Or, if that didn't work, he'd be charming. She'd always thought him charm-ing, although most people didn't. They thought him too abrupt, too direct—not understanding that time was an enemy to him. He wanted to get what he wanted without delay.

Jack suddenly turned his back on the open door and the crowd that had been attracted by the noise of the ice machine. His assistant moved out of the way, making a point of hiding behind the wall of the machine before peering out at the onlookers.

Macrath rounded the corner and stood with hand pressed against the metal sheath.

"Who are you looking for?" he asked Jack. "Or avoiding?"

His assistant glanced at him, face reddening.

Before he said a word, Macrath smiled. "A woman?"

Jack nodded, then looked toward the group staring up at the flywheel.

"I thought your mood due more to someone in Edinburgh. But it's closer to home?"

"Aye, sir. Or not."

He didn't know how to respond, so he kept silent.

"Women," Jack said. "They're confusing creatures."

Now that he could answer. "True," he said. "They are."

"She says she likes you and you make her smile." Jack glanced at him, his mouth twisted in a grimace. "Then, in the next instant, she's crying on your shoulder. What's a man to do?"

Macrath didn't know if he should offer commiseration, advice, or simply keep quiet.

It seemed quiet was the answer.

"She could leave any minute, sir. Then what am I to do? Go to London after her?"

"Hannah," he said, finally understanding.

Jack nodded. "Hannah."

"Does she know how you feel about her?"

"How can she, sir, when I've no idea myself?"

Macrath smiled. "You'd be surprised what they understand, Jack. Sometimes even before we know what's happening."

Did Virginia know how he felt about her?

"What I don't understand is why you're avoiding her."

"I've no sense around her, sir. I can't think. I can't speak more than a word at a time. My brain goes to jelly."

He hesitated, then gave Jack some advice. "Maybe you're afraid she won't feel the same."

"She might not."

Macrath nodded. "There's only one way of knowing, though, isn't there? She's not going back to London, Jack. That I can promise you."

Jack grinned, his color mounting as he glanced at the door.

"Go," Macrath said. "Find her and tell her how you feel."

He watched as Jack threw his gloves down on the workbench, then pushed through the people at the door.

Maybe he should follow his own advice.

He'd gone about this all wrong.

He'd open up his heart and tell her how he felt. He'd expose himself to her. Women liked that sort of thing, didn't they? Did it even matter what other women wanted? Virginia was the only woman he cared about. What did she want?

Forgiveness.

The thought rolled into his mind like a boulder and refused to budge. She wanted acceptance and understanding. If he gave those to her, maybe she'd also want him.

The second maid he'd stopped knew Virginia's whereabouts.

"I saw her go into the library, sir," she said, smiling brightly.

After thanking her, he entered the room, only to find it empty. He noticed the letter on the table and was tempted to read it but didn't, dismissing his curiosity in favor of Virginia's privacy.

The door to the grotto passage was ajar and the lantern missing from its hook inside the passage. Had Virginia taken it? For that matter, why had she gone to the grotto?

He smiled. Was she waiting for him?

She wasn't in the grotto, but the lantern was, resting on the stone floor beside the passage to the beach.

The wind bearded the waves with a white froth and pushed the tide higher onto the shore. The blazing afternoon sun heated the air, glinting off metallic bits in the rock formations.

The beach was narrow here. Why had Virginia come in this direction?

When he saw the crumpled figure, he started to run.

When she surfaced, Paul was smiling down at her, blotting her face with a handkerchief.

"There you are," he said. "I understand you might be feeling ill. An effect of the chloroform, coupled with the motion of the carriage."

She closed her eyes but the world didn't steady. She could still feel him touching her face and the movement of the wheels beneath her. She wanted to be at Drumvagen. She wanted to be standing on the beach watching the waves rolling in. The problems she had earlier, before she saw Paul, seemed so much easier to resolve than this situation.

"You have to take me back," she said. The words had to be pushed from her lips, seemed to hesitate there before leaping into the air. An effect of the chloroform?

"We're not going back to Drumvagen. Or to London, my dear. We're going to America. The two of us, together."

"I don't want to go anywhere with you," she said faintly, nausea sweeping through her.

"In America, people won't know you're the Countess of Barrett. They won't care. In America, I'm no longer a servant."

"People do care who you are," she said, keeping her eyes closed. Her sickness was easier to cope with if she didn't see his smiling, triumphant face. "People will care you abducted me."

"They'll never know. You see, by the time we get to America, you'll be carrying my child."

She blinked open her eyes, staring at the ceiling of the carriage. A movement to her left made her realize they weren't alone. A young man sat opposite them. She closed her eyes again, realizing the enormity of her situation. She didn't just have to fight Paul, but a stranger as well.

Dear God what was she going to do?

She wanted away from him, as far away as the confines of the carriage would allow. Slowly, she sat up, pushed herself into the corner and drew up her legs. Thrusting her hands over her skirts, she pressed down on the hoop to collapse it. She didn't want any part of her touching either man.

"Come, my dear, I know you're feeling the effects of the chloroform. I would have done something else if I had thought you would be amenable."

When he reached out for her, she batted his hands away and wedged herself into the corner even farther.

Please, God, let him leave her alone. Let him change his mind. Let him suddenly announce to the driver they were returning to Drumvagen.

"Why me? I've never given you any hint of affection. Why

would you think I would want to go with you anywhere?"

"I've never forgotten our night together," he said. "I remember how you kissed me. I knew, then, how you felt about me. Regardless of what you say now, Virginia, that was real and true."

"I thought you were my husband," she said.

"Except Lawrence couldn't abide you," he said. "When he offered you, I leapt at the chance."

She'd been reared to respect the dead, but at this moment she loathed Lawrence Traylor.

"He was a fool," she said. "A vengeful fool."

"Oh, I can't disagree," Paul said. He reached into the basket and withdrew a flask, offering it to her. "Just a little medicinal brandy."

She wasn't going to drink anything he offered her, for fear it would be drugged. When she turned her head away, he laughed.

"Lawrence allowed his emotions to get the better of him, I'm afraid. But then, so did I."

She glanced at him. "Even if those emotions aren't returned? How can you want a woman who wants nothing to do with you? What can I say to convince you?"

"Nothing. You see, Virginia, I've paid a price for you. You're my reward for years of struggle. For bowing and scraping and being endlessly subservient. I knew you were mine the minute the marriage was announced. It took Lawrence a few months to realize that."

Was he insane? From the glint in his eyes, she could almost think he was. How did one reason with insanity?

If he could viciously strike Hannah, what chance did she have with him?

Paul glanced at the window. "Ah, we're here," he said, turning to her. "I am sorry, my dear, but you can't be allowed to make a scene."

He reached for her. She beat at him, using her hands and feet, but he dragged her back over the seat. The other man handed him something and the cloth was suddenly over her face again, the chloroform sending her mind spiraling somewhere distant.

Hannah lay sprawled on the beach. For a moment Macrath didn't know if she lived, but a pulse beat sluggishly beneath his fingers.

"Hannah," he said, rage racing through him as he knelt on the sand, placing his hand gently beneath her head.

Her lips were bloody and her nose appeared broken.

Her eyes blinked open. "Sir."

He raised her a little until she was almost sitting, supporting her with one arm. Gently, he brushed the sand from her face. Had she been assaulted? Would she tell him, if so? He didn't want to leave her, but he needed to summon help.

Thank God Brianag had some skill at healing.

"Who did this to you?"

A bloodcurdling yell like the Highlanders of old split the air. He glanced over his shoulder to see Jack racing toward them, his feet kicking up clouds of sand.

Jack dropped to his knees beside Hannah, his hands trembling as they stretched toward her. He stopped inches from touching the girl, fingers curved around the shape of her face.

"Hannah. Oh, Hannah."

Tears streaked her face as she blinked up at Jack.

"Who did this to you?" he said.

"The countess—" she began.

"What about her?" Macrath asked. His rage disappeared. Instead, fear punched him in the chest. "What about her?"

Hannah grabbed his shirt. "The countess," she said. Each word took a week for her to utter. "He's taken her."

"Who's taken her?" Macrath asked

"Paul. Paul Henderson," she said slowly, enunciating each word around her bloody lips. "He's taken her, sir."

He nodded, outwardly calm while his mind raced. He'd have the fastest coach readied for the trip to London.

She gripped his shirt when he would have stood.

Patiently he listened, then altered his plans, hoping what she told him would lead him to saving Virginia.

When he would have lifted her, Jack shook his head, taking his place and gently raising Hannah into his arms, cradling her damaged face to his chest.

All the way back to the grotto, he heard Jack speaking, soft words to reassure her. He doubted Jack could take away Hannah's pain as he promised, but he understood the need for the other man to believe it.

Sometimes a man had to pretend to be powerful even when he wasn't.

In the grotto, before they sought out Brianag and endured the questioning sure to come, he turned to Jack.

"I'm going after him. You'll look after Hannah?"

"No sir," Jack said. "I'll leave Hannah to Brianag. I'd be in the way. But I'll see to the bastard myself."

Jack had aged in the last ten minutes. Gone was the lad he'd known, and in his place a man with a face as stony as the rock formation around them. His gaze was direct, his rage barely checked.

"I'm afraid you'll have to wait until I've had my turn, Jack," he said, clasping the other man on the shoulder.

Jack nodded. "You can have him first, sir. But I get him next."

"**M**acrath?" Virginia groggily asked, blinking her eyes.

She was being carried somewhere. Above her was the

wide blue sky, seabirds circling. Was she at Drumvagen? She closed her eyes as a wave of nausea swept through her.

After a moment she opened them again to see tall masts filled with sails.

Sails?

Was she dreaming? Was she back aboard the ship carrying her to England? No, that made no sense.

Why was Macrath carrying her? Had she fainted?

"You'll have to forgive my bride," he was saying. "She's had a bit too much excitement today, I'm afraid. Could someone show me the way to our cabin?"

She turned her head. That wasn't Macrath's voice. She blinked up at the man. Nor was that Macrath's face.

"Paul?"

She tried to raise her hand, but it felt too heavy.

"Don't worry, my dear," he said. "We'll soon have you somewhere you can rest."

"What am I doing here?" she asked, dizzy again. A sour taste lingered in the back of her throat and her tongue was swollen and dry.

He smiled down at her, turned sideways and spoke to someone, before descending a series of steps with her in his arms. She closed her eyes as the sky vanished and a timbered ceiling appeared.

What was she doing here? She couldn't remember. The lack of memory frightened her almost as much as he did, crooning to her.

"I'll take care of you, my dear," he said. "All you need to do is rest now."

He turned sideways again and the ceiling changed once more. She moved her head to find it was a room, dominated by a wide bed placed up against a wall. A cabin, she corrected herself. If she was aboard ship, it was a cabin, and the bed was a bunk.

What was she doing aboard ship?

What was she doing with Paul?

Elliot. Where was Elliot?

"What did you do to me?" she asked, not surprised to hear her slurred words. Talking seemed to be a difficult task. Not simply speaking, but forming the words in her mind.

A bottle. A rag. He'd put the rag over her face and she'd smelled something overpoweringly sweet. Simply recalling it made her nauseous.

Chloroform. He'd given her chloroform not once but twice.

"You tried to kill me," she said as he placed her on the bunk.

"Of course I didn't," he said pleasantly. "I merely had to convince you to come with me, my dear."

She tried to slap his hands away when he started to unfasten the buttons at her neck, but she was so weak she couldn't stop him. To her horror, he continued all the way down her dress.

"No," she said.

"Just rest, Virginia," he said. "I've no intention of taking you when you're unconscious. I want you to know who I am and remember our loving."

She didn't want to remember him touching her. She didn't want to remember anything about him. The words, however, were stuck on her tongue and didn't escape.

The sour taste was there again, a warning she was going to be ill. Afterward, Paul helped her to sit, placing a cool cloth on her forehead.

She wasn't going to be grateful to him for anything. Had it not been for him, she wouldn't be here, nauseous, dizzy, and confused.

Hannah.

The sudden image of her maid was important. She

closed her eyes and tried to remember. Hannah had been injured. Paul had struck her.

"Let me go," she said. "I want to go home."

"Where is home, my dear? Scotland or London?"

"Scotland." The answer came so quickly it surprised her. Anywhere Macrath was.

Dear God, where was Elliot?

"Where is my son?"

"Don't worry about your get, my dear. He's safe with his father. Maybe he'll think you're dead, rather than simply abandoning him."

She wouldn't do that. She wouldn't leave Elliot behind.

Perhaps it was best if he wasn't here, though, wherever here was.

Someone was at the door. She turned her head with difficulty to see a tall young man with a shock of black hair and intent eyes staring at her.

She knew him. A moment later she remembered. He was the man in the carriage.

He handed a metal box to Paul, who placed it on the floor beside the bunk.

"I hadn't intended to bring you along, William," Paul said. "But you've proved invaluable to me." He opened the box, retrieved a few coins, and placed them in the younger man's palm. "See if the captain has any accommodations in steerage."

"I'd rather be a skipper than chained to a scurf," William said. "'Specially one who drugs a nemmo. It's a crooked cross. Besides, I never said I was for America."

"You'd have a future there, a better one than on the London streets."

"I'd rather be in for a vamp," William said. "I'll take this, though," he added, rolling the coins on his palm.

With that, he disappeared.

Paul stared after him for a moment, then slammed the door.

"Ungrateful whelp," he said. He turned toward her, smiling in an odd way. "But you, my dear, you're a different matter, aren't you? I think you're going to show your gratitude soon."

"Please," she said, "I want to go home."

"Rest, my dear. You're not going anywhere without me. Ever."

He left the room, closing the door softly behind him.

She lay on the bunk, drawing her knees in, fear enclosing her. A wave of dizziness overcame her, and she found herself sinking into nothingness again.

Chapter 32

From what Hannah overheard, Henderson had already booked passage to America. Macrath hoped he'd reasoned this out correctly and Henderson wasn't on the way to Inverness or Edinburgh. If he'd been in Henderson's position and kidnapped someone, he'd opt to set sail quickly to lessen the chance of being apprehended.

Kinloch Harbor was deep enough to berth large ships, some of which were bound for foreign ports.

Since pubs were no longer permitted to open on Sunday, a few of the ships served as taverns, fitted up with tables, stools, and enough whiskey to satisfy hundreds of thirsty sailors.

When Jack went to find the harbormaster, Macrath questioned the drinkers at the dockside taverns.

At the first, no one recalled seeing anything out of the ordinary. In the second, however, one man remembered seeing a carriage.

"In the way of being in a hurry, it was," he said.

"Do you remember any of the occupants?"

The man shook his head. "Didn't see 'em. You might want to ask the lad over there," he said. "Stranger to Kinloch. Came in a little while ago."

Macrath went to stand at the table, directly in front of

the man sitting there alone. The man didn't look up, concentrating on the tankard clutched in one fist.

"I'm looking for a man named Henderson. Do you know him?"

"What's he done?"

An odd question for a stranger to ask.

"Why do you think he's done something?"

"I want to go back to London," the man said. "I'd rather be in my own rookery than here."

Macrath hooked his boot in front of one chair leg, pulled it out and sat.

The man's ears were so large his hat perched on them. Macrath studied him for a minute and offered a deal.

"Tell me where Henderson is, and I'll make sure you get back to London."

"Without being in lumber? I don't want to be in lumber."

"If you haven't done anything worthy of going to jail, you've no need to worry."

"I saw you dabbing it up with her. Is she yours?"

"Yes, she's mine," Macrath said, biting back his impatience.

"He thinks she's his. A bit nickey about her, he is. I never meant to be part of this."

"If you'll show me where she is," Macrath said, "I'll see you get back to London in style with a reward."

The other man looked slightly less morose at that news. He took a last sip from his tankard, then wiped his mouth with the back of his hand, stood, and nodded at Macrath.

"Best be about it, then."

Macrath couldn't have said it any better.

Virginia didn't know how long she was unconscious.

Blinking open her eyes, she discovered Paul was on

the bunk, kneeling over her. She was down to her black trimmed shift. Somehow, he'd managed to remove the rest of her clothing and his fingers were busy unfastening the bow at the top of her last garment. She tried to stop him, but he merely held her wrists with one hand.

"Stop it!"

"You're not the Countess of Barrett here, my dear. You're simply my beloved wife."

She stared wide-eyed at him, her stomach clenching. "I'm not your wife."

"But you will be," he said. "We're perfectly matched."

He didn't appear to be mad, only determined.

"Paul, please," she said. "The chloroform is making me sick."

"I didn't give you that much, Virginia, and a few hours have passed. I doubt you feel the effects as much as you say."

Appealing to his sympathy wasn't working. She wasn't as strong as he was. If she didn't do something, he was going to rape her.

The idea of him touching her was sickening.

"You're mine, Virginia. You have to understand that."

"I've never been yours," she said. "Never."

"Oh, but you have. You were mine the night Lawrence didn't want you. You've been mine ever since. Lawrence didn't understand and had to be handled."

He was smiling at her but there was a glint in his eyes that frightened her. Almost like he was warning her he could do anything.

"What did you do?"

"Why are you asking, my dear? You've known all along."

She shook her head.

"I can't say it was all for you, my dear, although it

would sound a great deal more chivalrous, wouldn't it? Does anyone care about chivalry anymore?"

"What did you do?"

"I was tired of Lawrence," he said. "He was ruining all of you."

Her muscles stiffened and her breath caught. Her gaze fastened on him and she couldn't look away.

She shook her head. "No," she said in a halting voice. "You couldn't have."

"Kill him?" He smiled. "It wasn't a difficult feat to simply place a pillow over his face," he said, unfastening the cuffs of his shirt. "With his weak heart, he didn't have any strength at all."

She was dizzy and nauseous but it wasn't the chloroform.

"But you've been unfaithful to me," he said, pulling off his jacket then starting to unbutton his shirt. "We need to rid you of the taste of Sinclair, I think, as soon as possible."

"So you'll rape me all the way to America? Even if I don't want you?"

"You wanted me once," he said. "I'll just remind you."

"I don't want to go to America," she said, trying to move away. He had her trapped, one knee on either side of her legs.

"I can still talk while I undress, Virginia," he said, removing his shirt collar. "Don't think to distract me with words." He tossed the collar to the floor. "America is your home. Don't you want to see your homeland again?"

"There's nothing there for me," she said.

"No friends? No family?"

"No."

"We shall have to make our own, then."

"I won't marry you," she said. "Nothing will make me marry you."

"Very well. I'll continue to plant my seed in you. I don't care if our children are bastards. The world will never know. I'll simply say we were married on the voyage. Who's to say we weren't?"

"I would."

He smiled. "You're a very good mother, Virginia. I shall have to train you to be a good wife."

She fought him, becoming a frenetic ball of arms and legs. She connected with him more than once, feeling a vicious surge of joy at his grunts of pain. She didn't care if she broke her arms or legs.

Paul Henderson was not going to rape her.

Her hand fumbled for something to strike him. At first she thought the ledge above the bunk was empty.

Metal, she felt cold metal with her fingertips. She reached up and grabbed the neck of a lantern as he lowered himself to her. She struck him with the lantern, but the blow hit his shoulder, not his head as she'd aimed, and fell to the floor.

He slapped her hard with his open hand.

"Don't make me punish you, Virginia. Don't make me do this."

She screamed. He clamped his hand down over her mouth, grinding her lips against her teeth.

He kneed her legs open. She arched upward, trying to dislodge him. He ground one knee against her pubis. When she cried out in pain, he slapped her again, his eyes dark, his face contorted with a frightening smile.

She tasted blood and it galvanized her, pushed her to scream again and bite at his hand.

He grabbed her hair, loosened from the struggle, and jerked on it until she cried out in pain. His fingers scraped at her shift, tearing it, exposing her breasts. His hand grabbed a nipple and twisted it.

She sagged against the mattress, giving up the fight.

He said something to her, but she couldn't understand the words. He was going to win. He was going to rape her when he wanted and there was nothing she could do.

Her hand dropped off the bunk, knuckles brushing the floor.

No, not the floor. Something he'd brought on board. The metal box. A heavy metal box that made a thunk as it hit the floor. Would it work? She didn't have time to worry about it because he was unfastening his trousers.

She hooked her fingers in the handle, grabbed it and prayed she was strong enough. Lifting the strongbox in an arc, she slammed it into Paul's temple.

He didn't make a sound as he crumpled to the side.

Pushing him off her, she slid out from beneath his weight. Had she killed him? Dear God, she didn't care. No, she hadn't, because he made a sound.

She scrambled from the bunk, ran to the door and escaped up the stairs.

The deck was crowded with people, men and women, sailors and servants, all standing at the railing watching as the sails caught wind. She could feel the movement of the ship beneath her, knew they were leaving the harbor by the panorama of masts they passed.

"Help me, please."

Several people turned. A woman cried out, and soon the entire crowd was staring at her. As well they should, since she was dressed only in a ripped shift.

A man came forward to offer his coat. She took it with gratitude.

"I need to speak to the captain," she said. "I need help. I've been kidnapped."

"That's not necessary," Paul said.

The man who gave her his coat stepped back.

She turned to see Paul standing in the doorway, blood

from his head wound coating the side of his face. Two people rushed up to him, but he pushed them away, grinning as he approached her.

"Virginia, dear, you must dress. You know you shouldn't appear in public in your undergarments."

She grabbed the lapels of the coat, holding it around her as she stepped away from him.

"My wife has been ill lately," Paul said. "You'll have to excuse her. I'm taking her home to be with relatives."

She glanced around and saw only concerned faces. He was going to convince them they were married. Or worse, that she had delusions and he was caring for her.

No one was going to help her.

She felt where her lip was still bleeding.

"You brought me here against my will. You hit me and tried to rape me."

The word caused several gasps from the onlookers. She could just imagine the story they would tell. Let them talk. Let her be the brunt of a thousand jokes. Just let her escape.

"Come, Virginia, you know that's not true," he said. "You're just overwrought." He glanced at the crowd. "She's a new bride and a bit shy."

More than one man chuckled, but the women looked either worried or horrified.

"Get away from me," she said when Paul took two more steps.

"You're making a scene, dear. People are scandalized."

"He kidnapped me," she said to the closest woman, a matron dressed properly in traveling coat and hat. For a moment she thought the woman might help her, but then she said something to the man next to her and moved away.

"I'm not your wife," she said to Paul, the comment eliciting gasps from the assembled women. "I'm the Countess of Barrett."

"I do apologize for her," he said, glancing around him.

"She has fits on occasion and I think the excitement of going on her first voyage is telling on her."

He kept advancing, the crowd parting to allow him to approach her. She took a few steps away, only to feel the railing at her back.

The ship was nearly at the mouth of the harbor. Once they were out to sea, she wouldn't be able to escape him.

The breeze skittered across her skin; she wanted to clap her hands over her ears to silence the clamor of conversation and speculation. Her heart beat too quickly. Her skin was tightening with each shallow breath.

A man dressed in a dark blue coat with a slouch hat over his gray hair pushed his way through the crowd and strode toward her. Beside him were two burly men. The man spoke to Paul, who nodded and remained where he was.

The captain was going to subdue her. That wasn't difficult to figure out. They were going to place her in Paul's cabin, where he could rape her whenever he wanted. No one was going to hear her or understand what he'd done. As far as they were all concerned, he was her husband and had full rights over her. He could say anything and they would believe him, but they wouldn't believe her.

They would think she was crazy, and laud him for his care of her.

She hated him more than she'd hated any man in her life. More than her father, who'd considered her a commodity. More than Lawrence, who only saw her as an instrument of revenge. The only man who'd ever treated her with decency, kindness, and love was Macrath, and she'd repaid him by being deceitful.

The captain was only a few feet away. Before he could reach her, before anyone could grab or stop her, she threw her legs over the railing and plunged into the sea.

At the harbor's mouth a ship was heading for open water. Macrath was on the pier when he realized it was the *Oregon*.

A woman stood at the railing, and although it was too far to see her clearly, something told him it was Virginia.

His heartbeat thudded in his ears.

As he watched, she turned and, in a slow and terrifying act, jumped off the ship, disappearing into the water.

"Stay there," he said, turning to the young man who'd told him about Henderson.

He stripped off his boots and dove into the water.

He was damned if he was going to let the woman he loved drown.

Virginia sputtered to the surface, the desperate need to get away from the ship blotting everything else from her mind. All she had to do was swim, that's all.

She pushed a bobbing crate out of her way, treaded water for a few moments to get a second breath. The chloroform was making her light-headed, or maybe it was the sudden, exhilarating freedom she felt.

Still, she had to pace herself. She was out in the middle of the harbor and had to swim to the pier. Pausing a moment, she thought she heard her name being called and started swimming again. She wasn't out of reach of the ship. Someone could lower a boat and Paul could come after her.

Debris floated in the harbor: oranges and pieces of something green, shards of wood not yet waterlogged. A tankard floated by, as if a sailor had simply finished his measure of grog and pitched it into the sea. She didn't like seeing the hulls of the ships coated with barnacles and green slime disappearing into the murky water. Nor could she abide the smell of fish.

Her legs cramping, she rested again, floating on her back. The distance hadn't seemed so far before. Now it looked almost unattainable. She told herself she could reach the dock. All she had to do was concentrate on swimming, then resting, then swimming again.

At the closest pier, fishing boats clustered like nursing puppies suckling at their mother. All except one ship, larger than most, nearly the size of the one she'd escaped.

The teak figurehead caught her attention. A woman emerged triumphant from the waves, arms thrust behind her, her smile joyous and free, the face a duplicate of her own.

She started to cry.

He'd said the figurehead resembled her. He hadn't said how magnificent it was.

Something was coming in her direction, splashing furiously. Not a something after all, she then realized, but a person, someone who knew her name. Was the chloroform giving her hallucinations? Suddenly, she saw it was Macrath, fully clothed and swimming toward her.

When he reached her, she stretched out her hand to cup his jaw, then pressed her fingers against the frown on his forehead.

"Are you really here?" she asked.

"I'm really here, but I might ask the same of you."

Macrath turned, shouted something at the ship looming nearby, and a rope slapped into the water. Pressing her hands around it, he moved behind her, guiding her toward the hull. She didn't like ships. She didn't like the ocean, either. Did he know that?

It seemed like he did.

"You can swim," he said. "You would have saved me

some bad moments there if I'd known. Why do you hate the ocean yet know how to swim?"

"My father insisted I learn," she said, "since we lived so near the Hudson."

"Well, thank God for your father, then, and I'd never thought to say that."

What a foolish reason to weep again. Truly, it was the chloroform.

"There's a ladder," he said. "Can you manage it? If not, I can carry you on board."

She turned to face him, still treading water.

The sight of Macrath, hair slicked back, his blue eyes intent, was the most stirring thing she'd ever seen.

"You're very handsome," she said. "Have I ever told you that?"

"You might have. Shall I return the compliment? Or concentrate on getting out of the harbor?"

"How did you know I'd be here?" she asked. "Hannah told you," she said before he could speak. "How is she? You really must arrange to have Paul Henderson arrested. He struck her viciously."

His fingers traced her bottom lip and she winced. "Did he strike you, too?"

"Can we stop the ship? Or send word to America? He can't be allowed to go around doing awful things to women."

He didn't answer, but his face changed, became the stern Macrath she'd heard about but rarely seen.

"You're very fierce with your expression. I'm not afraid of you, though. I never was."

"Good. I don't want you to be. Henderson's another matter."

She contemplated the thought of Macrath pummeling Paul again, and realized the idea didn't disturb her at all. When she said as much to him, he smiled.

"Can we continue this conversation once we're on deck?"

She looked up at the ship, and didn't like the fluttery feeling in her stomach when she saw how far up she'd have to climb.

She could reach out now and touch the hull, but would much rather have just swam to the pier.

What a pity she couldn't simply decide to be courageous and everything might be magically easier. She would have to work on overcoming her fears, starting right now.

She turned, kissed his mouth softly, given her swollen lip, then forced herself to face the rope ladder stretching straight up into the sky.

As she gripped the first rung, it occurred to her that she was already brave. She'd given birth nearly alone, stood up to Enid, come after Elliot, descended a cliff, stood her ground with Macrath, and jumped from a ship.

What was a silly ladder?

"You have to look away," she said. "I'm nearly naked. I've only my shift on."

There was that severe look again. She had the feeling Paul Henderson should go somewhere very far away, where Macrath couldn't find him.

Chapter 33

Virginia stood at the ship railing, staring at the *Oregon* as the vessel entered Moray Firth.

Macrath studied her silently. Even here, hair slicked back and drying in the warm salty breeze and wrapped in a blanket, she was the most captivating woman he'd ever known.

And perhaps the most troubled.

He wanted to erase the last day from her mind, but he couldn't. He wanted to take all the pain from her memory, but he couldn't do that, either. All he could do—and he had every intention of doing it—was remain at her side and give her comfort and support whenever she needed it.

The crew of the *Princess* kept their gaze away from her. He wore borrowed clothing, but at least it was dry. She didn't have that luxury, though the blanket covered her well enough. He didn't want to think of how she'd appeared on the deck of the *Oregon,* nearly naked and fleeing from Henderson.

If he could have pummeled the man again, he would have.

"I've sent Jack to Drumvagen," he said. "He'll send the

carriage back for us. As soon as I've spoken to the harbor-master, we'll go home."

She nodded but didn't turn or look at him, and when she spoke, it was almost like she addressed the scene before her.

"Will they send a ship after the *Oregon*? Will he be arrested?"

He wished he had a good answer for her. The fact was, once the other ship was out to sea, the harbormaster had no influence. The captain was law. Boarding the ship would be tantamount to declaring war on the *Oregon*.

"They'll send word to America," he said. "That would be the most practical thing to do."

"But it doesn't mean they'll arrest him, does it?"

"No."

She took a deep breath. "It's a great deal of water, isn't it? Some of it is very deep. I imagine you could drown easily there."

"You could drown in a lake, a river, or a basin as well," he said.

She nodded. "With the aid of a madman you could find a great many ways to die, none of which you'd expect."

He stood beside her, his hands on the rail, so close he could move his little finger and touch her. He didn't, however, feeling like these moments were poignant and profound in a way he didn't completely understand.

"I was never afraid of the river near my house, isn't that strange?"

"Had you ever seen the ocean?"

She nodded. "I had. But I hadn't loathed it as much as when we traveled to England. Maybe it wasn't the ocean I feared as much as a new life. Or maybe it was both. I don't like the dark, either. Or heights."

"I remember," he said. "But you acquitted yourself well on a rope ladder."

She didn't smile or otherwise acknowledge his comment. She turned to face him, keeping one hand on the railing.

"I want to overcome all my fears. Otherwise, Alistair will be afraid as well."

"I don't think we teach children our fears as much as our limitations," he said. "My father never wanted to succeed in a grand way with his newspaper and printing business. He didn't want to have an empire."

"But you did. I wonder why."

He smiled, as fascinated by her questions as he'd always been. "Because doing so challenged me? Because I wanted to be someone I wasn't?"

"I can't get over Paul killing Lawrence," she said, having already told him of Henderson's confession. "I feel responsible."

"You probably were."

She glanced at him, her eyes widening.

"I'm certain you were there, encouraging him, helping him hold down the pillow."

She frowned at him. "You know I did nothing of the sort."

"However, you insist on taking responsibility for a murder you didn't even know about until a few hours ago."

She sighed, her shoulders slumping forward. "It does sound idiotic, doesn't it? Still, if Paul hadn't had an obsession with me, Lawrence might still be alive."

"But Alistair wouldn't be, or hadn't you considered that?"

She shook her head. "No, I hadn't."

"I don't want to build our happiness on top of someone else's misery. Or death. So don't claim responsibility for something you didn't do, Virginia. Henderson decided on his own to kill Lawrence. He decided, on his own, to come after you. None of those actions were your doing."

He put his hands on her shoulders. "Now, let's address you calling our son Alistair," he said.

"It's all your fault. He's begun to look like an Alistair, don't you think? All prideful and Scottish."

"It could be his American half," he said.

He pressed his lips against the worst of the scars on her upper cheek, near her eye. They were tangible reminders of how close he had come to losing her forever. He would never have known if he hadn't gone to London, if he hadn't pushed his pride down, out of the way.

Moments such as these were rare, when the world stilled around him, when it felt like he commanded time. He wanted this moment to last, to pull on each second until it stretched. Could he freeze the minutes? Could he hold them, frozen, in his hands and offer them to her?

She pulled away, staring out to sea again.

Was she thinking about what Henderson had done to Lawrence? Or what he'd done to her?

She'd been at the mercy of the man.

She'd been at his mercy, too.

"I've handled this all wrong," he said, stepping back. "You should remain at Drumvagen because you want to, not because I've forced or charmed you into it."

She spoke without glancing at him. "So now you'll let me return to London, but without my son."

"You can take Alistair with you."

She gripped the railing tight enough he could see her knuckles whiten.

"You would let us go?"

"Yes."

Did she realize it would nearly kill him to lose either of them?

"I want you to stay, but I can't compel you to do so. I could tell you that you'll learn to become a Scot. Or that

Drumvagen isn't nearly as isolated as you think. Or I'm wealthier than you realize."

"It was never about money, Macrath. Don't you know that?"

"Then what was it? A title?"

"A family," she said, surprising him.

Turning, she faced him. "I didn't have a choice about coming to England. What my father decreed was law. I was to simply acquiesce without a word spoken. I found myself married to a stranger, a man I grew to dislike intensely."

She clasped her hands together.

"Yet he had a family. Two sisters who embraced me warmly. I grew to love Eudora and Ellice as dearly as the sisters I never had." Her smile was barely a curve of her lips. "I feel the same about my mother-in-law, even though Enid occasionally makes me want to scream. She and my father negotiated my marriage settlement. Lawrence retaliated by beggaring us all. He spent my father's money, all my inheritance, on properties that would go to his cousin."

He'd learned that from Hannah, but hadn't realized that Virginia had felt responsible for saving all of them.

"So coming to Scotland and getting yourself with child was the plan."

She nodded. "At the time, it seemed like the only thing to do."

"Did you never think of the consequences of your actions?" he asked. "That you brought a child into the world who would never know his father?"

She glanced away, then back at him. "No," she said. "I thought about a child in an abstract way. I didn't think he would be Alistair and I would care more for him than myself. I didn't know I'd feel guilty from the day he was born." She hesitated. "How did you know he'd been born?"

"I didn't come to London for Alistair," he said. "I didn't even know about him until I reached your house."

She bit at her bottom lip. What words did she bite back?

"Why did you come to London, then?"

"That was our destination," he said.

There, a partially true answer, one sparing him somewhat. He needn't confess he'd thought of her endlessly. Why tell her he saw her face when he stared at the night stars? That the surface of the ocean seemed to reflect her smile, and the sigh of the winds her gentle whisper?

"So you decided to visit me."

"I thought of nothing else for the last year," he said, abruptly deciding to expose himself.

Let there be nothing but the truth between them now, since there had once been an important lie.

"If we'd been destined for somewhere else, I would have come to London for you. I wanted you enough to beg. I wanted you to marry me and come back to Scotland with me."

She didn't look at him, concentrating instead on her clasped hands. Her head was bent, and he wanted to place a kiss on the nape of her neck, ease her back against him and hold her. Would he always feel empty without Virginia in his arms?

He had won at everything he'd touched.

He'd never won at her.

Perhaps love wasn't about winning or losing. Perhaps it wasn't a game or war at all. If you were lucky, you found someone who made you think and laugh, with whom you wanted to spend your hours. If you were truly fortunate, loving that person changed you, made you better, softened your rough edges and fueled your ambition even further.

Dear God, but he loved her. He loved everything about her, from the way her nose wrinkled when she was reading to her habit of touching him on the arm while speaking.

When he entered a room, she stopped what she was doing, sending him a smile that made his toes curl.

How could he live without her?

"Stay with me," he said. "Stay at Drumvagen and make it your home. If I need to travel, you can go with me. You and Alistair."

"They're depending on me."

"Your London family?"

She nodded.

"So, you intend to let the lie continue?"

She surprised him by shaking her head. "I can't. Because you're my family, too. More than anyone else."

He hated the worry in her eyes.

"I have a solution," he said. "Tell them to come to Drumvagen. Tell them all to come. They'll be part of our clan. Anything they want, they can have."

"You would do that?" she asked, her eyes widening.

"I would do anything for you, Virginia. Don't you know?"

"Enid is beyond stubborn, and insists on her own way. She's used to having her own household and it wouldn't be an easy transition."

"I can't wait for her to butt heads with Brianag."

A look of amusement lit Virginia's face, curving her lips and banishing the sadness. "Oh, dear, it will be a war, won't it?"

"And Ellice? What is she like?"

"Young," she said. "Untried and unformed, like I was at her age."

"I would have liked to have known you then," he said.

"I'd have shown you Cliff House. All my little secrets. The place in the woods where I hid from my governess, and the attic window looking out over the Hudson." She glanced away. "I'm sorry it was sold. It was such a lovely place. I wish Alistair could have seen it."

He would buy it for her as a wedding present. They'd travel to America to inspect it, and while he was there, he'd make inquiries into Henderson's whereabouts.

When he reached for her, she stepped away, shaking her head.

"Your man will have to offer Hannah marriage," she said. "Hannah's a good person. She's not the type to be trifled with."

"Jack?"

She nodded. "Jack. Nor will I stay at Drumvagen without marriage."

He stared at her, disbelieving. "What do you think I meant? Bloody hell, Virginia, I've been courting you."

She blinked at him. "Have you?"

"I gave you a book of poetry. I gave you gifts. I designed a rose garden."

Her cheeks flushed.

He wrapped his arms around her, intent on getting this right. "I love you, Virginia Anderson. You occupy my mind. I smile, thinking of your laugh. I want you as my wife. Is it plain enough for you now?"

She glanced away. Every time she got that look on her face, he was greeted with news he didn't like.

"I promised myself I'd always tell you the truth," she finally said. "Even the little bits. I should have written you about Alistair. I knew what I was doing was wrong." She stared down at the deck, then took a deep breath. "But I don't regret those days with you. I don't think I ever could."

He gently turned her face up. "I would have come to you the minute I heard of your husband's death. You came, instead."

She smiled, a strange expression given the one solitary

tear that fell down her cheek. He swiped at it with a finger, cupped her face in his palm. She held his happiness in her glance, his future in her answer.

"Will you be stay with me, Virginia Anderson Traylor? To be my wife, my love, and my friend?"

"I haven't told you the whole of it yet," she said. "I came to Drumvagen because I couldn't bear staying away. A year was decades long without seeing you. A defect of my character, to be in love with one man and married to another."

"Do you love me?" An eternity of seconds passed before she answered.

"Oh, Macrath, I love you with all my heart and parts of my soul."

When he would have pulled her into his embrace, she shook her head, her smile fading as well as her tears. Her face was still, her lips thinned, her eyes direct.

He steeled himself for her words.

"I'll try not to be afraid of anything, Macrath. Not people. Not tall places. Not dark places. Not spiders." She shuddered. "Perhaps spiders."

She took one step back from him, placing her hand on his chest.

"But I've decided I'm not going to be at the mercy of anyone. Not even you. Not even if I love you above all people. I've changed from the girl who always did what she was told, who was timid and afraid of everything."

He didn't say a word, but he could feel joy spread through him. He'd chosen well, this woman with the beautiful eyes and flushed cheeks.

His smile deepened, glowing from inside out.

"I'll decide what's right for me," she said. "That means you and I will differ from time to time."

"Undoubtedly," he said.

"You don't look disturbed by the thought."

"On the contrary, I'm anticipating our first argument."

She frowned at him but her eyes were sparkling.

"Are you now?" she said, in a credible imitation of Brianag.

As the harbormaster made his way to the deck of the *Princess,* he was surprised by the laughter he heard, especially coming on the heels of such a serious affair. He stopped, transfixed by the sight of the two of them, the man so tall, bending tenderly to the woman who had her palm on his chest.

She was smiling up at him, her expression radiant and a match for the joy in her eyes. He, too, was smiling, his stance one of a protector.

The sun glowed brightly on the horizon behind them, casting them in a brilliant light. The harbormaster had the feeling that what he was seeing was the face of love, unadorned and perfect.

Author's Note

The Married Women's Property Act, which would have allowed Virginia to retain an inheritance from her father, was not passed until 1870. The act was not retroactive.

The hymn quoted in Chapter 4 is the third verse of the hymn "All Things Bright and Beautiful," which was first published in 1848 in *Hymns for Little Children*, by Cecil Frances Humphreys (London: Joseph Masters, 1848). In modern versions of this hymn, this verse is omitted.

I've manipulated the date of the last smallpox epidemic. According to the *Encyclopedia of Plague and Pestilence* by George C. Kohn, the last great outbreak of smallpox in the British Isles began in 1871, causing 10,000 deaths in London. The epidemic continued in Scotland, where approximately 6,300 people died.

The Vaccination Act of 1853 required smallpox vaccination in England and Wales and was probably the reason why the 1871 epidemic was not larger. Smallpox vaccines were the first mandatory vaccines in the U.S. In 1809, Massachusetts required all its citizens to be vaccinated.

Macrath Sinclair's invention of an ice machine was taken from real accounts of the day. James Harrison, a

Scottish born newspaperman, immigrated to Australia and developed one of the first ice machines. While cleaning movable type with ether, he noticed that the metal type would be cold to the touch. His first mechanical ice-making machine began operation in 1851, but his patent for an ether vapor compression refrigeration system was granted in 1855. In 1873, in an effort to make Australian beef competitive with American beef, he prepared the *Norfolk* for a beef shipment to the UK. Instead of installing a refrigeration machine aboard ship, he chose to use a simple cold room. The experiment failed and he returned to the newspaper business.

The SS *Strathleven,* on which the *Fortitude* was based, was actually built in Glasgow in 1875. Her famous voyage, which ended in her arrival in London with forty tons of frozen Australian beef, mutton, lamb, and butter, took place in 1880. The refrigeration aboard the ship was a dry air machine built by a Glasgow company.

I thought her demise was sad for such a memorable ship—she foundered in 1901.

Broadsides were single sheets of paper printed on one side and sold on the street by peddlers or chapmen for a penny or less. Designed to be read unfolded, broadsides carried proclamations, the news of the day, local crimes (the more salacious the better), as well as songs and poetry. They're a fascinating look into what people thought important or interesting.

The broadside featuring the murder of Thomas Newbury near Haversham was published in London around 1870.

The broadside entitled "Murder of Betsy Smith" was published by Robert McIntosh, Printer, Stationer, Librarian of Glasgow, sometime in the mid to late nineteenth century. Betsy Smith's murder took place near Manchester, England, but the Glasgow publisher printed the story, no doubt due to its gruesome nature.

The poems in Chapter 15 are by Elizabeth Barrett Browning: "Sonnets from the Portuguese" and "The Lady's Yes."

Want to know more about the Clan Sinclair?
Keep reading for a sneak peek at

THE WITCH OF CLAN SINCLAIR

Chapter 1

Edinburgh, Scotland
October, 1872

Nothing about the occasion hinted that it would change Mairi Sinclair's life. Not the hour, being after dinner, or the day, being a Friday. The setting didn't warn her; the Edinburgh Press Club was housed in a lovely brick building with an impressive view of the castle.

Still, she should have somehow known, possessing an inquiring mind as she had. She should have seen the carriage pull into the street behind them. She should have felt something. The air should have been different, heavy with portent. Hinting at rain, if nothing else.

Perhaps a thunderstorm would have kept her home, thereby changing her fate. But on that evening, not a cloud was in the sky. The day had been a fair one and the night stars glittered brightly overhead, visible even with the glare of the yellowish gas lamps along the street.

A gust of wind brought the chill of winter, but her trembling was due more to eagerness than cold as she left the carriage. Straightening her skirts as she waited for her cousin to follow, Mairi wished she'd taken the time to order a new cloak—her old black one was a bit threadbare at the hem. She would like something in red, perhaps, with oversized buttons, and a hidden pocket or two for her notebooks and pencils.

Her dress was new, however, a blue wool that brought out the color of her eyes and made her hair look darker than its usual drab brown. At the throat was the cameo that her brother and sister-in-law had given her on their return from Italy.

"We saw it and thought it looked like you," Virginia said.

She'd responded with the protest that it wasn't a holiday or her birthday.

Macrath had merely ignored her and pinned it on her dress. "The best presents are those that are unexpected," he said. "Learn to receive, Mairi."

So she had, and today she was grateful for the thought and the gift. The brooch enhanced her dress.

She didn't see, however, that the finely carved profile looked anything like her. She didn't have such an aristocratic nose, or a mouth that looked formed for a smile. The hairstyle was similar, drawn up on the sides to cascade in curls in the back. Perhaps that was the only point of similarity.

Fenella joined her in a cloud of perfume, something light and smelling of summer flowers.

Her cousin was a pretty girl, someone people noted even though she rarely spoke in a group. Fenella's blond hair created a halo around her fine-boned face, accentuating her hazel eyes.

Mairi had seen a swan once and the gentle grace of the bird had reminded her of Fenella.

In addition, Fenella was far nicer in temperament than she was. Whenever she said that, her cousin demurred but they both knew it was the truth.

Fenella's cloak was also black and the severe color only accentuated her blond prettiness, while Mairi was certain she looked like a very large crow. However, she wasn't going to be deterred by her appearance or any other miniscule concern on this most glorious of occasions.

She strode toward the building, clutching her worn copy of *Beneath the Mossy Bough* in her left hand, her reticule in her right. Her hated bonnet was atop her head only because Fenella had frowned at her in censure. Otherwise, she would have left it behind on the seat.

Before they could cross the street, three carriages passed, the rhythmic rumble of their wheels across the cobbles a familiar sound even at night. Edinburgh had quiet hours, but normally only between midnight and four. Then, the castle on the hill above them seemed to crouch there, warning the inhabitants to be silent and still, for these were the hours of rest.

She knew the time well, since she was often awake in the middle of the night working.

"Are you very certain this is proper, Mairi?" Fenella asked as they hurried across the street.

She turned to look at her cousin. Fenella was occasionally the voice of her conscience, but tonight, nothing would stop her from attending the Edinburgh Press Club meeting.

"It's Melvin Hampstead, Fenella," she said. "Melvin Hampstead. Who knows when we will ever have the chance to hear him speak again?"

"But we haven't been invited," Fenella said.

Marie waved her hand in the air as if to dismiss her cousin's concerns. "The whole city's been invited." She shook her head. "It's Melvin Hampstead, Fenella."

She climbed the steps to the top, opened the outer door, and held it ajar for her cousin. Inside was the vestibule, a rectangular space large enough to accommodate ten people. Yellow tinted light from the paraffin oil sconces illuminated the door at the end, guarded by an older man in a dark green kilt and black jacket.

At their entrance, he stood, folded his arms across his chest, and pointed his gray threaded beard in their direction.

"Is it lost you are, then?"

Mairi blinked at him. "I don't believe we are. This is the Edinburgh Press Club, is it not?"

"That it is, but you're a woman, I'm thinking."

"That I am," she said, clutching the book to her bodice. "We've come to hear Mr. Hampstead speak."

"You'll not be hearing him here," he said. "The meeting is closed to women."

The man didn't even look at her when he spoke, but a spot above her, as if she were below his notice.

"That can't be true," she said. "Otherwise, it wouldn't have been publicized so well."

"This is the Edinburgh Press Club, madam. We do not admit women."

"I'm a miss," she said, stepping back. "Miss Mairi Sinclair, and I've a right to be here. I'm the editor of the *Edinburgh Gazette*."

"You're a woman by my way of thinking," he said. "And we don't admit women."

She had the urge to kick him in the shin. Instead, she batted her eyes ever so gently. She'd been told she had beautiful blue eyes—the Sinclair eyes—plus she was occasionally gifted with the same charm that Fenella effortlessly commanded.

"Are you very certain?"

Evidently, he was immune to both her eyes and her lashes because he frowned at her.

"It's Melvin Hampstead," she said. "I adored his book," she added, holding it up for him to see. "If we promise to slip in, not speak to anyone, and simply stand in the corner, wouldn't you allow us to enter?"

"No."

No? Just no? No further explanation? No chance to convince him otherwise? Simply no?

She frowned at him, one hand holding the book, the other clenched tight around her reticule and the notebook inside. She carried her notebook everywhere and the minute she could, she was going to record everything this man said, plus his refusal on behalf of the Edinburgh Press Club to allow her to enter.

"Is there a problem?"

She turned her head to find a man standing there, a bear of a man, tall and broad, with a square face and eyes like green glass.

"No, Provost Harrison, no problem. I was just telling this female that the Edinburgh Press Club did not allow women."

She'd listened to tales of Scotland's history from her grandmother, heard stories of brave men striding into battle with massive swords and bloodlust in their eyes.

This was one of those men.

He, too, was attired in a kilt, one of a blue and green tartan with a black jacket over a snowy white shirt. She could almost imagine him bare chested, a broadsword in his right hand and a cudgel in his left. The sun would shine on the gleaming muscles of his arms and chest. He'd toss his head back and his black hair would fall over his brow.

There were men and then there were men. One was male only because he wasn't female. The other was the definition of masculine, fierce and a little frightening, if her heartbeat was to be believed.

He braced his legs apart, folded his arms and regarded her with an impassive look.

She knew who he was, of course, but she'd never seen the Lord Provost of Edinburgh up so close. If she had, she'd have been prepared for the force of his personality.

If he meant to intimidate her, he was doing a fine job of it, but she would neither admit it nor let him see that she was wishing she'd thought to remove her cloak so he could see her new blue dress.

Nonsense. Was she turning into one of those women who couldn't be bothered with anything more important than her appearance?

Perhaps she should ask herself that question when she wasn't standing nearly toe to toe with the Lord Provost, with him looking half Highland warrior, half gentleman Scot. Or if she could have ignored his strong square jaw, full lips, and his sparkling green eyes.

"Is there a problem, miss?"

At least he'd gotten the miss part correct.

"No problem. But I don't understand why I can't attend Mr. Hampstead's lecture."

He raised one eyebrow at her.

"The Edinburgh Press Club does not allow women as members, I believe."

"Mr. Hampstead's lecture has been promoted throughout Edinburgh."

"For men to attend."

She could feel her temper rising, which was never a good sign. She had a tendency to do and say foolish things when she forgot herself.

She was very aware that there were inequities in society. For that reason, Macrath was the titular owner of the Sinclair Printing Company. For that reason, she signed her columns with either her brother's name or another male's. For that reason, she pretended Macrath was out of the office temporarily when men came to call to discuss a matter with the owner of the Gazette. She always took the information, made the decision, and wrote the supplicant with her answer, once more pretending to be her brother.

She had to hide behind a man to do her daily tasks, run a business, be a reporter, and publish a newspaper, but she'd never been faced with the situation she was in at the moment: being refused admittance solely because she was a woman.

It should have occurred to her but because it hadn't, she felt the curious sensation of being blown off her feet.

"What does it matter that I'm a woman?" she asked. "Does Mr. Hampstead's lecture only appeal to men?"

Right at the moment, she didn't like the Edinburgh Press Club very much. Nor did she like the gatekeeper or the Lord Provost. Most of all, she didn't like the burning feeling in her stomach, the one that felt like humiliation and embarrassment, coupled with the knowledge that she wasn't going to win this skirmish.

Fenella evidently noted the signs, because she grabbed Mairi's elbow. "Come, Mairi, we should leave."

"I believe that would be the wisest course," the Lord Provost said.

She narrowed her eyes at him.

Did he think he was the first man to have tried to put her in her place? She was faced with criticism every day, and every day she had to deflect it, fight it, or ignore it.

"I would have thought, in your position, that you would speak for all citizens of Edinburgh, not just the men. Or is it because I don't have the ability to vote that you dismiss me so easily?"

He didn't say a word, the coward.

"Your silence indicates that you can't dispute that."

His lips curved in a faint smile. "On the contrary, my silence might be wisdom, instead. I have found that it isn't wise to argue with those who are overly emotional."

The breath left her in a gasp. "You consider women to be overly emotional?"

"I do not address women, miss. Only you. The Club is a private organization, not one funded by or for the citizens of Edinburgh. I have nothing to do with its workings. I am simply a guest. Had I the authority, I would allow you entrance."

She smiled. "Then you do think women should be admitted."

"I think it's the only way to silence you."

She almost drew her foot back, but a soft sound from Fenella stopped her.

"Thank you, sir," Fenella said, stepping in and preventing Mairi from responding by grabbing her arm and pulling her toward the stairs. "We'll be on our way."

In her daydream, she sailed past the Lord Provost with dignity and poise while he wistfully stared after her. The truth was somewhat different. She left, but when she looked back, he was grinning at her.

Want even more? Then keep reading for a peek at

THE VIRGIN OF CLAN SINCLAIR

Chapter 1

Drumvagen, Scotland
May, 1874

Ellice could not tolerate any more.

Really, how much was one person supposed to bear? Day in and day out, all she heard was sniping.

The two women had been companionable for a year, almost friendly. When their book had been published— *The Lady's Guide to Proper Housekeeping*—she expected the amicable behavior to continue, especially since the book had become popular in Scotland and England.

Macrath's suggestion, a few years earlier, for the Dowager Countess of Barrett and Brianag, housekeeper to Drumvagen and wise woman of Kinloch Village, to pen a book between them had been considered odd. No one, least of all her, had expected the book to succeed as well as it had. Macrath told her they'd received orders from as far away as Australia.

Instead of feeling grateful for their good fortune, her mother and Brianag were at each other's throats again, each taking credit for their success.

Even now she could hear them although they were probably in her mother's sitting room.

"Of course the Scots would want to know how an English woman manages a household," her mother said. "The Scots always look to the English."

Brianag was not to be outdone. She muttered something in that unintelligible Scots of hers, followed by, "Only if they want to know how to ruin something."

Macrath had urged them to work on another book in the futile hope that activity would keep their antipathy at bay. Ellice thought this newest venture was doomed to failure. They couldn't even be in the same room for more than five minutes.

When a door slammed somewhere, she closed her eyes. Who had made a grand exit now?

How could they be so short sighted?

If she had the opportunity they'd been given, she would have leapt at the chance. She would have done anything Macrath wanted in order to get her book published. As it was, her manuscript remained a closely guarded secret. She was the only one who knew of its existence.

She moved from the window seat to her secretary, unlocked it, then placed the manuscript inside, locking the desk again and pocketing the key.

"Glib i the tung is aye glaikit at the hert," Brianag said, her voice just this side of a shout.

"What is that supposed to mean?" her mother said. "Would it be too absurd to hope that one day you would speak the Queen's English? Even a Scot can learn that."

Ellice rolled her eyes. Couldn't they pick another place other than the hall to quarrel? Or at least insult each other in a softer voice?

Because of Macrath's kindness and generosity, she and her mother had been given wonderful quarters at Drumvagen, almost as if they were family in truth, instead of claiming only a tenuous relationship to the owner of this magnificent home.

Virginia had once been married to Ellice's brother. After Lawrence's death, Virginia had fallen in love with Macrath Sinclair, a Scot who made even Ellice's heart pound occasionally, especially when he looked at Virginia across the room with that certain look in his eyes.

Perhaps it was that look that had sparked her imagination. What would she feel if a man looked at her in that way, or treated her as if there was nothing more important in the world than her?

Her mother chose that moment to open the door to her suite. "Are you daydreaming again, child?" her mother said, bustling into the sitting room. "Have you no other occupation to mark your time?"

"I've been reading," she said, feeling a twinge of conscience at her lie.

Reading was considered the occupation of a gentlewoman. Even here, in the wilds of Scotland, she was to comport herself as the sister of an earl.

"You and Brianag have to stop arguing," she said.

Her mother raised her eyebrows.

She was not given to correcting her mother. Enid was, after all, the Dowager Countess of Barrett and quite a formidable personage. But something must be done before Macrath decided to act. Virginia was heavy with her third child and Macrath was on edge, just the kind of mood where it wasn't wise to tweak his nose.

"The woman is a cretin," her mother said. "She wants to have a chapter on laundry in the new book."

Ellice frowned. "Why would you object to that?"

Enid shook her head, looking up at the ceiling as if for divine interference. "A gentlewoman hires a laundress, my dear child. She supervises. She doesn't do the work herself."

"But shouldn't she know everything about it, to ensure the work is done correctly? Otherwise, she might be fooled if a laundress states that a stain can't be removed. It's like having a lady's maid, Mother. Shouldn't you know how to care for your own jewels, in order to prevent them from being damaged?"

Her mother stopped and stared at her, such an intense regard that Ellice wished she would blink. Enid finally nodded, just once, a signal that Ellice wasn't to be chastised for speaking out.

"I've been giving some thought to your future," her mother said, changing the subject from her own shortcomings to something more terrifying.

Ellice stood and very calmly walked to the other side of the room, sat on the window seat and regarded her mother.

Calm. She needed to remain calm, that was all. She wouldn't fidget, which was—as her mother had often told her—a nervous habit. She didn't particularly want her mother to know she was terrified.

"You're of an age to be married," Enid said, moving through the sitting room, touching objects Ellice had brought from London to give her a bit of comfort in the Scottish countryside. A book her sister, Eudora, had given to her on her fifteenth birthday. A sketch of her brother, Lawrence, framed in silver. A small porcelain statue, called a Foo Dog, if she remembered correctly, that resembled a wrinkly lion more than a dog.

She was aware of her own age and her circumstances, perhaps a bit more than her mother who occupied herself with quarreling for most of the day.

As lonely as she was at Drumvagen she couldn't summon up one iota of interest in a purchased husband. Macrath wouldn't hesitate in providing a dowry for her. That's the kind of man he was.

She wanted exactly the same kind of man for herself.

Where did she go to find another Macrath?

Enid was still walking through the sitting room, her substantial hooped skirt grazing the tables and brushing against the wall.

"Why should I marry?" she asked. "I'm perfectly happy." A bit of a lie but her mother didn't need to know that.

Her mother drew herself up, shoulders level, and hands clasped tightly in front of her. Enid was a short woman, one whose bulk made her appear squared. A small and formidable enemy if she wished to be.

"Marriage is a woman's natural state, Ellice."

"You're not married."

"I have mourned your father all these years, child. I do not wish to replace him in my affections."

Not once had she ever heard her mother talk about the late earl fondly. Whenever Enid referred to her long-dead husband it was in an irritated tone, as if his demise had been planned to annoy her. Now she was claiming to feel affection for him? Ellice didn't believe it. She was not, however, unwise enough to say that to her mother.

Enid, Dowager Countess of Barrett, never forgot a slight, even one from her own daughter.

If Eudora had lived, no doubt her older sister would have known some calming words. Or by this time, Eudora would have married and made Enid a grandmother several times over.

"Would you be pleased to be a grandmother?" she asked.

"Without benefit of marriage?" Enid abruptly sank into a chair. "Tell me you haven't done anything so precipitous. It was bad enough that Virginia bent the rules of society, but you?"

If Virginia hadn't bent the rules of society, they wouldn't be living in this grand house, each given a lovely suite, and treated like family members. Another comment she wouldn't make.

"No," she said. Should she tell her mother she was still a virgin? That was a word never spoken about in polite company. People merely assumed you were maidenly until you weren't.

Society, and she would freely admit that she hadn't been out in it very much, seemed like a giant organization whose members all knew secret rules, the purpose of which was to shield everyone from real emotions.

"Thank the good Lord and all the saints for that, at least." Enid fanned the air in front of her flushed face.

NEW YORK TIMES AND USA TODAY BESTSELLER

KAREN RANNEY

A Scandalous Scot
978-0-06-202779-5

After four long years, Morgan MacCraig has returned home looking for solace. Yet peace is impossible to find with the castle's outspoken new maid trying his patience ... and winning his love.

A Scottish Love
978-0-06-202778-8

Gordon MacDermond has everything he could ever want—except for the one thing he most fervently desires: Shona Imrie, the headstrong beauty he foolishly let slip through his fingers.

A Borrowed Scot
978-0-06-177188-0

Veronica MacLeod knows nothing about the breathtaking, secretive stranger who appears from nowhere. Montgomery, Lord Fairfax, agrees to perform the one act of kindness that can rescue the Scottish beauty from scandal and disgrace—by taking Veronica as his bride.

A Highland Duchess
978-0-06-177184-2

Little does Emma, the Duchess of Herridge, know that the dark and mysterious stranger who bursts into her bedroom to kidnap her is the powerful Earl of Buchane.